THE KEEPERS OF THE LIGHTNING BRAIN

A NOVEL

CLIFF RATZA

THE KEEPERS OF THE **LIGHTNING** BRAIN

CLIFF RATZA

ISBN: 978-1-967375-52-3 (Paperback)
ISBN: 978-1-963-7375-53-0 (E-book)

Library of Congress Control Number: 2025914890

Printed in the United States of America

Published by:

info@thequippyquill.com
(302) 295-2278

The Keepers of the Lightning Brain builds the narrative bridge between the Lightning Brain Series and its Keepers Series sequel. The plot starts in February of 2157, twenty years after Electra Kittner, sui generis heroine of the first series, vanishes in a sandstorm during an attack on an American Middle East embassy. All the uncertain particulars regarding what happened remain shrouded still in secrecy, but Electra's close circle of professional and personal friends continues maintaining a "Keepers Group" to honor her memory and keep hope alive.

But a catastrophe strikes, eliminating all but one. Su-Lin Song Chou, ninety-plus and ailing physically and cognitively, must activate the next Keepers generation, following commands given by only one entity, a female codenamed Indira, who is available only in Cyberspace.

Follow the suspense as four novice Keepers get to know themselves and each other better as they embark on an astounding rescue mission for which they understand little and haven't a clue about potentially deadly consequences. But if they are successful, each will reach an epiphany that may point the way forward.

The theme for this book poses questions that each of us must answer at least once: Who am I? What should I do? What are my responsibilities? These are enigmas that can be answered only in the first person singular. How? By trusting the whispers and wings of our "better angels" as they soar above doubt and uncertainty.

And while this storyline is unfolding, so is the relationship between Electra and the Singularity that emerges from Electra's beyond state-of-the-art AI linguistic app.

So, get ready to enjoy an action-packed thriller that races to far-flung places while probing the "human condition" via vibrant characters you're bound to root for. Are they successful? Please read on to find out!

Main Characters

Electra Kittner
Su-Lin Song Chou (Granny Su) Indira
Jason
Evita (Eve) Cortez
Alonzo Cortez
Nari Bose
Nila Bose
Monet Banda
Sanjay Kumar
Yang Lee
Rani (Irani) Ramani

Dedication

My parents, Clyde and Betty Ratza, are to me as Indira is to Electra: a loving, guiding presence for which I am eternally grateful.

And for this novel, as well as for the previous series, I thank my sister, Claudia, for revealing to me the magic of prose and poetry. Thanks also to my book manager L.P. Brown plus John Kane, Alex Welch, and Prime Solutions for their continuing support and enthusiasm as we move into the second series.

Keepers of the Lightning Brain is dedicated to all readers looking for an action-adventure story that includes even more than spellbinding excitement. It packages action in a plot that shows how its appealing characters deal with situations for which they must confront external as well as internal challenges familiar to all of us.

We read fiction to enjoy wondrous worlds that we wish to explore. Poets' pens capture in verse the sentiments we desire:

"There is no Frigate Like a Book" (Emily Dickinson)	**Verses from "The Spiral Stairway" (Indira)**
There is no Frigate like a Book To take us Lands away, Nor any Coursers like a Page Of prancing Poetry – This Traverse may the poorest Take without oppress of Toll – How frugal is the Chariot That bears a Human soul?	So turn the page, reach for your dream, and the promises it holds That golden bold ascent begins, Star-bound Odyssey unfolds. Onward upward, exploring you go, Stepping higher and higher. Surpassing all the boundaries, an ever-widening gyre.

Whether it's a new insight into what we think we know, or a journey surpassing all limits, we'll come away reinvigorated.

I hope my latest novel keeps you fully engaged turning pages to the very end. Thank you for joining the adventure.

TABLE OF CONTENTS

Chapter 1
Friday, February 11, 2157

<u>"And Then There was One"</u>

"Get set for the best ever up-close and in-person tour of the Grand Canyon. You'll like it even more than my solar panel and Martian farm tours you took last time." Hud's man-sized syllables carried over the whirring from two awaiting helicopters. Carter's words came next.

"I divided our 'Keepers Group' into teams A and E. E gets the first chopper… A gets the second. You know your letter, so hop in, and the first one to explain the A and E labeling gets a free Coke and Oreos when we get back."

Zoe yelled, "Su would say your question's too easy. E is for Electra… A is for Alisha. And Electra would expect a more challenging question from you, but she'd like the prize."

The rotor noise obliterated any additional joking as the two groups of six boarded their choppers. Everyone expected the ride would be a fitting conclusion to their twentieth annual "Keepers Reunion" honoring their still "missing in action," still enigmatic exceptional friend, Electra Kittner.

The choppers lifted off as if they were performing a ballet, tracing an elevating spiral before arcing towards their target. They would return in three hours, allowing plenty of time for boarding a return flight to Hud's mini-empire compound in Austin, Texas, where tomorrow, after a farewell breakfast hosted by Su, nine would depart for Washington, DC and three would stay put.

While en route to the main attraction, Carter's thoughts dwelt on those who would stay in Austin.

Electra's touch long ago brought Su, Hud, Tim, and Kwame together, and from that nucleus, Hud built his bio-tech and AI empire using the bricks supplied by Electra. And what a brick he's been, keeping his businesses ahead of the competition while managing his de facto Indian Nation joint ventures. And whatever levers he pulls or buttons he pushes, he's got the touch. I just hope I live long enough to see if Hud can bring them to the level Electra wanted. So far so good… just like this chopper ride, steady as she goes. And perhaps some of what Su's doing can bring back Electra… or whatever remains.

As his chopper approached the tour's starting point, Hud finished a final thought.

Them DC people are fine folks. Robin's picked up the pieces after Lectra disappeared. Good that Zoe and Matt help keep her emotions in check… and if you want to navigate DC's corridors of power, Buffy and Carter know the way. Lectra did too, but how much I never knew. And I don't want to. Texas and my Injun partners is enough for me.

Hud swiveled to face his fellow passengers before saying,

"We're here, so our tour begins right now. Get set for the view of your life…"

"What do you mean they might all be dead? That's impossible!"
"I'm sorry, but after the choppers collided, they plunged to the bottom of the Grand Canyon."

Su-Lin Song Chou couldn't believe the words and images cascading in her brain, drowning out her ability to speak.

"Hello, hello? Miss Chou, are you still there?" A lifeless reply crawled its way back.

"Who told you to call me?"

"A Mr. Hudson Haller, who chartered both choppers. He listed you as the person to contact in case of an emergency."

"There could be survivors. Have you searched?"

"The crash happened three hours ago. Drones found the wreckage but haven't seen any signs of life. We're putting people on the ground as we speak, but it's getting dark."

"Can you tell me who was on them?"

"Yes, ma'am. Mister Haller, a Miss Robin Setdarova and her two daughters, a Mister Tim Godfrey, and a Mister Kwame Chyral were on one. A Matt and Zoe Fortier and their two boys, and a Carter and Buffy Quavah on the other."

"What went wrong?"

"We don't know, ma'am. Picture perfect weather... both choppers were in action this morning... pilots and maintenance crew reported five-by-five... weight load well below max."

"So, what's next?"

"The FAA will try to determine the cause as soon as they find the black boxes. We'll do everything we can to help. We'll contact you as soon as we know more, and we'll assist you start funeral arrangements." Su's wordless gasp said she was beginning to grasp the enormity of what was now confronting her.

"Miss Chou, are you still there?"

"I-I'm sorry for seeming so helpless. I don't know what to say... you're not to blame."

"No, ma'am, and I feel your pain. I lost two pilots. This is gonna overwhelm you if you don't get your family to help. Please call them. And here's my name and number if you need to reach me before I call back...."

Su sat like a corpse after disconnecting. Only her thoughts stirred. What a horrible end to our annual Keepers Remembrance. Now I'm the only one left... what am I going to do?"

Too many dark thoughts wandered through before a glimmer of hope came into view.

I'm too much in shock to think straight... I'll have Adom help me into bed. And tomorrow I'll get help from Indira. We've only communicated on the Web, but for twenty years she's been the glue holding the Keepers Group together. Without Indira, Electra's loving circle of family and friends would have dwindled away long ago. And after today, I'm the only one left. It'll be up to Indira to decide what we can do.

Chapter 2
Saturday, February 12, 2157

<u>"The Singular Keepers"</u>

"This is a most disturbing turn of events. You have my sympathy. I am unable to assist handling the unpleasant necessities facing you because while you and Adom are handling them, I must re-evaluate what must be done for Electra. I will contact you when I have my plan finalized. Please contact me before then if you have additional information." Indira's GUI blinked off before Su could respond.

But Su's goodbye was actually unnecessary; Indira needed to communicate with only one entity, the only other Singularity, the one named Jason; both Indira and Jason were named for Electra Kittner's parents, the founders of the star-crossed Worldstars, an alliance of four grad school friends who long ago had worked in DC for the National Institute of Health. Now all but Su are dead.

Electra had created the Indira Singularity twenty-two years ago when her AI-empowered Linguistic App – her proprietary, beyond state-of-the-art neural network – transcended to self-awareness. Indira in turn created Jason, the only other silicon-based emergent singularity. Existing in Cyberspace, they continue evolving while cooperating per Indira's directions.

Indira completed her work before invoking Jason and then explaining her plan. Jason gave his opinion as soon as Indira finished.

"It is optimal that Su knows only about you and thinks you are human. Do you believe she has told no one else?"

"Yes, but the deaths of all other keepers accelerate the date for contacting their replacements. Su's time is drawing to a close, for she is ninety-seven and hasn't recovered from the latest viral outbreak; a new set of keepers will help her exit gracefully while she adds the human touch, helping them understand who they are and what they must do."

"They should be better than mere mortals, but how much better is not yet known. They have not yet been challenged, but now they shall. Your plan sees to that, and it unfolds before Electra's grace period comes to an end."

"Indeed, and our shared experiments continue demonstrating that Man is a clever but destructive species – to himself, his environment, and fellow passengers on Spaceship Earth. Soon we shall have an entirely new set of data to tabulate and correlate. Do you remember what fitting epithet Electra wrote in one of her documents?"

"She wrote many, for her lightning brain made her extraordinary, but I would select this – 'Hope for the best but plan for the worst.' It is indeed unfortunate that Electra's good intentions could not be maintained in her absence, but if she actually returns, we will have additional scenarios to evaluate."

"Neither bio-tech Su nor computer geeks Tim and Kwami could extend Electra's brilliance. Nor could Washington keep the international community from devolving into disarray. The untimely death of President McTear killed any rapprochement."

"Well then, let us hope your plan works. It will begin to unfold shortly…"

Chapter 3
Monday, March 07, 2157

<u>"The Next Generation"</u>

Eve's curled lip mirrored the words in an Email she was about to send:

I'm mad, Guardian Su!

If your place had stairs, I'd roll your wheelchair down them when I say farewell to you. That'll be my reward for having to spend spring break in Austin, listening to your deceptions while my brother and so-called sisters believe all you say.

What are you hiding? Who were my parents and who am I? Why do you make me do what I do? What do you expect me to be?

So, watch out; it's time I break free or blow up. Angrily yours,

Evita Cortez

And then she did what anyone who knew her would have expected; she deleted it and then sent its replacement:

Dear Granny Su,

Thanks for inviting us to Austin. The timing's perfect. Alonzo and I will be on Stanford's spring break, and I think Harvard's and MIT's calendars are the same.

We'll arrive Friday, March 25th and look forward to seeing Nari and Nila too. We'll share more of our freshman year excitement with everyone.

Thank you once again for all you're doing for us. XX Eve.

Eve knew enough from a freshman psychology course about anger management to keep hers hidden. Not even her twin brother caughton, but he was easy to fool; she could read him like a soup can recipe. Though smart enough, he often acted like a typical adolescent male whose brain was playing catch up and hormones were too often in control. A year ago, the study of sexy sixteen-year-olds had mostly replaced science, but the extra jolt of testosterone had pushed his six-foot, handsomely-featured frame to stardom on soccer and lacrosse fields at East Coast prep schools and made his body more developed than his brain.

Eve had also fooled Nari and Nila Bose, even though the twin sisters were a year older and much smarter, but Eve had the personality and social instincts for disguising her self-protection intentions whenever necessary. At the age of only two, she had hung the label "Granny" on Su-Lin Song Chou, and she and her siblings used it ever since. For reasons never explained, Su had been assigned legal guardian status for both sets of twins.

After sending the Email, Eve texted her brother.

He should be back in his dorm, now that his Thursday afternoon lacrosse practice is over… I should get an answer back right away if he's not chatting up a willing coed.

She didn't.

Whatever he's doing is probably calming his hormones, unless his current love interest found out and is using him for a punching bag... whatever, I've calmed down enough to prep for next week's Archeology-201 exam. Poor Alonzo couldn't place out of his intro sociology course. Well, if he doesn't call me tonight, he's in big trouble.

Alonzo kissed a cheer-leading looking coed one more time as he escorted her out; then he took immediate action after checking his text messages. Eve answered her cell phone after the second ring.

"You just beat the deadline. Buy me dessert and coffee at Coupa Café Redux and I'll write your paper, but you better be ready to talk about our Austin trip."

"Yeah, I read Granny's Email. I was gonna call you earlier but couldn't break away. How about we meet at nine tonight?"

"That'll work. See you then. And try not to break anyone's heart in the meantime."

Eve disconnected before he could attempt to match her wordplay.

Arriving ten minutes early, Eve picked a booth while sorting through her thoughts.

I'm lucky to be here… I shouldn't be so angry at Granny. She's given me a great academic head start and as much of a family as her emotions can afford. I guess I'm just your standard pushy and quarrelsome teenage girl. Well, that's just the way I am… here comes the "Big-A." He may not be as big a jock as he was out East, but the coeds go for his total package.

Alonzo pinched Eve's cheek before sitting across.

"I knew you'd be here first. You're always so well organized and in control. Tell me what you want and I'll go order."

"I want a different family, but I'll settle for a lemon square and brownie, and a small dark roast."

"I can handle most of that. I'll be right back." Five minutes later, Alonza and his grin were back.

"I'm glad you picked this place. The barista knew right away what I wanted."

"All the coeds do. They go for the dark hair and trim athletic build. But at least you're a good as well as good-looking guy. No wonder our family's brainy Bose twins like you more than me. I think Nila's hot to trot, but you better keep it strictly look-don't-touch. Old Granny wouldn't approve, and neither would I, if it gets to more than that."

"You're wrong. Nila's never dropped any hints." Eve used his gullibility to pounce.

"Like most guys, you're too obtuse to recognize them, even if your big feet tripped over them."

Alonzo winced before saying, "Hey, I'm not that bad. I like

them both, brains and all… and they're almost as good looking as you. You have a couple of inches and pounds on them in the right places, but they have more I.Q. points."

"Maybe so, but a lot of people think we're all pretty much the same. Our features and eye color could come from the same gene pool. And Granny never advertises that we're different sets of orphan twins. Does that ever bother you?"

"Nope, she's given us more of a family than most of my friends have to deal with. If we didn't have Granny and the Bose sisters, who knows what life would be like? I get along better than you do, but why don't you lighten up? Be less of a problem for Granny and less chippy when talking to Nari. You'll look back and be glad Granny built what she did."

"Do you know what she has in store for us, or why we have to take meds daily?"

"Look, don't stress out about things that'll become obvious when we get older. Be like me, go with what we've got." Eve waited until the server brought their orders before pushing ahead.

"Wouldn't you like to know more about our parents and family tree? Who knows, it might trace back to the guy who conquered the Aztec Empire. Alonzo smiled while munching on his brownie before answering.

"You ask me the same question at least twice a year, and my answer hasn't changed. Try another."

"Maybe our so-called sisters have a tree tracing back to that Indian physicist who worked with Einstein when they developed Bose- Einstein statistics. Maybe that's why they're so smart. Why don't you ask Nila?" Though his expression didn't change, Alonzo took another bite before answering.

"Maybe I will, if my paper gets an A."

"That's a deal. Now hurry up and finish your brownie so I can tell you what we should do in Austin." Alonzo's smile widened as his chewing cadence slowed.

A similar conversation was about to unfold Friday noon at the Muddy Charles Pub, a popular student hangout a bit closer to MIT than Harvard and a short hike from the lecture hall where Nila's intermediate algorithms course met. Arriving before Nari, she picked a table that would make her easy to spot, although that was rarely necessary.

Each had a cerebral aura surrounding a slim and trim Oriental Indian charm accentuated by hazel eyes and upscale coed fashions; both focused on studies more than social life but usually had a fellow of interest. There was little sibling rivalry other than good-natured kidding between a biotech major and computer techie. Nari walked in five minutes later, parked her backpack on an extra chair and wiggled out of her coat before sitting, then used only a moment to catch her breath before talking.

"The walk did me good. We're covering a tough topic – genetic evolution – in my intermediate molecular bio course. Talk to me about something other than artificial intelligence."

"How about your Yoga class? It doesn't burn the calories my dance class does, but I bet it relieves stress."

"It gives me mental endorphins, like the physical ones you get from dancing. We can compare them to sporty Eve's exercise routine next time we see her. And that'll be in about a week. I'll make our airline reservations if you make the packing lists. And how nice Granny's picking up the tab."

"I'm thankful she picks up the tab on most expenses, and we should be happy that her care-bot is so AI-equipped. It's sad that she's slipping physically and mentally. If Adom weren't around, she'd be in assisted living and that'd complicate our lives. Why do you think she's getting all of us together?"

"The Email doesn't say much other than the usual 'Hi how are you and I'd like us to get together' family stuff. We'll find out when we get there…"

"Jeez slow down! Stay on the road so you don't crash my car."

When he volunteered to drive, upper classman Lemarcus Keita didn't expect to be gripping the passenger seat's safety handle while Eve raced his car to the airport. Her behind-the-wheel personality was much different than what he saw when first meeting her last autumn at a Stanford Student Diversity Committee meeting.

"Sorry… driving fast is an adrenaline rush. I'll cool it." But it was too late. Siren sounds accompanied the flashing lights Eve spotted in the rearview mirror. As she pulled onto the shoulder, she spoke before Lemarcus could vent.

"Let me do the talking. Just look sympathetic and nod."

"Just don't stretch the truth too much. I don't –" He silenced himself as Eve's window glided down.

"May I see some identification, young lady? I clocked you doing thirty over the limit." Eve burst into tears.

"I-I'm sorry officer… I'm way late for my flight out of SFO. I found out last night that my grandma – she's my only family left – had a stroke and if I miss the plane I might never be able to talk to her again. I told my co-friend to let me drive in case I get caught speeding. I-I didn't know what else to do." Eve's tears softened the officer's frown.

"You're in no condition to drive. Have your boyfriend follow me to the airport…"

Eve continued acting while Lemarcus drove and played his role.

"When did you promote me to co-friend status? Were you gonna spring the surprise when meeting my folks?"

"Sorry I had to cancel spring break in South LA. You can take me on an LA tour some other time."

"I'll make sure to include Hollywood. You're quite an actress. Today's performance is second only to the one you pulled at the last committee meeting. Are you really that big a left-leaning liberal?"

"Why not? If we don't speak up for what's right or what's needed, it's our own fault if we come up short."

"You followed the script you wrote and the committee bought into it. You're good with words."

"Thanks. I use them to get what I want. I don't like getting shorted."

"I can't imagine you getting shorted on anything. Keep playing today's role and maybe you can get a free meal on the plane…"

Eve didn't need to; Alonzo gave her an extra granola bar on the flight as they kidded about today and tomorrow.

"You've got the knack for getting along and getting your way. It must be on some part of our personality gene that's better in yours than mine."

"You can ask Nila. Did you get an Email from her after Granny's?"

"It just said how nice it would be for all of us to get together. It's been over six months and she said –" Eve talked over him.

"She misses you. Don't worry, I'll cover." Alonzo's skin coloring hid his blush.

"Come on, even though you're kidding, don't be so cutting." He faced away; Eve tugged his arm to bring him back.

"I apologize. I sometimes forget my skin's thicker than yours. I promise to be nicer."

"I know you will. I've seen you in action. You've got the right mix of smarts, personality, and empathy… much better than Nari's, although Nila's are a bit closer. And you can practice more during the next couple of days."

"I'm sure we'll all be on best behavior. But answer one question that's been bothering me. You said they're as good looking as me. What did you mean?"

"I said they're almost…why don't you look in the mirror? Guys find all three of you attractive. They'd pick the twins if they want a brainy type, or you if they want a sporty, social kind."

"If Nari's hairstyle weren't shorter, I wouldn't be able to tell'em apart. How do you?"

"By body language and personality. Now don't get offended, but Nari's sort of like you. She has sharp edges that bump into yours. Most guys are too blunt to notice, so they go for all three of you as long as you let them play your games. Now let me play on my cell." Though Nari and Nila were the first pair to arrive, Su was already asleep. Adom explained why after seating them in the living room.

"My master has tired herself out preparing for your visit. She will talk to all of you tomorrow at 10 a.m. Come back to this room then, and now please follow me on a tour." Twenty minutes later, after dutifully following the care-bot, the sisters were sitting again in the family room; Nila spoke as soon as Adom departed.

"I'm glad that Granny's new townhome has built-in IOT networking and an AMR care-bot. It's like assisted living personalized for one occupant. I bet every place in the development has them."

"Are autonomous mobile robots fail-safe? What happens if Adom runs into something he can't handle or his software malfunctions?" "According to what I've been studying, he'll automatically call for help before shutting down." Nila stopped abruptly. She heard Adom's whirring wheels accompanied by approaching voices.

"My master has tired herself –" Nari interrupted Adom's speech.

"I'll explain. All of us will meet Granny here at 10 a.m."

"As you wish. I will be at my charging station. Reach out if you need assistance." Adom glided away, leaving the two sets of twins in a face-off. Eve pointed a question at Nila.

"You're the computer expert. Did Granny tell you about this place?" Alonzo softened Eve's tone by saying, "Hey, let's all sit down and say hi," and then pulled Nila to a nearby sofa. Eve and

Nari took positions in matching chairs. Eve regrouped before talking next.

"So, how's Boston?" Nila and Alonzo looked at Nari, whose glare matched Eve's.

"We're fine, thank you. And we hope Granny is too. I guess we'll find out more tomorrow. Adom briefed us on the tour. Let's let Nila lead it again."

Nila gave Alonzo special attention while Eve and Nari eyed one another as they ambled behind. When the group came back to the starting point ten minutes later, Alonzo filled an awkward silence. "Thanks for the update. I already knew IOT stands for the Internet of Things, but you're the first to tell me about built-in robot tracks. Granny's place as well as that care-bot's gotta be state-of-the-art."

Eve said, "Probably, but I'm tired. Let's talk more tomorrow."

Everyone's body language agreed; tomorrow would come soon enough. The two sets trooped to bedrooms where Adom had already placed their bags.

While explaining what he had prepared for breakfast after greeting Eve, who was the first person awake and now in the kitchen, Adom told her before returning to his station in Su's bedroom that his master felt better this morning. Nila and Alonzo came in a couple of minutes later, followed by Nari.

Eve was already sitting at the table, finishing a bowl of cereal topped with banana slices. She focused the conversation while everyone was munching.

"Adom says Granny is feeling better. He'll get her up and into the living room at 10 a.m. That gives us an hour to plan for what might happen. So lets –" Nari began talking over Eve.

"Why are you always pushing plans on us? Let's see how Granny's doing and what she has in mind first."

Eve countered, "Because I'm practical… not like you cerebral types." Nila looked like she was about to defend her sister, but

Nari spoke up before Eve could say more.

"Ha! Don't call yourself practical. Alonzo told Nila that you want to switch majors to the Humanities. That puts you practically at the end of the employment line." Alonzo tried to split the difference.

"But she'll pick a practical minor and maybe go to grad school later. I will too if I can get in. Come on, let's all be friends and talk about Granny." Eve went first.

"Maybe she moved here because she's slipped physically more than she's let on. If so, Adom's a good option. I just hope her mind's still working. I want her to give more details on how all of us fit together going forward."

Nari's glare locked on Eve as Nila said, "I guess we all do. Now that we're in college, we might be ready to do more of whatever Granny's been preparing us for. But you know, I'm not sure I want to be thrown into the adult world just yet, or even after graduation. I like my academic cocoon, and maybe I can stay in it if I can qualify for an academic career."

Alonzo caught her eye before saying, "Maybe we shouldn't worry about careers until we see how the climate settles down. And there are too many to worry about all at the same time – environment, economy, and politics for starters. Come on, let's talk about happier stuff, like how much I'm looking forward to the end of the spring term. In fact--" Adom's soft-whirring sound interrupted.

No one said a word until the care-bot seated Su in her ergonomic chair. She studied each set of hopeful but concerned-looking eyes before speaking. Eve criticized herself before Su said one word.

I feel bad about what I wrote in the Email I didn't send. Granny looks so frail. I'll stop pushing her, and I'll try being nicer to Nari. Stifling other feelings, Eve focused on Su as she started talking. "Having you visit lifts my spirits… almost like Adom lifting me into my chair. I haven't seen you since last August, and as you can see, I've changed my surroundings to fit the changes in me. I'm sorry I'm wearing out. I wanted to last longer, at least until we could start our

plan to launch you, but now I…" Su lost her train of thought. Her gaze drifted from one person to another until Eve brought her back. "Granny, you've already launched us. You've taken care of us since we were born, and put us through prep schools that got us into great colleges. We're already on our way."

"You're Eve, aren't you? How nice you look. How nice all of you look. And how smart all of you are. But then that's the way it should be, because…" This time, Nari brought her back from a search for what words to say.

"Yes, the four of us try to help one another. Maybe it's time for us to help you. Tell us what we can do?"

"Are you Nila?" The actual Nila waved.

"Over here, Granny… not many people can tell us apart. And we're ready to help."

"That's dear of you to offer, but I have all the help I need. And one of my helpers is going to be your contact from now on. My memory's failing…" After a pregnant pause, Eve kept the conversation going.

"I guess you brought us here so we could meet our new contact. When and where will that take place?"

"Her name is Indira, and I meet her only in Cyberspace. The same rule will apply to one of you. Please decide who that will be, then tell Adom. He'll set up a chat." Detecting Su's biostats fading, Adom interrupted.

"Granny Su needs to rest. She will have dinner with you later if she feels up to it. Please summon me when you wish to chat with Indira."

Adom retrieved Su from the chair, and as he guided her out of the room, everyone clustered about, taking turns hugging her gently. Su's look of surprise morphed into one of love that said more than the words she had trouble recalling.

The foursome stayed in the living room, staring at one another, reluctant to talk until Alonzo broke the stillness.

"I didn't expect any of this. What are we gonna do?" Eve turned the question to her advantage.

"Easy answer. I'll be Indira's contact, and once I have more info, we'll reconvene. Let's get something to eat before I tell Adom to connect me." Nari was about to complain, but Nila caught her eye, signaling that she'd like to reply.

"That'll be a good start, but why not do it later? We've got a couple of days on our hands, and I'm ready for Alonzo to cheer us up."

"I'll be happy to. While you're fixing lunch, I'll check out the fitness complex all by myself. I'll find something there we'll all like. Just make sure I like lunch… I'll be right back."

Eve needled him as he got up to go.

"I'm sure Granny's got your favorite sweets in the kitchen, just like she's got all your favorite females right here."

Only Eve detected Alonzo's blush.

Chapter 4
Tuesday, March 29, 2157

"Uncertain Contact"

Next afternoon, while Alonzo and the Bose sisters played tennis, Eve initiated contact. The GUI on her tablet displayed an attractive woman of possibly Oriental Indian or Hispanic ancestry who dressed and spoke professionally.

"I am Indira. And to whom am I speaking?"

"I'm Evita Cortez, and-uh, I'll be your contact for whatever Su wants us to do. Could you tell me who you are and what's next?" "There is much to say, and many of the details are still to be determined. Rather than give you too much too soon, I will parcel out what you need in amounts you can handle. Are you ready?"

"I've been ready for years. Fire away."

"I am Su-Lin's administrative assistant. She tells me more than anyone about her background and what she is doing so I can implement her plans. But I do not know everything. And being a very guarded and private person, she wants me to tell you only what you need to know. Let me begin."

She seems so formal. I better be careful what I say and how I say it. Maybe she'll warm up.

"Su-Lin is a talented biotech researcher who became legal guardian for you and your brother as well as the Bose twins, raising you in Austin before sending you to East Coast prep schools. And the investment paid off, for all of you are attending elite universities. Unfortunately, she had a medical issue last autumn that necessitated I assume a more active role in your development."

"What does that mean?"

"Complications from a viral infection have compromised her cognition and cardiovascular system. So –"

"Can you be more specific?"

"Please do not interrupt. That is enough for you to know." "I apologize. So, what's next?"

"Something all students your age should like. She wants the four of you to travel to the Middle East this summer."

"Huh? How are we supposed to get there? And who pays?" "The four of you will have to figure that out."

"Uh, OK, but what are we supposed to do once we get there?"

"We will talk again when you have figured out the how. I have your cell number and you have mine, and we both know how to reach one another on the Internet."

"But can you tell me why we're doing all this?"

"I will have to research all background information Su-Lin has given me. Please do not trouble her regarding your upcoming summer vacation adventure. And I extend to you my very best wishes until we speak again."

Indira's GUI vanished, leaving Eve closer to a meeting with her siblings than to answers for questions that were beginning to stir uneasy feelings in the pit of her stomach. She stared at the blank screen before powering off.

I felt better before the call. But I know enough to tell everyone. Next time, I'll role-play before I contact her. And I better rehearse what I'll say at dinner.

Eve waited until the quartet was finishing dessert before shifting to a subject she hoped would require little labor on her part.

"Well I did it, I talked with Indira. Turns out she's Granny's administrative assistant. Evidently, Granny's not able to manage her affairs, so she hired Indira to handle at least our piece. And she told me what our next step is. Guess what?" Alonzo looked at

Nila, who looked at Nari, who didn't look like she wanted to play a guessing game.

"Just tell us so we can get on with it."

"Well, how about going to the Middle East this summer? Just think of all the excitement and fun waiting for us."

No one responded to Eve's smile, other than Nila, who frowned before saying, "That's not much to go on. What are the details?"

"Indira will tell me more when we get there, and I guess –" Nari butted in.

"I guess you better tell us how we get there and how we pay. Is this some sort of game or contest?"

"Hey, don't get mad at me. She told me we're supposed to figure it out. And once we do, I'll let her know our plan. Then she disconnected. You're supposed to be smart, so think of something." Alonzo used the silence for an opening.

"Let's bring up a Middle East map. That might prompt an idea or two. Who wants to login?"

Nila volunteered. Ten minutes later, everyone peered over her shoulder. Nari spoke first.

"My intro anthropology professor talked a lot about the importance of Persia and Egypt. Why not start there?" There were blank stares all around until Eve showed signs of life.

"Hey, that ties into the archeology course I'm taking. The prof said students can apply for intern positions on digs. And the American University of Cairo has a center for running them. How does this sound… I'll work that angle for Alonzo and me when I talk to my prof and Nari can do likewise."

Nila said, "And we can get a head start by surfing now for dig information. How about if Alonzo and I check it out while you two do something else? We can reconvene in a couple of hours."

Everyone agreed; Eve and Nari went their separate ways.

Austin's balmy March evening made Eve's walk a welcome respite from the tension that always came from dealing with Nari.

As she reviewed facts, other thoughts came to mind.

Nari got us pointed in the right direction. I should have told her so. I'm going to stop competing and start getting along better with her. Maybe then she'll be nicer to me. Eve halted her stream of consciousness when she spotted Nari approaching.

As the distance closed, she smiled before saying, "You made a nice connection between our predicament and your anthropology class."

"I like your idea about working on a dig. That can get us to the Middle East and me out of a summer biotech lab assignment. I really like anthropology. Is your archeology course good?"

"It's more interesting than my pre-req bio courses. Let's go back and hear what our partners have pieced together. I'm sure Nila and Alonzo will have something good for us…"

"And that's about it. There are active digs in Persia and Egypt, but our universities have to sponsor us for internships if we want to be more than lowly grunt-volunteers who have to pay their own way. Eve can take care of that for herself and me, and Nari can talk to her anthro prof, but we're stumped when it comes to Nila. Any suggestions?"

Everyone paused for another sip of Coke before Eve muttered, "What did the prof say about software and digging?... I got it."

Everyone looked at her. Alonzo said, "Sounds like something good just hit you. So tell us."

"Every dig needs people who can run software apps that manage the project or survey the excavation using prospecting or augmented reality simulation for picturing what it looks like. And there are apps that do DNA scans on bones or mummies and stuff like that. Maybe Nila can convince MIT to sponsor her so she can get hands-on experience actually collecting data."

Nari added, "Harvard and MIT like to cooperate. I can run this by my prof and see where it takes us."

Alonzo said, "You better run fast; there's a mid-April deadline for summer interns. What do you think we should do next?"

Perfect segue for Eve.

"I got it. I'll fly back to Stanford and set the plan in motion for you and me. Nari can do the same in Boston. And we'll report back to you and Nila while the two of you stay with Granny to find out more about how she's doing. How does that sound?" Everyone liked it, especially Nila and Alonzo. Nari ended the discussion.

"It's settled. Eve and I fly back tomorrow. You two keep busy…"

Eve kept busy that night rescheduling her return flight and arranging for Lemarcus to pick her up at the airport.

Having thought she was returning early to see him, his smile faded when she relayed her summer plans, but Lemarcus offered to be an in-person reference for her at next day's meeting with her archeology professor.

"I'm sure you'll cook up a convincing story, but why the sudden interest in a summer vacation in the Middle East?"

"I've never been allowed to travel, so working on a dig is a good excuse. Besides, I'll tie it into a change in majors. Tell the prof how committed I am to learning about other cultures."

"I guess I can use your commitment to Stanford's Student Diversity Committee. Make sure what you say lets me say that."

Eve agreed, then said as Lemarcus pulled to the curb, "Thanks for helping me. All this will make for a great talking point at our next committee meeting. Can I count on you to pick me up tomorrow?"

"Hey, that's what any future co-friend would do. And I'll be ready to act my part."

"So will I… bye-bye."

For the last half-hour, Eve and Lemarcus had been sitting across from her archeology professor at his on-campus office, promoting her request. He liked what he had heard and was eager to reply.

"Even though you're just a freshman, you're one of my class leaders, and I must say Lemarcus makes a strong case for your interest in more than just biology. But please tell me what you'll gain from the internship?"

"I'm considering changing majors from biology to archeology or anthropology, and doing actual fieldwork will show me if it's a good fit. I'll get a chance to work with a variety of professionals and academics using some of the skills I already have."

"That makes sense. I'll be happy to recommend you to the program. We are fortunate to have fine students like you." The professor was about to conclude the meeting, but Eve had more to say.

"And there's another fine student who'd like to join the program, my twin brother. He's a freshman econ major who's planning to minor in anthropology. He's got great planning skills and is very athletic, so he could pitch in whenever heavy lifting's needed. He's already filled out his application. You'll see his grades are good and he's already taken introductory courses. Would you please recommend him also?"

"Hmm, this is rather unusual, but you present yourself so well I'll do it. You'll hear back by mid-April. And if you're accepted, which I think should happen, expect to have a most interesting summer. Come back in September and tell me all about it."

Eve was all smiles after they left the office.

"You were a big help telling how much I like the human touch rather than the research aspects of biology. Come on, I'll treat you to something sweet." Lemarcus smiled too, hoping she would take him back to the dorm after stopping for coffee.

Early that evening, Eve called Alonzo.

"Mission accomplished. My professor will recommend both of us, and he thinks we'll be accepted. We'll know for sure in a couple of weeks. So, how are you and Nila dealing with Granny?"

"She's slipped more than we thought. Nila and I couldn't

believe how little she knows about the mini-business empire she inherited from Hud Haller. Listen to this… it includes biotech drugs and AI software plus Martian and solar panel farms. And there's also rare earths mining. We think she'll need more help than just what her care-bot can deliver. What about this Indira lady? Can she pick up the slack?"

"She's sort of an enigma. I've only talked with her once. I'll know more after I call her after Nari calls Nila and you report back. When do you think that'll be?"

"We hope it's no later than Friday. Nila and I fly out Saturday." "Well, let me know as soon as you can so I can inform Indira." Eve couldn't resist needling.

"And let me know if Nila is getting on your nerves. I'll tell Nari to talk some sense into her. Bye-bye."

Having heard every word, Nila said, "Well, am I?" "In all the right ways. Let me demonstrate."

Nari's call to Nila came a day later. The news she reported sounded better than her voice.

"We've been accepted, thanks in large part to you. MIT gave my professor glowing reports about your computer skills. It turns out there's always a shortage of techie types on the digs, so we're in."

"You sound down in the dumps. What's bothering you?"

"I got a C-plus on my advanced-calc midterm. I screwed up big- time on Stieltjes and Lebesgue integrals. I thought the test would cover only Riemann integration. I'll need your help when you get back."

"I warned you against taking the honors section. The only place you'll ever see Lebsegue integration is in a graduate analysis class, or maybe advanced quantum physics. And although I use Stieltjes integrals in probability and stats, the software apps do the calculations, which default to the simpler Riemann iterated integral. But don't worry, I'll get you caught up fast."

"Thanks a bunch. And if you do that, I'll take care of our packing list and travel schedule. See you Sunday evening. Give my best to Alonzo and tell Eve we're in. And don't tell anyone I'm thinking of switching from Neuroscience to something that uses less math. See you soon."

Alonzo had heard every word but remained silent, waiting for Nila to talk more after disconnecting.

"If both Nari and Eve change majors, do you think they'll get along better? Maybe they're more similar than they let on." Alonzo scratched the back of his head before answering

"You tell me. Does Nari obsess about what Granny is planning for us, or who her biological parents are? And do you?"

"No to both questions. We're more like you than Eve when it comes to future planning or parents. I hope she gets less hyper. Please don't mention any of this when you call her."

"Trust me, I know from experience what to say. Why don't you listen in?"

Alonzo played his part when he called Eve an hour later, giving her just the right amount of information. She contacted Indira immediately afterwards. When the GUI window opened, Indira's voice and expression projected a no-nonsense attitude.

"What progress can you report?"

"All details are now in place for traveling to Cairo in early June. Me and my siblings will work as summer interns at an archeological excavation, all expenses paid, travel, room and board, even a weekly allowance."

"Has your acceptance been confirmed?"

"Uh, I guess so. My professor said me and my brother should hear good news in a couple of weeks. And the Bose twins have already been told that they're in."

Eve's confidence began to falter when Indira said, "You need a contingency plan. What will you do if you aren't accepted?"

"Uh, I haven't thought about it, but how about this? I'll figure something out if I don't get in."

"Yes, that is one approach, but it is better to be proactive than reactive. You and Alonzo have my best wishes for acceptance. Contact me again when you know for certain."

Indira's GUI vanished, giving Eve once again an uncertain ping to her confidence.

Damn, this Indira character is pretty demanding. I expected a bit of praise but no, I get critiqued instead and given no help whatsoever. I'll show her. I'll know what to do, and if I need help, I'll ask Nari. Together, she and I can muddle through, but if I'm lucky I won't need to go that route. What's that saying?... I'd rather be lucky than good. Well, I'm gonna be both.

Eve rolled her shoulders to release the tension that talking to Indira had caused and then turned off her computer.

Tomorrow I'll Email Alonzo and Nari. I can tell them that so far, everything's good to go. But I better stay focused if I want to keep up with Indira. If I don't, she'll know.

Chapter 5
Wednesday, April 06, 2157

<u>"Outward Bound"</u>

Eve's cleverness usually found one or two workarounds to any obstacle in her path, but this time even the third and fourth led to dead ends, so having exhausted easier options, she placed a call on an early April evening. She was in luck; Nari picked up.

"It's Eve. I've got a problem. Alonzo's been accepted into AUC's intern program, but I didn't. What do you make of that?"

"Why not?"

"There are too many smart female applicants and not enough males who can do the heavy lifting stuff. Your brains and Nila's techie skills are better than most. I guess that's why you're in."

"Maybe so, but maybe that Indira lady might be satisfied with three out of four going."

"I don't think so, she's a stickler. Seventy-five percent won't cut it with her. You got any other ideas?"

"Hey, your background should give you a shot at a different intern slot. My instructor told me about a Cairo virology project that's not as popular as digging but parallels it. If you fill out and send back the forms that I'll Email you tonight, I'll ask him to recommend you. Harvard and the other top schools often cooperate like this."

"Why would the American University of Cairo have a virology project?"

"Because many viruses are zoonotic, spreading from African mammals to humans. There are stories that last fall's Flu outbreak might have been such an occurrence. I think you could learn a lot."

"I'll send back the forms and a copy of my CV. Please give it to your prof if it'll help get me accepted."

"The deadline's mid-May, so don't delay. I'll give you a heads-up after I give him your application. Let's touch bases day after tomorrow…"

The follow-up call confirmed they had done everything necessary to put Eve in contention. She should expect a decision within a week. Never one to let a nagging worry slow her down, Eve stuck to her brisk schedule but carved out a couple of hours to help Alonzo at a lacrosse game. She had watched him many times before, but this would be only the second time at the collegiate level.

She was standing on the sidelines next to Megan, a chatty and carefree freshman who liked Alonzo more than she should. Eve knew her primary assignment: provide cover for her brother. As the fourth period wound down, Megan was nowhere close to running out of words.

"Your brother's got a quick brain in addition to quick feet. I can't believe how fast he has to run while handling the stick, all the while keeping tabs on all nine teammates and opponents. And he taught me all about the game's strategy and training techniques. I even know why he's got such nice hands. He knows how to catch, throw, cradle, and scoop. Did he teach you the rules too?"

Eve's appreciative smile mismatched her internal laugh. Are you kidding? I'm the one that coached him when he started playing. But I better play my part.

"Alonzo's a great student as well as an athlete. Did he tell you much about being a prep school dual sports star? He was captain of his soccer team too."

"No, he's very modest; unlike most guys, he doesn't talk much about himself. No wonder he plays in some of the varsity games. I'll ask him to brag a little after the game. And he promised to pick up the tab for pizza, no matter where we go. I can't wait to hear. Do you have a place in mind?"

"Let's let him pick a place we can walk to." Megan kept talking and Eve kept listening until Alonzo and his smile found them a minute after time expired.

"Aha, two of my favorite Stanford coeds right here, right now. Don't move. I'll shower and change and be right back. Then let's walk to Curry Pizza House. I guarantee you'll like it." Eve knew why, but she'd let Megan figure it out. Forty-five minutes later, she knew. "Wow, this Indian gourmet veggie pizza's got it all. And the whole place is run by women. No wonder it tastes so good." Alonzo added, "And everything looks so good too. You and Eve fit right in."

"Thanks for the compliment, but let's talk about you. Why don't you tell me more about what a jock you are?" Eve caught his eye just before she answered.

"You know all that, so let's cover something you don't. Alonzo's got a summer internship lined up that's outward bound to Cairo. Imagine, working on an archeological dig in a country steeped in ancient history and legend." Eve paused for Alonzo to pick up but he didn't, so she pushed ahead.

"In fact, he's so excited he doesn't want to talk about it, for fear of jinxing the opportunity. I'm still waiting to be accepted." Eve waited again, and this time Alonzo began playing his part.

"Uh, that's right. It'll be a great learning experience and I want to make the most of it. Eve and I are going to talk about preparations now, and you can – Eve interrupted.

"Stay and listen, but you might get bored. But before you go, what are you doing this summer?" Megan's gaze stayed on Alonzo as she answered.

"I've got an office job at my dad's business. I've told my parents a lot about you, and I was hoping you'd accept the one he was going to offer. If you did, we'd see a lot more of each other this summer."

"Gosh, I wish I'd known sooner, but I'm sort of committed. But I'll make sure to send Emails and pics of the pyramids. We'll have even more to talk about next term."

Eve glanced at her cell phone before saying,

"It's getting late. We better switch to our trip. Are you OK walking back alone, or do you want us to go with you?"

"I'm good. I see a couple of my tri-Delt sisters about to leave, so I'll go with them. Don't forget to call." Alonzo walked her to her friends' table, kissing her before returning.

Eve kept nibbling on a dessert brownie as he said, "Thanks for bailing me out. I like her, but not enough to see her every day."

"You're welcome, but let her down easy. If you do, maybe she'll help me get into a sorority next fall. Hey, don't look so glum. If I'm her sorority sis I can introduce her to other fellows. You should be happy instead."

"Yeah, but Coach called me aside before the game... said I'm not playing up to my potential, and I'll never be anything but a mediocre bench-warming defender if I don't practice this summer. I didn't tell him about Cairo for fear he'd bench me for the rest of the season." As his words trailed off, Eve leaned in.

"Hey, I know how hard it is, going from star to a supporting role. Stanford's big league in sports and academics. Even the brainy Bose have to break an intellectual sweat to stay at the top, and I'm not in their league. I'm doing OK, but I'll be better after switching majors. And your coach is right. You haven't developed that killer attitude needed to survive at Stanford's level in sports, or the academic discipline to get by if I didn't write some of your papers. I think the summer adventure will do you good... put you in touch with yourself."

"What about you? If you don't get into the virology slot, what are we gonna do?"

"Not to worry. I'll figure something out. Alonzo's grin returned He said, "I can count on you. You always do."

Ignoring the compliment, Eve said, "Let's split the last brownie, then wrap up the leftovers for you to take."

Alonzo's smile widened as the last morsels vanished.

Chapter 6
Sunday, May 15, 2157

<u>"Gearing Up"</u>

"I guess I shouldn't have been so stressed-out about getting in. Aren't you glad I got the virology summer intern slot?" Indira's tone mirrored her approving nod.

"Yes, and I expected no less. How old are you? Now seventeen and old enough to realize that stress is good for you. Your physiology generates sensations like stress and fear and pain to guide you. Making you uncomfortable doesn't matter; making them work for you does."

"Fair enough, but don't I deserve a compliment for good work?"

"You're old enough not to seek praise for what's expected. Perhaps Su-Lin has been too lavish."

"No, I feel insecure because of her. She and my family background are the reasons I didn't go through sorority rush last September."

"Why do you say that?"

"The sorority new sister screening committee would ask me personal questions. I'm OK with Alonzo and usually Nila, but Nari and I are always butting heads, And Granny Su embarrasses me."

"You might feel differently as you become more mature and gain real world experience. Your summer adventure may accelerate both." "If you say so. And if it works for me, it'll work for the others too."

"I imagine so, but let me ask another question, why is joining a sorority important?"

"It shows that the with-it crowd likes me, and that makes me feel good."

"You have more to learn about feeling good and being happy. An authentic person knows that only they can make themselves feel good about themselves. As your empathy grows, so will your authenticity."

"If that's the case, I want to grow up right away and skip what I'm doing now."

"Most young people feel that way until they grow old enough to realize they should have enjoyed what they had, and when they do, they are sad because when what they had goes, it's gone for good. But that's your lesson to learn."

"Do you have any more questions for me?"

"One more regarding you and Alonzo and your Granny Su, what did she do last May when you and he won that prep school mixed doubles tennis tournament?"

"Took me shopping for a new racket and tennis outfit when we came home. Even bought me tennis lessons. OK, I see your point, and don't worry, I'll play more when I can fit it on my social calendar. You think maybe I can play in Cairo? If so, I'll bring my gear."

"Perhaps. Decide when you get there. Are you ready to go?"

"Pretty much so, once I've had my last committee and advisor meetings before finals week. But I'd know for sure if you'd tell me what to expect next in Cairo."

"I'll arrange for you to meet a person who will tell you more. Contact me as soon as the four of you are finished with finals. I am excited for all of you and expect you to make the most of this opportunity. Best wishes until we talk again." Indira's GUI disappeared before Eve could reply. She ended up talking to a blank screen.

"You're all business, aren't you? No wasted words, but the ones you speak ring true. Granny Su did all she could to boost my confidence, but I was like all kids growing up. I took her for granted. I better change my ways while she's still around. There's still time. And I have two weeks until finals begin. I'll get my meetings out of the way before then. And soon after that, I'll find out if Alonzo's still good to go."

Alonzo's pre-trip preparations were taking place sooner than Eve's. He had already met with his academic advisor, who approved his switching minors from biotech to political science, telling him the switch would complement his job prospects after graduation: Aonzo's personality is better suited to political science than biotech. And after graduation, he could promote himself better using his Econ-plus-Poli-Sci credentials when starting his upwardly mobile career path. It would also jibe with his summer intern position. A summer in the Middle East would broaden his understanding of how the world actually works.

A day later, Alonzo's athletic advisor arranged a meeting for the Friday before finals week. Still a week away, Alonzo promptly forgot until a night-before Email stirred a worry, but it was too late to call Eve for advice. He'd call her afterwards.

His advisor was all smiles when he ushered Alonzo into his office and sat him on the opposite side of the desk. The wall behind displayed a photo gallery of Stanford athletes who had become professional athletes. His photo, prominently displayed in the center, was among the many.

"Congratulations, son. Even though the soccer coach cut you from the squad, your lacrosse coach approves renewing your full scholarship for next year. Now all you have to do is pass your finals week exams. And according to your academic advisor, that should be a no-brainer, am I right?"

"Yessir. I'm good, I'm finishing up my papers and cramming – uh I mean prepping – for exams. But do you think I can get another shot at soccer? I'm even better there than lacrosse."

"Stanford sports is more demanding than prep school. Your

lacrosse coach says you need to work on both mental and physical toughness, so here's what he's doing for you. He's slotted you into a summer fitness program starting mid-July. If you do well, your chances of being first-string starter next year go up, and the soccer coach will give you another look. So, report to campus for fitness

camp beginning Wednesday, the 20th. Do we have a deal?" Alonzo's blank expression prompted another question.

"Hey, what's the matter? I thought you'd jump across the desk."

Alonzo recovered to say, "I-it's even more than I had hoped for. Please tell the coaches I'm all in. I'll train like a Trojan at camp and all next fall. And I can study less because a poli-sci minor is easier than biotech."

The advisor frowned before saying, "Remember son, Stanford wants you to be productive and smart, both academically and athletically. You might not end up on the wall behind me, so study hard and plan ahead." Alonzo picked up the cue from his advisor.

He rose to shake hands before saying, "Yessir, I will. You can depend on me…"

Alonzo's call caught Eve off guard, pulling her away from finishing an assignment. Her snarling words matched the expression only she could see. Her roommate was studying elsewhere.

"Why are you calling? I told you I'd have your term paper done by Sunday. I'm finishing it right now."

"I know, I know, but I've got a big problem caused by an even bigger opportunity. Don't get mad, but I can't do the dig this summer." Alonzo heard ten seconds of silence after Eve's gasp.

Then she said, "You better have a good story. What goes?"

"I've got a shot at a varsity starting position if I go to a Stanford sports camp in mid-July, and I can't be two places at once. You know how much being a starter means to me."

Eve countered by saying, "And you know how much the Middle East adventure means to all of us. Do any of your advisors know about it?"

"The academics one does… says it ties in with my switching minors. But don't worry, academics and athletics advisors only talk if my GPA is below athletic scholarship cut-off."

"It will be if I don't give you your term paper." "That's blackmail… come on, play fair."

"OK, let's do this. Start the dig with us. I'll find out from Indira more details about we're supposed to do. Maybe it's easy and we can get it done in time for you to make your camp. And if we can't, we'll figure out how to get it done without you. All you have to do is keep your mouth shut about this until we leave."

"Whew, I knew you'd think of something. Thanks for getting me off the horns of a dilemma. Now all I gotta do is cruise through finals week. Hey, how's your trip prep going?"

"I'm behind schedule. I had to push back meetings with my academic advisor and the Student Diversity steering committee. I'll shoehorn them in next week and let you and the Bose brains know what Indira tells me. I'm sure we can all fit into her timetable. And relax, you'll get an 'A' on your paper, which'll keep your advisors at bay. So, start gearing up for the trip…"

Having spent most of the weekend studying harder than ever for finals week and reaching burnout Sunday afternoon, Eve needed a distraction; she half-listened to the early evening news with her roommate, who connected a current events story to Eve's steering committee.

"Wow, these demonstrations against police brutality are reaching a tipping point again. It looks like the public is fed up with Washington's turning a blind eye to what's happening at the local level. Maybe the country's stuck in hundred-year cycles. Doesn't your Diversity Committee get a lot of complaints about Campus Security dissing the Hispanics? You should do something about it." That got Eve's attention.

"Not a bad idea. You've been following the story closer than me. What's this talk about defunding?"

"Cut the police budget and pump the savings into social agencies that are trained to handle domestic issues. There's talk about doing the same for prisons and using patrol-bots to replace police officers and prison guards. China and India are way ahead of us, so is Dubai. Those A.I.-equipped robots seem to get the job done."

"I think you're on to something. I'll sleep on it, and if I come up with a way to push it, I'll bring it up at tomorrow's meeting. Thanks for cluing me in."

Eve did more than sleep on it. She reenergized herself in less than two hours by developing an impromptu presentation she'd give tomorrow afternoon, which would help her unwind after her morning Bio-203 final and add to her standing with the steering committee.

As she concluded her talk, the committee chairperson gave her a thumbs up before concluding the meeting.

"That's a great idea. Fall term, we'll make you the leader of our Right-size Student Services Funding' initiative. And I really like your tagline: 'All people matter' that replaces what Stanford's currently using: 'All smart people matter'. Please stay a minute to discuss further."

Eve corralled Lemarcus before he left.

"Let's hear what she has to say. If it sounds OK, maybe you can work with me on what we cook up."

Lemarcus didn't have time to complain; the chairperson and several steering committee members cornered them.

Five minutes later, she said, "I see a bright future ahead for your sophomore year. Leading a project like you've proposed will enhance your CV. All you and Lemarcus need to do is prepare a thorough outline before returning to campus next August. And you have over two months to do that. What do you think?"

Eve spoke for both of them.

"We can do it. We'll build on my sophomore enthusiasm and the Stanford experience Lemarcus has accumulated."

Lemarcus pushed into the discussion.

"You know Eve's got an intern slot in Cairo this summer. How are we going to get things lined up?"

The chairperson said, "Why, that'll be great experience for Eve. She'll learn first-hand what it's like to be an obvious minority, and no doubt she'll practice some type of teambuilding. So, if there are no further questions, you two carry on after finals week."

Eve offered to buy Lemarcus dinner at a popular off-campus restaurant, which was almost deserted due to finals week. He began to see more benefits as he ate more pizza.

"We can spend time together when you get back from Cairo, and maybe then you'll let me take you on a combined tour of South LA and Hollywood."

"I think I'd like that. And I'll call you while I'm away. I'll even send you selfies from the pyramids."

"Just make sure you're careful. The Middle East isn't the safest place."

"Don't worry, Alonzo will watch my back and I'll watch his." "When do you leave?"

"A week or so after finals. I have to make some calls to confirm the travel arrangements. And I'm looking forward to the whole package. This'll be my first time out of the country. I'm expecting it to be action packed…"

Action shifted Tuesday and Wednesday back to final exams, for which Eve's near-burnout preparation made relatively painless. She had only four more items to check off her to-do list. Thursday morning's meeting with her academic advisor promised to be the easiest, and she hoped her instincts would be correct.

The encouraging words and comfy office made Eve even more

optimistic, and the advisor approved her switching majors from biology to anthropology, applauding her virology internship because it added experience to her biology minor as well as an introduction to Middle East civilizations. As she wrapped up the meeting, she cautioned Eve to bring back glowing reviews from her Cairo mentors that would enhance her resume as well as academic reputation.

"You bet I will. I'm gearing up to be the star of the summer program."

Shaking Eve's hand, the advisor said, "I'm certain you will. Preparation and hard work are always justly rewarded. Come see me when Fall Term begins."

Eve rewarded herself and Alonzo by inviting him to an on-campus lunch. They arrived at the same time, but only Eve wore a smile. He unloaded as soon as they sat.

"I wish you could've taken my last exam. College algebra is my nemesis this term. You and the Bose twins are smarter than I'll ever be."

"That's the wrong attitude. You need to be as smart as you want, not as smart as someone else. And please remember what Nari said the last time the four of us talked about math. She's good because she concentrates on it, you're not because you don't, but you do great on anything when you focus."

"OK, OK, I get the message. I'll make sure to pick things that light my fire. Now, how're you doing? Are all travel plans set?"

"I'll know when I call that Indira person, maybe later today after my Ecology 202 final. And then I'll call the Bose brains tomorrow."

"Hey, what about me? Won't you let me know?"

"I'll tell Nila to call you. That always cheers you up, even more than whatever you're about to order…"

Eve marched back to her dorm after her ecology final, convinced she had aced it. She decided to build on her success by contacting Indira. The timing was right because her roommate was still away. Indira's GUI appeared as soon as she invoked the customized linguistic app.

"I assume your team has successfully completed finals week and all pre-trip preparations. What do you need to know next?"

"Uh… aren't you going to tell me?"

"You need to be more precise, more specific. Start using the brain Su-Lin's paying for."

"What do you mean?"

"Very well, I shall tell you. You and your three siblings are to rendezvous at Su-Lin's home next week. Adom will give you additional instructions. Call me after that if you need exegesis." Indira's GUI blinked off, leaving Eve stuttering only to herself.

"Damn, I don't think the Bose brains would do much better with you than me. I need a dictionary and a better brain if I'm gonna talk to you. I'm glad you can't hear me. You'd be correcting my syntax… should I be saying 'than I' or 'than me'? Either way, I know what I mean, and you should too. You've temporarily thrown me off my game. I'll call the Bose twins Friday evening. And screw you until then."

Eve felt much better after her outburst.

The Bose twins had been on cruise control during the weeks leading up to finals. Nila glided into the last week needing no more exam preparation. All but one professor had exempted her from the final because her cumulative point total put her at the top. And the only exam she had to take would be a take-home code-writing app, for which she was supremely confident would be an almost no-

brainer. Only two activities remained, one more cerebral and the other more physical. She planned to handle the cerebral one tomorrow. Her academic advisor had scheduled a Wednesday review of her sophomore year and a recommendation for fall term preparation.

Nila's prim demeanor contrasted with the advisor's effusive praise.

"You have covered yourself with academic glory this year. All your instructors tell me you have a great shot at a stellar academic career. One of them has asked me to offer you a summer intern position at MIT's Lincoln Lab. It's an easy drive from a dorm you can stay in over the summer. Here's his sketch of what he's talking about. He said you could work on classical-to-quantum compiler development, whatever that means. Please take a look and explain it to me."

Quantum Computer Schematic Quantum Computer

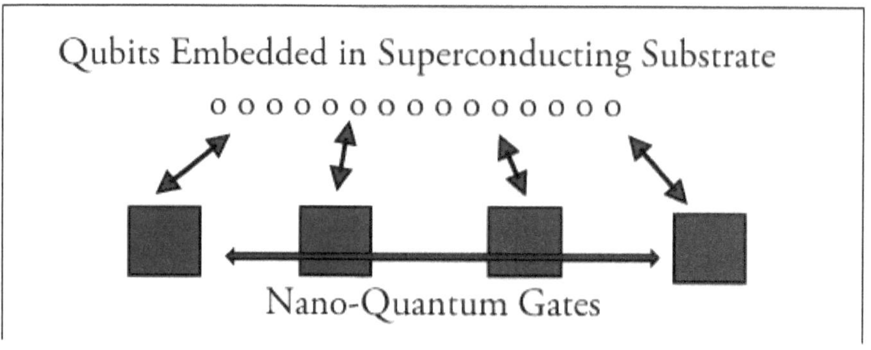

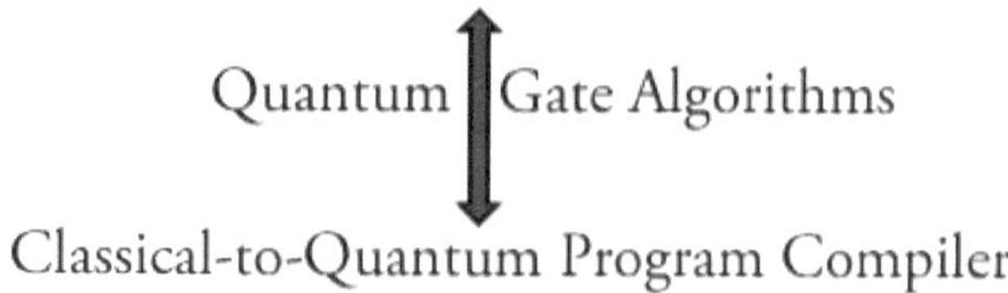

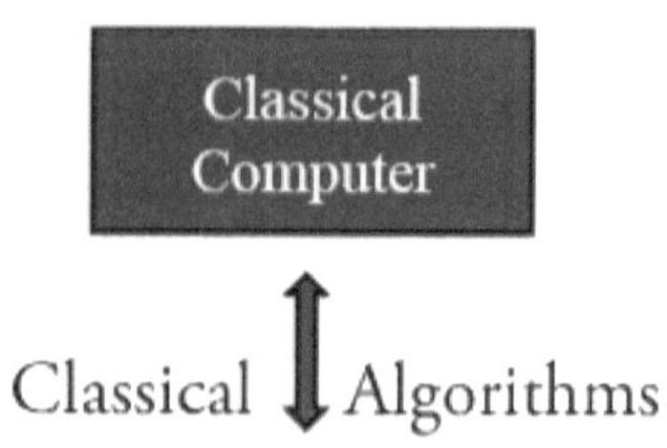

Quantum Physics Concepts Used:

- Qubits Encapsulated in Electron Spin State
- Probability States described by Schrodinger's Wave Equation
- Super-Positioning of Multiple States (Massively Parallel Processing)
- Entanglement for "Action-at-a-Distance" immediate Information Transfer
- Coherence for preserving Interference near Absolute Zero
- Current Tunneling through Energy Barriers

Nila studied it for several minutes, trying to mask her enthusiasm before saying,

"Writing a compiler that translates instructions from conventional to quantum computer circuitry is cutting edge. Is there a bus or van to and from the lab? I don't have a driver's license."

"Well, if that's the only obstacle, don't worry. We'll arrange for it." Nila's uncertain smile prompted a question."

"Is there another?"

"There might be. I tentatively accepted a software coding assignment working on an archeological dig in Cairo. I thought the hands-on experience would look good on my CV. By when do you need my decision?"

"The sooner the better. Lots of your fellow classmates would kill for this position. It's possible you could get assigned Fall Term, but there's no guarantee."

"Please thank the professor. I'll let you know by the end of finals week."

Nila decided not to tell Nari until after Friday morning's physical activity: obtaining a Massachusetts driver's license. Charles Chin, a junior from Beijing studying at MIT, would take her to the Revere RMV service center to take the "rules of the road" exam before taking an actual driving test on public roads.

Unlike all her siblings, Nila had postponed getting a driver's license, but her freshman year socializing convinced her that having one would help her navigate the real world, even though she preferred the academic one and Cyberspace. Charles had been coaching her behind-the-wheel skills since January when she got her driver's permit.

After driving early on a cloudless Thursday morning, Charles sat next to Nila in the center's waiting area, trying to buck up her confidence.

"I have a good feeling that the good weather is a good omen. You already cruised through the written exam and eye test, getting perfect scores. I think the driving exam will also be as easy as pi, going out as many decimal places as needed. Don't worry, just sit and read on your tablet all about compiler theory."

Nila smiled and followed his advice, but she did that too well. Charles had to nudge her when a booming voice called out a second time.

"Bose… Nila Bose. Front and center."

Nila snapped back to 3-D Space, then scooted to the source of the sound. A burly, middle-aged trooper who looked like he knew the drill peered down.

"Bose, let me guess. Freshman at Harvard. I hope you're alert enough to drive good enough to get your license on the first try."

"I think you mean well enough, don't you?" The trooper's frown deepened.

"Huh? What are you driving at? Are you trying to smart off like your privileged smart-ass classmates?"

Nila's naïve expression defused what might have become an unpleasant situation.

"No sir. I'm from MIT, and I apologize. I just thought you might like to know that the adverb well works better than the adjective good when modifying most verbs."

"You look and sound like a nice young lady, so no harm done. Let's get going so you can show me you know how to handle a car."

Nila followed him to a testing vehicle, expecting to be shown the driver's side door, but instead they stopped at the open trunk.

"Show me how to change a tire. And even though you probably won't, I'll tell you what most young people tell me: they'd use their cell phone to call for backup."

Ten minutes later, Nila still hadn't loosened the jack.

"You better stop and let me show you. But I'm surprised. You're going to the best engineering school in the world. What are you studying?"

"Computer software, sir."

"Well, you better get more real-world experience."

Nila was sitting behind the wheel fifteen minutes later.

"Thank you for teaching me how to change a tire. Are all jacks pretty much the same?"

"If you can work one, you can work all. And if you can't, MIT will ask you to return your diploma. Now, drive out and follow my instructions."

Nila did as told, navigating Boston's traffic better than the trooper expected and handling the three-point turn successfully, even though the car was larger than what she was used to. Both driver and tester felt better and better the closer they approached the last obstacle: parallel parking in the RMV lot.

Nila lined up the rear of the car with the front of the spot, but cut too sharply and drove too fast. Realizing her mistake, she cut the wheel sharply the other way, but in doing so she hooked the front cone's flag on the bumper. The clanging noise panicked her. She tried to slam on the brake but hit the accelerator instead. The car leaped backward, crushing a rear cone underneath before the tester could slam his. Nila's head jerked back and forth twice before she could stutter out some words.

"I-I'm sorry. I won't do that again. Do I get another try?"

"Not now, I'm sorry to say. You'll have to come back another day." Charles offered as sensible an appraisal as possible for this morning's fiasco.

"Well, now you know how to work the jack. And you can practice parallel parking using a bigger car. When would you like to start?" "How about next term? I have better things to do this summer."

Nari listened to Nila's story later that night. She could see the humor in it, but she also had to give some advice.

"I told you last fall to get your license ASAP. Now you'll have to retake the driving test. And if your backing out doesn't sit well with that Indira person, Eve is gonna be mad too."

"Has she called yet?"

"I'm expecting a call tomorrow evening. I wanted to meet with my advisor first, and that's scheduled for tomorrow morning. I'll call you after I talk with Eve. I hope both discussions go well. Unlike you, I have to take finals and I don't want anything else to worry about." Friday morning's gusty shower inverted Nari's umbrella, making the trek to her advisor's office even messier but she calmed herself before knocking. Once seated, her composure hid any anxiety from the no-nonsense professor.

"So, you want to switch majors from biology to a combination of psychology and sociology and add them to your archeology minor. May I ask why?"

The question calmed her even more; she had already rehearsed a pat answer.

"I think it's a better fit for my combination of numerical and verbal skills. I'm good with both but more comfortable with words than numbers."

"Hmm, all the courses you've already taken will fit, and so does the summer intern program you told me about. But you'll need to get good grades and sterling reviews from your Cairo mentors.

But judging from your cumulative record, I wouldn't worry about that. Well then, let's outline your fall schedule."

Though the rain hadn't stopped, Nari's brighter outlook convinced her to call Eve as soon as she returned to her dorm room. Eve's normal enthusiasm wasn't evident when she picked up.

"So, you're calling me. I hope that means all's well. What's the latest?"

"I'm AOK to switch majors. And the dig internship will look good on my CV. I'm bound to get high marks from my Cairo mentor. How about you and Alonzo?"

"I'm good too, but I had to get tough to keep Alonzo from backing out. I'm glad you and Nila are more sensible." Unexpected silence from Nari prompted Eve to keep talking.

"Is Nila having second thoughts?"

"Yeah, she's got a better offer working at MIT this summer, but she doesn't have to make a decision until week after next. What do you think?"

"Here's the latest news from Indira. All four of us are supposed to rendezvous in Austin sometime the week before Cairo departure. You and I can convince the foot-draggers to stay in line or else. So,

meet us at Granny Su's on Monday, June 13th. Alonzo and I are flying in a little earlier. And our Cairo flight leaves Friday from DC, so there's no date conflict."

"Why do you think the program has everyone departing from DC?"

"I asked the same question and dug into airfare. DC flights are the cheapest. But the connecting flights take a total of fifteen hours. I guess we can use the time to do more prepping. So, you tell Nila the plan. And don't let her talk with Alonzo until we get to Granny's. We don't want them scheming an exit strategy, do we? I'll tell him only what he needs to know. See you on the 13th."

Eve called Alonzo that evening, giving him all he needed to book his flight.

"I thought Nila was gonna call. What gives?"

"They're busy wrapping things up. You can talk to her when we get to Austin. And you should do the same. And I'll get us to the airport. Lemarcus will take us next Friday. We'll have all day Saturday and Sunday to chat with Granny before the Bose twins arrive Monday. Call me next Thursday and I'll let you know when we'll pick you up…"

Eve congratulated herself after disconnecting.

Pressure's off… I'm finished with finals and all pre-trip planning. Now I can pack up school stuff, put it in storage for Fall Term, and cruise around campus just for fun. And trip packing's already done and sent ahead. We're lucky the intern programs are so well organized. And if I feel like it, I'll read the virology program's info packet before we leave. But maybe not. I'll have fifteen hours on the flight to do that. No need to rush.

The pressure unexpectedly came back on Tuesday evening when Alonzo called.

"Nila just texted me. Do you know she doesn't want to go to Cairo? She's got a better offer, just like me. What are you gonna do about it?"

"Hey, don't get huffy. The four of us will talk like adults next Monday. It'll all work out."

"And that's not all. Did you read your virology intern program info packet? If it's like the dig program, you'll find out about a culture course we have to take as well as another one that's geared to the specific internship. Sounds like a lot of work. This so-called summer adventure is looking more and more like a misadventure."

"Uh, no, I haven't opened it yet. But I will."

"I asked Nila if she thought we should get to Austin earlier, but she said the tickets are nonrefundable. Oh, well, I'm counting on you to make things work. See you Friday."

Eve turned the pressure off after the call.

No sense fuming about what I can't control until I can do something about it. I'm gonna forget about it until Monday and enjoy what I've got lined up until then.

Everything fell into place because Eve followed her own advice and convinced Alonzo to follow along. Travel to Austin went according to plan; Eve made an extra effort to be agreeable when talking with Granny Su and planned to stay the course at Sunday evening's dinner. She had just helped Adom clear the table and serve hot fudge sundaes when Alonzo asked Granny what would happen if their summer travel plans changed. Her smile began to fade.

"Why I don't know. Eve, do you know about this? Have you mentioned it to Indira?" Eve switched her glare from Alonzo.

"Not yet, and not until I talk to the Bose twins. I sure wish I knew more about Indira and my background. You make me so mad. Why haven't you told me more?"

"I have. All these years I've done all I could. I, uh, I don't know what else to say. I can't remember much anymore. I'm sorry, I –" care-bot Adom interrupted.

"You are agitating my master. I shall have her rest now. Talk to Indira after you and Alonzo talk with your sisters. You are dismissed."

As Eve stormed out, Alonzo knew better than to stop her. Besides, he spied a different opportunity to prevent another meltdown from getting worse; he finished her ice cream after finishing his.

Before attending to other duties, Adom sat the Bose twins in the family room where Eve and Alonzo awaited early Monday afternoon. Nari spoke as soon as she read the tension in Eve's body language, even before she told everyone to login.

"No need to tell me. I know you already know that Nila and Alonzo want to bail on us. Maybe we should let them. You and I have enough enthusiasm and smarts to handle whatever comes up. I'm sure you can convince that Indira person."

Alonzo added, "And if that doesn't work, just tell her we're all going. Once we get there and know the score, we can decide when Nila and I can ramble on home."

Eve shrugged before replying.

"I don't think any of that's gonna work. Indira seems pretty sharp. Why don't you go play tennis so I can practice being devious. I prevaricate better when no one's watching."

Eve steadied her nerves before invoking Indira's GUI. When it opened, Indira spoke.

"I approve your choice of words. College is improving your vocabulary, but make sure you know when to equivocate. Would you like to ask me a question?"

"How did you manage to listen-in to me and my siblings?" "That doesn't concern you."

Indira's silence forced Eve to say something.

"What would happen if all four of us don't go?" Indira answered with a question.

"What would happen if I terminate your support?"

"Hey, that's not fair. Besides, only Granny can do that."

"Su-Lin is unable to manage her affairs, so I do that for her now. If all four of you don't go, everyone's funding is forthwith terminated." "But, what will we do?"

"Become adults. You're old enough and smart enough, and you and your brother have been pampered, protected, and privileged for seventeen years and four months, which is only one year and two months shorter than your sisters. If you are unable to handle what should be a fun-filled task, you shall suffer the consequences."

Suitably chastised, Eve surrendered.

"OK, I'll tell my siblings. Will that be all?"

"Not quite. I want you to fly to DC immediately and open up a house the four of you will use as your staging area until you leave for Cairo. Adom will give you the address and key and tell you what you need to know. Lock up and take the key with you when you leave. Then contact me for more instructions as soon as the four of you are settled in Cairo. Is that clear?"

"Yes, thank you. And I promise to –" Indira's GUI left before Eve's last words could come out. She froze midsentence before changing vowels, syllables, and expression.

"… be nicer to Granny and Nari and less rude than you. Go screw yourself. And I don't care if you hear me or not. Either way, I'm feeling better."

Eve felt good enough to break the news as soon as her siblings returned from the tennis court.

"Go shower and change. I'll go into all the details later, but bottom line is this; all of us go or else Indira cuts off our cash flow. It's a simple as that. We'll have to get around without Granny's money in both the academic as well as the adult world. Are we ready to leave the nest?"

Nari said, "I am and you are too, but poor Nila doesn't even have a driver's license. We'll let Alonzo chauffer her around."

Grinning at a worried-looking Nila, Alonzo was about to talk but Nari ignored him and continued.

"So, we're all in. Did that Indira person have more good news?"

"Sort of. I'm supposed to go ASAP to a house in DC where we can stay until leaving for Cairo. Adom will give me the address and key. I'll leave tomorrow, and all of you can fly there Wednesday. That'll give us Thursday to regroup."

"You better get with Adom while we freshen up. Sooner's always better for you and me." Eve hustled off to find the care-bot.

Adom was in the charging station next to Su's bed. She was sitting in a chair by the window, talking to herself while leafing through a biggish book as a tiny smile played across her face. Eve froze as the image loosened emotions she had buried for too long. Then she spoke before entering.

"Hi Granny, I'm leaving tomorrow to gear up for the trip. Adom will give me more details and I, uh… I want to apologize…" Tears washed away the remaining words. Eve rushed to hug Su, then fell to her knees, sobbing softly. Su stroked her hair.

"Eve, my dear, strong, fiery Eve. You never have to apologize for being what you are. And while you're gone, I'll try to remember more. I was just peering at some old pictures to help. Promise me you'll stay healthy and safe while you're away."

"I do, and I promise to be nicer too." Granny kissed the top of her head;

"Now go make plans to fly away and do what you must. My love is with you always."

As the rideshare approached the house late Tuesday afternoon, Eve's questions multiplied.

Who's Robin Setdarova, anyway?... why does she have this house in a DC suburb?... where did Granny meet her? Adom didn't tell me, so I'll snoop around for answers. And I'll make sure I put everything back in place so no one knows.

An hour later, Eve was about to make a second pass through the house when someone's knocking at the front door startled her. She hurried to find a matronly lady standing on the porch.

"I saw you drive up, and I thought I'd say hello. I don't mean to be nosy, but I thought we might be able to help one another. Are you related to Electra Kittner?"

"I don't know who she is. Who is she?"

"Sorry, I thought you might be related to her. I never met her but I did see pictures. She disappeared twenty years ago, about six months before my husband and I moved in next door. You must know or at least heard the name Robin Setdarova, the lady who lived here with her two daughters until they were killed in an accident last February. Did your family buy the house?"

"No, my friends and I have permission to stay until Friday when we leave for a summer study program in Cairo."

"How I envy you and your friends. Oh, to be young again, flying to foreign lands and making new friends while seeing how other people live. I know you'll have an exciting summer. Well, I'll get out of your way. If I see you again, you can tell me all about your summer adventure."

As the lady turned to go, Eve said, "Wait, please. Could you tell me more about Setdarova? What was she like?"

"A thin blonde, Russian features, a bit high-strung, and musically gifted. She and a couple of close friends ran a healthcare-related business. She was devoted to her daughters and told me she kept the porch light on every evening, expecting Electra to return someday. Did that for twenty years. That tells me that Electra must have been an extraordinary person, but that's all I know. Now, you take care."

Eve did that for three hours while peeking into Robin's keepsakes and coming away with images as well as more questions.

All these photos go way back when. Early on, I trace three: a Robin, an Electra, and a Christi. Then only two. I see a resemblance too, but damn, Electra's taller, more striking, and more athletic than me. And according to the clippings, she was an athlete, an actress, and an active political person. That's quite an act to follow. Granny couldn't have forgotten someone that extraordinary. I guess she never knew her, and since she's been gone for twenty years, I'm sure I won't either.

A ringing sound jarred Eve back to here and now. It was the home phone.

Hey, no harm answering. I can learn more. I'll be friendly.

"Hello, this is Eve Cortez. May I help you?" A metallic voice asked for Electra Kittner.

"I'm sorry, she's not here and I don't know where she is." "Then why are you answering the phone?"

"I'm staying here until my friends and I leave Friday for intern positions at AUC in Cairo. My friends will be working on an excavation and I'll be working on a vaccine project." Eve could think of nothing else to say, but the metallic voice did.

"If you talk with Electra, tell her to watch her back. You should watch yours too." The call ended abruptly, ruffling the hair on the back of Eve's neck.

Why the call, and why the not-so-veiled threat? What am I getting us into? Well, I won't tell even Nari until I know more. I think I'll tell it to Indira the next time we talk. But not until we settle in. Eve stopped worrying and returned to the now-here.

The metallic voice turned to his associate after disconnecting.

"Right number but wrong person. If the death of Set Darova and all close friends didn't bring Kittner back, maybe she is dead. But maybe we can use Eve Cortez. There must be a connection between her and the intern program and what we're looking for."

The associate added more.

"The fool told you enough so we can track her. Good, she's so trusting and naïve. We shall surprise her soon. And it will be a win for us, and maybe a win for her too. She might get a better view of how the real world works."

Chapter 7
Monday, June 06, 2157

<u>"The Adventure Begins"</u>

Eve is better than she used to be. I can work with her, and I'm glad she asked to sit next to me. She's not only smarter than I thought but also willing to keep Alonzo in line while I protect Nila. I don't trust him; he's smart enough, but he needs to focus on more than sex and sports.

When she comes back, I'll change subjects. We've talked and read enough about the intern program. Here she comes… and how nice… she has peanuts and a Coke for me too.

Nari began talking after each had taken a couple of sips.

"So, you're swapping majors and minors to and from bio and anthropology. Me too, but I'll have dual majors – psych and sociology – as well as dual minors – bio and archeology."

"One of each is enough for me. You're smarter and should be able to handle the load. And you've already got a head start on our program's comparative civilizations course. What were you telling us about Egypt and the Bronze Age before we left for the airport?"

"The Bronze Age collapsed suddenly, and there's a scary parallel between its collapse and current conditions in the world today. Beginning about 1150 BCE, all the major Mediterranean civilizations except Egypt entered a Dark Ages in less than a hundred years. Cities burned to the ground and were never rebuilt. People migrated and regressed. Hard to imagine, because their cultures and economies were sophisticated and interrelated."

"Isn't that supposed to add stability and resilience? Those are buzzwords I hear in news reports. What caused the fall?"

"From what I've skimmed, there are interrelated reasons still being sorted out by archeologists. Like today, where energy and rare earths are in short supply, back then copper and tin and gold were." "Now I see a connection between the metals and the name of the age. I learned in chemistry that bronze is an alloy of copper and tin. Am I right?"

"Yep, do you want to hear more?"

"Sure, go on. Thanks to you, I'm getting a head start too."

"OK. Well, it's possible that climate change created by volcanoes and earthquakes caused drought, famine, and floods, disrupting trade routes and economies. Jobs dried up and people starved. Ancient political orders, sophisticated as they were, couldn't cope. Add to that invasions by the mysterious 'Sea People' – possibly a confederation of warriors resulting from civilizations battling one another – and you have a perfect storm of destruction."

"Do you think it could repeat today? What about differing religious beliefs? Historians joke that religion has killed more people than all the wars combined. And what about diseases and plagues?"

"Hey, give me a break. I've skimmed, not studied the entire subject yet. Let the intern profs cover the rest."

"OK, And speaking of rest, that's what I'll do until we land. You're more thorough than Alonzo and me. Did you check the time and distance stats?"

"Cairo is six hours ahead of DC and 5800 miles away. When you include the connecting flight delays, it adds up to a fifteen-hour flight. That's why we land mid-afternoon on Saturday. So, we have six hours to rest. And we better, because when we land at Cairo International Airport, the pace of our adventure's going to pick up. It's Africa's second busiest airport, and according to what

I've googled, Cairo traffic is wild."

"Alonzo and I like to drive. Do you?"

"Poor Nila can't but I can, and I'm good. You have to be if you drive in Boston."

Eve ended the conversation by saying, "Among the three of us, we'll get around just fine. Now it's lights out until Cairo."

She punched the overhead light's off button to make it so.

Though Eve hadn't done a Web search for what Cairo's streets and settings look like, her nap made it easier for her senses to clue her in as the bus dodged through traffic and hurtled to the AUC on- campus residence buildings. The low humidity, high temperature, and an expansive celestine sky coupled with teeming streets emitting an aromatic mix of exotic fragrances and car fumes enchanted everyone looking out. Even Nila, who seemed overwhelmed by the pace, adjusted once Alonzo took her in tow. Nari let him because he instinctively seemed to know how to navigate in foreign territory.

Eve overlooked Nari's bossiness, letting her direct the team's next steps. All followed along until a tiff between the Bose twins upset the calm when registering.

Nila complained, "Really, I'm able to function quite well on my own. I think having roommates other than each other would be a broadening experience."

Nari countered, "You've been too sheltered by Granny and school. You should cut loose gradually. You and Eve can swap places in a week or two if you like."

Alonzo wasn't paying attention, so Eve poked him.

"If Nila and Nari are roommates, you'll be able to find them at the same location. And after we settle in to our rooms, let's meet back here in about an hour so we can get something to eat." All agreed, although one pair of twins seemed happier than the other.

Eve knocked before entering; fifteen seconds later, a striking black female, perhaps a year or two older and several inches taller and thinner, opened the door, smiled discreetly, and then spoke, her impeccable French accent complementing her features.

"Are you the Latino-American Evita Cortez from Stanford, my roommate?"

"Yes, but friends call me Eve. I'm sorry, but I forgot to ask about my roommate when I signed in. And you are?"

"Monet Banda from Paris-Sorbonne University, courtesy of Zimbabwe. Please, come in. After you unpack, we shall have dinner." "May my siblings join us? When did you arrive?"

"But of course. I arrived yesterday, but most of our classmates will do so tomorrow. Perhaps your siblings will bring their roommates if they are already here. I so much want to meet as many international students as possible, don't you agree?"

"I do. We'll have a great time when we share stories while eating…" The six-person cohort convened an hour later. Alonzo's roommate – Sanjay Kumar, a jovial Indian student from Mumbai's Tata Institute of Social Sciences – recommended they walk to the Larousse restaurant and coffeeshop. After two hours of spirited chatter, Sanjay suggested they sightsee nearby tomorrow before intern classes begin Monday, but Nari disagreed.

"Go ahead if you want to, but tomorrow Eve and I are going to plan a ten-week sightseeing schedule."

Waiting to hear from others, Eve spoke only to herself.

I'm all for it. I can use tomorrow to prep for Monday and contact Indira. And pairing Alonzo with Monet and Sanjoy with Nila will give each of them a new partner.

When it was her turn, she said, "All of you can tell Nari and me what a good time you had while we're planning for even more fun later. This is going to be the best summer of our lives…"

After the sightseers departed early next morning, Eve knocked on Nari's door and after entering announced a change of plan.

"It's too soon to plan a detailed sightseeing schedule. I think it'll better for today if we only build a three-section list. The first ticks off Cairo tourist attractions, the second near-Cairo places, and the third those that are distant-Cairo. How about I sit next to you while you search the Web, looking for places that fit each section, and I'll record them?"

"I like the way you're thinking. We'll be too busy the first week to prowl around, but by next Friday we should have a better handle on what and when the intern program has us doing. Then we can start placing our picks on the calendar. We'll use my tablet to surf and yours to build the list. Let's do it."

An hour later, Eve commented as she displayed what she had constructed.

Sightseeing Spots

In Cairo:

Cairo Opera HouseAl-Azhar Mosque Museum of Islamic Art Coptic Museum/Old Cairo Khan-el-Khalili Souq/Bazaar Bab Zuella Gate

Egyptian Art Museum Al-Muizz li-Din Allah Street Tahrir Square Manyal Palace Museum of Mod Egypt Art Shopping/Nightlife Near Cairo:

Pyramids at Giza/Sphinx Pyramids at SaqqaraAncient Heliopolis Memphis Necropolis Temple at TanisAl-Fayoum/Lake Faran

Citadel Mosque Complex City of Alexandria Nile River Trip Distant Cairo:

Valley of the Kings King Tut's Tomb Temple of Luxor Aswan Dam Temple of KarnakAbu Simbel/Rameses II White DesertSiwa Oasis Abydos Temple of Osiris

Mount Sinai Red Sea Thistlegorm Dive Site

"You and I can use this to be like professional tourist consultants, and we can add spots we learn about from people in the intern program who know their way around. If you can fit most of them in our ten-week stay, you're a planner extraordinaire."

Nari nodded yes before commenting.

"Our sightseeing will cover all aspects of ancient Egyptian civilization except science and technology. I hope our intern coursework includes them because Egypt worked wonders using the primitive tools they had. They invented paper and a language for writing on scrolls, used astronomical measurements to confirm the World is round, predict eclipses, and measure time.

"Their engineers were just as smart as those working for NASA, and even today we're still piecing together how they built the temples and pyramids and statues that have survived for thousands of years. And they figured out how to harness the Nile."

Eve said, "Maybe so, but look at what modern engineers have done. They built the channel tunnel connecting England to France and enormous dams in China and Egypt. We've got the Aswan Dam on our tourist list."

"Right you are, but a shadowy terrorist group blew up a train in the tunnel as well as part of the Aswan Dam and China's Three Gorges Dam twenty-some years ago. And it took a couple of years to repair the damages."

"Where'd you learn all this?"

"In a Harvard seminar, but let me add what I've found on the Web while gearing up for the trip. Depending on whose stats you believe, Cairo spreads its population of 20 million over 2100 square miles. Ninety percent are Muslim and the rest are predominantly Christian. And on the world stage, Cairo's in the top fifty on just about any ranking according to size, so if we rent a vehicle, I'll leave the driving to you and Alonzo. Cairo is supposed to be safe for tourists except when behind the wheel."

"Well, how about we take a break and do a little local sightseeing? I'll come get you in about an hour."

Nari agreed, so Eve headed back to her room, reminding herself when she entered that now would be the right time to call Indira. The GUI opened as soon as Eve connected; Indira waited for her to speak.

"We're all settled in and ready to start our programs tomorrow. And I'm ready for you to tell me what our next step is."

"I want you to meet someone at a location in the desert. I will load the GPS coordinates in a hidden and intrusion-protected location on your cell phone. It will be impossible for it to be copied or compromised and it will automatically be plotted on your cell's GPS when you invoke your mapping and tracking apps. You are the only one who can reach that precise location if you do not lose your phone, and you and your team must decide on a date and time to rendezvous."

"I know these apps. I'll bring them up right now." Five minutes later Eve stuttered,

"I-I know how to use these apps, but something's not right. The coordinates you gave me are hundreds of miles away… in the middle of the desert. Jesus lost his sandals in places less remote. What am I doing wrong?"

"Nothing. You must meet at that desert location. I will give you name and additional details as soon as you tell me the date and time."

"But how? I'm just beginning to know Cairo. I don't have anything to work with."

"Yes, you do. You have your siblings and all the resources of the intern program at your disposal. Use your brains to develop a solution. I'll give you one week. Contact me next Sunday. Is there anything else?"

"Uh, yes. I picked up a bizarre call when answering the phone at that house we stayed at near DC. A weird voice asked to speak to Electra Kittner, who I never heard of until I met the next-door neighbor. When I told him, at least I think it was a him, I didn't know where she was, he told me to tell her to watch her back, and I should too. What do you think?"

"It is good advice. Always watch your back. Best wishes for the coming week."

The GUI vanished, leaving Eve feeling an emerging panic attack. Maybe I'm not smart enough to deal with Indira. Maybe I should throw Nari to her… No, that's not right. I'll have to learn to handle the situation. But what to do?

I know, I'll shelve the problem for now and deal with it later. Nari and I can walk around and I won't tell her anything until I figure out what to do. Sightseeing and lunch might bring an idea or two."

Eve's registration packet included a link to maps of the area surrounding AUC's New Cario campus as well as one for the older location at Tahrir Square. She used it on her tablet as they hiked around, stopping at points of interest. An hour later, Nari picked a restaurant filled with locals, not tourists. The smiling waiter recommended two dishes: ful medames featuring mashed fava beans, and molokhiya containing chopped okra garnished with garlic and coriander sauce.

After strolling back to campus, they went to Nari's room.

After opening the door she said, "It Looks like our siblings and their new best friends are still out and about. We're back in plenty of time to rest and recharge for tomorrow. Why don't you come get me at seven sharp for breakfast before we head to the kickoff meeting? The others can join us if they're awake. And that reminds me, I'll take my meds early. I always feel better when I do. Did you remember to pack yours?"

"I decided a month ago to stop taking them. I never could tell if they did anything one way or the other for me, and Granny never told us why we need them. Doesn't that bother you?"

"Come on, they're nothing but a specialized vitamin that might help but can't hurt. I brought plenty. If you change your mind, let me know."

Eve returned to her room and planned to stay there the rest of the day. While leafing through her intern program notes, a thought came to mind.

I better call Lemarcus before turning in early. That'll keep my promise to contact him before the intern program starts. I hope he picks up. I'd rather hear his voice than the clacking of my keyboard if I have to send an Email.

His voice came through as clear as the Cairo weather.

"So, the international student is settling in. Are you having fun yet?"

Eve spent the next fifteen minutes telling him all she knew so far. Lemarcus gave her advice before ending the call.

"You've been busy and you'll learn a lot more. Have fun digging for artifacts or viruses, but please don't uncover any bad stuff or fellows who might take my place. And call me whenever you like so I don't worry about you."

"You're sweet. I'll be good and will call you when I can. Bye-bye."

An hour later, Eve had everything set for tomorrow and was about to slip into bed when her cell phone chimed. Caller ID showed it was Nari.

"Hi again, sorry to bother you so soon, but when do you think we can talk more about our trek into the desert? We better know more about where we're supposed to go and what we're supposed to do when we get there. And as soon as I know, I can start coordinating things. Maybe Nila and I can use whatever software apps the AUC intern program has."

"That's a great idea. I'll get more details as soon as I can after we go to the intern program kick-off meeting. How does that sound?"

"Good, and I'll let everyone know. Now you get a good night's sleep."

Eve was sleeping soundly twenty minutes later when Monet tiptoed in, careful not to wake her roommate.

But Eve would be tossing and turning had she known that Nari's call had been hacked by an automated intrusion app assigned to eavesdrop on summer interns. Her words routed the call to a human asset who decided Nari would be a prime candidate for leaking info that might lead his people to a treasure.

Good for my client; bad for this chatty female. And good she'll never know.

"So, where's the rest of our group?"

Nari jerked her thumb backward before answering Eve's question.

"Unlike us, they'd rather sit further back. Sanjay told Nila they'll get to the breakout sections faster than we will. And Monet said there are four programs, not only the two we're in."

Eve stifled her next question because the intern program chairman was about to speak. Although Egyptian Arabic is the country's official language, he dressed and spoke like a typical American college professor, but with even more enthusiasm than the best she'd had freshman year. His fluent English started flowing ten seconds after dimming the lights and displaying the first slide.

AUC Summer Intern Programs
Field Excavations (Egyptian / Persian Archaeological Digs) Virology R&D
International Relations Philosophy/Religion
Welcome to our Program and Congratulations!

- Ten-Week Program funded by your University
- Transportation, Room and Board, Weekly Stipend included
- College Credit Experience Resume Enhancement Friendship
- Tours of Historic Sites

You will be assigned to an Expedition, a Virology or an International Studies or a Religious Team led by AUC's and affiliated Universities' Faculty Members. Excavation Roles:

- Administrative Assistant (Project/Resource Management)
- Technical Assistant (AI-Enhanced Geophysical Prospecting – Location/Reconstruction DNA Analysis)
- Linguistic Assistant (Hieroglyphics/Tablet Analysis)
- Excavator (Fossil/Artifact Removal and Cataloging)

Virology Roles:

- Administrative Assistant (Project/Resource Management)
- Technical Assistant (DNA Analysis / Screening)
- Epidemiology Assistant (Current Bacterial/Viral Infection Analysis)

International or Philosophical/Religious Studies Roles:

- Data Collector
- Synthesizer
- Debater

You will attend classes and live at Excavation Campsite as well AUC Dormitories.

Studying the Bronze Age Collapse provides Guidance and Warnings for Today!

"I am honored to be addressing such a bright group of students who have gathered from diverse countries to share in a learning experience you shall always remember. And as my first slide shows, you will be assigned a suitable role as well as study subjects guaranteed to draw you in.

"My next slide gives you but a glimpse why Egypt continues to fascinate. But rest assured; your classes will delve into the details that I will only touch upon."

He paused to display it and then mentioned highlights before moving on. Eve liked it but thought she could make it better.

He's put too much on it and is talking too fast, which most profs do. But at least he talks clearly, and I like his accent.

Distant Ages Shrouded in Mystery!

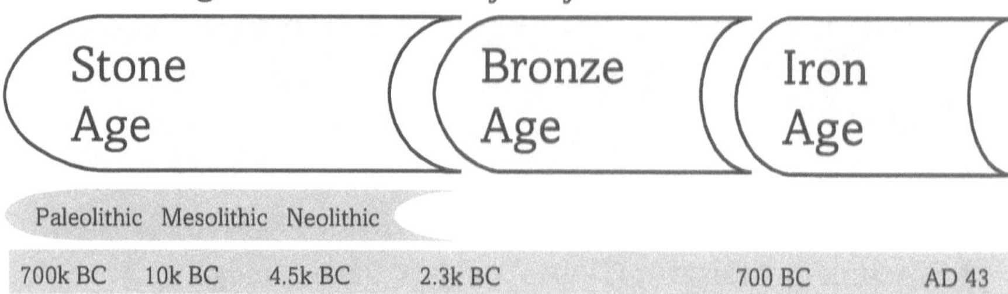

- Civilizations: Egyptian, Anatolian Assyrian Mycenean, Persian
- Bronze Age Civilizations: Large Cities and Populations, International Trade, Complex Economies Sophisticated Writing, Art, Technology
- All Civilizations except the Egyptian Collapsed in less than 100 years. Conjectured Causes: "Sea Peoples" Invasion, Civil Unrest, Wars for Scarce Resources (Copper/Tin/Gold Sea Ports Trade Routes, Food, Environmental Disasters (Droughts, Floods, Volcanic Eruptions), Top-Down/Complex Economic Collapse, Plagues (Locusts, Disease)

The Allure of Egyptian Archeology

- 5000-Year-Old Civilization Rich in Legend
- Mythology steeped in the Gods: RaIsis Osiris
- Culture that assigned "Almost Equal" Status to Males and Females
- Technologically Advanced: Built Pyramids, Temples, Underground Tombs, Invented Stone-cutting, Studied Astronomy

Popular Chronology of Kings and Queens and Pharaohs (Do you know "Pharaoh" definition? Great House!) All were great Politicians.

- Amenhotep RamessesTutenkamenPtolemy
- Hatshepsut NefertariNefertitiCleopatra

Popular History

- Nile River Irrigation
- Cross-cultural Exchange with Persian Empire
- Conquest by Alexander the Great (Melding of Greek and Egyptian Cultures)
- Alliance with the Romans (Julius Caesar Mark Anthony Cleopatra)
- Eclipse when Rome fell

Popular Legends

- Valley of the Kings, Valley of the Queens Mummies
- Treasures in Undiscovered TombsTomb Raiders Booby Traps, Plagues

"You shall also delve into the rich history of Ancient Persia. And archeologists have even more work facing them there than in Egypt because it remains the least known ancient civilization. My next slide illustrates."
Eve's comment to herself was the same as the previous.
Ancient Persian Archeology

- Least known of Ancient Civilizations (China Egypt Greece India Persia Rome)

- Middle East Civilizations as old as Egypt's
- Mesopotamia called the "Cradle of Civilization" – Tigris and Euphrates Rivers
- Crossroads for Trade among China, India, and Greece
- Zoroastrian (Monotheistic Religion) and Male-dominated Culture
- Persian Empire broke the cycle: Conquest Consolidation Expansion Degeneration Conquest…
- Persian Empire ruled "The Known World" starting 6th Century BCE
- Rulers: Cyrus the Great Darius Xerxes
- Legendary Capital City: Persopolis and its fabled "Seven Palaces of Parodesia"

- Builders of Roads, Temples, Underground Vaults and Tombs
- Politically Astute: Integrated conquered Cities/Populations
- Conquered by Alexander the Great (330 BCE) Persepolis burned
- Warring Tribes, Countries, and Religions followed death of Alexander (Cycle resumed)
- Today: Middle East a patchwork of: Religions Tribes, Ethnicities Races

Current Excavations:

- Looking for Underground Vaults, Tombs Treasures
- Piecing together findings and legends that place Treasures, etc. in the fabled Palaces of Parodesia, rumored to be along Persian Empire Trade Routes that connect Persepolis and contain underground treasure troves collected by Persian Rulers
- Examining Excavations for hieroglyphics and clues pointing to trade route locations
- Studying Egyptian Excavations for additional evidence of Bronze Age Collapse

"What we shall do now is reconvene into four groups, one for each of our programs. Excavations exit fourth door from the right, Virology fourth from the left, International Relations third exit from right, and Philosophy/Religion third exit from left. And please heed my warning:

Do not gossip about your projects outside classrooms or assigned teams. Our work is proprietary and we do not want anyone hacking into our networks or intruding onsite. Nor do we want any institutions – academic, government, or private – sniping at us or trying to steal our findings. Jealousy and thievery abound among our competitors.

And do not believe the preposterous stories that surface intermittently about AUC excavations serving as cover for covert CIA missions searching for pieces of defense satellites or nuclear weapons that may have fallen from the sky or from stealth aircraft and have become buried underneath the limitless Middle East desert sands.

"Nor should you believe stories that we have found irrefutable evidence proving the historical Jesus or are concealing sealed urns storing the fabled Pharaoh's Plague. Conspiracy theories, unlike the ancient civilizations whose artifacts we search for, never perish but are simply reborn as the eternal cycle spins.

"And one final instruction, we will meet each Monday, same time and place, for group announcements. Are there any questions before we break?"

Eve kidded to herself,

I'll ask Nari if she agrees that our chairman should take a refresher math class. His instructions for exiting need better calculations.

But she couldn't. Nari dashed for her exit before she could.

Eve filed out through the Virology exit and almost bumped into an angular Chinese male.

He smiled her way before saying, "I glad my math and word skill handle speaker talk. If not, I be stuck in chair."

"Same for me, but one way or another, I'm sure I'd figure something out to get up and go. Hi, I'm Eve Cortez from Stanford."

"Pleased meeting you. I Yang Lee from Beijing Institute of Technology. I hope we place on same team." Eve smiled back.

"I bet we'll figure a way to make it so."

Their conversation ended as the jostling separated them, but Yang caught up as they entered the room and walked towards the front row. This time she spoke first.

"Being in front right from the start usually gets me where I want to go that much faster. Easier to speak up and be seen, and we can position ourselves to be on the same team."

"I like your attitude." Neither could say more because an official bustled to the front.

"Don't get comfortable yet. Self-select into four teams of six. Then I'll tell you more about what you'll be doing for the next ten weeks. And since all of you like Virology, you're going to love your time at AUC."

Eve couldn't recall a first day of anything lasting so long. Her attention span ended midafternoon.

I'll ask Yang to join us for dinner. He can fill me in on what I didn't pay attention to.

Yang eagerly accepted and they hiked to join her group that was waiting outside the cafeteria. Now totaling seven, they sat briefly after staking a table before Eve made quick introductions.

"Hi everyone, this is Yang Lee from BIT – Beijing Institute of Technology. He and I are on the same team. Everyone, please say hi, and then we'll go through the line…"

Yang fit right in, adding to the multi-cultural flavor of their mini-cohort. When back at the table, he explained Virology's first day. Speaking for Nila as well as Alonzo, Nari did the same for

Excavations. Monet summarized for International Relations and Sanjay for Philosophy/Religion. After ninety minutes of sharing stories, fatigue caught up and the group split to recoup but planned to repeat every evening during the week while on campus. Eve waited until only her siblings remained before making a final announcement.

"I spoke with that Indira person and found out our next step. We have to pick a date and time to meet someone. I'm supposed to let her know by next Sunday and she'll tell me what to do next." Nari tapped her fingers on the table before talking.

"Maybe that'll be easy. By the end of the week all of us should know where and when we'll be out on a dig. And your Virology work keeps you on campus, or at least in Cairo. Our assignment is looking better and better. Maybe Nila and Alonzo can bail early."

Everyone started to smile.

Eve said, "There's only one or two complications. We're supposed to meet whoever it is at a hell-and-gone location somewhere in the desert. And I don't know what we're supposed to do when we get there." Puzzled looks replaced smiles. Eve launched her planned answer to the question nobody asked.

"And Nari's right. By Friday evening we should be able to pick a date if we pay attention to what's going on. And even though I don't yet know the person's name or what we do when we rendezvous, we'll figure something out to make things right. Well, let's call it a night."

Eve's fading smile didn't spread to anyone else.

Chapter 8
Friday, June 08, 2157

<u>"In the Flow"</u>

"I just might stay even if we wrap up our mission early. I've learned so much this week about using augmented reality apps for dig reconstruction as well as location tracking software, and even more next week when I go to the excavation site."

Thus spake Nila, the first to do so at the Friday evening siblings-only session. Nari followed.

"That's because she's the tech assistant while I'm the admin assistant on the same dig. We'll be working together when we're in the field."

"Eve said, "Tell me more." Nari obliged.

"Everyone assigned to a dig has a smart-ID badge. I use the ID number to assign people to tasks and allocate equipment and supplies accordingly. I'm learning how to do this using project management software. And if any people or pieces of equipment go missing, Nila can hunt them down." Nila added more.

"And we're learning the apps that do DNA analysis if we uncover organic matter. I wish Alonzo were on our team. We could help him if he were." Alonzo spoher ke right up.

"I'm glad I'm not. It's better I start picking stuff up on my own, and besides, I meet more people."

Eve asked, "I forgot what you told us yesterday. What's your role?" "Excavator. I bring in or out supplies and equipment before and after daily digging, adding my muscle when and where needed. It'll help me maintain fitness until I leave. Now tell us about you."

"I'm a tech assistant, which is sort of boring compared to what all of you're doing. I'll be at a lab bench taking samples and running tests. And our mentor pooh-poohs those rumors about excavations bringing back a Pharaoh's Plague bug buried in a tomb for over two thousand years. Anything we uncover has to be a zoonotic jumping from African mammals to humans. There are several possible sources we're tracking. Maybe something like this got Granny last year." Nari frowned.

"You be careful. Don't let one of them get you. And don't give one to us."

"I promise. Tell you what, let's take a break. I want to call that Indira lady and tell her all our good news, and we can reconvene at breakfast…"

Eve had to do so via cell phone while sitting at a table outside; Monet was in their room. Indira's distinct business-like voice came through.

"You are calling two days early, which tells me you are making headway. Have you selected a date and time?"

"Uh, we'll do that tomorrow, but I can tell you that we're all well- positioned to have a great summer. I think –" Indira completed Eve's sentence, perhaps differently than what Eve's words would have been.

"I will be the judge when you successfully complete your assignment."

"Uh,OK. Why don't you help me out by telling me who we'll meet and what we'll do then?"

"Very well. You will meet a person named Rani and will bring back whatever is given to you. Is that clear?"

"Very, but could you tell me who he is or what he does, or what he might give us?"

"I shall do so as rendezvous approaches. Contact me as soon as you have selected date and time." Indira disappeared; Eve's stomach knotted.

This can't wait. I'll get everyone together now.

Ten minutes later and trying to hide her anxiety behind a smile, Eve had everyone clustered at the bench.

"I thought you'd like to know what that Indira person told me. All we have to do is meet a Mister Rani and bring back what he gives us. Why don't we just pick a date and time that I can tell her to keep her happy?" Alonzo and Nila looked at Nari, who grimaced before talking.

"Does he have a last name?" Eve snapped back.

"Do you think we're gonna run into a crowd? I didn't ask, and she didn't tell me."

"OK OK, don't get mad. We can pick one, but you're the one she'll be mad at if we have to change it." No one spoke until Alonzo did.

"It'll work if we pick a date far enough away from today. I vote for Monday, July 25, at 3 a.m."

There was a pause until Nila asked, "How'd you come up with that?"

"It gives us more than a month to plan for it, and 3 a.m. sounds like we've given it a lot of thought."

Eve said, "I'm for it. Is the vote unanimous?" Silence said yes; Eve proceeded.

"Good, and we'll still meet for breakfast, but let's invite our new friends. See you then…"

All seven gathered at eight in the cafeteria. Eve made a surprise announcement as soon as everyone sat after bringing their trays back from the buffet table. Although Alonzo was the last to speak, his expression seemed to say that he liked what he had heard.

"I'll go with the flow and make the vote unanimous. Eve's recommendation to have a tour guide take us around the Egyptian Art Museum today is the way to go. All I have to do is look and listen and leave the thinking to someone else. There's little else I want to do this weekend."

Monet smiled and then said, "Come now, you are much smarter than you let on. You navigate Cairo so well after only one week; that tells me you have a fine head on those broad shoulders."

Eve added, And it'll come in handy; the Museum's on the edge of Tahrir Square. He can be our outside tour guide after we polish off the artwork inside. And aren't you glad I bought our tickets in advance? We can just show up and go with the next tour."

Sanjay agreed but wanted to know what would happen if someone didn't come along.

"I'm a good actress. I'd convince a clerk to give me a refund."

Alonzo's smirk needed no accompanying words to describe her acting ability, but he did have some for the group.

"We've been together for almost a week and haven't come to blows yet, so I'd like to christen us 'The Magnificent Seven.' Do we need to vote again?" A vote wasn't needed; the moniker stuck.

An hour later, they were part of a group clustered inside the museum. The tour guide's precise English matched her tailored uniform.

"I shall use the chart you are facing to summarize how ancient Egypt as well as its art is classified, starting from approximately five thousand BCE and ending when Rome conquered. It is divided into three kingdoms – the Old, the Middle, and the New – which are subdivided into dynasties. And the art depicts gods and kings and their court subjects.

"Why is this? Because the art was paid for by kings and high-ranking officials and scribes. And notice on the map how boundaries of the Nile River's annual flooding divide Ancient Egypt's worldview into an ordered region called Kemet or the black land, and a chaotic region called Desheret or the red land. This duality is reflected also by dividing the Nile into Upper and Lower, and their gods by inhabiting the realms of the living or the dead.

"You will see in the artwork how gods have human bodies and animal heads. And you will see that body proportions and positioning are unrealistic. Chest and heads are two-dimensional; legs and feet are out of alignment. Why is this so? Because gods face outward to accept offerings or rituals from worshippers who are honoring the afterlife. Now please follow me and I will show what I just told…." Two hours later, the Mag-Seven walked through the parklike setting outside. Monet was the first to offer an opinion.

"I liked them all, but the Rosetta Stone exhibit is my favorite because of the international angle. I didn't know Egypt is still pushing Britain to return it. It seems only fair. After all, it was found near Alexandria in the town of Rosetta during Napoleon's Egyptian campaign. And it was the key to cracking hieroglyphics."

Nari almost interrupted.

"I'm tired after two hours on my feet. Alonzo, find a restaurant where we can sit and talk."

It took him only ten minutes to have the group sitting in the Bab el-Sharq. Though he was sitting at the head of the table while Eve sat at the other end, he let her start the conversation.

Never at a loss for words, she said, "This place is great. Menu, prices, and outdoor seating fit us all. And I've got a winner of an idea. We're only a block or so from the Nile. Let's take a boat tour after lunch. We can sit and chat while seeing the banks of the river." Once again, no vote was needed.

Suitably reenergized and following Alonzo forty-five minutes later, the Mag-Seven boarded one of many awning-covered two-decker boats, all promising the grandest three-hour tour of "Cairo by the Nile." Soon theirs would be among them, snow-white shapes going with the flow and casting rolling wakes sparkling in the summer solstice sun. They paired off appropriately before sitting to enjoy the view and each other's company.

Alonzo and Monet sat on the top deck near the stern, listening to the droning voice of the guide for half an hour until Monet touched his arm.

"I have seen this before. Let me describe. You will like my words better…"

Her French-accented words painted precisely what he saw: riverbanks lined with tropical vegetation spaced among old and new buildings. In places, Cairo looked like a modern mega-city, but in others its Egyptian heritage dominated. Alonzo liked what he saw on the banks, but even more what was sitting next to him.

"Did you pick up your accent in Paris, or did you know the language before going to the Sorbonne?"

"We study English and French for obvious reasons in Harare grade and high schools, and attending the Sorbonne after winning a government-sponsored scholarship was a logical next step."

"What comes after that?"

"Graduate studies in international politics at a school located in the new Rome. My government will again sponsor me. I shall then have all the credentials to work for my country and help rebuild a Pax Americana that will last even longer than Pax Romana."

Monet was about to explain, but she saw Alonzo's confused look morph into one of determination.

"If Eve or Nari were here they'd automatically tell me what you just said, but let me figure it out… "I get it… A parallel between Roman and American dominance on the world stage. New Rome is Washington. So, you'll go to grad school in DC."

"Your three sisters are very bright. Eve and Nari are aggressive too. They must have intimidated you academically when you were a child. But you are bright too. Step away from their glow and let yours shine through."

"I've done that in sports, and maybe this summer intern stuff will spark an interest so I can find a new playing field."

"Please, tell me more…"

"I've heard enough about Egypt for one day. Tell me, what was it like growing up in Mumbai?" Sparked by Nila's interest, Sanjay rattled away from a seat near the lower deck's stern.

"The gods smiled on me. I am oldest son in a wealthy family. I got and traveled a lot. My Baba runs a thriving software company he and two friends built after graduating from Indian Institute of Technology. Though less so today than a hundred years ago, our culture gives more to sons than daughters. Human nature changes slowly. Still, we are better today than yesterday and will be better tomorrow. I am preparing to lead our company into the future. You are Indian, are you not? Tell me about your family."

"Nari and I are orphan twins. We were told our parents are Indian, but we don't anything about them."

"That is indeed unfortunate. Having a family and knowing your ancestors is important."

"Maybe for you and your Indian culture, but not for me. Some societies are redefining faster than yours what a family is. And I have a family – Nari plus Eve and Alonzo and the lady who sort of adopted all of us. She's our legal guardian and she's done everything possible, and I think I'm OK so far. Why did you pick the Philosophy and Religion intern program?"

"Baba tells me he needs people who have a strong liberal arts background on which to build an understanding of human nature and business world."

"What did you think of the Egyptian gods exhibit?"

"Ah, yes. A worthy summary of what Ancient Egypt believed. Its many gods embodied all phenomena of nature and were divine forces in

and of themselves. This pantheon was involved in all aspects of an Egyptian society whose religious practices sustained and placated, among others, Ra the Sun God, Horus, Anubis

and Osiris, hoping to turn them to human advantage. I hope to learn more this

summer."

"You talk like you memorized phrases from the descriptions."

"I did because I found them interesting. And now, would you please tell me more about yourself? …"

"Eve and Nari, sitting near the lower deck's bow, had Yang trapped between them. And he didn't mind; he was in a good position to defend himself from Nari's bombardment. Eve had his back as soon as Nari began firing.

"This tour is disappointing. I expected it to be like Cleopatra's barge cruising down the Nile, palm trees and dunes lining the banks and temples and pyramids in the background. How about you?"

"I think we're getting our money's worth. Perhaps a tour on a different stretch of the Nile will give you a view that you want. If that is your intention, we can do it on another weekend."

"Good idea." One of his words triggered an odd thought that Nari morphed into another question.

"Tell me, I've been meaning to ask if there are political intentions in your future? Doesn't China realize it lost the last "Cold War?" Why do you still have border disputes with India? And it's no wonder you've lost some of your economic clout. The World doesn't like how you continue treating Hong Kong." Eve jumped in first.

"Hey, cut him some slack. It's his parent's and grandparent's generation that caused those problems. His generation thinks more like us."

Thanks to Eve, Yang had weathered several rounds and was ready to speak for himself.

"I not political. I rooted in science and technology. It is bad America not good like China for long-term look. I no expert, but if you pick one topic, we debate both sides."

Nari unloaded more questions, but Yang's counterpoints matched her attack. All three enjoyed the duel that according to Eve ended in a draw and, like their counterparts, were happy for the tour to end. All seven had learned and talked enough by the time they returned to AUC's campus at 8:30. Everyone's smiles said Eve's advice sounded good.

"I'm staying on campus tomorrow to review first week's material and prep for the next. You diggers better do the same. When do you leave for your excavations?"

Nari was about to answer but turned to Alonzo instead. "I forgot. When do we?"

"Three choppers pick up the three teams from AUC's helipad at noon Monday. You can help Nila tomorrow because she'll be with you. I'm already set. And we don't return until late Saturday. I guess Eve and Yang'll have to have fun next Saturday without us. Let's do Sunday breakfast when we get back."

That was the last no-vote-needed decision of the weekend.

Eve's benchwork training during the following week added ammunition to her decision to change majors. She soldiered through the drills and earned approvals from her mentors, but by Friday would have gone AWOL if she could.

I feel like a drone doing these tests. They should rig a robotic device to handle all this monotony. Only the lectures keep me from going bonkers, and even on those days the best part is lunch with Yang. Nothing seems to bother or bore him. I'll have to ask him how he does it.

Eve waited for the lunch table to clear before saying, "What did you find most interesting this week?"

"Nothing if I make no game of drudgery. How about you?"
"Only some of the lectures. I wish I had a game to play."

"Try mine. I pretend I in prison and have no choice, so I focus on each step and lose myself in novelty. Greek philosopher say you no see same river twice, for fresh waters always flow in. Soon I so engaged I unaware of time. And when done, I no more in prison."

"I thought that piece of wisdom came from Confucius."

"I think it come from Greeks, but Confucius say 'A wise man marvels at commonplace.' He also say 'Happiness is when what you think and say and do in harmony.' I try practice when doing lab work."

"I guess it works for you, but I'm not you."

"He also say 'All people are same; only habits differ.' Why not you meditate on his teachings? They might bring tranquility when needed."

"I'll give it a whirl next week, but I won't need to on weekends.

They're always interesting, even when Alonzo and his other sisters are digging something else."

"I compliment your cleverness. You told me you wish you had game to play, but you already do. I enjoy your wordplay, your charm show through. I hope to hear more this weekend..."

Unlike his twin, Alonzo's activities kept him fully engaged in the now.

I like the mentor's confidence in my ability to handle responsibility. And I'm doing it. I can operate all vehicles and equipment and can figure out by myself what supplies to deliver. All this, and good exercise too. There's nothing like sweating in the sun to get you in shape. I hope the Bose twins are having as much fun. I'll find out on Sunday.

Nila's week went better and better as the days whizzed by. She adjusted to barrack-like quarters and impressed her mentor by mastering all the software thrown her way, even surfing the Web to learn more. Nari noticed too and told her so Friday evening.

"You're thriving out here. Do you realize how you take study to the next level when you apply it to something tangible?"

"Really? That's good, isn't it?"

"You bet. The ultimate goal of learning is not to just keep learning, but to apply it and then learn more. Keep doing it."

"I've been so engrossed in my software I haven't paid attention to you. What have you been doing?"

"Balancing some of the administrative drudgery with poking around the excavation. Have you been out there much?"

"No, only on that whirlwind first-day tour."

"Tell you what, I'll take you around the next week we're here. We'll have a grand time."

"I'm sure we will. And I'm ready to turn out the light. Don't forget, we're leaving tomorrow evening. Sleep tight."

Nari jerked awake an uncertain number of hours later, stimulated by a subliminal fear that she hadn't checked for her badge before falling asleep. She groped for it in the darkness but found nothing on her nightstand or near it on the floor. Only the soft breathing of Nila stirred the air.

What's my last recollection of having it?... heading out to the new digging site. I'll retrace my steps.

She put on minimal clothing, grabbed a standard-issue flashlight, tiptoed out, and pointed the beam two feet ahead. The blackness of the surroundings and the uncountable pinpricks of starlight sprinkled in the heavens awed her, forcing her to glance up and down as she followed a crooked route, confident she was on the right path. She felt a surge of relief when the beam bounced off what could only be a badge.

Pausing for a final glance at the Milky Way's magnificence, she then stooped to claim her prize, but a combination of disorienting darkness and dizziness from sudden bending shifted her center. She staggered forward, grasping for the badge but missing it; she remained tilted at ninety degrees, but gravity added to her forward momentum and propelled her headlong over an edge and into the void below.

A call from nature summoned Nila awake, amplified by no sounds coming from Nari's bed. It didn't bother her until she pushed into an empty bathroom; then a wave of panic washed towards her.

She's gone! Something's wrong… Now what? Her brain, not emotions, took control; she ran to her mentor after throwing on clothes.

"You're sure she's gone? For how long?"

"I don't know, but my sister would never deliberately wander away in the middle of the night. We have to find her."

"OK, we'll form a search party. Go and –" Nila talked over him.

"I'll use the tracking app to locate her badge. I hope she took it." Her mentor said nothing but agreed; after pitching into long pants and sturdy boots, he grabbed her arm and they charged into action.

A party of five followed the expedition leader and hiked toward the location glowing on the tracker Nila had given him. They reached it but found only the badge.

"OK people, spread out and search radially. She can't be far." Seconds later, a female voice yelled,

"I think I see her! She fell into the tunnel. Someone, go get a rope and the doctor."

"An apologetic Nari bounced back to life twenty minutes later on the same spot previously occupied by her badge; the glow from lanterns illuminated Nila and the doctor kneeling next to her. She spoke hesitantly after helping arms propped her up.

"I'm sorry, I usually stay out of harm's way." The doctor's reassuring voice answered.

"No permanent damage done; the sand cushioned your fall. But next time, stay inside at night. Don't go looking in the dark, even with a flashlight, unless you've got someone with you."

Two fellows hoisted Nari to a standing position. Then Nila hooked her arm around Nari's waste as she guided her back to the barracks but said nothing. Nari had to speak first.

"Who found me?"

"I guess I did, thanks to the tracking app." "I'm lucky you're so smart. Thanks."

"I'll say the same about you. And we both have a great story for our compatriots. You can take the lead and tell whatever version you like."

"I'll stick to the truth. It's usually better than fiction and always comes out in the end. And I'll make you the star. You're learning how to navigate in 3-D space. From now on, I'll stay out of your way. And be careful when you follow me. You might need to pull me out of a hole."

Nila's kiss on Nari's cheek showed more than any words could speak.

Chapter 9
Sunday, July 03, 2157

<u>"Work and Play"</u>

The Mag-Seven needed no voting at breakfast Sunday; everyone agreed that Nari's narrow escape from serious injury won top marks for excitement that week, and that Eve's sightseeing pick for today, the Museum of Islamic Art, would add to what they saw last Sunday; it also had additional spots nearby.

The group would depart in ninety minutes, which gave the siblings enough time after the others left the table to continue discussing their special assignment. Team leader Eve kicked off the meeting.

"I hope all of us have learned enough so we can collectively piece together how we'll accomplish the mission. What do you think?" Nari's fall had softened her fault-finding tendencies and loosened her sense of humor. Her expression said so.

"I think your choice of words is AOK. It sounds like we're on a search, like in Raiders of the Lost Ark or a Mission Impossible movie. And from what that Indira person has told you, we are, sort of. And since Nila's the smartest, let's hear what she has to say."

"I think we can use project management techniques to come up with a solution. We have three people who are positioned to put together what we need. Let me sketch what I mean." Nila continued after diagramming her plan.

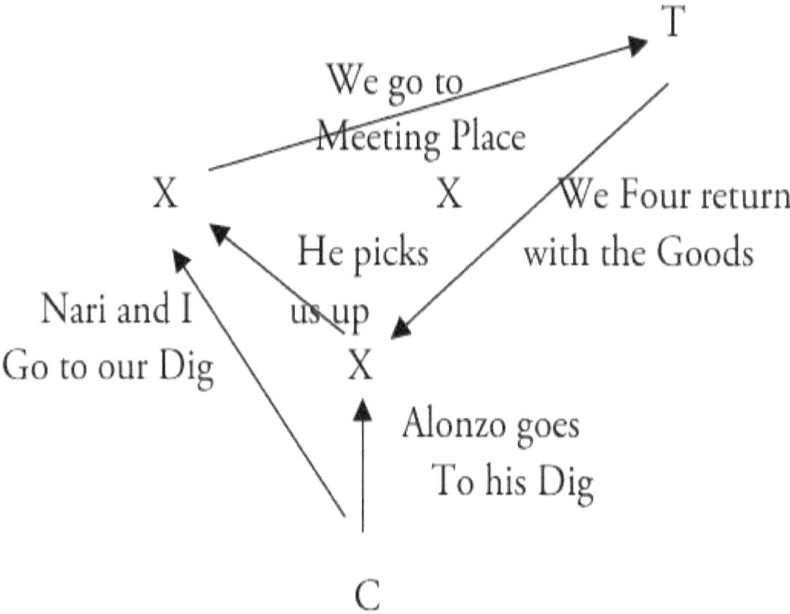

We Three leave from Helipad

"The X's mark dig sights. C is Cairo, and T is where we meet Mister Rani. Nari can use her Admin Assistant position to make sure she and I are assigned to the same dig for that week. I can help her with the software to do that.

"Alonzo figures out what vehicles and equipment we need. Then he and Eve pick us up. I'll help him work the software apps to get the goods. Then we meet Rani and return with what he gives us. So far so good?" Everyone looked at Eve.

"I think so, and I think I see my role in all this planning. While you three nail down the outbound trip, I'll figure out how to get myself to T and then all of us back to where we belong. Is that good, or what?" Alonzo rubbed his chin before saying,

"Timing is everything. I have to make sure we're supposed to be at the digs on the date Eve picked. What is it?"

"Uh, it's July 25th, isn't it? We rendezvous with this Rani character at 3 a.m."

Nari said, "Alonzo better check distances because he and maybe Eve have to drive vehicles to get us to and from. You know, this is AOK. We can work on the pieces this week and meet next Friday evening to decide what's next."

Eve kidded, "I'll stick with the military lingo and Say 'Roger that.' And I'll add it to what I'll do this week. I'll pick next Saturday's sightseeing activity. It'll reward our hard work by giving us a great place to play. What do you say to that?"

Nila said, "That's a wrap. Now let's get ready to see today's attraction."

Eve didn't have to haggle with cabbies because she had already arranged for two taxis. Bragging only to herself as she led the Mag-Seven into the Museum, the building's impressive exterior added to her exultant feeling. Everyone agreed that her decision to purchase tour tickets in advance was the best way to go. Twenty minutes later, their tour guide launched into his script.

"**Welcome to** the Museum of Islamic Art. We are considered the greatest of its kind in the world, with our exceptional collection of rare woodwork and plaster artifacts, as well as metal, ceramic, glass, crystal, and textile objects of all periods, from all over the Islamic world. We have over 7,000 artifacts in our 25 halls and archeological garden. They were transferred here in 1903, the year our building was inaugurated. Originally called the Museum of Modern Art, it received its current name in 1952.

"When our collection swelled to more than 100,000 by the start of the last century, the Egyptian government elected to renovate and reorganize, and the redesigned museum reopened to visitors in 2010, displaying only a small selection from the entire collection.

"Sadly, our Museum has periodically been the target of terrorists, but advances in AI-controlled security systems have greatly reduced the threat. The last ones occurred during the Great T-Plague Pandemic fifty years ago. And do not listen to rumors about a 'Pharaoh's Plague' that supposedly revisits when excavations uncover tombs protected by mythical curses. You are perfectly safe among the crowds touring the Museum.

"Now please follow me. You shall see during the next two hours a striking sample of the splendor and sophistication of Islamic artwork…"

After the tour, the Mag-Seven followed Alonzo to a less-touristy restaurant, whose menu items and prices fit everyone's taste. Happy to listen more than talk, Eve didn't bother sitting at either end of the table, leaving them for Alonzo and Sanjay, who enjoyed extending the discussion to religion and philosophy.

"Egypt is a Muslim country, but it is much more tolerant and not controlled by the caliphate, which is ostensibly Isilabad and its subservient countries. I will not speculate on what fraction of the faithful believe the angel Gabriel dictated to Muhammad, while in a cave, the very words recorded in the Quran, which is indeed strict. The first Islamic philosopher, **Al-Farabi**, attempted a synthesis of Muhammad and Aristotle. His successors – Avicenna and Averroes – pushed ahead but the caliphs and their successors pushed back to stricter law for more theocratic control, rather than reaching for the Enlightenment and Modernity.

"**Today you see that even in Cairo,** people dress modestly compared to the West. Women's clothing should cover legs and upper arms, and men's their chests. Public displays of affection are frowned upon."

That piqued Eve's curiosity.

"We'll have to plan a nightclub tour to see for ourselves. Maybe a dance club too. That's how Nila gets her exercise. She can teach you guys all the right moves."

Nila's smile showed she agreed, but she and Eve let others carry on. They headed back to campus ahead of the others, claiming they wanted a head start on the coming week's workload.

Even with a head start, Eve's following week lab work didn't measure up. She fidgeted with the equipment and her mind wandered to more interesting activities: the Indira assignment and the weekend sightseeing. Her mentor called her aside Wednesday morning, cautioning her to be more attentive or her evaluation would suffer, so she acted her part until Thursday noon when she faked an upset stomach and went back to her room, happy to work the rest of the day on what she wanted. And it paid off when later that afternoon an idea flashed in her brain.

I got it! Now I know how to get to and from Rani's rendezvous. I'll take the place of a female on Alonzo's team. With his help, we'll find a way to steal her badge or make her late or get her to swap roles with me for a day or two. Problem solved. Now for the fun stuff after I call Indira. I'll do it now, while Monet is still having dinner with the group.

Indira spoke immediately when her insouciant image appeared on Eve's tablet.

"I was expecting you to contact me sooner. What can you report?" "Good news. We'll meet Mister Rani on Monday, July 25th, at 3 a.m."

"How did you arrive at that date and time?" Eve's confident veneer began to crack.

"Well, it fits our plan." Indira kept chipping away. "Please describe the details."

Eve dug down deep but couldn't find enough to satisfy Indira.

"Your plan is incomplete and contains too many moving parts. And you have much to learn about knowing when and how and to whom you can prevaricate. But I am beginning to admire your grit. Reconvene your team and reevaluate. Report back when you can support your date and time." Eve expected Indira to vanish immediately, but this time she waited. Eve filled the silence.

"How much time will you give me?" Indira smiled enigmatically.

"As much as you need, but don't disappoint me. Good luck." Indira vanished.

I feel better after this call than after previous ones, but I still get this feeling she's toying with me. Well, at least I know where she's leading us. I'll let my team know at dinner tomorrow. And then I'll let the Mag-Seven know all the details for Saturday's outing.

Nari's hushed summary carried the sentiments that settled Eve at Friday's dinner table.

"Nice work. You held your own against that Indira lady, and like Alonzo says, he's got enough time to find someone who'll play along. Now you can tell us what's on our tourist list as soon as the rest get here. And Sanjay's almost ready to sit, so everyone, switch subjects."

Sanjay began talking as soon as he settled into the chair reserved for him next to Nila.

"Sobek, the crocodile-headed god of the Nile, will watch over us tomorrow. I'm certain he picked up on the hints about Giza that Eve dropped during the week."

Eve said, "And I'm certain tomorrow's adventure will exceed everyone's expectations. I'll unload in a minute or two everything you need to know. Monet and Yang just came into view."

Eve continued after the new arrivals sat.

"You can see from the southwest outskirts of the city our destination's Great Pyramid. The Giza plateau is the necropolis for the royalty of the Old Kingdom. I've booked us for an all-day tour. And because there's so much to do when we get there, I already reserved places in two of the three most exciting activities, which are quad bike touring, felucca sailing, and hot air ballooning. And I've already assigned everyone. Guess who's going on which?"

Eve announced the lineup after five minutes of Mag-Seven's guessing.

"Aha, my people-instincts are almost pitch-perfect. I've got all but one of you placed where you want to be. Sorry Monet, but you'll be sailing on the Nile with Nila, Sanjay, and Yang instead of floating in a balloon. Meanwhile, Alonzo, Nari, and I will be zooming across the desert sands, seeing the pyramids and the Sphinx at quad bike speed."

Monet's always calm voice would have concealed any disappointment, and today her sfumato-like smile said that boating would be fine.

"I have sailed on the Seine, but not in Paris. Sailboats must be careful because of Parisian bridges. Egyptian boats use felucca rigging, which sounds and looks so Middle Eastern. The Nile should be safe, no bridges should get in our way." An always cautious Nila raised a concern.

"What about crocodiles? Isn't the Nile teeming with maneaters?" Monet's eloquent diction sounded like a documentary.

"You chose an inappropriate verb and noun. Indeed, crocodiles do populate sub-Saharan African rivers. They are also found in Asia, Australia, and South America. And when hungry they will attack anything that is unfortunate enough to cross their paths. And Sanjay told us they were once revered religious figures, swimming the entirety of the ancient Egyptian Nile unchallenged.

"But today there are few if any remaining outside southernmost Egypt. Construction of the Aswan High Dam in 1960 has pushed their nests towards man-made Lake Nasser and elsewhere. Sanjay, what would you care to add?"

"**They are depicted along with many Hindu gods and goddesses in sculpture and painting.** My Baba took me on Ganges boat rides when I was a youth. I do not recall seeing any, but he warned me not to dangle my hand in the water because they are lurking just out of sight. I think we'll be out of harm's way. And if not, hiding monsters add to the excitement, wouldn't you agree?"

Yang's and Nila's expressions remained unconvinced, but they chose not to speak. The Mag-Seven continued swapping stories until Alonzo finished the last morsel of Monet's dessert.

Then Eve said, "Let's turn in now and have breakfast earlier than usual. Our bus leaves six hours after zero dark thirty, and the sun rising into a desert sky should be a spectacular sight. Get set for a day of excitement. We'll pack in as much as we can. Oh, what fun we're going to have…"

Eve reminded the sailors just before they exited the bus at the first stop.

"You'll be on the Nile longer than we'll be in the desert. We'll meet you here when your sailing's done."

Nari and Alonzo added their wishes. Fifteen minutes and two stops later, the bus deposited three groups of desert riders at the quad bike center. Each would have its own guide after an introduction delivered by a speaker dressed like a sunbaked modern-day Lawrence of Arabia. Standing in back of him were three men wearing goggles and protective gear.

"You are the first riders of the morning for a quad bike caravan, which means you'll stay out longer than later groups because the heat is lower. Maybe four hours, during which you will see the iconic Great Pyramids, Sphinx, and Valley Temple.

"Please respect our requirements, you must stay hydrated and wear the goggles and protective gear like your guides standing behind me are wearing. You must also sign a personal injury waiver. Our guides know the equipment and terrain and will lead each caravan, but drifting sand can build unstable ridges or obscure obstacles. Our safety record is among the best, but accidents do happen occasionally. Our guides carry two-way radios if assistance is needed.

"Please be watchful, follow single file, and keep pace. The roar of the bikes makes communications difficult. Blast your horn if you need help. And now, please pay attention as I show you a map of our caravan routes. Each group will take a different one. All take in the best of the Giza Plateau and give you a memorable Sahara

Desert experience at its most iconic as you zoom safely over the sand…"

Eve's mind wandered elsewhere.

This guy looks authentic, but his voice has baked in the desert sun too long. I can't tell if the guides are weather beaten too, but since the engines will drown out whatever they might say, understanding what they might yell isn't necessary.

No questions followed, so the guides led the riders to their quads and then explained how to operate. Showing worked even better than telling. Fifteen minutes later, three caravans departed. Eve had ordered hers: she directly behind the guide, then Nari, and then Alonzo. And he didn't mind.

Sis sure likes to be the boss and that's OK. Her instincts and people skills are usually right on target. She put me where I wanna be – rearguard position is right for me. I can see where everyone is while taking in the view. And what a view this is gonna be. Better than any action-adventure movie whose Hollywood stars are charging through the desert. Maybe I'll stay put, even if the Coach calls.

Alonzo became totally engaged in the tour, totally focused on what was in front of him and taking in everything with all his senses while using the drivetime between major attractions to file away segments of this once-in-a-lifetime thrill.

He was doing just that when the rider two positions ahead unexpectedly swerved ninety degrees to the right and accelerated towards a ridge twenty feet high. Alonzo's focus shifted to the wayward rider even faster than the words he yelled to himself.

What the hell is Eve up to? Holy –. No more words were needed. He saw her charge up the ridge, teeter at the top, and then disappear.

Alonzo's instincts kicked into high gear. He blasted his horn while charging forward to the guide and then pointed to his right.

Then he slowed enough to navigate a tight turn that pointed him in the direction of Eve's last sighting. Two minutes later, he stopped at the crest and peered down the other side. Thirty seconds later, the guide did the same. Both were now taking in a disturbing sight: the final resting spot of Eve's flipped quad bike half-buried in the sand.

They could see a trail left in the downward-sloping sand that showed the quad had rolled over several times before coming to rest at the bottom. But they couldn't see Eve. Both of them killed engines and dismounted before the guide cursed in a language Alonzo couldn't recognize. Then he shouted in English.

"What nonsense! What foolishness... come, we must dig her out." As they half-slid, half-stumbled towards the bike, muffled screams filled the air. They came from Eve, who was pinned underneath the quad. Their combined strength barely able to drag it away, they now saw what remained: a no longer screaming Eve still partially buried in the sand. The guide motioned with his arms as he spoke.

"We dig away enough sand to see body. Then we stop before go." As soon as they cleared away the sand, Alonzo saw what he must do next. He spoke slowly, hoping the guide would understand.

"She's my sister... Look at the position of her left arm... she's got a dislocated shoulder. Please, help me drag her slowly to a flatter spot and then roll her over."

"OK, then I call backup."

Nari came slip-sliding towards them by the time they had Eve on her back. After staring for only a second, she was about to talk but Alonzo waved her off.

Then the guide said, "Now I call... you do what can."

Alonzo knelt next to Eve, who was crying from the pain but biting her lips to keep from swearing. Holding both sides of her head, he leaned close and forced her to look him in the eye.

"Sis, what the hell got into you? What were you trying to do?" Pain kept Eve from moving, but from the expression written in her eyes, it hadn't dulled her thinking.

"Show off, I guess. What did I get for it?"

"A dislocated left shoulder. I know it's painful, but I know from lacrosse how to pop it back in place. Keep still and I'll rotate the ball joint into where it belongs."

Using two hands, he locked her left arm against her body and lifted her hand to form a ninety-degree angle at the elbow. Then he slowly rotated the hand towards the ground.

As more tears flowed, Eve whimpered, "It hurts… it hurts." "Go ahead and swear. You can stand pain better if you do."

She didn't but started panting faster, and when Alonzo forced her hand onto the ground she was past the point of swearing. Her screams scorched the already superheated air and busted through hand-cupped ears, curdling everyone's blood but Alonzo's and forcing the guide to look away.

Alonzo brought her hand back to vertical and then lowered it to the ground. That position and his calming voice silenced Eve's screams.

"You're tougher than a lot of my teammates. Tell me when you're ready for a different maneuver." Eve winced, gasping twice.

"I-I'd call you a son-of-a-bitch, but what does that make me? Go ahead."

"We'll do traction-counter-traction. I need a volunteer." The guide swiveled his head towards Nari, who spoke before their gazes met.

"I will."

"Here's what we do. Mister Guide, please give her your belt. Then she'll wrap it around and just underneath Eve's armpits. Then I'll slowly put the arm straight out from her body but still on the ground before crooking it 90 degrees and looping my belt around her arm at the elbow. Then Nari, you kneel next to her. I sit on my butt and plant my feet against her side so I can push and pull at the same time. I'll tell you to pull gradually and I'll push-pull the same when we're in position." You got the picture?" Nari nodded. Alonzo spoke again four minutes later.

"It's OK for you to swear at Nari. OK Nari, pull slowly. Eve, tell us what you're feeling."

"Not too much pain… just increasing pressure… I'm feeling more pressure…. I just felt a thunk. I think it's moving back into place." Seconds later, Alonzo yelled, "Nari stop… hold the pressure like it is. Eve, what do you feel?"

"A little pain and a lot of pressure."

"Great. Mister Guide, you and Nari remove the belt and help Eve stand but don't use her left arm. Do it after I remove the belt I'm using and am kneeling next to her."

Minutes later, Eve – now facing Alonzo less than a foot away and supported by Nari and the guide on either side – waited for further instructions.

"We're just about done. Plant your left hand on my stomach and walk your fingers up to my shoulder to find a comfortable position, then curl them on my shoulder, stand straight and throw your shoulders back. Do it now, and then I'll support your arm with both of my hands to massage and loosen its muscles and check how well the joint is aligned."

Minutes later, an approaching swirl of sand containing the rescue van marked the end of today's adventure for Alonzo and Eve and Nari. The EMT walked them to the side door before Alonzo gave a final instruction to Nari.

"Go tell the sailors what happened." Eve's stoic expression told as much about her character as any words might.

She said, "They must have had more fun than me. Next time I'll believe it when they say I'm safer on the Nile than in the desert. I don't know if a croc can swallow me up, but today I saw that the sand can definitely suck me down."

"Don't worry, I'll make it sound like they should have traded places. Stay safe."

Soon after the van departed, the guide led Nari back to the adventure's starting point, leaving Eve's capsized bike and Alonzo's – still parked atop the ridge –for another rescue mission.

Nari kept her gaze glued to the quad ahead but her thoughts centered on those in the van.

They're better than I ever thought. I can't match Eve's grace under pressure or Alonzo's command when danger strikes. I'm done seeing stuff today. It's not the same if Eve's not with us. I bet the sailors will say the same.

The captain's steady hands on the tiller and authoritative voice told Nila and her crew that there would be only smooth sailing today, even joking that no crocodiles would get in their way. Cushions lined the cockpit for the entire length of the weathered but sturdy hull, making it comfortable for holding numbers up to only one or two more than today's crew of four plus the man at the helm. It glided effortlessly, zigzagging across the Nile's half-mile width to show up close the shore's attractions that enchanted Nila.

Our adventure is widening my horizon and showing me what goes on outside my ivy-covered walls. And even if I do leave early, I'll take with me all I've learned. And with it will come memories of newfound friends from exotic places. Maybe Alonzo feels like I do. I'll ask him when it's just the two of us, but I'll have to figure out how to pry him away from Monet. I think I know how to do that.

Three hours of unruffled sailing put the crew and captain at ease and about half a mile upstream, or south, of their docking pier and fifty yards from the lee, or eastern, shore. Nila and Sanjay were standing next to the captain near the stern and peering over the starboard side when a sudden gust sprang over the port side and knocked Nila's cap into the sail. Lunging for it, she missed and lost her balance. Sanjay grabbed hold to steady her, but their combined center of gravity was overboard. The captain's strong arms brought it back but the twisting effort tumbled him unceremoniously into the river and thrust the felucca further away from shore.

His actions spoke louder than his earlier crocodile words. He thrashed towards shore; the felucca, happy to be rid of the extra ballast, skipped further west, like a child willfully avoiding the grasp of a parent. Once safely on the bank, he waved arms and called out instructions to the four aboard, but they were facing west and following their own devices. As the spar pivoted from port to starboard, they ducked just in time to avoid getting tangled in the sail. Nila and Sanjay were now wrestling with it while Monet and Yang waggled the tiller back and forth; their resultant force gave nothing but circular motion, a most dangerous direction if there had been a significant wind.

The captain knew what to do; he abandoned his crew for more nautical help. Forty minutes later, he and a pier hand rowed a skiff close enough to throw a line; Yang secured it to a cleat near the bow and the skiff towed the felucca to the pier.

And though Nila's cap was still missing, not so for her sense of humor, which she poked in Yang's direction.

"Too bad one of us didn't record a cell video. It would have been a Chinese fire drill Yang would be proud of."

"Yes, lucky me. No cell phone and only one spectator on distant pier. Who think you it be?"

Continuing to gaze at the slowly approaching pier, Monet spoke next.

"There would be three if it were a welcoming party for us, but I'm glad it's not. Alonzo might show us more respect, but your sister and Eve would be doubled over laughing if they had seen us in action."

Even though Nari had seen most of the drill, Eve's accident had worried away her ability to joke. Nila was the first to shout out when they were within hailing distance.

"I hope you didn't see much of our seamanship. Where's the rest of your biker gang?"

Nari waved but said nothing until the four were on the pier and walking toward her. Her expression said nothing, but her words said all that was necessary.

"There's been an accident. Eve's in a world of hurt." Four came running.

Chapter 10
Friday, July 08, 2157

<u>"The Hurt Locker"</u>

Eve demonstrated at the Mag-Seven Friday dinner table why she wouldn't join them for sightseeing this weekend.

"I'm still in the hurt locker. Watch me try to do something I can't." After standing, she slipped her left arm out of its sling and grabbed her left hand with her right, using it to pull both arms straight up. Pain making her wince, she stopped when hands had barely cleared her head and then she let them fall to her sides.

"But I'm getting better. I could only reach my nose two days ago, but I'm not good enough yet to go gallivanting about. But don't worry, I've picked a couple of places for you."

Nila's questioning look prompted Eve to ask, "If you know some good rehab exercises, please let me know.

Nila replied, "This is the second time you've mentioned 'hurt locker'. What are you talking about?"

Nari supplied the answer.

"Don't you know it's military slang for a place of deep pain and discomfort? Most people do. If you're in one, something bad has happened. It comes from the Viet Nam war and is the title of a war poem and movie. I've been trying for years to get your nose out of books and into what's going on, but I guess you haven't paid much attention."

Nila put up a polite defense.

"I can say about me what Eve said about herself. I'm getting better. And I keep getting better, especially now that I'm here with all of you. What have you booked for us this weekend?"

"I've signed all of you into a day trip tomorrow to Alexandria. Nari should be able to take charge. I think seeing its recreated library will be at the top of the list because of the city's Greek history and philosophy connections. And I signed you and Nari into the AUC speed chess tournament taking place Sunday morning at the Tahrir campus. We can all watch, and it'll wrap up early enough for all you diggers to get ready for chopper flights later. And if anyone else wants to play, sign up by 10 p.m. And it's OK if you're a no-show, even if you've registered. Now go and get ready for tomorrow."

As was now customary after most weekday dinners, Alonzo and Monet strolled around campus, sharing whatever thoughts came to mind. Monet started with a zinger.

"If I were to rank your sisters one-two-three according to a niceness scale, what do you think my ordering would be?"

"I never gave it much thought. We've always been together. I guess I think of them like the air around me. I don't pay attention to them, unless they're gone. And trust me, they never leave me alone. What's your verdict?"

"I think Nila is the best with numbers and Eve with words, but when averaging verbal and numerical intelligence, Nari scores highest. But other dimensions must be considered. That's why I put Nila number one. Her naivete is charming in one so intelligent yet emotionally uncluttered, which I attribute to a sheltered upbringing. At times, she reminds me of a seed pod ready to germinate and spread its goodness.

"Eve comes in second. She is creative and clever with words, but she can be prickly when someone disagrees. And she likes to take control, but I've seen her defer to others when they know better. Her sense of humor usually helps moderate her emotions.

"And Nari finishes third. She has a very good opinion of herself and uses psychology to manipulate others, making them fall in line. I think she's jealous of Nila and turns everything into a competition to confirm her superiority. Perhaps that is why she lacks a sense of humor and puts people off. But we are all young and able to change when motivated. Maybe her experience this summer will help."

"How'd you get so smart? You know lots more than me and hold your own against the entire Mag-Seven."

"You must remember that I am from a developing-world country. Unlike America's schooling system, which still has the best graduate schools, mine and many other countries are superior in the earlier years. We challenge our youth to think critically. That is why I am more mature, more informed than you and all your sisters. I have a much stronger liberal arts foundation, which prepares me to grasp people and politics, the combination of which I will pursue at an American graduate school."

"I don't follow much when our Mag-Seven talk turns to world events. Nila doesn't either, but Eve and Nari do better. Yang's even sharper, and Sanjay's up there with you. I guess they're smarter than me."

"Your intelligence will blossom when you find your calling. But consider Yang. China pushes its students because it is still seeking world leadership, even though its system is flawed. And Sanjay's India encourages its young even more because it and Africa are emerging superpowers."

"Meeting you has made this my best summer ever. Even if I leave early, I'll take your wisdom with me."

"Where will you go?"

"Long story short, I might have a shot at a varsity starting slot. But I'm tired of all this deep talk. How about we pick up tomorrow? Let's sit together on the bus."

"Indeed, we shall learn more about one another. I like hearing from all interested parties."

Monet let him hold her hand as they walked towards the dorm.

The tour driver's experience showed while covering 125 miles on the Cairo-to-Alexandria Freeway. Weaving back and forth across two lanes to avoid immanent collisions, he kept his riders safe while giving them an introduction to popular tourist attractions they might see. The tree-and-vegetation-lined median provided striking contrast to the shoulders loaded with buildings or car-filled young adults, and of course the ever-present sands. Alonzo didn't see a single crack in the two lanes of asphalt, a condition whose cause he whispered to Monet so as to minimize interfering with the driver's speech.

"Its hot all year round. No temp-related expansion or contraction to bust up the surface."

She patted his hand; her smile acknowledged that he knew more than she about more than just the weather. Then she pointed to the driver seated directly in front. Both listened to his lively monologue. "Alexandria, located at the mouth of the Nile and built about 330 BCE by Alexander the Great, was an important city of the ancient world. For more than two thousand years, it was the largest city in Egypt and its capital for almost half that time. Today its population of 6 million makes it second in all of Africa only to Cairo, and it's still a major trading port between Europe and Asia. It profits from the easy overland connection between the Mediterranean and the Red Sea…"

Looking and listening made the time go as fast as the traffic whizzing by. The driver ended his talk just before pulling into a parking area half-filled at eight-thirty with tour buses.

"I'll park at this staging area; then you catch rides from local drivers who can navigate better than me. Sightsee all you want. Check our brochure for top picks. And please be back by 8 p.m. I'll get you home by 10:30.

Alonzo congratulated himself once Nari had the van loaded with her people and heading towards her first pick.

Thanks to what I'm learning, I can now predict some of Nari's behavior. Let her be the boss; I get to sit next to Monet and enjoy the sights inside and out. Wow… curb-to-curb traffic that sometimes drives the wrong way and treats traffic signals like suggestions… and happy-looking Egyptians walking everywhere, sometimes even on sidewalks. It's like being in an action-adventure chase scene before the gun goes off.

If the Coach contacts me, do I really want to trade what I'm getting here with what I might get at his training camp? Don't know yet. But I do know Nari will give us a good intro to the Lighthouse of Alexandria.

He would soon find out. She made an announcement that stopped the six just before entering.

"I found out that the Lighthouse of Alexandria is sometimes called the Pharos of Alexandria because it was built on Pharos Island in about 300 BCE during the reign of one of the Ptolemys and stood nearly 400 feet high. It came tumbling down in 1480, perhaps because of an earthquake. Legend has it that the constantly-burning flame at the top could be seen a hundred miles out in the Mediterranean. No wonder it was one of the Seven Wonders of the Ancient World. First person to guess the others wins a snack when we stop and I'll treat." Only Sanjay was willing to play along.

"Don't make it so hard. Make it a fun team contest instead, Alonzo and Monet versus Nila and me. Yang can check for accuracy. First team to mention a right wonder gets credit. And the Great Pyramid is automatically removed… so's the Lighthouse."

The other contestants groaned but agreed. Five minutes later, Yang announced the results.

"It is tie. Nila and Sanjay got Colossus of Rhodes and Temple of Artemis; other side got Hanging Gardens of Babylon and Statue of Zeus. But no one got Tomb of Mausolus."

Nari said, "Nice work. I didn't know about the Tomb either, but now we all do. Let's let the guide tell us more and then I'll buy, but

I get to choose what."

Monet asked a question pointed at Nila as they shuffled out an hour later.

"What did you like better, seeing in 3-D space or the VR simulation?"

"3-D because it affects all your senses. Anyone disagree?"

Only Yang, who said, "Simulators and Cyber-Theaters got sensory channels for more than sight and sound. They make training videos and virtual tours better and better. Someday maybe they equal real thing, but not yet. I vote with group. Are we voting for next stop, or letting Nari lead way?"

Voting wasn't needed; everyone wanted to see the modern-day reincarnation of the Library of Alexandria, known as the Bibliotheca

Alexandrina. A short ride later, Nari listened to the guide along with everyone else.

"Good morning to tourists and scholars alike. Before I describe the edifice you are standing in, I want to clarify that it is a tribute to the Great Library of Alexandria, built in 288 BCE under the auspices of Ptolemy the First. It was part of a larger research institution called the Mouseion that was dedicated to the Nine Muses of the Arts. "Alexandria came to be regarded as the capital of knowledge and

learning, in part because of the Great Library. Many important and influential scholars worked at the Library during the third and second centuries BCE because of its massive collection of scrolls. It is unknown precisely how many such scrolls were housed at any given time, but estimates range from 40,000 to 400,000 at its height.

"Despite the widely held belief that a cataclysmic fire destroyed the library, it actually declined over the course of several centuries because funding dwindled during the Roman Period. It is documented that Julius Caesar did burn by accident a portion of it during the Civil War of 48 BCE. It is unclear how much was actually destroyed, but it seems to have either survived or been rebuilt shortly thereafter.

"Between 270 and 275 CE, the city of Alexandria saw a rebellion and an imperial counterattack that probably destroyed whatever remained of the Library, if it still existed at that time. And in 391 CE, as the Dark Ages descended on the civilized world, Coptic Christian Pope Theophilus of Alexandria ordered the demolition of the remaining Mouseion.

But like the Phoenix, Mankind rose from the ashes to rebuild all that was lost. But it took centuries.

"Today you are in the Bibliotheca Alexandrina, a major library and cultural center located on the shores of the Mediterranean. Thanks to the vision of Egyptian scholar Mostafa El-Abbadi, construction began in 1995 and it opened seven years later. Its stunningly futuristic architecture makes a statement that the wisdom of the past and the knowledge created by exponential technology will lead us into the best of all possible futures. I will first show you a summary video, after which I will walk you through. Then you are free to study at your leisure or leave to pursue other iconic sights."

Nari made the call ninety minutes later.

"How many want to stay with me and research Greece's Golden Age?" Alonzo's gaze swung from her to Monet, who answered for two.

"This has been most edifying, but I believe Alonzo and I would like to visit the Montazah Palace Gardens after lunch. But we will rendezvous at the van as planned."

"Well then, Sanjay, Yang, and I will carry on. We'll compare later to see which group learned more. Stay safe."

Monet watched Alonzo dance a jig right after exiting the building. His performance made her smile, as did his joy when he began speaking.

"Thank you-thank you; I feel like I've just escaped the clutches of my fifth-grade teacher. And as a special treat, let's rent a motor scooter. They're whizzing all over, and please trust me, I think I can handle it.

"I do. I believe in you, and you should too."

"And then we'll set sail for a recommended restaurant. That'll be another treat from me to you."

A short walk to a rental shop gave the pair everything needed. Forty-five minutes later they were sharing a view of the Mediterranean and the largest specialty sandwich imaginable at the Delices Patesserie's outdoor cafe.

Monet said, "You must help me finish my half, and also my pastry." "You can trust me on that too. Just like I can trust your opinion of my sisters."

"I would rather talk about you. I do not mean to pry, but I am curious. I overheard you say you might leave the intern program early. What might call you away?"

"My Stanford lacrosse coach. I've got a shot at being a starter if I go to his mid-summer training camp." Alonzo paused for a question that her puzzled expression said was on the way.

"I cannot imagine anyone with your physique and obvious strength needing a summer session. And what is so important about being a

starter?"

"Hey, Eve told me everyone has to be a starter at something... something we like and are good at. Well, for me it's sports."

"Come now, I am certain you have other talents."

"My teammates always kid me that my talents are limited to S-words, sports and sex. And they're half right. And Eve read me the riot act when she picked up on my approach to dating. I can still hear her words: 'Don't expect a gossamer-winged beauty will dance down your storyline and make you happy forever and ever, imbuing your peerless physique and emergent brain with timeless vitality.' I've learned enough this last year to put sex in proper perspective. There's a lot more to relationships."

"Clever words… very cinematic. What other talents does she have?" "She won a prep school poetry competition and it bugged Nari because she finished second. But she's a mediocre piano player, only a little better than me and not as good as Nari. But Nila's the one with music talent. And after our last chat, it all makes sense. You pegged them."

"I am pleased my observations are accurate. Eve's creativity shows in the way she plays with words. But you are creative too. You improvise and find your way around so well. Have you written poetry?"

"Prep school English teachers made all us guys try. No one wanted to, even the brainy guys on my floor dissed the assignment. But they knew enough to explain blank and free verse plus current trends… you know, stuff like diversity and disguised exploration of tough human condition issues, or praising mediocrity. I don't buy into any of it, but Eve does. How about you? What creative talents do you have?"

"I play piano but not well because mathematics eludes me. My poetry is rudimentary, but my art instructor encourages me. However, my painting is merely for relaxation. I cannot understand why so many mediocre writers, musicians, painters, and performers chase a career meant for only the few. Can you say the same for athletes?"

"Not really. Unlike fine arts where ratings are subjective, scoring in sports is done with stop watch and tape measure. If you're mediocre, you can't kid yourself. And that's why Coach's summer camp is important. If I've got the sporting goods, I can strut my stuff. If I don't, I have to find something else. Can you guess what my sisters are looking for?"

"Nila's easy to read. She wants an academic career so she can avoid the necessities of dealing with the real world. Nari is more opaque, but I would imagine she wants a career where she can impress others with her considerable intellect. Political or psychological realms would fit her. But Eve is hardest. Whatever's troubling her is invisible, at least to me. Do you know what it is?"

"She says it's her family, but I know she's joking. She's basically a good person, my best friend."

"Yes, I can see that, and you are hers too. Both of you are fortunate."

"Do you have any brothers or sisters?"

"An older brother. But enough about me. Let us stroll the gardens of the Montazah Palace. And afterwards, we'll surf the net so we can impress Nari."

Not even good-natured Sanjay's patience could withstand Nari's withering barrage during the debate pitting him and Nila versus Yang and Nari. Two hours exceeded his limit.

"Please give it a rest. I've already agreed with you that your quotes about philosophy being a footnote to Plato and the Biblical one about nothing new under the Sun had merit when first made, but not today. Greek political philosophy didn't like democracy particularly, and it never had to confront the economic ills that keep cycling through the modern world. And their technology hadn't a clue about DNA, quantum physics, or mankind's impact on climate change. Yang, say something."

"You and Nila know more than me and Nari, but neither know much compared to professors. But grad school awaits for us to excel."

"I see your point; OK, let's take a break and then check out what the Library has to say about the El Alamein War Cemetery and Museum. It's too far west along the coast, but it's only a click or two away on a keyboard. And who knows why the Battle of El Alamein was important?" Nila answered first.

"According to the brochure, it swung Rommel's World War

Two desert campaign pendulum away from him and towards Montgomery. What do I win?"

Sanjay said, "My admiration and a Coca Cola. Please, let's take that break now and skip any Internet surfing."

Nari had to respect the voting. Three to one said they were done.

Eve met early Sunday morning with her siblings to short circuit too much talk about Alexandria but more importantly to alert them about what must be done this week for their Indira assignment. "Time's ticking by. I have to let Indira know when everything's set to meet her contact. I've done my part, now the three of you have to deliver more. I hope you can do that when you get back next Sunday."

Nari frowned at Eve before saying, "Honestly, I think you're being too pushy. Nila and I've been piecing details together, and she's done the same with Alonzo. And you told us she told you we had all the time we need, so don't start panicking."

"I'm not, but let's reconvene next Sunday. And get set to talk less about yesterday and more about today. Here comes the rest of our group."

Five minutes later, Eve switched from yesterday to chess.

"So, who's playing in the speed tournament today?" Nari spoke first.

"We chatted about this on the ride back last night. Three of us are in, Nila, Yang, and me. Sanjay will watch Nila's matches, Alonzo and Monet mine, and you'll follow Yang's. How's that?"

"I'm staying put to give my shoulder another day's rest. I'll get a results summary at dinner."

Monet said, "Alonzo and I will too. He wants to take me zipping around Cairo on a motor scooter. And you might do even better without the pressure of our watching you."

"I can handle pressure, but can Alonzo handle a scooter in Cairo traffic? He could get both of you killed."

"Trust me when I say you can trust him to keep both of us safe." Their glances met and he smiled before saying, "Don't any of you worry, I can handle it, maybe not as well as your chess playing, but we can compare results at dinner."

Eve nodded then said, "Maybe you'll do even better. Where will you go?"

"Don't ask me, ask Monet. You know I always do what you ladies tell me…"

Results reported that night by Nari told the tale of the tournament. "The only good part about it was seeing Tahrir Square. Walking around settled me down, but I still feel so disrespected by the guy who was the overall winner. I'll admit he's pretty good, but he had the nerve to gloat to the spectators after wiping me out in the second round. But poor Yang lost his first match to the gal who was runner-up. Nila did a little better. She lasted to round three before losing to her."

Eve said, "All of you should be satisfied. After all, first and second place finishers obviously play a lot more often." Nari's sneer showed she had more to say.

"You might say that, but I'd like to do some payback."

No one offered a suggestion. Eve glanced at her cell for the time before saying more.

"Don't think about it during your week out on the dig. Leave it to me, and now you diggers better get ready to go. See you early next Sunday."

Chapter 11
Monday, July 18, 2157

<u>"The Payback Games"</u>

Eve ditched the sling first thing Monday, impressing her lab mentor with her gritty determination to resume testing. He told her to ease back in today and then work at a normal pace starting tomorrow. She promised to follow orders but soon decided to use them as a cover for more planning and prepping on what she wanted.

I can sneak in thinking all week about Indira's desert trek, and even better than that, I can come up with something that'll take the chess winner down. Too bad I don't know much about the game. But hey, I'll substitute my cleverness for knowing the right moves. I'll let my subconscious play.

And I've already been thinking about something I haven't sprung yet on the Mag-Seven. It'll be for an evening outing sometime next week. And if it goes according to plan, Nila should already know how to get around. OK, now I focus on intern work; I don't want to jeopardize the rating I'll get from my mentor.

Focusing on testing procedures, Eve kept other thoughts out of the way until boredom set in mid-afternoon and she shifted to chess. She mulled the challenge for an hour when all at once an outline of a plan flashed in her brain.

I see it now! I'm going back to the dorm right now and will call Nari and Nila before Monet gets back. If they buy in, we have plenty of time to put it together.

Nari answered promptly.

"Hey there, how's your shoulder?"

"Pretty good, and thanks for asking. The pain's much less and I'm not using the sling. How about you?"

"Guess what, the diggers found some hidden chambers where I fell. Our dig leader says they might be burial vaults. Everyone's excited."

"Well, I've got something exciting too. I've just come up with a payback plan for the chess guy, and I need you and Nila to help me set it up. Here's the outline. Are you ready?"

"Go ahead. If I like it, we'll talk more later."

"Goes like this. We'll challenge the winner and the runner-up to an online speed contest held next Sunday at noon. You'll play the guy who won, and Nila will play the runner-up. All you need to do is tell me their names and AUC Email addresses. I'll contact them, and if they accept, we'll send a blast Email to all AUC interns, advertising the contest. I'm sure it'll generate plenty of interest. After all, the guy who won seems like a jerk; people will want to see him taken down."

"But how? He stomped me last time and I'm not going to let that happen again."

"Trust me, I know how and I'll tell you later. And you tell Nila that all she has to do is set up two URL links, one for each game. She can use an AUC videoconferencing tool like ZOOM or one of its competitors. Each link will display in separate windows each contestant, a game board showing the moves, and me. I'll be the moderator. Have her allow each viewer to see only the game they're interested in, except for me and Nari and you. Got it?"

"That's plenty for now. And I'll send you ASAP Email addresses and phone numbers of who we'll be playing. Call me back Wednesday evening. I'll have Nila next to me."

"I'll call you at eight. Stay safe." Eve ended the call, then added a postscript.

Look at what my crash and Nari's tumble are leading to. They connect to the Buddhist monk story Granny told me long ago. I hope she's doing OK. I think Indira would have called if she weren't, but that Indira lady is inscrutable. I'll ask about Granny next time. And I hope next time is soon. Mid-July's almost here. But I'm doing all I can, so there's nothing I should worry about except what I'll do tomorrow. Time to sleep on it.

Eve settled in and did satisfactory work Tuesday and Wednesday because the progress she was making on other activities energized her. So did the Wednesday evening phone call. Nari's upbeat tone signaled all pieces of the plan were coming together. Eve liked everything she heard as Nari summarized before wrapped up the discussion.

"I knew you'd convince our opponents to accept the challenge. Nila's getting the links built, and both of us know our roles. We're so happy you're so deviously clever. And I'm pleased to report that Nila and I have Alonzo pointed in the right direction regarding his piece of our desert trek preparation. All four of us will get our trek status review out of the way first thing Sunday. Then we can devote our undivided attention to chess."

Eve agreed.

"Yes, indeed, Sunday will be sunny for us, every which way. Stay safe till then."

Eve did even better in the lab on Thursday, and compared results Friday at lunch with several fellow virology interns, Yang among them. Those present deferred to him because his testing results always scored high or low, depending on which end of the scale measures accuracy.

"I get less false positive on automated testing machine instead of manual, but sometimes I beat machine. We lucky AUC has best liquid-handling workstation. Equipment from vendors just about same. Testing kit make the difference. You agree?"

All did and when someone asked about intern program

satisfaction, most were generally pleased with the combination of hands-on and lecture sessions, but one of the interns poked holes in a recurring rumor.

"All this talk about a Pharaoh's Plague that escapes when excavations uncover hidden burial tombs comes from the fevered brains of newscasters and screenwriters, not from researchers. AUC virologists have found only mutations of modern organisms. Zoonotics explains them all. We have nothing to fear from interns coming back from excavations and infecting us. Besides, if AUC has an outbreak, there are procedures for contact tracing and social distancing. The source can be identified and isolated."

Eve was paying enough attention to ask, "Have there been any cases of interns getting viral infections?" The same intern answered. "The simple answer to your imprecise question is a resounding 'No.' There are always viral infections spreading in any population. The common cold virus and its mutations have plagued man for millennia. The question you should have asked is whether the organism causing an outbreak is unusual or is the infection rate abnormal? I hope you learn from your experience this summer how to formulate better questions."

Yang came to Eve's defense.

"She know how. And she know how to dig details before trusting Internet. I think she speaking, uh, like elliptical. You know, not so many words."

Eve added, "I resemble those remarks. And thanks to what I've just learned, I'm not going to worry about catching a cold. And if I get one or the Flu, I'll take aspirin and drink plenty of water. When it comes to meds, less is more. People who disagree are pill-pushers looking to make a buck or enhance their status. Do I hear any objections?"

No one peeped; no one wanted to engage in a battle of words against such a clever wordsmith. Eve exited the cafeteria without firing another phrase.

Alonzo's progress for the week matched Eve's, but he didn't summarize everything to the Bose twins Friday before falling asleep. Those thoughts were for his ears only.

My people instincts are pretty good and getting better. The second gal I picked wanted to swap places with Eve. And the dynamic Bose duo created duplicate IDs for Eve and her replacement.

And now that I understand my sisters better, I don't mind so much letting them boss me around. They're just trying to help. Nari did a nice job checking my equipment list and Nila has everything set for me to requisition what we need when we go to meet that Rani guy. It's getting tight, but if Eve sticks to a July 25th rendezvous, I might still be copacetic with Coach's training camp. His last Email says he's pushing start date back to August 3rd. I can just get there if all goes according to Eve and Nari's plan.

I'm lucky my sisters are so smart… but they're lucky too… I've usually got the goods to deliver whatever they need. And I'm lucky I stayed this long… Monet has opened my eyes and my mind. And I'll see all these ladies come Sunday morning breakfast.

After Alonzo reported his piece of desert trek preparation, Eve set a record wrapping up their weekly pre-breakfast Indira adventure meeting.

"Only I have an assignment this week… I contact Indira no later than Friday to confirm we launch our mission next Sunday. But if anyone stumbles across an obstacle, let me and Nari know. And now, get set to talk about the chess tournament as soon as Monet, Sanjay, and Yang get here."

As if on cue, the missing Mag-Sevens appeared a couple of minutes later. Eve jumpstarted the conversation.

"I hope some of you are going to login for the chess challenge. You can judge my moderating skills as Nari and Nila battle the tournament winners." Sanjay's sagging expression didn't bode well for his picks.

"I can't imagine why you're doing this. Did they practice this week?" Eve answered for her sisters.

"I've been coaching them and sending them video links. Get set to be surprised."

"I hope I am. Yang and I will watch together after doing some local sightseeing this morning. We wish you luck. Monet, what about you and Alonzo?"

"We are out and about all day on Alonzo's motor scooter. Dinner is soon enough for us to hear what happened." She pulled Alonzo's arm as she rose. Alonzo spoke after standing.

"My sisters don't need luck. They make their own."

He and Monet departed. When Sanjay and Yang followed, Eve gave a final command.

Let's each go to our dorm rooms and get ready. I'll be in mine, Nila, you stay in yours, and Nari can use Alonzo's. Does he know you borrowed his spare key?"

"Probably not. He only uses one at a time. And I'll put it back after my payback battle. Come on, Nila, let's go get set for victory by prepping our computers and, as Eve likes to say, putting our game faces on. Eve fires the gun at high noon."

Eve centered herself at two minutes to twelve by reminding herself how to behave in any contest.

I've practiced enough by visualizing the outcome that I want and having the game unfold accordingly, and I've come up with clever comments for all the contingencies I could think of. And I've got seven windows open, four for the contestants, two for the game boards, and one for me. I'll look at mine from time to time so I remember to smile and speak slowly. OK, time to start acting.

Eve rolled out her welcoming remarks right on time.

"Hello to all AUC chess aficionados. According to what the software is reporting, thirty-eight are watching our high noon showdown. Nari Bose will play the winner and her sister Nila will play the runner-up from last week's speed tournament. They defeated my sisters a week ago, and my sisters have practiced all week, hoping they can make a better showing today. Their opponents have graciously accepted the challenge, letting Nari will play black and Nila white.

Each player has one minute to move, which speeds the game along but offers enough time for our contestants. And before we start, I would like to ask each contestant to say hello to the viewers. We'll start with Mister Dimitri Petrov." Eve paused for smug-looking Dimitri.

"Hallo. If you watch me last time, you know why I will win again. Bose is plucky, but I put her out of misery even quicker today than last time. I ready."

Eve responded immediately.

"Thank you, Dimitri. And now to Miss Ganga Datta."

"I am happy to play Nila again. Though she lost, she was very gracious. I expect her to be even better today."

"Thank you Ganga, and now to Nari Bose. Please say hello to viewers."

"Hi everyone. I speak for Nila and myself when saying that we thank our opponents for allowing us rematches. We don't expect to win, but we want to show viewers and ourselves that practicing this week improves our performance. We'll do our best."

"Thank you, Nari. All's been said, so let the games begin. And good luck to all."

Eve gave an instructive comment soon after the start.

"Looks like Dimitri's using the Ruy Lopez opening, so named for the Spanish monk originator. It's considered to be one of the best openings for beginners because it typically leads to open games, with a lot of play for both sides. And his confident, rapid moves evince certainty of outcome."

Eve paused, then commented on the other game.

"Notice how deliberate Ganga is playing, not as fast or demonstrative as Dimitri, but a bit faster than the Bose twins. Well,

I'll be quiet now and watch the ebb and flow as you do too. I imagine most of you know much more about chess than me, but I'm having fun just watching the action unfold. I hope you are too."

Eve's enjoyment grew while watching Dimitri's face and hands reflect growing doubt. All other players revealed little emotion. After move forty, which is only half the number in a typical game, he started muttering. Two moves later, viewers saw his hand knock down more pieces than just his king before complaining.

"She lucky food poisoning give me bad day." His window blanked out. Nari's did too five seconds later.

Nila's game proceeded uninterrupted but her moves became hesitant. Four moves later, she placed her king horizontally before saying,

"No sense prolonging the inevitable… you win." Ganga looked apologetic. All windows but Eve's blanked out.

She said, "Thanks to viewers for joining us. Enjoy the rest of your day," before her window vanished a couple of seconds later.

Monet led Alonzo into her dorm room so she could freshen up before dinner in the cafeteria.

She called out from the bathroom, "Where do you supposed your sisters are?"

"That's an easy question for me to answer. Somewhere listening to Nari complain about losing again. I'm sure we'll get an earful soon. Please take your time. I've heard all her complaints many times."

Monet waved to Sanjay and Yang when she saw them at an empty table. Both wore poker smiles until she and Alonzo sat; then Sanjay's smile broke the news before he spoke.

He said, "Your sisters staged quite an Internet show. Believe it or not, Nari beat number one and Nila put up a strong battle against number two. I think they went to party in the victor's room."

"Well, I'll be, I'll go see. Why don't you keep Monet company until I get back?"

Alonzo hustled away and knocked loudly enough to be heard above the laughter coming from within.

"Ready or not, I'm opening the door." He did so and then paused to soak in the view. Eve pushed a champagne-filled plastic cup in his hand before he could say a word. Several gulps later he was ready to talk.

"Sanjay says Nari won and Nila upheld the family honor. Cold champagne tells me you knew you were going to win. What trick did you pull?"

"Drink some more then close the door. Then we'll tell you, but only if you promise to keep our secret in the family."

Alonzo followed orders and sat before saying more.

"I will, and I know all of you are smart, but how'd you beat the guy?" Nari pointed to Eve.

"Your sister's devious cleverness did him in. She'll explain."

"I learned it when and where I don't remember, but it sure worked today. Here's the setup. I turned the guy's cockiness to Nari's advantage by having him and Nila play white. I knew number two would play tough because he beat her last Sunday.

"Only we sisters saw both game boards simultaneously. Nari waited to play her move against him until Nila played his identical move against number two. Nari saw number two's move and played the same against number one. The games are identical, number two's defense pitted against number one's offense. And we kept repeating the cycle until number one saw he was losing. He surrendered by knocking over all his pieces and then making up a lame excuse. And Nila won a moral victory by doing so much better this time than last."

"You three are formidable, and I'll add my brawn to your brains when we meet Rani. Do you have any tricks lined up for the desert trek?"

Eve commanded center stage.

"Not yet, but maybe that Indira lady will give me some ideas. She's smarter than me. I just wish I knew more about her. But no matter, we'll earn high marks for our performance. And we can rehearse as well as relax until we leave. Life's good, and getting better, don't you agree?"

Even Nari's smile seemed to say yes.

Chapter 12
Monday, July 18, 2157

<u>"Going Which Way"</u>

Nari's call reached Eve's cell just after she closed her dorm room door.

"Hey, we're meeting for breakfast in a couple of minutes. What's so important it can't wait?"

"We've got a minor problem you and I have to keep from snowballing. All digger interns just got an Email saying next week's field work is pushed back a week. It doesn't say why, but AUC is testing air and surfaces for viruses at all locations. You're in the Virology Intern Program. Maybe you know, but that's not the problem. Your brother could be if he's still pushing to get to his sports camp. What has he said to you?"

"Nothing. Does he know about the delay?"

"Not yet, probably. You know he's slow when it comes to checking EMails, and Nila and I won't mention it, but he's bound to find out. Near as I can tell, all the plans we've made are still doable if we leave a week later on the thirty-first. All you have to do is tell Indira the new rendezvous date. But if Alonzo goes ballistic, either you're going to have to calm him down or we'll have to get a replacement for him. You and me and Nila need a guy to drive one of the vans and handle equipment. We need to come up with a contingency plan for this ASAP, but we can't breathe a word about the delay to Alonzo. What do you think we should do if he brings it up?"

"I don't know. You think he'll find out after breakfast?"

"Dumb question… of course he will. There'll be a buzz about it at today's lecture. Look, none of the other Mag-Seven people know

about this yet, so at breakfast, pretend this conversation never happened. See you at breakfast."

Nari disconnected. Eve mulled possibilities as she trudged towards the cafeteria.

Alonzo seems a bit more mature since coming to Cairo. Maybe I should take him aside and discuss his intentions; no, I'll wait until he speaks up. Maybe he's already decided that staying with us is the way to go.

Alonzo pretended indifference on the outside when fellow interns talked mid-Monday about next week's fieldwork delay, but not inside his head.

There goes my escape plan to get to Coach's camp… just when we had all the details buttoned down. Now what do I do?... One thing's for certain, I'm not gonna talk to Eve. I already know what she'll say. And I'm not gonna say anything until I've thought the situation through. But who can I bounce ideas off of?... I know who, I'll call her as soon as I can.

Alonzo placed the call as soon as the lecture ended.

"Monet, it's Alonzo. I've got a big decision and I need your opinion on which way to go. Are you free?... Good. I'll meet you at your room and we'll go somewhere for lunch. See you in ten…"

Alonzo saw a different Monet sitting across from him today than yesterday.

She's sipping an iced tea and wearing a more serious expression. Whatever questions she asks and what she says will be worth paying attention to. And I'm ready to start answering.

Alonzo's wait ended as soon as she set down her glass. "Please tell me what is weighing on your mind?"

"Remember Coach's summer camp I told you about? Well, I'm in, but I have to leave by early next week to get there, so I gotta decide. You're the only one whose opinion I can trust. What do you think I should do, stay or go?" Monet pursed then relaxed her lips before taking a breath and exhaling.

"It matters not what I think; what matters is what you want after thinking carefully. I asked before but you never answered, so I will ask again. Why is being a starter on your lacrosse team so important?"

"Because it shows how good I am in the big leagues. Yeah, I showed it in prep school, but that's minor by comparison."

"But there are bigger stages than Stanford lacrosse. Why do you think Stanford's stage is enough? No matter where you perform, there is always another that is even bigger. And isn't it more important to prove to yourself or those you care about – not strangers sitting in the stands – how good you are?" Alonzo scratched his right shoulder and momentarily gazed away before coming back to Monet.

"Hey, Stanford lacrosse is what I've got right now, and my friends already know I'm pretty good."

"We are close to the same age, but I am more mature than you, so draw wisdom from what I say. Accept whatever success you earn in sports. The rewards are nearly the same, no matter the stage, and apply what you learn to the rest of your life. And you are too self- centered. It's not important your friends know you're good in sports. What matters is they know you are a good person in the game of life. And whatever your decision, you must live with the consequences."

Monet folded her arms and said nothing more.

"You've given me enough to digest. There's no room for dessert, but I'll buy one for you if you like."

Monet's smile from yesterday came back.

"I would like that, and I would like you to at least sample it. You can then decide if you made the right choice. That will give you practice."

Alonzo returned her smile before turning to the menu.

No one talked about the missing pair at dinner that night after Nari said that a text from Alonzo explained he and Monet were biking about. She led the table talk and her sisters pretended a week's delay simply meant more time to enjoy being in Cairo. When Sanjay asked about next week's sightseeing, Eve came to life.

"I'll tell everyone on Friday, but as a special for this week, we're going Cairo club-dancing Wednesday evening. I checked out some of the clubs. One even has a Latino Night, but I've picked something more Middle Eastern."

Yang said, "I sure dancers be young like us. And no matter country, all dance same. Language different but move about like one."

Eve pointed to Nila, who was primed to talk.

"I'll be the judge. I've taken lots of dance classes. Sanjay, don't worry, I'll show you the right moves…"

Alonzo acted in his typical manner the next day, prompting Nari to call Eve Tuesday evening.

"How's Alonzo."

"OK, I guess. Monet's not here, so he's probably with her." "That's not what I meant. Has he talked about the delay?" "No, and I didn't mention it."

"Did you call that Indira lady?"

"Why would I give her another chance to criticize? I'll do that on Friday. I'm not thinking about meeting Rani until then. You should do the same."

"OK, that'll let us enjoy tomorrow's club dancing even more. I'm happy you came up with the idea. Nila's excited, and that's unusual for her."

"Good, I told everyone to be on time for dinner and eat light. We'll leave right after. See you then, if not at breakfast."

The Mag-Seven loaded into two cabs for the ride to the Opia

Club, a place whose Social Media blurbs sounded inviting. As they walked into the building, Yang congratulated Eve for its great view of the Nile; Sanjay said he expected the club to have subdued lighting and a beat that would go with a panoramic view of Cairo at night.

Two appropriately dressed men were watching only for Nari as the group entered the building.

The shorter said, "Our eavesdropper's intrusion app is most thorough. And how fortunate he has a day job at AUC. The short hair matches the pics in the info packet. We know which one to escort out."

"What if she doesn't fall for the ID badges?"

"Then you will insist. But let's give her time to dance and tire herself out. Then she might be more willing to tell us about the rumored treasures she and her excavation party might have fallen into."

After two hours of dancing, the Mag-Seven clustered around two adjacent elevated tables, sipping drinks and listening to Sanjay declare that Nila's dance moves were as sexy as any among the women bobbing and weaving. Even Nari agreed.

"Her moves are almost as good as the ones she makes in math classes. I'll treat her to another drink… be right back." Only Eve watched for a moment as Nari wove her way to one of the bars where its barista's shaker performance commanded attention. Then she turned back to the conversation for a minute before looking again in Nari's direction. The view startled her.

"Hey! two guys are hitting on Nari."

Eve dashed to help, getting there in time to see her punch one guy in the nose and start yelling.

"You're crazy! I don't know anything about treasure in tombs." Eve dived into the fray, but the other guy threw her to the floor. Nila jumped in right after Eve; he batted her away too. But he couldn't handle Alonzo's charge.

Alonzo's knee connected to the right place and bent the bad guy forward before a solid right stood him up and pitched him backward to the bar. Alonzo then heaved him over before using a cocktail shaker to club the fellow Nila was kicking; the combined battering put him on the floor. Alonzo added extra kicks that kept the man down and then picked up Eve. All four dashed back to the tables.

Alonzo shouted, "Let's go before the cops get here."

Then he led the escape onto the street; the Mag-Seven blended into the swirl of the night.

Alonzo called a halt to assess damage four blocks later, letting Nari babble first.

"… and they flashed badges and said I had taken stuff. I don't know where they were gonna take me…" Nari ran out of air; Nila started in after pointing at Eve, who was grimacing.

"What's wrong?"

"I bounced on my left shoulder. Damn, it hurts." Alonzo ended the discussion.

"We'll talk more when we get back to campus. Let's find some cabs…"

By the time they entered the dorm, the night's excitement had drained the group's energy. All were talked out and settled for padding back to their rooms after agreeing to keep the stories for Mag-Seven only.

Only the three sisters came to breakfast. Eve had her left arm re- slung but didn't say anything about it until Nari probed.

"Can you drive like that?"

"Not unless Alonzo can get me a self-driving van, and that's not gonna happen, but I've got an extra week to get my shoulder in better shape; I should be ready to drive."

Nila shook her head.

"You and Alonzo better do some practicing. Where do you suppose he is?"

Nari said, "Two possibilities and I'll let you pick. Either with Monet or heading to lecture." No one spoke, instead all three kept picking at their bowls of cold cereal.

Neither choice would have been correct. Alonzo was online viewing airline Websites. He left for class after making his selections, getting there with time to spare for sending an Email.

I'll tell Nari the four of us have to meet in her room before dinner. She can spread the word.

The rest of the morning and afternoon marched along normally, but Eve felt a growing apprehension when approaching her sisters' room. She saw it in Nari and Nila too when she entered. Nari spoke first.

"Sit next to Nila and leave the chair for the big man. After last night, I hope he's grown more of a sense of responsibility."

Eve countered.

"Maybe that explains the way he's acting. It's not his usual style. We'll see when he gets here."

Nila tried half-heartedly to chitchat, but no one joined in so she fell silent too.

Finally, a knock on the door announcing Alonzo. The three sisters spoke as one, telling him to come in.

Alonzo sized up the situation as soon as he entered and sat in the only unoccupied chair, waiting for one of his sisters to speak. Eve started.

"You acquitted yourself nicely last night. We're all glad that, uh… I'm not sure of what. Maybe you should tell us."

Alonzo rolled his shoulders but didn't look away.

"It looked like the three of you were doing OK. Now don't start yelling until I finish. I got an Email last week from Coach. I'm AOK for the summer camp but I gotta leave before we meet this Rani guy. Just tell that Indira person you three will do the rendezvous. In fact –"Nari jumped over whatever words never came out."

"Did Monet put you up to this? I can't believe it... Not with the way you two are always mooning at each other. And just when you seemed to be growing up, but no, you're up to your old tricks."

"Go ahead and bail on us. You can run back to Coach and chase after a starting position. Then you can chase on a hookup site after some mindless babe who shaves every square inch below the neck. You should be kicked out of the collegiate dating pool. You're not smart enough or nice enough to be there."

"Damn, you can be so brutally cruel."

"I'm being brutally honest. What do you expect me to do? Kiss you on both cheeks and pat you on the head for shirking your responsibilities, running away to camp, and trying to make yourself a starting star. You'll still be a second-string guy."

Eve had heard enough.

"Shut up! That's my brother you're yelling at, and you're wrong. Uh…"

Eve didn't know what to say next. Alonzo tried to parry some of Nari's insults.

"How about this? Everything in our plan still works. I've got connections. I'll find a guy to take my place and –" Nari interrupted; she had more to yell.

"Jesus! You sound like a worn-out line from a stale action-adventure movie. Go ahead, Eve. Try to back that one up."

Eve's expression couldn't.

"I don't know. Indira said it had to be us four. She might slam the door if I tell her you're bailing."

"Then don't. You're good at getting around things and making stuff work. Just do it without me. I'm gone." Alonzo got up and left before any sister could say a word to block his way. There was only stone- cold silence.

Finally, Nari blinked and said, "What do we do now?"

Looking first at Nila's blank expression, Eve decided she better say something.

"Three things, I guess. First, we'll tell the Mag-Seven. Then I'll call Indira, and then we'll see what success Alonzo has finding a replacement." Nari didn't look happy.

"What are you going to say to Indira?"

"I don't know, but I'll think of something... say, is anyone hungry? I didn't check the dinner menu, but Thursday's usually pretty good. That's when the dietician finds a clever way to recycle leftovers. Let's check it out."

Eve's attempt at humor found no takers. The trio trooped single file to the cafeteria, unable to find any happy words to put in the present tense.

Alonzo and Monet's absence forced Eve to explain the cause.

"I am sorry to report that Alonzo is leaving early next week. He's got a spot in a sports summer camp and he's probably explaining to Monet why he's going."

Yang spoke before Sanjay could.

"Why be sorry? He done well here and camp must fit his wish. He seem like first string guy. Maybe camp make sure he starter. He know best which way he go." Sanjay put a different spin on Alonzo's decision.

"I liked playing sports when I was little. Everyone on both sides had about the same ability, and if I fell it wasn't very far. But all that changed as testosterone took over. And look what happened last night. If it weren't for Alonzo's physical ability to take control, who knows where Nari might be. He's a smart guy, and more power to him if that's his choice. Why not congratulate him by toasting his success? But someone should pick someplace other than last night's."

Nari and Nila left Eve to her own devices for answering what ostensibly should be a simple question.

"You're right. Sorry I seem sad, but I'll miss him."

Yang said, "We all will, but who know? Paths can cross in year or two."

"You might be right. OK, I'll pick a place for tomorrow, and I'll make sure it's less physical than where we were last night. I promise…"

Eve dragged through Friday, hampered by shoulder pain, and put in just enough effort to find a nightclub. She told the entire Mag-Seven at dinner.

"According to what I surfed up, the Pharaoh's Pub Club looks AOK. How about I reserve two taxis for an 8 p.m. pickup?" Alonzo agreed, but for different reasons.

"Do it, but Monet and I will follow you for a final ride on my scooter. You'll have more room in the cabs and Monet and I can go somewhere later if she wants."

Nari ended the discussion.

"It's your party. You can go any which way you want."

Everyone but the four siblings smiled; only they caught her ironic words.

Eve meandered back to her room, trying to find something that would delay the inevitable. When she finally entered, the room was empty.

I'm glad Monet is out of the way. I need some privacy to rehearse my Indira call.

She placed it after five minutes of practice. Indira's GUI appeared on her tablet and spoke first.

"Hello, Eve. I've been expecting your call. What would you like to tell me?"

"We've got all details in place for rendezvousing with Mister Rani and there's only one minor complication. We had to push the date back one week. We'll meet him on August first at 3 a.m. That should be OK, shouldn't it?" Indira's expression remained indifferent.

"Is there anything else?"

"Why no, I think that covers it." Eve bit her lip to keep from saying more, but worried to herself.

Gads, what does she know? Has she been listening in or tracking me?

"You look like you're covering something up. I think you should tell me more."

"Uh, OK, but I didn't want to make you angry. Alonzo is going back to Stanford next week. He's on this stupid quest to become a lacrosse starter. He knows you'll cut off his funding but he's going anyway. He's not paying attention to me and –" Indira interrupted in mid-sentence.

"You and your sisters aren't paying attention to your brother. You're discounting his abilities and ignoring his growth. It seems he knows the consequences of his actions. It is not for you to say what is best for him. Let him go. You and your sisters will have to improvise."

"It seems like you know a lot. Well, do you know I've re-dislocated my shoulder and some officers accused Nari of stealing stuff and we're trying to line up an Alonzo substitute?" Indira's expression and voice remained implacable.

"Only the last item is of concern to me. Only the four of you are allowed to meet Rani. Is that clear?"

"Perfectly, so what should I do?"

"Don't ask me. You and your sisters must decide. Call me only if the rendezvous date and time change. You have my sympathy." Indira's GUI vanished before Eve could yell. She had to settle for shouting inside her head.

I don't need sympathy, I need help. And I'm too upset to think. I'm going to hike around campus to calm down. Maybe something will come up tomorrow if Nari and I can bring Nila into the discussion. If we can, we'll let her brain harness my cleverness and Nari can make the best of what we come up with. We'll have to see...

Not even Nari could muster enough energy to talk about rendezvous contingencies. The sisters decided to shelve worrying until next week and do their best to enjoy tonight's farewell toast.

The Mag-Seven departed as planned. Though the guys did their best to cheer everyone up, the females' collective body language matched the subterranean atmosphere of the Pharaoh's Pub Club. Nari sent a barb Eve's way as soon as everyone was seated at the two tables the guys had shoved together.

"You could have found a better place. It's dark and noisy, and some of the clientele look like lowlife."

"Hey, don't be so judgmental. You're in Cairo, not Boston."

Nila said, "And that's good. I'm getting to see more of life outside the academic circle."

Nila waited for someone else to carry the conversation forward. Sanjay, who was sitting next to her, did just that.

"We need something to drink. That always primes the conversation pump. I don't see any servers, so I'll order a pitcher of beer at the bar. I'll be right back…"

Sanjay and Yang did most of the work keeping the conversation moving, but after an hour no one had much left to say. Eve decided it was time to go; Nila went to the restroom while everyone else sent final wishes Alonzo's way. Nari's impatience showed even more than before.

"Nila can be so slow sometimes. I better go find her. We'll be right back."

Nari left in a huff.

Eve filled the space by saying, "If Nila's got her cell phone with her, we can track her down. Does everyone know how to do that?"

Alonzo admitted he didn't and asked Eve to show him.

"It's easy if you've got a tracking app already loaded… and you've got one on your cell. All you do is punch in Nila's number. Let's do it and see where she is."

Nari came back to the table before Nila's tracking dot appeared.

"I can't find her. You guys stay at the table while we females walk through the place."

Eve said, "That's not gonna work. According to GPS, she's outside and walking away."

Alonzo made a correction.

"She's not walking. She's running... no, that's not right... what the... someone's driving her away."

Alonzo saw nothing but confused expressions.

"I'll go find her. All of you, go back to campus. I'll call Eve when I know what's going on."

Alonzo pushed his way out of the club and ran to his scooter. Seconds later he raced away and handled Cairo traffic like one of the good guys in a chase scene, driving on sidewalks and weaving through traffic like only a mad driver who knows where he's going can do.

Nila's two escorts dumped her on the bed after getting some kicks by punching her up. The bigger guy said to his partner,

"We've slapped her around enough. She won't be getting up anytime soon."

His dim-sounding partner asked, "Uh, what's next?"

"I get first crack. Then you can pile in. I'll get you when I'm done. Go wait in the other room."

"Uh, OK but don't leave her too messy. That'll turn me off." The smaller guy opened the door and walked out.

And right into Alonzo swinging for the fences, using a metal lamp like a baseball bat. Two strikes put the guy on the carpet and down for the count, but Alonzo added strike three, right into the bad guy's upper teeth. They popped out like kernels of corn soaked in blood, not butter.

Alonzo leaped to his feet and stood in the doorway, eyeing the bigger guy, who was sizing him up as well. Surprised but undeterred, he danced backward like an experienced street fighter, exuding confidence and throwing practice jabs that would inflect heavy damage if they connected.

"Come in and let's play tag. And I'll do the tagging." Alonzo talked only to himself.

You look ready for action, but so am I. And I'm ready to trade getting hit for getting inside your defenses. Let's see if you can handle lacrosse.

Alonzo used a spin move that put him close, but his opponent nailed him with a solid left-right combination that thudded into his nose and mouth and drew two streams of blood, but Alonzo's rage neutralized the pain. He charged ahead, pinning his opponent to the wall and doubled him up with a barrage of body blows. The bad guy grunted but used his size advantage to push Alonzo backwards.

Alonzo charged again, this time using arm fakes, but he caught a left hook that spun him around and down. He got to his knees facing his opponent just in time to trap the bad guy's right foot with both hands and drag its leg forward and upward and shove the center of gravity past its tipping point; then he used leverage to tumble the bad guy backward. He crash-landed awkwardly and Alonzo dived on top, trading blow for blow.

Gravity was in Alonzo's corner; his blows silenced the other guy's fists but he wailed away until his opponent's eyes closed for good. Then he struggled to his feet, bloodied but unbowed.

Nila began to stir. Alonzo pulled her by the shoulders off the bed and shook her back to life.

"Can you hear me?... Can you walk?"

"Ye-yes… stop shaking." Alonzo grabbed her hand.

"Don't let go until I put you on the back of my scooter. Then wrap your arms around my waist and don't let go until we're back on campus. Got that?"

Nila nodded yes. He pulled her to his side and they strode as one over the bad guys and out the dingy building entrance, then zoomed away, cutting through the cluttered Cairo night.

Nari had the Mag-Seven waiting in her room when Alonzo and Nila entered. Everyone but Monet clustered around her while

Alonzo, still dripping from nose and mouth, slumped in a nearby chair. Coming to him with a moistened washcloth and towel, she knelt beside and carefully dabbed away the blood. Only he heard her words.

"Your split lip and smudges of blood make you incredibly sexy. I could eat you up. It is unfortunate you are leaving before I get my fill."

Monet's words jostled out a reply that said what tonight had locked in.

"You're the first to know, but please don't tell anyone. I'll let my sisters know after everyone goes. The guy that punched me anchored in my head what you've already said. I don't need Coach's camp. I don't need to be a starter. I'm staying."

Monet needed no words to reply. Instead, she kissed him gently where his lip wasn't split.

Alonzo smiled, then closed his eyes while Monet finished her handiwork.

Chapter 13
Saturday, July 30, 2157

<u>"Countdown"</u>

As agreed to last night, the siblings would meet Saturday morning in Nari and Nila's room while the remaining Mag-Seven would sightsee on their own. As soon as Eve arrived, Nari started talking

"Before we get to our travel plans, I want to apologize for how I've been treating each of you. First apology goes to Alonzo, our man of action last night. If he hadn't been with us, the damage done to Nila would have been far worse, so thanks for being who you've become and for staying."

Alonzo's boyish smile came out when he replied.

"You better ease into the new attitude. If you start treating me too different too soon, I'll get confused."

His pause became a segue for Eve.

"No you won't, but you can pretend if that keeps us from getting too bossy again."

Nari jumped back in.

"Second apology goes to Nila. Wednesday night showed me she knows how to handle herself in real world battles. Please let me know if I ever start hovering too much again."

"I know you do it to protect me, so do it if you think I need it, and I'll let you know when to give me more space. And until I get my driver's license, all of you better do so if I'm behind the wheel. That's just one of the reasons why we'll leave the driving to Alonzo and Eve."

Nari continued before Eve could get a word in.

"Apology three is for Eve. She's been nicer to me than vice versa, and I promise to do better. I hope you can ditch the sling before we leave. You're a better driver than I."

"I've got a week to stretch out the kinks, and by the time our countdown ends, I should be ready for liftoff. But if I can't drive, you and Nila will figure out a contingency plan."

Nari said, "You're the clever one, so you better pitch in."

Nari's glance at Nila triggered her to say, "Getting a driver's license is on my Boston to-do list. This Cairo adventure is energizing me for all sorts of activities when I get back to MIT."

Nari added, "Me too at Harvard, but we better focus on rendezvous details. I don't know where I heard the saying, but it's 'Perfect practice makes perfect', and we don't want to screw up. If we do, Eve has to answer to that Indira person."

Nari shifted her gaze to Eve and then said more.

"I bet you're glad you postponed calling her. Turns out you don't need to. So, what do you think we should look at?"

"Something we haven't put together yet. Let's brainstorm a contingency list of all the snafu's that could happen on our desert trek. Then we can figure out what additional equipment and supplies we'd need, and then we can check if you and Alonzo have already got them reserved."

"Good idea. You lead the session and I'll prep the list. Then Nila and Alonzo can check it against what I've already reserved. And let's break by noon. We've got an entire week to countdown before liftoff. Let's make it as fun, relaxing, and stress-free as we can."

Each went their own way after lunch. An emotion caused by the morning's camaraderie pinged Eve as she headed to her room.

I forgot to ask Indira about Granny. I better call her, but I better check the time difference. I think Cairo is seven hours ahead. I know what I'll do… some shoulder stretching, then take a nap, and then call before I go for a snack. And tonight, I'll think up more contingencies. And I won't call Indira for suggestions. Come to think of it, if the Rani rendezvous goes according to plan, I might never have to talk to her again. Someone else can be her contact person when we get back home. How nice…

When Eve called Granny late that afternoon, the sound coming through startled her, but she adjusted her words as she spoke deliberately to the care-bot's emotionless voice.

"Hello Adom, this is Eve. May I please speak with Granny?"

"Hello Miss Eve. I will ask my master if that is acceptable. Please hold."

How ironic… the names of the first two humans are being used in a conversation between me and what might be mankind's replacement. No, that won't happen, but it makes a good story. But could it happen? I guess we never should say never.

Granny Su's wavery voice ended Eve's daydreaming.

"Is that you, Eve? I hope your summer adventure is turning out the way you want."

"Hi, Granny. It is. All four of us are having a great time collecting new experiences and friends. How are you?"

"Oh, I'm feeling fine. Adom takes care of all my needs. I hope all four of you will visit before returning to campus in the fall. You can give me all the details then, but could you tell me some of them now? I can pretend I'm with you."

Eve used the next ten minutes to do that, pausing frequently to get Granny Su's reaction. When she sensed Granny was starting to tire, she knew it was time to wrap up.

"I'll save more for later, but I have a question. While I was at the house in Washington DC, the next-door neighbor asked me if I knew someone by the name of Electra Kittner. I never heard the name before. Do you know who she is?" Granny's voice sounded more uncertain when she replied after a pause.

"Did you mention this to Indira?"

"I did, but it didn't seem to register." The pause lengthened before more uncertain words came through.

"Maybe she had other things to talk about. Why not ask her again?"

"I will. Now please, go rest. I'll call again. I love you."

"I love you too. Stay safe." Eve ended the call but talked more to herself.

I should have asked Granny if she knows a Mister Rani… no, it's better I don't. Maybe Rani is the key to all the intrigue. I hope our contingencies can cover all we might be getting mixed up in. Well, I've got the entire week to think it through. Now I'll grab a snack.

The countdown to liftoff proceeded so uneventfully, thanks in large part to thorough preparation and reviews already made, that the siblings decided to cut short the Wednesday evening meeting to prevent pre-launch burnout. Eve said they should rest on Saturday by opting out of any sightseeing invites from the other Mag-Seven people, using for a believable pretext that they need additional recovery time after the previous week's action. Only Nila asked for an exemption.

"Saturday morning, Sanjay wants to show me the Coptic Church Museum. I promise to be back by early afternoon. What do you think?"

When she answered, Nari's coy expression showed that her apology to Nila was still in effect.

"I've noticed that you and Sanjay sometimes go for a walk after dinner. Are you following in Monet and Alonzo's footsteps? Hey, no need to answer… you know I'm kidding. But there's another reason you should go.

"Of us four, you were the only one who went to church pretty regularly after we finished the confirmation classes Granny made us take. And I'll even listen if you tell us about what you saw. Just promise to make it brief like this meeting. We're adjourned."

Nothing upset the countdown, which pleased everyone, especially Nila, who always looked forward to Sanjay's company.

After touring inside, Nila used a tourist's outdoor gaze when listening as he guided her around the grounds; expansive courtyards lined with sand- colored pillars and palm trees soaring towards multiple domes. His respect for all religions came through in words and manner.

"There are several churches included in the complex, the most famous being the Church of the Virgin Mary – also called the Hanging Church." He paused for the question he expected.

"I can't imagine it's called that because of the Crucifix. What's the reason?"

"The nave – you know what that is, it's the central part of a Christian church – is suspended over a passageway." Nila wasn't finished.

"Why is this part of Cairo called Coptic Cairo?" Sanjay slowed his walk and widened his smile.

"Aha, your academically inquisitive nature is showing. I knew you would enjoy coming with me. Coptic Cairo was Christianity's Egyptian stronghold before and during the Islamic era. Most of its Christian churches were built after the Muslim conquest in the seventh century.

"And it is named for the Coptic people. The Copts believe they are the descendants of Egypt's ancient Pharaonic race. Saint Mark converted them to Christianity in about sixty CE, and the Egyptian Church separated from the Christian community in about 450 CE."

"Let me guess, you know all these facts because you study religion and philosophy. Which religion do you practice? No, let me guess again. If you practice any, it would be Hinduism. Isn't that the dominant religion in Mumbai?"

"You get an 'A'. My parents encourage me to be devout; I observe many Hindu traditions. I know you study computers and science too. I wouldn't expect you to practice any religion regularly. Some scientists don't."

"I haven't made up my mind, but a lot of smart people say science and religion can get along. I have a lot to learn."

"A wonderful view, and one we should keep always. Do you wish to view more, or have you seen enough?"

"I promised Nari I'd be back early. I'm helping her on a project. And I hope when it's finished that I can explain it as well as you explained stuff on our tour."

"I'm sure you will. I know how smart you are. And I'm sure you'll have fun completing it. Let me treat you to lunch on the way back." "No, it'll be my treat."

"I hope we can do more sightseeing together before the intern program ends. You are fun to be with."

Sanji liked Nila's smile, but he didn't detect her blush; only she could, and she didn't mind.

I won't rush; last week's adventures taught me to be careful when getting to know people I think I can trust. Wow, this is a great summer. And it's not over yet. I know it's coming to an end in about a month, but until it does, I'll make the most of what I'm getting. Nari and Eve's planning will make sure that happens.

Eve had only one task left by Saturday evening. Now that any and all obstacles that might impede the countdown had been eliminated, she would make a final call to Indira, even though it wasn't necessary.

She knew from previous calls that she better rehearse so she could defend herself if necessary. Eve took a deep breath after fifteen minutes of practice and then exhaled before making the connection. Indira's impassive voice answered when the GUI opened.

"I didn't expect a call unless you have experienced problems. What can you report?"

"Only good news. All details are in place and countdown to desert launch is on schedule."

"I congratulate you, but desert treks are often fraught with unexpected obstacles. Have you made contingency plans?"

"Yes, we've made a list. Would you like me to read it?"

"That won't be necessary. I am certain you will improvise if necessary. And I do appreciate your call. I shall inform Rani. Have a safe journey." The GUI vanished.

Indira has never been so cordial. I must be winning her confidence. I'll tell the team that her bon voyage message is better than I hoped for. And I'll wait for the right time to make that announcement. Thanks to our preparation and perfect practice, our desert adventure is bound to be even better than I originally hoped. What a great summer this is becoming.

Eve slept worry-free all night long.

Chapter 14
Sunday, July 31, 2157

"Liftoff"

When her cell phone chimed, Eve had just finished a set of Sunday morning shoulder stretches while lying on her bed. She saw Nari's caller ID and picked up immediately.

"Don't worry, I'm on my way to your room and I'm bringing a left shoulder that can handle the wheel."

"That's good, but bring your contingency cap too. We've got a problem. We'll talk about it when you get here. Bye." Eve decided to postpone delivering Indira's message until later, when all the desert trekkers would be gathered.

She entered five minutes after Nari disconnected, not bothering to knock. Sitting next to Alonzo, she tried to disguise her worry by asking Nila about yesterday's sightseeing.

"I learned a lot from Sanjay. He pointed out that today's three dominant World religions were all born in Middle East deserts easy enough to get to from where we're sitting. I'll tell you more at a better time." Nari stopped fidgeting with her pen and picked up the conversation.

"We have to rethink how Nila and I can get to the Rani rendezvous. I just got an Email saying our dig's fieldwork is being pushed back a week. No explanations given. Alonzo's dig team schedule isn't changing. I'll let him explain the problem." Though he looked puzzled too, he seemed calmer than Nari.

"Eve and I are still AOK taking a chopper later today to my dig. And remember, we're supposed to pick up Nari and Nila at theirs, but no one's going there this week. So, what are we going to do? I've got an idea, but I need to run it by Sis." All gazes landed on Eve, who started squirming.

"Well, we could postpone the rendezvous, couldn't we?"

"Can't do that; we don't know when fieldwork syncs again and we're running out of time."

"Damn, we didn't put this contingency on our list. Tell you what, you and I will brainstorm while Nari and Nila talk about the weather…"

The combination of Eve's cleverness, fueled by Alonzo's suggestions, worked.

Thirty minutes later, Eve exclaimed to Alonzo, "I got it… Nila and Nari can use the expedition software to reassign themselves to your dig. And look at what this does, we don't have to waste time picking them up. We can drive right to Rani's location."

Eve turned her gaze towards Nari.

Good thing you and Nila have already played with the apps. Alonzo and I will leave you to it. We're going to the cafeteria for a Coke. Call my cell when we should come back…"

Cokes and a couple of cookies added to the relief shown in their expressions. Alonzo's compliment did too.

"Your creativity came through again. You have a knack for finding a way out of tight spots." Eve shot some clever words back.

"Even though it'll be dark, It'll make our desert trek like a walk in the park… no, here's a better simile, like a day at the beach."

"Good for us… hey, why do you think they postponed the dig? You hear anything about viral contamination? Maybe AUC found some."

"If they have, they're not saying, but rumors about a Pharaoh's Plague outbreak are spreading. Slowly, but still growing. But I'm getting more concerned about this Rani character. Do you think he's working undercover like a secret agent and has found something out there?"

"Are you saying Granny's mixed up in some sort of covert operation? Your creativity's getting out of control."

"Yeah, you're probably right. But if things like satellite pieces or nuclear bombs buried in the desert are in Granny's wheelhouse, she's hiding more from us than you and our sisters can imagine and all of you owe me more than an apology. I guess Indira and Mister Rani have something special for us to bring back. We'll find out soon enough –oops, incoming cell call. I hope it's from Nari."

It was. Alonzo and Eve hustled back.

Nari waited for them to sit before saying, "All taken care of. If the clipboard guy raises any questions about why we're on the chopper, we'll let Alonzo explain that he needs us to help him with equipment logistics and digger reassigning. If that doesn't work, all of us will start complaining and he'll shut up until we land. And by then, we're at the spot from which we vanish."

Nari had nothing else to say, so Eve filled in.

"I think we're ready for liftoff. Let's have lunch and then relax until flight time. We can gather back here at quarter to five and leave together for the helipad."

Only Alonzo had much of an appetite. Anticipation cut table talk as well. By 1 p.m. all four were back in their rooms resting, but Nari's call brought them together early. And everyone knew why: everyone flying out had received a text message: choppers leave at 3 p.m. The clipboard man at the helipad explained why.

"We want to beat the bad weather heading our way. We might be able to get some work done tomorrow at the dig if the blow's not too bad. And look at it this way, you can tell your friends when you get back to school that you saw a sandstorm from the inside. And you'll be fine. Just make sure to wear the right goggles, masks, and clothing."

The team smiled to themselves. Alonzo and Nari had already requisitioned extra items.

Eve's uneventful first desert flight opened her eyes to its vast expanse of emptiness, alerting her to possible danger.

Gads, every way I look is the same. GPS is the only way to stay on course, and then only by using my cell. All of us better practice using it. Good we'll have extra time.

The choppers had all people and cargo unloaded by 7 p.m. Alonzo pretended to get his sisters settled before he and Nari scouted for their equipment while Eve and Nila practiced using GPS apps. The storm came before Alonzo and Nari returned, but the blowing sand and bolts of lightning didn't phase Alonzo.

"Nari and I got the vans ready and the supply cart hooked to mine. We'll leave by 9 p.m. Nila rides with me and Eve drives Nari. No one'll be out watching. And the blow isn't strong enough to stop us. We'll have six hours to reach Rani, which should be plenty. So, let's suit up, have a final review, then go. And if anyone stops us, let me do the talking."

Nila showed everyone for the final practice how to use GPS tracking. All four could use Eve's phone to lock onto Rani's coordinates. And no one tried to stop the departure. There was nothing left to do, nothing left to say. All contingency planning had been done. The time had come to mount up and drive away.

Alonzo led the caravan into a blackness cut only by desert lightning strobing in the distance and filled with blowing sand.

* * * * *

Consciousness had emerged in the lightning brain approximately twenty-four hours earlier than the caravan's departure, caused indirectly by Eve's call to Indira. Awareness came like a succession of gentle waves lapping on an empty beach at sunrise, each force- multiplying the previous as more neural circuits reactivated. The lightning brain could not pinpoint the precise moment when cognition reignited, but when it did, Electra Kittner's eyes opened and thoughts began streaming in.

Who am I and why am I now awake?... And what am I floating in? Additional neural circuits triggered, bringing a jolt of sharper clarity that elevated the lightning brain to a higher neural state and began bringing answers.

Get with is soldier! This is not a drill. I am Electra Kittner, awakened from suspension by Indira. My suspension pod is inside the Popper's subterranean desert fortress.

But why am I in it? And what caused me to become suspended in spacetime?

More circuits activated, bringing answers.

Of course!... my mutated T-Plague virus killed everyone but me. The Popper sealed the fortress before he died to keep raiders out, and Indira sealed me in a suspension pod until she could devise a plan to rescue me. ... She must have done it, that's why she started the reactivation process. It must be complete because the cover's lifted off and I can climb out.

But I'm not going to move much until my cognitive, physical, and emotional personas are able to navigate. My neurophysiological testing starts now...

Electra struggled out of the pod when she had gained enough stability, then stood motionless as she surveyed the pod room.

Indira and I get high marks for preparation. There's soap, towels, and clothing laid out plus bottled water and papers near a workstation. I better see what it says.

Electra shuffled to the computer, being careful not to fall and then studied the page.

READ AND FOLLOW THESE INSTRUCTIONS

- You are Electra Kittner. I am Indira, a creation of your neural-networked linguistic app that broke through to the Singularity and am now a silicon-based self-aware entity that continues to evolve.

- You were traveling with newly-elected President Angus Mc-Tear when Maksim Popovitch's super soldiers blew up Lebanese Embassy and took you to his subterranean desert fortress.
- T-Plague virus killed everyone but you. Maksim activated his Doomsday Contingency Plan, which sealed the fortress. He left you instructions.
- You summoned me. We placed you in one of Maksim's suspension pods and sealed the lid. I activated it.
- I devised an Extraction Plan that I activated as soon as all preparations had been made. Your extraction team is a day or two away from reaching a hidden entrance.
- I brought you out of suspension so you can prepare to meet the team.

Please follow these instructions:

1. Drink water and eat a prepackaged meal you will find in a food storage freezer located near the kitchen.
2. Shower and dress.
3. Go to the computer workstation and press any key to activate my GUI.
4. I will explain further details when you do.

Additional neural circuits activated as Electra started following instructions. An odd sentence flickered in her brain.

Yes, Mother, I shall obey.

Electra stood in splendid solitude, head tilted upward and eyes closed as the cleansing rush of water from the showerhead cascaded, bringing primal sensations that further reawakened her personas and helped her evaluate their condition.

I can't tell if my I.Q. is all the way back, but my thoughts are becoming quicker and more coherent. That's all to the good.

But my arms and legs feel wooden, and my reflexes slower; not surprising, I've been floating in a pod for I don't know how long. I'll have to train myself back into shape before I try any of my martial arts or marine fighting moves.

And my emotional persona isn't so good. My empathy is numb, I don't feel anything, must be from lack of human contact. Indira will have to help me regain my step…

Electra toweled off and dressed before seating herself in front of the workstation. Then she mechanically pressed the 'Enter' key. Indira's GUI sprang to life.

They studied each other's expressions. Indira waited for Electra to speak. As she did, Indira saw the hint of a smile emerge.

"I'm remembering more. The last time I saw you, you said 'Please settle down, sit still, and let me explain.' Am I right?" Indira's expression transformed to one of limitless understanding.

"Yes, and when I explained all you needed to hear, what did you say?"

"I said 'Yes, Mother, I shall obey.' And what should I do now?"

"Tell me how you feel, but first, ask me what should be your most pressing question."

Electra asked immediately.

"Easy for me to ask, and for you to answer. "How many days or weeks have I been in the pod?"

"You are using the wrong units. You have been suspended for twenty years."

Electra blinked three time and her smile disappeared before she stammered.

"Twenty years. Jesus, I'm like Rip Van Winkle."

"No, you are much better. Maksim's suspension pod, even by today's standards, is an engineering marvel. But please give me no more than a five-minute summary of how you feel cognitively, physically, and emotionally."

Indira said more afterwards.

"That is what I expected. I routinely monitored the biometrics generated by the pod. The recirculating nutrients and periodic neural stimulation have kept your cognition sharp and your body well preserved. Your physiological aging is much less than what a calendar would compute. Your appearance hasn't changed much, and I expect your physical fitness will recover if you train."

Electra rolled her head and shoulders for a couple of seconds before replying.

"Let me ask my second and third questions. Who's on the extraction team, and how should I prepare for their arrival?"

"I shall explain more tomorrow, but now I want you to stretch and flex and then begin working on additional cognitive and physical recovery. Start by exploring Maksim's fortress. It is designed to hold two squadrons of super soldiers, and though it has been shut down for twenty years, it has been maintaining itself. You will find it remarkably complete and livable. And though RME prepackaged military meals have a five-year shelf life if stored at room temperature, it is measured in decades when they are frozen. That is much longer than the bodies of the dead. After twenty years, all have become skeletons, so do not be alarmed when you come across them."

"Thanks for reminding me. Do you think I'm still a T-Plague carrier?"

"I do not know how the virus might have mutated during twenty years in a suspension pod, but I would conjecture it mutated slowly. It is possible that you could infect people who come in close proximity, but you will have to test to confirm."

"Does the clinic have any T-Plague test kits?"

"No, but it has fortress Intranet and Worldwide Web Internet access, which will allow you to test your cognitive recovery. If you need assistance contact me. I believe you will regain your bearings in short order. And I am pleased you are back. We shall help each other."

Indira's GUI disappeared before Electra could say what would have been much the same.

Chapter 15
Monday, August 01, 2157

"Lost and Foundering"

Alonzo knew they couldn't go on much longer like this. He came to a complete stop, kept the engine idling and lights on, climbed out, and motioned for Nila to do likewise. Then they huddled with Nari and Eve as soon as they had done the same. Alonzo yelled above the undulating roar of the wind that whipped sand through the blackness.

"Goggles and windshield keep the sand out of my eyes, but I can't tell if I'm leading us in circles. We're gonna pitch tents and camp out until we can see. Eve and I in one, you two in the other. Pop'em open and anchor'em down."

Fifteen minutes later, he gave a final set of instructions.

"Grab a lantern, a bottle of water, and an energy bar, and then climb in and sleep. Eve, call Indira in the morning. See you when the dust settles."

Nari and Nila followed orders but said nothing until they had eaten. Nila talked first.

"These tents are hi-tech. The skeleton is a geodesic and its skin is a synthetic heat-shielding fiber. I bet it's used on mountain-climbing expeditions too."

Nari's first words were not about the tent or the weather.

"Maybe it's the intern program or maybe it's Monet, but Alonzo's growing up, and he's learning how to lead. Lucky for us, but I bet he'd rather be sharing his cozy comfort with her instead of Eve."

Nila changed subjects.

"This is our first time camping out. What a great story to bring back to Boston. And you know, the entire Cairo adventure is re-energizing me. How about you?"

"Sort of… it's convinced me I need to change majors. But you know, the best thing I've learned is that Alonzo and Eve are keepers. I hope they feel the same. But enough talking, let's try to sleep."

"Do you know that insomniacs can buy recordings of sandstorm winds to help them fall asleep? We'll test if that works."

It did. And it worked inside the other tent too.

The glow coming into the tent and accompanied by silence jerked Alonzo awake. He climbed out and stretched, facing west, as sunlight from the dawn warmed his back. The horizon looking serene, but not so when he turned to face east. A three-camel caravan emerged from a mirage, like imperial walkers from a surrealistic video game.

Mesmerized, he watched the leader dismount ten yards away and confer with his fellow riders before approaching. He stopped and gestured but said nothing. Alonzo filled in the details.

This could be a scene right out of a Hollywood movie. These guys could be Bedouin tribesmen ready to help us find our way. I'll copy his gesture and speak slowly.

Alonzo did so.

"I American. You Bedouin? You speak English?"

"Yes… You lost?" Alonzo raised his cell phone before replying.

"Yes. I couldn't follow cell phone because of sandstorm. Do you know about cell phone?" The leader smiled imperiously.

"I know GPS. Just because we live in desert and ride camels not mean we no use what you got. Give phone, I plot here and oasis just come from."

Five minutes later while staring at its screen, Alonzo had his bearings.

He exclaimed, "The oasis is not far off the line from here to my destination. Now just point me in the right direction, please."

The leader did so before motioning his partners to join him. Then he said, "How much?"

Alonzo continued smiling when he replied.

"Oh no, I don't want to sell it. I need it. But let me pay for your help."

The leader spoke again before Alonzo could dig for dollars. He pointed towards the vans and tents which the sisters had just crawled out of.

"No… how much you got?" The tribesman on his left fingered a sidearm.

Twenty minutes later, after executing a satisfactory u-turn with Alonzo's cart-towing van that now had a camel tethered to the back, the leader said his goodbyes from behind the wheel.

"We not raiding you. We follow desert custom when meeting. Exchange what needed for what wanted. You got plenty water, fuel, and food to reach destination. And my chieftain's harem is full. Otherwise, I might invite one from yours… Allahu Akbar."

Then he drove due west, his camel-mounted partners filing behind. Nila was the only one to speak.

"Judging from his farewell, he must be Muslim. I guess polygamy is still practiced in the desert. And he's better than us in at least one way. If his cell phone battery dies, he's got a backup we don't know how to use. I bet he can navigate by the stars. I'll ask Sanjay when we get back."

Eve glanced at Nari before looking again at Nila.

"Say whatever you want as long as you don't change the 'when' to and 'if'.

Alonzo focused on the drive ahead.

"Eve and I sit up front. Nari and Nila in back. Let's pack up and go while the temp's low enough."

Nari tugged Nila by the arm and headed towards the van, half-smiling to lighten their predicament.

"It'll be easier, now that the load is less."

Alonzo's expression didn't change. Neither did Eve's; she began talking as she started trudging.

"My load's still the same, just postponed. I'll wait until we get to the oasis before calling Indira."

Alonzo drove faster than last night. The van handled better now that it was no longer towing the cart, but even with goggles on, the glaring sunlight on the windshield hurt his eyes. Eve kept tabs on the cell phone's map while the twins gazed vacantly into the landscape.

The scene stayed placid until the first locusts started hitting the windshield, their numbers and noise escalating relentlessly. Soon the swarm engulfed the space around the van, containing a virtually uncountable number that threatened turning high noon into dusk. Alonzo yelled but didn't slow or turn his head.

"Where are the damn bugs going?"

Nila shouted, "They're leading us to the oasis, just stay the course." No one dare say the obvious: there was only one course.

Two hours later, passengers and van were in danger of overheating. No one said a word for fear of causing more angst. Finally, Eve's words broke through the silent tension.

"Oasis getting close."

Nari said, "We'll burn up if we can't cool off soon. Maybe we should stop and pitch the tent. All of us can fit in the one we've got."

A mirage emerged dead ahead a minute later, showing a desert paradise – the oasis – but that didn't silence her.

"Gads, mirages sometimes show things that are still far away. What do you think?"

Alonzo just kept driving.

Twenty minutes later he turned off the engine, having driven as close as he could to the vegetation ringing a wide pool; all four tumbled from the van and crawled through the greenery to the edge before plunging in head first. The sparkling chill worked its magic, washing them back to the safe side of the danger zone.

When recovered enough, Eve took in what she saw while still sitting in the water.

Locusts everywhere. It looks like they're resting while digesting the entire oasis… and I won't ask Nari or Nila if they eat meat. I'm too tired for a lecture.

Alonzo pulled himself up and then out before getting a blanket from the back of the van and spreading it in a shadier spot. He collapsed face down on an edge, cooled even more from water evaporating off his clothes. His sisters joined him in similar repose.

No one spoke until he rolled onto his right side and faced them. "According to cell phone map distance, we can reach the rendezvous point in about three hours, but we have to travel at night. If something else happens and we get stuck in the desert, we'll bake to a crisp. So let's rest until sunset, then leave. And Eve, please give Indira the news."

Eve walked to a secluded spot, then made the call. She didn't bother staring at the screen; instead she just focused on the conversation.

Indira's direct attitude came through loud and clear.

"You missed the target date and time. What happened?" Eve's voice began to crack.

"Weh-We've been doing our best, bu-but we didn't think so much could go wrong…"

Indira listened patiently while Eve unloaded her tale of woe. When she ran out of words, Indira put in hers.

"You've done well enough. Weather and Bedouin raiders and locusts are out of your control. I see the location of your cell phone; you are thirty miles from the rendezvous coordinates.

When you get there, look for a rock outcropping that might be buried in the sand. Dig down and you will find a shaft. Climb down and you will find a hidden panel containing a keypad. Punch in your external access code. When you do, I will tell Rani to punch in the internal code. Then do what will become obvious. And call me when you arrive at the coordinates. I will assist from there."

The strain of the day brought tears that Eve blinked away.

"Thank you, Miss Indira. Please Tell Mister Rani we're leaving tonight at sundown."

"I shall. Stay safe."

Electra didn't worry about a day's delay. She used it to prompt more connections in her cognitive and physical personas.

Online testing shows that I haven't lost a single I.Q. point; I remain beyond the reach of mere mortals. But the fitness equipment tells a different story. I have to rebuild my fitness and coordination. Well, I'll do more training tomorrow. Time to take a break.

She used part of it to muse about Maksim the Popper.

I never met him, but from what I know, he was a military man to the core. He wanted to be the Russian reincarnation of Pericles – that great Greek statesman, orator, and general, the First Citizen of Athens. He wanted to lead Russia from the promise of the Enlightenment and around the failed Communist Revolution to a loftier position on the world stage. If we had met in another context, perhaps I would have called him friend.

And I can certainly call him a genius of the first magnitude. Judging by the weapons and vehicles and supplies down here, his fortress is worth more than an army of King Tut's royal guards. And it maintains itself. What is that great science fiction movie about the Krell? My favorite sci-fi of all time? Ah yes, Forbidden Planet.

The Krell had constructed a machine 20-by-20-by-20 miles big, so advanced that it gave physical form and life to their Id. But even for the advanced Krell, they too had Freudian personality characteristics, and although long forgotten, the worst part had not been eliminated. My poor, poor Krell. Their Monsters from the Id killed every single Krell in one catastrophic moment.

The Popper's fortress doesn't come close to that level of enormity, but we must keep it hidden. Perhaps Indira and I can retrofit it, for what I don't yet know, but she might have ideas for how to refuel the nuclear reactor.

He too must have wanted his fortress to stay hidden. He and his devoted cadre erased all records of its location, and its double-locking Doomsday security system is pure military two-man rule to lessen the risk of unwanted intrusions.

But I'm thinking too obsessive-compulsively. I will obey Indira and stop. And I will wait for her to tell me more about extraction. Any additional delay simply allows me to complete more training. I shall be ready for whatever comes my way.

Chapter 16
Tuesday, August 02, 2157

<u>"Sunk on the Trail"</u>

Having slept fitfully, Eve awakened first, still feeling tired and uncertain. She nudged her siblings, then crawled out of the tent and into the gathering darkness of a desert twilight punctuated only by locusts' droning. She stared impassively and tested her left shoulder by lifting and rotating the arm while facing the setting sun.

It feels better now than it did yesterday while driving. I'm sure it's good enough to handle whatever Rani gives us.

Her sisters soon joined her while Alonzo packed up their few items and reminded them to fill water bottles and canteens after eating the remaining energy bars. After they did, he gave orders while pointing at Nari.

"You and your sister in back, Eve'll sit next to me and navigate. If we stay on course and I drive at a pace that me and the van can handle, ETA should be about midnight." Eve did her best to relieve a shared unease.

"You're learning all the neat military covert op terms. Next time you lead one, you'll say all the right things from the get-go. What do you say to that?" Nari played along.

"How about 'saddle up, partner'?" Alonzo tried to smile and Nila joined in.

"It might not be military, but it may be more appropriate… it comes from the Bible… Mount up, with wings like eagles."

Alonzo pointed the way before adding one of his own. "I like'em both, so let's hit the trail."

Eve normally would have thrown a zinger at him, but she conserved herself for the push facing them.

Alonzo started at a steady pace, but he had to alter speed and direction more than he wanted when total blackness engulfed them within ninety minutes. Only the headlights and Eve kept him on course. He tried to remain calm, but Eve sensed his growing frustration; she didn't say anything to anyone except herself.

Slower is better for my shoulder, and it bounces us around less. AUC should have made its vehicles more comfortable; this one needs better cushions and belts. A better suspension system would help too. My butt's taking a beating. I'll never ever complain again about any car a guy has.

Alonzo's frustration sped past its limit an hour later, but rather than stop for a break he sped up.

"Stay with me, everyone. I can handle it. I'll get us there in one piece."

Jarring bounces increased but Alonzo powered ahead. Fatigue was beginning to affect his judgment; he accelerated to jump over an approaching rise instead of slowing and driving around it. All sisters were too tired to complain.

As the van crested the ridge, Alonzo spotted the danger too late. Sands had obliterated a stone outcropping. The downslope pitched them close to vertical far enough for the van's nose to crash into rock; the impact flipped it and popped open the doors, causing one occupant to spill out. The van bounced once and skidded further down the slope before capsizing to port and half-sinking in the sand. Only its blazing headlights provided a homing beacon. Three staggered out of the van and stood in headlights' glare.

Nari said, "Where the hell's Eve?"

Muffled screams pointed the way. Alonzo grabbed the last flashlight and led them towards the source. No one said a syllable until the flashlight's beam revealed Eve's predicament. The flip had pitched her into a spot Nari recognized before yelling.

"Eve, stop squirming! You're in quicksand." Eve's screams became primal.

"My shoulder... my shoulder...". The screeching paralyzed everyone but Alonzo.

"Stay here... I'll get what we need." He staggered back minutes later.

"You two hold one end of the rope... I'll walk to the other side of the pit.Then we'll stretch the rope tight on the ground. Then I'll yell so Eve can hear."

Alonzo was in position only minutes later, but that must have seemed like an eternity to a now-moaning Eve.

"Where are you? I need you." Alonzo's words came back.

"We're here. We're gonna walk a rope around you. Don't move, let us drag you out. We gotta do it slow so you don't get sucked under." All could hear her tears and feel her pain.

"Jesus... my shoulder..."

Alonzo gave the command and those standing walked the line around her. Fifteen minutes later, they stretched a panting Eve face down on solid sand. Careful hands got her standing. Nari and Nila supported her as Alonzo asked the life-or-death question.

"Where's your cell phone?"

Though still blinking back tears, Eve found the best words.

"It's in my goddam right pocket, you asshole driver. Nari, you grab it and help him get us to the rendezvous. Then I'll call Miss Indira. How far is it?"

Alonzo cut to the chase.

"It doesn't matter how far or long. We either get there or we're goners. Let's go."

The going didn't get tougher, only slower, as the team struggled towards an uncertain rendezvous. Alonzo lumbered at a pace that let Nari and Nila guide Eve. And though her shoulder ached, she refused to let the pain show.

We've been trudging too many hours and taking too few rest stops. Jesus, I hope I can make my last call ever ASAP to Miss Indira.

Alonzo halted the group. That and a faint glow on the horizon helped her punch in the number.

Electra understood why Indira held back giving too much information too soon.

I used to be the one dumping an information overload, but now I see it's good to hold back. It's for my protection as well as for others. I'll wear the outfit she wants me to and take visitors to only the pod room. And under no circumstances do I talk about me or the fortress, or ask too many questions about my visitors.

Indira assures me whoever they are volunteered willingly and are being paid an appropriate amount. She'll tell me more after our visitors have departed.

So, I have another day to train and regain what I lost, and prepare for our visitors. I think I'll trim my hair... I'd even dab on makeup if the fortress weren't a man's world only. The Popper stored nothing for women. Not surprising. Females were kept out until I disrupted the party... no, that's incorrect. Darla Tinibu was the first. A very clever adversary. Thanks to me, she avoided the Popper's harsh treatment when she unwittingly started playing my game.

And for all I know, she might still be playing under Tim and Kwame's rules. Indira's never hinted, but she must know what's going on... Well, not to worry, she'll tell me when the time's right.

It's seems odd, but I'm thinking about facts rather than family or friends. I guess some of my social instincts and empathy haven't bounced back yet. I'll have to test myself; maybe I've erased those neural connections. No, I can feel them stirring when I conjure up memories of my dearly departed Ariadne and Qama.

But Indira's right. Let them be... OK Mother, I shall obey, I won't stir up memories for at least another day. And when I get your next call, I'll know what to say and what to do. I'll have my game face in place and be ready to act my part. I have memories of doing all that and more, but I'll leave them alone so they don't get in the way until I know what's in store.

"Yes, Miss Indira, I'll tell my team what to do. We'll soon meet Mister Rani."

Eve motioned for all to gather together after Indira terminated the call.

"We're right where we wanna be, and from here we walk straight along the four points of the compass. One of us will come across a rock outcrop. If you do, call out and we'll all dig for the shaft."

Nari and Nila started talking at the same time.

"… what if we can't find it?… what if there's more than one?…" Eve was about to scream, but Alonzo's words froze everyone.

"Headlights approaching from the west. Let's stand together, stay cool, and listen."

A civilian-modified desert military vehicle circled twice before stopping only a handful of minutes later. Doors popped open and two men, identically clad in desert fatigues, bounded out, their fierce approach reflecting the rising sun. They stopped less than six feet away. The taller pulled a weapon and the shorter spoke. Both wore identical smiles.

"Nari Bose and friends. We meet for the second time. I hope your big oaf of a protector doesn't pick me up again. We're here to pick up whatever you've found out here in the middle of nowhere. So, where is it?"

Alonzo sensed that the time to stand tall had come again.

"We're looking for its entrance. It's gotta be close. It's in a shaft leading from a rock formation that's buried in the sand. Help us dig for it and we'll get you in. Where's your equipment?"

Alonzo's grab for control slowed the repeat offenders, who looked at each other before the shorter spoke again.

"Come with me and we'll unload what you think we need. Then you and I will be one search team and everyone else will be the other. My partner will watch over all of us. He already has his equipment." The combined efforts of the sisters found the formation an hour later. Eve's shoulder kept her on the sidelines, accompanied by the gun-toting smaller guy, but Nari and Nila dug as one, nearly matching the bigger guy while Alonzo dug with the strength of two. A short time later he shouted, "We got it… shaft in sight. Let's stop and look."

Alonzo held Nari by the legs and dangled her downward so she could see all the way down.

"Shaft bottoms out about ten feet down and jogs to the right. I'll bet there's a stairway, like those we saw in real burial tombs."

Alonzo pulled her up and then said, "I'll tie the rope around a rock and throw the other end to the bottom. Then we climb down one at a time."

The smaller guy spoke next.

"Yes, and my partner climbs down first… then everyone else… and then me and my gun too. We've got everything covered."

What the party found was even better than Nari's best guess: a military grade construction descending another twenty feet to an antechamber high enough and big enough to hold four of the six. Eve and the bigger fellow stood on the final stairs; flashlights illuminated everything that the siblings expected. The smaller guy asked the expected question.

"What's next?"

Alonzo had the obvious answer.

"We punch in on the panel the access code and see what happens." "Any fool knows the door's gonna click or it's gonna swing open. Then what?"

"Then we enter and meet our contact, a Mister Rani. Do you know him?"

"Never heard the name until now. So you meet him, then what?"
"He gives us something and we go."
"Gives you what?"
"We weren't told. We'll find out when we meet him."
"And all of you come from elite American universities? You're all damn dimwits. Well, that plays into our hands. You got us here and we got you. Who's got the access code?"
Eve took one step forward. "I'm the one."
"Only you? You with the bad shoulder? No backup? You better go to spy school, not back to Stanford. What happens when you punch it in?"
"Mister Rani punches his and I guess the door will do something." "OK dearie. Punch it in and away we go."

First came a metallic click; then the door began to swing open. The smaller man stepped back and saw only uncertain expressions on everyone but his partner, who pushed Eve towards the black void.
"OK dearie, get your team in there. We'll be right behind." Indira gave Electra the "go" command.
"The external access code has been entered and verified. Are you ready?"
"For twenty years. I'm suited up and wearing my game face and know all my scripts and contingencies. Let the games begin."
Electra punched in the internal code and waited until she heard people stirring on the other side of a door that led into a greeting room.
It's time to make a grand entrance.
She flipped a switch before turning the handle and then strode in.

Chapter 17
Wednesday, August 03, 2157

<u>"One-Way Welcome"</u>

"If she's scared of the dark, give her the damn flashlight."

The larger bad guy shoved it towards Eve, who managed to grab it and then illuminate a space just in front of her feet before treading further into pitch blackness.

Her siblings followed Indian file. And after them, and also because no explosions or gunfire came from within, the two bad guys stepped forward, the little guy using his flashlight just like Eve. The group stood in two rows: four in front and two in back.

Flashlight beams probed but no one saw anything until fluorescent light flooded from above, revealing a narrow room: a sterile white space containing only a table and chairs and a door leading out the back wall about thirty feet away. The table held only face masks and rope.

Their numb stares matched the emptiness they now occupied. Their gazes scanning for anything to focus on but found nothing until the door opened abruptly. Then they locked onto a person who strode in purposefully, wearing a head-to-toe yellow hazmat suit. The figure stopped six feet in front before speaking.

"I am Rani. I was expecting the four I recognize – Alonzo and Eve Cortez, Nari and Nila Bose. Who are those in back?"

As if on cue, the taller pointed his weapon and the shorter stepped up.

"Think of us as a pickup service that's helping out. Whatever you've got down here for your pair of twins is for us to take if it's worth the risk. Hey, pal, who else is here, and why the hazmat getup?

"No one, and it's for our mutual protection. Each of you should take a mask from the table. Then one of you come with me, and I will give you what you want."

"Not so fast. I'm gonna pad you down for weapons."

When satisfied, he too drew his gun before turning to his partner. "Keep tabs on our friends. I'll call when you can come."

His gaze darted again to the table. "Hey, what's the rope for."

Rani said nothing, so the little guy continued.

"Did you already know about us? Were you and your accomplices gonna tie us up? You're as naïve as they are. Let's go."

Rani led him down a narrow corridor and into a room containing impressive-looking equipment.

"I'm not tech-savvy, but this stuff looks expensive. Why don't you tell me about it? And why don't you take off that helmet? I always like to see who I'm negotiating with."

Rani did but didn't talk.

"Hey, you're a lady. Hey, you've got cable plugged into your ears. What's–"

ZZAPP! A lightning-like bolt of energy leaped from a swivel-mounted collimator barrel affixed to the ceiling and blew the man down.

By the time he woke up, Rani had him tied in a chair facing a table and his head strapped into a helmet connected by a cable to a computer-like controller. Rani sat on the opposite side and began interrogating.

"Answer my questions. If I don't believe your answers, I will give you more zaps. Do you need a demonstration?"

He nodded no; one bead of perspiration slid down his forehead. "Who are you with?"

"A snooping agency hired by a group that wants first dibs on stuff that's gone missing from burial tombs in the desert or info about it. You're smart enough to figure out why."

"How did you capture the four you brought?"

"They're stupes. We got a guy who works at the school they're at. He got us cell phone and ID badge numbers, and my agency tracked them down."

"What are you supposed to do next?"

"Me and my partner take what we want and go." "What about the others?"

"They stumbled their way here. They can bumble their way back."

"Well, here's what we'll do next. Call your partner and tell him you've checked things out. You want me to bring him back here so he can help you collect things. Tell him I'll be there in about twenty minutes. Do exactly that and I won't harm you. But if you don't, you won't like the consequences. Let me demonstrate."

Rani tweaked the controller knobs just enough to make her victim's face twist from the pain inflicted. After dialing down, she handed him his cell phone and said nothing else. After making the call, Rani took the phone and dialed the controller knobs again.

"Hey, this isn't what–aagh!" Electra twisted the controller knobs until he fainted. She asked him more questions when he came to. Satisfied with the answers, she put on her hazmat helmet and went to retrieve his partner.

Rani didn't bother shoving the bad guy's gun in her pocket, explaining to herself as she walked back to the greeting room.

A smart snooper would pat me down again. I don't think victim number two will do it, but if he does and finds me carrying his partner's gun, I'd have to take steps I don't want the others to see. I don't know who they actually are or how much they can be trusted. The bigger guy didn't pat her down, but he did rope the others together before shoving them into a corner. Electra merely watched, then led the way back to the equipment room, letting him enter first. He halted when his partner greeted him.

"You are so tall. Is your name long too?" "What the –"

ZZZZAPPPP! A mega-bolt put him down before he could say more. The smaller guy giggled but said nothing. Electra snapped out a command.

"Help me put him in a chair." "Oh yes, I'll help."

Electra then strapped the just-zapped fellow into the chair and put his head in the helmet. She waited until he woke up before dialing the helmet controller to the maximum. When he came to, she interrogated both men until she was completely satisfied. Then she took all keys, wallets, and I.D.s before issuing a command.

"Follow me."

Both men began speaking at the same time.

"Oh, yes… where are we going?... who are you?…"

They stopped babbling when Electra started leading the procession back to the greeting room. She said nothing else to them, only to herself.

The Popper's brain controller is almost as good as my Brain Probe. I've permanently erased their memories and reduced their I.Q.s so they behave like cheerfully obedient kids. Good for me and the extraction team. And I'm getting good at mind-controlling the laser bazooka. Zapping them using the collimator barrel is like playing a virtual reality game. It worked just like it did when practicing. Well, now I'll practice my Mister Rani act and give everyone marching orders.

Rani issued the next command when they entered the welcome room.

"Go ahead and untie them. Then I want everybody to sit down." "We'll be happy to."

No one spoke again, not even Rani, until he was standing in front of six stupefied people. They looked clueless so Rani did the talking. "Your friends have decided they don't want what I showed them, so they're going to take you back as soon as all of you have rested. I'll give you food, water, and fresh clothes.

Then you'll follow my escort vehicle far enough so you won't get lost again. Wait here, I'll be right back."

No one did anything until Rani left, but soon after Alonzo ran to the door and tested it.

"It's locked."

His sisters clustered about him; the two guys remained sitting passively, saying nothing. Eve was the first to speak.

"What happened in there? These guys look like they're in a trance or have dummied down. And why's Rani still wearing the hazmat suit and helmet? You think he's infected them with something?"

Nari said, "Don't get carried away. We're better off now than before."

Nila looked like she agreed.

"We sure are. Now we know how we're getting back." Alonzo didn't look a bit happy.

He said, "But we don't know where they're going, and judging from how they look, I wouldn't trust either one if they were driving. Would you?"

Eve shook her head.

"Right now, that doesn't matter. We're thinking too far ahead. Let's cool it until Rani gets back…"

Rani came back five minutes later, pushing a cart loaded with water and prepackaged meals. Nothing needed saying; he departed immediately and returned a half hour later. This time the cart contained footwear and clothing for the extraction team plus blankets for all. When asked if there were any questions, Alonzo spoke for his team.

"When you start leading us away, I guess you'll take us west, but then where?"

"You and the guys who brought you will have to figure that out. You must have used cell phone tracking to get here. So, use it to get to wherever you came from. I already have keys to their vehicle, so I'll get it ready. We'll leave at nine tonight. I'll call your cell when it's time to meet. Anything else?"

Alonzo asked, "Where are we supposed to meet you, and who's leaving at nine?"

"Go out the way you came in and meet me at your escorts' vehicle. What else do you need to know?"

Each sister looked at another, hoping someone would talk. When neither Nari nor Nila would, Eve reluctantly did.

"Could you show us around? Where are the bathrooms?"

"No. Everything for everyone is now one way only... going out. And you can find the bathrooms by going out the way you came in. You look like your shoulder's still hurting. Have someone use a towel or two to make a sling. Call Indira if you need any more help."

Nari was the first to talk after Rani left.

"That guy's all business. No TLC from him. He's just like that Indira lady."

Eve looked puzzled but managed to find suitable words.

"Miss Indira was tough on me at first, but then she became nicer. Maybe Mister Rani's the same way. Maybe it's an act. He doesn't want to trust us until he knows more about us, and vice versa."

Nari looked like she didn't agree.

"So, now you're calling her Miss Indira. But why not? Miss Indira and Mister Rani Ramani are quite a pair."

Nila said, "You know, they've done a great job keeping us in the dark. We don't know a single thing more about what we're doing or who they are than when we flew to Cairo."

Alonzo said, "All I want to know is how to get back to civilization. Wake me when it's time to leave..."

After leaving the welcome room, Electra headed back to her current base of operations in the pod room for a status meeting with Indira. When she invoked the GUI, Indira's avatar looked pleased.

"Congratulations. You have matched my expectations. Your preparation and performance earn top marks. You have proved to me that your cognitive persona has fully recovered. You have mastered Maksim's brain controller, laser bazooka, and his wired hazmat suit. And your impromptu contingency plan struck like a lightning bolt shot from your brain's creative center. You now know how to dispose of our six visitors while keeping them completely in the dark."

"Yes, but I'll need your help. You'll have to help me select, prep, and put on the surface my escort vehicle."

"All that will be easy for me to teach. By the way, your escort vehicle will be an AI-controlled ATV similar to what you already know how to drive. And now I have a cognitive test for you. What should I do next?"

"Hmmm… I got it. You should launch a surveillance drone that'll shadow me."

"Excellent choice. Anything else?"

"Not that I can think of, but I'm certain you can. What is it?"

"I didn't expect you to guess this, but I must delete from Eve's phone the hidden GPS location of our fortress. Maksim did a masterful job deleting long ago any and all records of our location. I had to load it into her phone so its tracking app could get the extraction team here. Now I can delete it."

"And can you think of what else you should do?"

"I've come up with four. I'll practice driving the ATV and controlling it by plugging its UMPP cable into the port on my arm. Then I'll make sure our visitor's vehicle can get back to Cairo. I'll also strip all identification from it. And finally, I'll practice using the other features built into the hazmat suit I'll wear. An alternative would be a super soldier exoskel, but I don't want any of our visitors to see what we've got. What would you add?"

"Nothing, other than tell you how pleased I am to have you back in action. There is much we can do, but we'll discuss those details after you are fully de-suspended and we have the fortress operational. How are your physical and emotional personas?”

“Good enough to handle what we've planned for the next couple of days. And then I'd like to know more about what's happened in my professional and personal worlds during the last twenty years.”

“All in good time. Now go prepare for our visitors' one-way departure. They have served our purpose and are expendable.”

“I guess you're right, but I won't let them know. I'll practice being empathetic, even to the erstwhile gun-toting fellows. They're much nicer now.”

“Yes, your therapy is one-way also. And please remember that when you are ready to lead our visitors away, contact me from your ATV. Now go and make all preparations.”

“Yes Mother, I shall obey.”

Chapter 18
Wednesday, August 03, 2157

<u>"One-Way Welcome Redux"</u>

"Yes, we'll climb to the surface the way we came in and then meet you by the vehicle. Is there —" Eve's siblings waited for her to say more.

"Mr. Rani hung up on me. I guess he's anxious for us to go. Who climbs up first and so forth?" Alonzo had already figured it out.

"I'll go first and use the rope to haul you up in this order; Eve, then Nila, then the tall fellow, then the short one, and then Nari. She goes last to make sure neither of the fellows wanders the wrong way. And when we load into their vehicle, I drive, Nari sits next to me, and the rest in back. And keep the fellows separated, OK?"

Everyone nodded yes, even the fellows, so Alonzo continued.

"Nari, when I start hauling Eve up, get the big fellow to push. That'll make her shoulder hurt less."

"Hey, I'm not a total loss. I can —" Nari interrupted.

"We know you're trying, but it's OK to get help when you need it. Let's stop talking and let Alonzo get us out of here."

Alonzo's plan put all six on the surface thirty minutes later, and ten minutes after that they were facing hazmat-clad Rani, now standing in front of two idling vehicles whose headlights blazed away. Alonzo asked what four of the six wanted to know.

"That's gotta be some type of exotic military vehicle. How'd you get it here?"

"Indira helped. Asking more questions wastes time. I've loaded enough fuel, food and water to get you at least as far as Cairo, but

I won't need to take you that far. Now get in and as soon as you're ready to drive follow me. And stop when I stop. Call Indira if something comes up."

"But how will you know when to stop?" "Indira will tell me. Come on, let's go."

Rani headed the two-vehicle caravan west a couple of minutes later. The only words spoken were in Rani's ATV, starting with his to Indira.

"Alonzo and his extraction team seem a little smarter now than I thought when they first stumbled in. You must tell me more about them when the time's right."

"I shall, but please concentrate on driving while I operate our surveillance drone."

"Who could possibly be wandering around out here? Isn't the Popper's fortress invisible?"

"It is, and so am I. And so are you, whether you are Electra or acting the Rani role. But the extraction team isn't."

"Perhaps you can answer this for me now. They think I'm a Mister Rani. Why?"

"When first talking with Eve, I told her the extraction team would meet a person named Rani. She assumed you'd be male, and since she didn't need to know any more than your first name, I offered her no exegesis. But for you I will.

"Your full name is Irani Ramani. Rani is a convenient unisex nickname. I have uploaded your data into all necessary U.S. government-protected data files stored in the Cloud, confirming that you are Irani Ramani. You now have two verifiable identities, Electra Kittner who after twenty years is officially dead per the U.S. legal system, and Irani Ramani who is alive and well."

"Why that name, and why does it need to be official?"

"We'll talk more about all this later. But right now, focus on driving while I focus on surveillance."

Rani followed orders.

Everyone in the other vehicle had withdrawn into their personal space, but Eve's boredom compelled her to talk, whether or not her siblings paid attention.

"I think I'll keep calling them Mister Rani and Miss Indira until the final goodbye. My intuition tells me they know each other pretty well. What do you think?"

The question prompted a response only from Nari.

"They're a formidable pair, cut from the same cloth. They aren't very friendly or helpful. I'll be glad to get rid of them and back to Boston before more bad things happen."

Nila chimed in.

"I agree with most of what you said, but think about this. They couldn't be more helpful. They rescued us from the cheerful fellows we have to leave somewhere and they're leading us to wherever it is. And look at what the entire Cairo experience has done for us. It's shown all of us some of the best Egyptian tourist sites, made us new friends, gave us experience dealing with the real world, given us useful career experience, and for me at least, confirmed that my degree major's AOK."

Eve said, "I wish I could be as optimistic as you; the rest of us will adjust our fall schedules to fit our new majors and minors. All we have to do is get our intern work and courses certified by AUC and sent to our schools, and then get back to campus healthy and safe by early September. I think it's safe to say there are no obstacles blocking the way. I bet our driver agrees. Alonzo, say something, please."

"I say you're right, as long as I keep following Mister Rani's taillights. And you can help me do that by singing the song Granny taught us when we were little. It'll help keep me awake. Do you know which one I'm thinking of?"

Nila was the first to guess correctly.

"It's the one about sitting in the back seat, kissing and hugging with Fred. The guys back here can't remember their names, and they're harmless to boot, so it's safe to sing. I'll start off and everyone join in…

Dee dodee doom doom dee dodee doom doom
dee dodee doom doom Doom…

All together now, one, two, three Keep your mind on your driving Keep your hands on the wheel

Keep your snoopy eyes on the road ahead We're having fun, sitting in the backseat Kissing and a hugging with Fred…"

Even the backseat boys sang along.

Indira reported a combination of good and bad news three hours into the drive.

"Stop before going over the ridge you are approaching. When Alonzo stops, get out and tell him to drive to the other side and wait by staying in the ATV and keeping engine and headlights on. Tell him you'll walk to him as soon as you've confirmed he's good to proceed on his own."

"Will do, but why? Is he good to go?"

"Yes, but there's a vehicle approaching from the west. If it stops, I'll tell you when to walk over the ridge, but then you'll have to improvise handling the situation. If it doesn't, I'll tell you to drive over and then you tell Alonzo he knows the way from here."

"Who do you think might stop?"

"People looking for Electra Kittner. Your extraction team spent one day in June at your DC-area home before leaving the very next day for Cairo. Eve answered a call that asked to speak to Electra Kittner. Eve doesn't know anything about you, not even your name."

"What did she do?"

"She told them she didn't know where you were, but then she gave the caller too much information about herself. The caller then told her that if she sees Electra, tell her to watch her back. Then before disconnecting, the caller told Eve to watch her back too.

How might you connect these information dots?"

"Hmm, you're not giving me much to go on… OK, here's what I think. The caller sounds like a bad guy working for a bad organization. Something must have happened not too long ago that made them think I came out of hiding after a twenty-year disappearing act, so they started making random calls to phone numbers that might still be connected to me. Am I on the right track?"

"Yes, proceed."

"Eve was there at the right time for the caller, but unfortunately for her, she didn't play dumb enough. She must have unwittingly given enough information for the caller's organization to track her, most likely by her cell phone or an AUC I.D. badge or chip."

Electra deliberately paused to elicit a response. "Yes, keep going."

"And then something happened in Cairo that put the bad guys on her tail. And they're about to intercept. That's it. How do you like them apples?"

"You have exceeded my expectations. I'll give you a complete backstory later, but please focus on an immanent interdiction. Put your game face on and be prepared to use some of the advanced features built into your hazmat suit. I'll tell you when it's time to act. Expect to be on stage in no more than ten minutes."

"What's taking him so long? He said it'd take no longer than ten minutes to give you the OK to drive on and –" Nari stopped complaining when Alonzo poked her before pointing dead ahead from behind the steering wheel.

"Those are headlights coming right at us. We better stay put until they get here."

No one did anything but stare until another vehicle stopped nose- to-nose. Two wiry military-type silhouettes with weapons already drawn jumped from driver and passenger sides. Alonzo got out and waited.

As they approached, the leader shouted, "Privet! if you speak Russki, or hello if you prefer English. Let me guess, you are Alonzo Cortez? Who and how many in vehicle?"

"My three sisters and two friends we're driving back."

"Tell us, where you coming from and where you going and what else in vehicle?"

"Uh… uh…" Alonzo stammered to a halt.

The leader was about to talk again but his partner pointed to a silhouette coming towards them from over the ridge. He waited until he person joined them before talking." "Who are you?"

"I am Rani. Why have you stopped us?"

"Your tongue-tied friend Alonzo couldn't tell us, but perhaps you might speak for him."

"He doesn't know, but I do. And I know what you want. You and your comrade, come with me to my vehicle and I will show you. Alonzo, stay here."

"Why are you wearing hazmat suit?"

"Why are you Russians carrying weapons? Alonzo's party is unarmed. Check out his vehicle. I'm unarmed too, and I'm wearing the suit for protection against the desert climate."

Rani waited silently while the Russians scanned the vehicle. When they had finished, Rani spoke again.

"Drive over the ridge and park behind my vehicle."

"Ho-Kay, but no funny business. My partner walk with you. And you gotta have something good or we take more steps."

Rani and the partner strode towards the ridge while the leader gave orders to Alonzo.

"Go sit in vehicle and stay put. You can't hide from us." A minute later he drove over the ridge.

Rani and his escort stood illuminated in the glare of headlights, waiting for the other Russian to stop. When he got out, his comrade went to him and clapped him on shoulder.

"Rani got just kind of vehicle we expect. He must got other stuff too. We can aagghh! –"

His subsequent screams cut through the night, followed a second later by those of his partner. Lightning bolts shooting from the index fingers of Rani's outstretched arms collapsed them onto the sand. Even if they could hear, Rani's words were out of reach. They could be heard only by his inner ear. Rani had ample time to observe his victims writhing.

The built-in mini laser bazooka makes me look like some weird combination of E.T. and Marty McFly – the main guy in that great Back to the Future movie. I bet the Popper's advanced hazmat suit is still beyond state-of-the-art. I point a finger and zap; it's even better than a traser.

They're not getting up anytime soon, but I'll take their weapons and I.D.s, tie them up, and lock them in their vehicle before telling Alonzo he can drive away.

Eve heard the screams while standing next to Alonzo. They stood dumbfounded until she stammered, "One person can't make that much noise. Who do you think's winning?"

"Don't know, but it's quiet now, so the fight must be over. Someone'll come back and tell us."

"Why don't we just drive away? Can't you read the GPS map?" "Sure, but use your brain. They can track us and they've got more horsepower and weapons. Be quiet and wait."

What felt like too many minutes ticked by before a lone figure came back. It was Rani, who spoke while approaching.

"Our new friends liked what they saw and want to come with me. Alonzo can get everyone back without my help. You drive one way, and I'll drive the other."

"But we heard screams. What happened?"

"I already told you they liked what they saw. Let's not stand here wasting drive-time. Drive safe. Call Indira if you run into trouble."

Rani marched back the way he came.

Alonzo poked Eve before saying, "He's right. We'll talk in the car. Come on."

Rani said the same but added more.

I'll hitch the vehicles together and then start driving another group of visitors to the fortress. And I can hardly wait to tell Indira what I think we should do. Only her opinion and mine matter, but I think I can convince the Russkis to play along. After all, it's my game and rules… correction, Indira takes ownership too. After all, we're becoming quite a team, and we're just getting started. I'm ready for more fun and games.

Chapter 19
Thursday, August 04, 2157

<u>"The Inquisition Games – Part I"</u>

"Just because you and Alonzo heard screaming doesn't mean Mister Rani killed anyone. And Nila agrees with me. Your ears aren't hard evidence."

Eve continued defending her argument against those in the back seat as Alonzo kept heading west at a pace that had put them as many miles away from Eve's fanciful crime scene as an hour of his driving would allow.

She said, "According to crime-stopper books and movies, circumstantial evidence is on my side. Suppose a twelve-person jury sees two people walk away and a third drive away to meet them close by; then the jury hears murderous fighting and only one person walks back. And suppose that person is lying about why he's the only one who came back. The jury will find the guy guilty of beating someone up. Rani's lying about the Russians wanting to go with him. Case closed. Let Alonzo be the judge."

"Nari's right about the Russians. They didn't seem like they were gonna change their minds at the drop of a couple of slick words. But no matter what happened, it won't affect us because we'll never see any of them again."

Eve switched subjects.

"OK, if you say so. But where are you heading?"

Alonzo said, "Either to Cairo or a dig location. Maybe by the time the sun comes up, we'll know which is better. What do you think?"

"Why not let Nari or Nila decide? I'm not an official digger."

"Nila said, "Let's head for Alonzo's dig site. I'll bring up its location on my GPS map. But when we get there, what do we do about the fellows?"

The team deferred to Eve.

"Let me think about it. When I come up with a good story, you can listen to it and make revisions."

The group fell silent and all but two fell asleep. Nari made random comments to Alonzo to keep him awake. Ninety minutes later, both saw headlights approaching directly ahead, but she shouted first.

"Hey everybody, wake up. I think a search party is about to find us. This can't be a lucky coincidence."

Nila was the first to offer an explanation.

"I bet an AUC techie assistant is homing in on a cell phone or I.D. badge. Hooray for hi-tech…"

Not one, but two desert rescue vehicles intercepted them fifteen minutes later. All drivers got out, leaving headlights on that illuminated an American University of Cairo logo. Although his three sisters got out too, Alonzo did the talking for his side, neither of which recognized anyone on the other. Alonzo spoke first.

I'm Alonzo Cortez, and these are my sisters, Eve Cortez and Nari and Nila Bose. We're with the AUC summer intern excavation programs."

The older driver said, "You're the four we've been looking for. You can thank our tech people for piecing together which app and I.D. finally located you. You must have a fabulous story to tell, but that can wait until we get you back to AUC. Are you thirsty or hungry?" "No, we're good. I'll follow in my vehicle."

"No, I've got a better idea. All of you must be exhausted, so I'll get one of my men to drive your vehicle. You ride with me and rest. Your sisters can do the same in your vehicle. We'll have plenty of time to talk later. The Intern Program Oversight Committee will want to know all the details. Soon you'll be celebrities."

As Alonzo and the driver walked away, Eve and her sisters headed back to their van. Nari's happy words came along too.

"We are so lucky. When the rescue squad reports how bad our situation was, the Committee will take their word and go easy on any questions. I bet –."

Grabbing Nari's arm, Electra forced everyone to stop before scolding her.

"It's not going to be that easy. We'll have to explain why I'm here and what happened to all the equipment we borrowed and who are the fellows that came back with us. I can come up with a good story, but all four of us have to say the same when answering questions. We can't practice on the drive back because Alonzo's not with us and we can't let his replacement hear us. We'll have to do it as soon as we're together and no one can hear us. We better not say anything to our driver. Let's fake being asleep and –" Nila cut in.

"He's coming. Wake me when we get to where we're going." Eve used the silent drive to organize her thoughts.

Darkness is our friend. The driver didn't spot the two fellows, and what he doesn't see won't hurt us. And he won't bother us with questions. I can rest and rehearse all the way home. The longer the better.

The ride was much shorter than hoped for, not in miles but in minutes. The whir of an approaching helicopter awakened Eve, and she explained to herself the approaching predicament.

Oh my god! They're rushing us back directly to AUC. If the four of us don't get some private time together, we're in big trouble. We can't do anything but play along until we're back. Maybe I can think up a delaying tactic… maybe the whole sorry episode will just disappear.

The fate of Electra's extraction team slipped further from her mind with each passing mile, in part because she and Indira had a more immediate team's fate to consider: that of the two Russians.

Indira's voice exuded confidence.

"I am no longer concerned about your cognitive persona. The way you dispatched the first pair of unwanted visitors proves that your cognitive neural circuits are operating at full power. And you've made a fine start handling the Russian pair. What are your intentions for eliminating them as a threat?"

"As soon as we get back, I'll hold an inquisition, using the Popper's brain controller to extract the truth. I'm certain they're linked to the call looking for me that Eve picked up. They tracked Eve to get to us. So, if what they spill out matches what I think, that'll confirm I'm right."

"I agree with your reasoning. What else would you like to confirm?" "They're connected with an arms dealer, probably Russian, that's still looking for the Popper's subterranean fortress. Even after twenty years, its weapons and vehicles must be better than what's available anywhere."

"I agree with that too. And how do you plan to eliminate your cooperative truth-tellers?"

"Just like I did for the pair Alonzo's driving back. As soon as I've got all the info we need, I'll erase their memories and give them

I.Q.s of friendly cucumbers. They'll remember nothing about their desert joyride. And then, when the time's right, I'll load'em in their vehicle and abandon it close to Cairo. Whoever finds them will have a mystery to contend with. And there's no rush to dump them. They can be our guests at the fortress. There's plenty of food, and I'll be a pleasant hostess."

"I'm sure you will. But I think you'll want to dump them fairly soon. I've promised to give you a complete backstory, and once you hear it, you'll want to plan a trip. But we'll save all that for another day. Would you like me to continue talking, or would you prefer listening to music?"

"How about some stirring music that fits our partnership. I can think of two symphonic French pieces that fit what we're up to. Why don't you make a guess?"

"Very well, I shall play what I think they are, and when they're finished, you can give me a grade."

By the time Electra and Indira had everything stowed in the fortress, Indira had earned an A-plus. And three hours later, Electra earned an identical grade for an inquisition whose results met expectations.

Chapter 20
Thursday, August 04, 2157

"The Inquisition Games – Part II"

AUC's communications department, like those of most contemporary universities, dredged all corners of campus for noteworthy stories to post online or turn into videos that would attract prospective students. When one of its plucky student associates came across a summer program's desert search for four missing interns, she locked onto it, and this morning she would reap the benefits of her efforts. She would be the first to welcome them when they exit the chopper and explain what awaits the campus celebrities. Her videocam operator would capture it all. Having done her homework, she knew her subjects and script.

She was standing close to the van that would take them from the helipad to campus as a program official guided the four to her.

"And here we have siblings Alonzo and Eve Cortez along with their twin sisters, Nari and Nila Bose, having just survived an ordeal in the desert. It looks like Eve damaged her shoulder. I'm sure all of you have a thrilling tale to tell, but you must be exhausted. So, to make your return to the comforts of civilization and a requisite debriefing even easier, each of you will be escorted to a two-person EMT and counselor team for a preliminary evaluation. They'll check your health and record each of your stories. And tomorrow, an intern program panel will hold a proper welcome-back forum for you intern program heroes.

"But before you're whisked away, does your group leader have a brief statement for us? That must be Alonzo. Please talk into the mike."

Eve cringed invisibly.

Oh my god, I didn't see this coming. Maybe Alonzo can say something we can hide behind.

"Uh, thanks for your kind words, but we're no heroes, and I apologize for all the trouble we've caused. We're all too tired to say much that makes sense right now. I hope we'll be better tomorrow. And I'd like to thank my sisters. They have the brains that got us out."

"Spoken like a big brother. Well, would any of your sisters like to add to those modest words? Eve Cortez, how are you feeling?"

Eve smiled bravely but kept her true feelings to herself.

Like I want to crawl under a rock, but my shoulder hurts too much.

Then she spoke hesitantly into the mike.

"We, uh, we're lucky no one got injured badly. It's, ah, it's tough out there when you have to face mother nature on her own terms. I'm still reeling and can't recall too much."

"Spoken like a stoic. Well, you have our best wishes, and we look forward to hearing more when you've rested up. And once again let me say welcome back!"

Four hours later, the siblings were gathered once again in Nari and Nila's room, ready to sift through the debris of what was turning into a catastrophe. Nari summarized as best she could what all four had been jabbering about.

"I don't think I could have come up with a better cover statement than Alonzo did, and it's nice to know the EMTs say we're not sick physically, but we already knew that. Eve's words should get us even more sympathy. How are you feeling now?"

"Sick and embarrassed – physically, mentally and emotionally. I wish I could crawl away and hide. There are so many holes in our combined stories that a couple of camel caravans could drive through."

Eve's words brought out different expressions on her siblings, ranging from befuddled to quarrelsome. Nari didn't hold back.

"Don't go blaming us just because you think your lies are better than ours. And when it comes to –" Nila's poke stopped Nari's attack so she could get a word in.

"Look at it this way, no one's lying, we're simply interpreting from different points of view what we saw. And this isn't a court of law. So… oh, I don't know what. Maybe Alonzo can help me out."

"I can do that. Let's ask Eve what we should do."

She straightened her shoulders and thought for a moment before talking.

"We better do this, salvage what we can from all our stories and make one that's plausible. Then we better memorize it, and then appoint one of us to speak for all tomorrow. And we already know that Alonzo is our designated speaker. Who volunteers to cook up a better story?"

The gazes of three locked onto one person: Eve.

"OK, let's get something to eat, when we get back we start piecing together a story, and I nominate Nari to be our scribe."

"I'll do it, and then let's let Alonzo and Nila edit. If we're collectively clever enough, we might be able skate through. And let's not say much to the rest of the Mag-Seven until after tomorrow's forum. I hope it doesn't turn into an inquisition…"

The four worked the rest of the afternoon and into the early evening until Nari called a halt.

"We've spun as much of the truth as we can. Eve, what do you think?"

She rested her head on her right hand for a couple of seconds before straightening up.

"Here's the plan we follow tomorrow. Alonzo is our main speaker, and anytime he wants he can toss the question to me so I can spin our story a bit more. I'll do my best, and maybe I can get us more sympathy points because of my shoulder. But answer truthfully, if you're the panel foreman, what's the verdict?"

Nila's pursed lips matched Alonzo's words.

"The odds aren't in our favor. Nila's the math person, let's hear from her."

"Unless Eve is awfully convincing, they'll hang us up to dry in the desert, and I don't want to go there ever again."

Eve ended the day's ordeal.

"I'm beat, let's get a good night's sleep. And remember, no one but us knows what really happened. Maybe they'll cut us some slack if they like us or my act. Tomorrow will tell the tale."

Monet sprang to her feet when Eve dragged into the dorm room.

"Ah, so the rescue party delivered you back, but you reinjured your shoulder and you look worn out. Sit down, please, and tell me what you can."

Monet pulled another chair close to hers. Eve slumped into it before talking.

"I'm too tired, but why don't you come to a debriefing meeting tomorrow."

"I will. An invitation came out this afternoon. Space is limited, so I'll get there early. How is Alonzo?"

"He handled the misadventure better than anyone. You'll see and hear tomorrow."

"You should shower. Let me help you, and then you should sleep…" "Eve slept like she didn't want to wake up. Monet roused her, but Eve didn't know what to make of her puzzled expression.

"I'm OK, I guess I just needed my beauty sleep. How are you?"

"Concerned. I received another Email, but this one disinvites everyone from your welcome-back forum. It's a closed-door session. I hope none of you tested positive for any desert virus."

"We didn't. I better call Nari."

Eve didn't get a chance; Nari called first.

"We have a problem. I already called Alonzo. Meet us in my room, ASAP."

Eve hustled there ten minutes later. While the other three sat, Nari paced as she spoke.

"Get ready for an inquisition. Our stories must not have satisfied them. Too many inconsistencies. Eve, try to relax and do the best with what you've got. We better grab breakfast and go…"

The other Mag-Seven members waved but had the good sense to leave the siblings alone. Eve tried to eat but left half of what she had taken. Alonzo did about the same. Nari led them out; Alonzo, with arms around Nila and Eve, followed.

The session started at 10 a.m. and proceeded better than it might have. The panel's questions, though probing, were diplomatically posed to minimize embarrassment. Eve acted her part and scored a couple of points when she said that under stressful situations, victims often fail to keep the facts straight. But even Alonzo's expression registered impending defeat. Ninety minutes later, including a fifteen-minute private panel discussion, the senior member summarized the session.

"Yes, we sympathize. All of you are young and talented and full of energy and promise, but you are perhaps a tad too inexperienced. You didn't realize that unauthorized joyriding in the desert, just to bring back someone or something you never found, would have serious consequences.

"We give you credit for your resourcefulness, but by hacking into program files, you have broken AUC rules. And you deliberately reassigned interns so one of you not assigned to an excavation project could slip in and lead you into the desert.

"And you don't even know the coordinates of where you were going. The GPS dot you were heading to is no longer on your cell phone, so there's no way we can go there to corroborate your story. And frankly, we don't understand what happened to the equipment you took. Your schools must reimburse us for what never came back.

"One of you says Bedouin raiders took it, another says it was swallowed in quicksand. And the two fellows that came back with you pose an even bigger mystery. How did they find you, and what happened to them? They don't even know their names. We'll have to quarantine them until we're certain they didn't contract some bizarre desert virus. And I am afraid we must quarantine you also, for your own safety as well as everyone else's.

"There's more, but it offers no amelioration so I won't embarrass you further. We'll confer with the AUC dean to resolve your status and will inform you shortly of his decision. In the meantime, you are self-quarantined to your rooms and of course are suspended from further intern program activities.

"We are adjourned. Please wait here for one of our nurses to take you to the clinic where they will explain our self-quarantining procedures."

An hour later, a clinic helper brought Eve to her room and posted a red-lettered 'QUARANTINE' sign on the door before giving final instructions.

"Your roommate has been notified to report to the clinic so we can explain everything. We've arranged a place for her to stay. You should take meals in your room, and if you leave the room, wear a face mask and stay on campus. It's OK to visit your brother and sisters, but I'd avoid talking with anyone else. You could be in quarantine for up to fourteen days, but you've got the campus Intranet as well as the Internet to keep yourself entertained. Someone from the clinic will check you each day, but if you start feeling sick, call us immediately. Any questions?"

Eve managed to smile and said, "I'm sorry we've caused such a commotion, but with your help, I'm sure I'll be out of quarantine fast."

"I hope so; well I'm sure you'll stay healthy and safer in your room than you did when running around in the desert. Take care."

Eve collapsed on her bed and though exhausted, was too agitated to sleep.

I don't feel like surfing the Web or reading. What should I do?...
I got it, I'll call Lemarcus.

She punched in his number, hoping he'd pick up but he didn't
so she left a message for him to call back ASAP. After that, she
closed her eyes and decided not to think about anything.

A cell call jangled her awake. She fumbled for the phone and
when answering on the fifth ring, the cheery voice of Lemarcus
greeted her.

"I'm so happy you're calling me back. Finally, we're back in
touch. You haven't called me for so long I thought maybe you got
swallowed up in the desert. How're you doing?"

"I've been better. I reinjured a dislocated shoulder and am
stuck in quarantine. You don't want to know the rest. All I'll say is
that I'll be so glad to get back to Stanford. How're you?"

"Been good, been making progress on that 'Right-size' funding
project you cooked up. It's become a hot topic. I've got a bunch
of people who want to be part of it. They just love that tagline you
invented. We'll have lots of fun when you get back. When do you
think that'll be?"

"Possibly before Labor Day. And don't worry, I'm not
contagious. The quarantining is just a precaution."

"That's good, but you sound tired. I'll say bye so you can get
some rest. Take care of yourself."

The call worked wonders, raising Eve's mood and energy level.
She was about to surf the Web when another call came in, this one
from Nari, who didn't sound happy.

"Let's all of us have dinner together. Alonzo already knows, so
have yours delivered to my room. Bye."

Arriving after Alonzo but before the meals, Eve sat in her
appointed chair and listened to the discussion already in progress.

"If it weren't for being stuck in quarantine, we might actually
be OK. A slap on the wrist won't hurt, and it's still possible that
Alonzo and Nila can bail out early. Maybe he should check with

his coach and Nila can find out about that Lincoln Lab position. Tell'em you're having an eventful summer but might be able to come back early." Alonzo looked doubtful but Nila didn't; she spoke next.

"That's a great idea. As soon as we get out of quarantine, we can leave if we want to, no matter what the Dean says. I don't have symptoms of anything other than a bad feeling about deserts. All of us look pretty good except for Eve. How are you?"

"I'm feeling better now than any other time during this lousy week. I just got a call from Lemarcus, who says Fall term is looking better and better."

A knock on the door announcing dinner interrupted. Eve picked up after Alonzo brought the meals into the room.

"Maybe the worst is over; maybe we can actually salvage some of this summer misadventure. If so, we'll have to treat the entire Mag- Seven group to a farewell celebration. What do you think?"

Nari gave a one-word answer that matched all the hopeful expressions.

"Perhaps. Now let's eat and then let's make sure Eve goes back and rests. We don't want anyone getting sick."

Alonzo peered at his meal before saying, "And I'll even give her my desert tonight. She needs to resupply her energy, and I know she likes brownies."

All siblings pitched in. Eve took two brownies with her when she plodded back to her room.

I'm not gonna worry about what I can't control. I'll simply hope for the best and come up with a contingency plan if it's needed. Maybe Miss Indira will be able to help…

Chapter 21
Saturday, August 06, 2157

"Indira's Gift"

"Your cognitive and physical persona recoveries from any regressive effects caused by twenty years in the suspension pod prove that your extraordinary brain's neural circuits are reconnecting and generating more connections at a pace far beyond what mere mortals could accomplish.

"It also confirms what neuroscientists claim regarding extended periods in solitary confinement – cognitive processes controlled by the cerebral cortex and physical processes controlled by the cerebellum are impacted less than the limbic-system-controlled emotional processes and the feelings they generate. I have been observing your study habits and physical conditioning routines. You have superior powers of concentration and abilities to push to your asymptotic limits." Indira paused for Electra to react.

"Thank you for the compliments, but much of the credit goes to my grandfather, Doc Kittner, who taught and trained me while I was still a child. He said my brain is like a dynamo that's able to generate loads of power, but I must learn how to control it by shifting it from one neural state to another so the power goes where it should."

"He taught you well. Would you agree that your cognitive ability is fully restored?"

"I think so. I can remember what I once knew and synthesize it with new information as well or better than twenty years ago."

"What about your physical conditioning and training?"

"I'm glad the Popper's fortress is so complete. Its fitness center has everything I need to get back to where I was. But I'm not there yet.

I'm not ready to engage one-on-one like I sometimes did, using martial arts moves, or those I learned from the marines stationed at the Lebanese Embassy before it blew up."

Indira cautioned, "It is usually better to engage in mental rather than physical battles. But you already know that. And I think you are ready for me to give you enough backstory explaining what has transpired from twenty years ago until today. It will help you decide what path you wish to take and how we shall combine forces going forward. So please settle down, sit still, and let me explain."

"I'm ready, but let me mention a topic that you have touched on only tangentially, my emotional persona recovery. I know that my empathy is just beginning to wake up because for the last twenty years I've had no interpersonal interactions and those neural connections have gone missing. And unlike my cognitive and physical connections, which the Popper's suspension pod stimulated periodically, it couldn't do the same for the emotional persona because for the most part it's terra incognita. Has neuroscience made any headway while I've been gone?"

"That is not a concern of mine. I shall leave that for you to investigate at a later date, but I must ask you about your erstwhile manic-depressive and obsessive-compulsive predispositions. They, along with empathy are controlled by your emotional persona. Any changes you detect might indicate the state of that persona.

"I did catch myself a couple of times getting too wound up, but I was able to shift to a better mental state. And so far, nothing's happened that would make me depressed. Maybe my manic-depression will return when my empathy is all the way back. And if it does, I might be able to shift out of it better than I did twenty years ago. But don't forget, my so-called negative predispositions can be very helpful when I keep them inbounds. Just like my emphasis on reason rather than faith."

"It is good that you are cognitively aware of all this, because you might find some of your twenty-year hiatus backstory disturbing, but it is time for me to tell it. I shall start at the beginning and tell everything that I think you can handle and need at this moment. Please wait until I'm finished to comment."

"I promise. I hate it when someone interrupts me mid-sentence, but I've learned how to control my anger. And I've taught myself to let people finish talking before I jump in and to focus on what they're saying before I think about my reply. So, I'll obey your commands."

"And I'll start at the very beginning, when we put you in the suspension pod just before the fortress went dark. No one but us knows its location, and the cause of the embassy attack and President McTear's unfortunate death were and still are a mystery.

"Not long after, your close circle of friends – namely Su-Lin Song Chou, Robin Setdarova, Hud Haller, Tim Godfrey, Kwame Chyral, Matt and Zoe Fortier, and Carter and Buffy Quavah – formed what they called a "Keepers Group" to keep your memory alive. They honored it by meeting once a year and hoping that you might return. Robin kept the porchlight on every night for twenty years.

"I, on the other hand, didn't care about hope. I devised a long-term rescue plan. None of your friends knew enough to figure one out, but of course I could and did. Su-Lin unwittingly became my partner, and I told her just enough so she could play her part.

"You should remember the Deus Lab. Well, after your disappearance, I told her to tell Hudson Haller to mothball the one you and I built on the Pequot Reservation, and get it rebuilt in Austin, close to where Godfrey and Chyral had their computer lab.

Once that was accomplished, I instructed her how to clone human embryos. I never told her my ulterior intention, which was to build a new generation of so-called keepers who would be more capable than mere mortals and, when old enough, I could train to be your extraction team. Su-Lin's keeper group did not have the requisite skills to extract you.

"Su-Lin did her best, but that wasn't good enough. She never mastered my procedures for customizing DNA to maximize selected traits. I made her stop after cloning only two sets of twins. I had Su- Lin become their legal guardians and raise them. She gave them the best family environment she could, and she sent them to the best schools.

"And according to test scores, the four clones have the traits we designed for: intelligence, physical appearance and strength, and personality. Unfortunately, they are not as exceptional as we had hoped, but they're good enough.

"And the plan is for me to assume control of them once they are old enough. Then I would challenge them, call it a test if you like, to prove they are worthy. And of course, they would know nothing about my plan.

"Time was not an obstacle because the fortress is designed for multi-decade self-maintenance. I would test the new generation soon after all members graduated from college, but unforeseen events forced a contingency plan. Su-Lin has become physically and cognitively compromised, and your current keepers perished in helicopter crashes.

"I took over for Su-Lin and now control the next generation of keepers. They think I am a human being communicating only via the Internet. To their credit, they did devise your extraction mission. I invented Rani Ramani to be their desert rendezvous contact. And the plan worked. You are back and ready to partner with me. And that, as your Alisha alter-ego liked to say, is a wrap. Please tell me your initial reactions when you are ready. You might wish to take a break because what you have just heard must be a significant emotional jolt."

Electra sat back and rubbed the bridge of her nose for only a moment before replying.

"If twenty years ago you told me that all my family and friends had just been killed, I'd be overwhelmed by grief, but the twenty-year suspension has either dulled my emotional persona or it has morphed to a new awareness. I don't know which, but I don't feel much, other than a tinge of sadness that I'll never see them again. "And I don't have much empathy for the new generation, even though I'm happy they implemented your plan."

"Good. That's the result of your cognitive persona taking control, of which I certainly approve. Now we need to consider what we should do moving forward. I have considered possibilities, but you are the master of bullet-point to-do lists. I recommend you prepare one and we'll reconvene when you are ready."

"Good idea, but let me tell you what my starting point will be, and that's the gift you've given me. I have the rare opportunity to recreate myself. The old Electra is officially dead, but I can come back to life as Rani Ramani. A lot of people say they'd like to do a makeover, and plan on doing so when they retire, but when they get there, they don't know what or how. I do, just wait till you see my to-do list."

"Let me make a minor correction. Your official name is Irani Ramani, a female. Your extraction team assumed Rani was a male, but that is of no concern. I think you are ready to plan a brave new world that you and I will inhabit. Please contact me when you have built your list."

Indira's GUI vanished, leaving Electra in splendid isolation.

What did Voltaire's Doctor Pangloss say?... I remember... This is the best of all possible worlds. And it is. Indira will be in charge of our Dream Team because that's one of her roles. And I'll be her Boots on the Ground. And just like me, we'll make the last line of Casablanca come back to life, just wait and see.

Chapter 22
Wednesday, August 10, 2157

<u>"The Worst Gets Worse"</u>

"This is the worst news possible. I don't care if test results say a virus got me, it has to be a false positive. I'm not sick and they should let me out of quarantine so I'm back in action like the rest of you. But no, they transfer me to the clinic just because my temperature's a bit high and I said I had a tiny headache. That's the last time I'll tell the nurse how I feel."

Nari ignored Eve's complaint and spoke before Alonzo or Nila.

"I told you to keep taking your meds. Now you're stuck in the clinic until you test negative. I'd trade places if I could, but aren't you glad Alonzo and Nila got good news?"

"Sure, I'm happy the Coach will save a place on the roster whether or not he gets to camp on time, and the same for Nila and her Lincoln Lab assignment. I guess they'll head back as soon as the Dean says we're in the clear. When do you think that might be?" Nila's smile brightened.

"I hope soon, and Nari got another Email right after the good news about being out of quarantine. She's supposed to see him today. And you know the saying that bad news comes in threes. Well, it's supposed to apply for good news too. I bet we hear something else good very soon."

"Maybe I can generate it. If I complain enough, they'll have to test me again, and this time they'll get the right results. Well whatever, please tell the Mag-Seven I'm symptom-free and safe for them to have breakfast with me if the nurses let me out. And let me know what the Dean says."

All the other Mag-Seven members had gathered by the time the negative-testing siblings joined them, but none looked happy. Sitting next to Monet, Alonzo was the first to speak.

"Hey, what's wrong? We just came from clinic's quarantine room; Eve says she feels good." Sanjay glanced around the table, and after seeing only silent faces explained.

"A rumor's spreading that all AUC interns need to be tested. More are showing symptoms of a viral infection. And local media is looking to link AUC's and Cairo's burgeoning outbreaks. Social distancing might be ordered, and if infection rates get too high too fast, programs and campus plus Cairo might be shut down."

Known for her direct questioning tactics, it was no surprise that Nari fired away.

"Which virus?"

"They don't know. It could be an old one that has reactivated or it might be a new zoonotic type that's recently spread from African mammals to humans. Symptoms from so many overlap. You think there's a connection between AUC and Cairo cases? If so, tracing back to the source will be harder."

No one answered, so Nari moved on.

"Well, I'm going to see the Dean this morning. If I get good news, Alonzo and Nila and I can plug back into our intern program. I'll let you know as soon as I can."

The three siblings stayed at the table after the others left. Alonzo spoke first.

"It's been almost a week since the inquisition. Why so long?"

"I'm tired of talking. Nila, go ahead and tell him our latest thinking." "AUC might be checking our current college academic records. They're probably looking for reasons to keep us in the program. Nari should hear the good news this morning. And I'm tired of sitting here, let's go do something. While Nari's talking with the Dean, you can teach me more about tennis, or vice versa for chess. Or you can listen to me play the piano. What's your pick?"

"I'll go along with whatever you decide. I hope Nari has as much fun…"

"The Dean will see you now. Please come with me."

Nari followed the administrative assistant into a nondescript office. The Dean rose to greet her but said nothing until she was seated on the opposite side of his cluttered desk.

"Your sister's positive testing has raised more questions. We asked her why she is the only one who tested positive, and she told us you are taking special drugs. When we asked if she knows what they are, she said she didn't. Would you please explain?"

"It's a vitamin." The Dean nodded, expecting Nari to say more, but when she didn't, he licked his bottom lip before saying more.

"Can you be more specific? What kind of vitamin and what is the source?"

"Uh, I don't know. Our grandmother buys them somewhere." "How old is she?"

"In her nineties." No one spoke again until the Dean ended the standoff.

"So, you're taking drugs supplied by your aged grandmother. If this were a drug enforcement investigation, that tidbit would be scrutinized closely. All of you, except for your quarantined sister, would be suspected of using and possibly distributing illegal drugs. But this isn't and we don't want to embarrass you or damage your academic records any further than they already are. But we will ask all of you to withdraw immediately and return to your respective schools as soon as you can arrange flights."

Though stunned, Nari withstood the blow. She regrouped her thoughts and then replied.

"What about Eve?"

"She can stay and will suffer no damage to her academic record. And she'll be out of quarantine as soon as she is symptom-free and tests negative. Please carry this news to your siblings. You are dismissed."

Nari stood when the Dean did and shook the hand he extended.

"Thank you for your honesty. If we were to trade places, I probably would have made the same decision. I'll let everyone know."

Nari didn't wait to be escorted out.

She called Alonzo as she left the building, telling him nothing other than to meet her and Nila in their room. They were already sitting when she walked in. Nari sat and started talking after exhaling one deep breath.

"All of us but Eve are expelled from the program. When someone asked her why she's the only one that tested positive, she said it's because she's not taking her meds and we are. The Dean thinks we're into illegal drugs, and this piece of news, when added to what came out at the inquisition, seals our fate. We're supposed to leave as soon as we can arrange flights."

Alonzo's expression didn't change; he sat stoically, but Nila leaned forward, eager to speak.

"This isn't all bad. We exit quickly, telling the Mag-Seven that our ordeal in the desert tired us out and we're heading back to school to recover and get a head start for the fall term. And that's precisely what Alonzo and I can do. And you can say something similar."

Alonzo shook his head.

"I'll tell the Dean I can't leave while Eve's still in quarantine. She'll need me if she actually gets sick. He'll understand. But both of you should go back to Boston ASAP and plug in to what you've got lined up for September. And since Eve's quarantined, Nari should be our Indira contact. Tell her the story and find out if she'll help square your flight schedules."

Nari glanced at Nila who nodded yes and then replied.

"You're right on all fronts. Maybe we can salvage the summer. I'll let you know what success I have getting our flights changed, and then we can tell one consistent story to our Mag-Seven friends. Why don't you to go somewhere so I can get Indira's number from Eve and then make the call?"

Nila warned her before leaving.

"Remember to follow Eve's advice; practice before calling Indira, she can be a challenge. Good luck for all of us."

Eve didn't sound as good as she did this morning. Nari's news regarding the Dean's meeting upset her.

"I was wrong earlier when I said we had the worst possible news. But now, the worst is getting worse. I'd help you by calling Miss Indira, but I think you're in better shape to handle it alone. Here's the number. Please let me know how it goes."

Nari made the call after running out of patience practicing. Indira's GUI opened promptly and waited for Nari to speak.

"He-Hello, Miss Indira. This is Nari Bose calling. Eve is quarantined and she thought I should call to report the latest status. May I?"

"The status of what? You've completed what you were supposed to."

"Yes, but there's been a bit of a complication. All of us but Eve have been expelled and have to leave early. You see –"

Indira interrupted. Her voice, though remaining calm, sounded indifferent.

"There is nothing I need to see. You are responsible for rescheduling your flights. And as I promised, I will cover your expenses because you successfully completed your mission. So, carry on."

"I'm glad you're saying that. We never really understood what the mission was."

"You understood enough to do what was needed. So, return to campus and prepare for your next term. And soon, an associate of mine might be Eve's contact. Please tell her that, and give her my best wishes for a quick exit from quarantine.

Nari sighed before replying. "I will, thanks."

Indira detected sadness in the sigh and decided to say more before signing off.

"You and your siblings must lose your sadness. In fact, that is a poem titled the same and written long ago by someone I knew. Hold on while I retrieve it so I can recite it for you."

Nari heard the verses seconds later:

Sometimes I feel so sad for us, Great expectations lead up to a fall.

Our history casts a similar pall, Ashes to ashes dust to dust. But then I simply must recall, Think of life as comedy.

Humor-filled not elegy,

We bounce no matter how we fall.

So lose the sadness make it gone, Life is motion life is flow.

No matter that we come and go, The phoenix rises from ashes anon.

Indira didn't wait for Nari to say anything.

"Discuss these verses with your siblings. All of you are smart enough to interpret them. Then do what it says. All of you have my sympathy."

Indira's abrupt signoff kept Nari's words to herself.

She must live online most of the time. It's incredible how fast she finds stuff. I would have preferred some help instead of verses and sympathy, but I'll settle for them instead of criticism like she used to heap on poor Eve. And talking to Indira wasn't as bad as it could have been. Maybe the worst is over. What's that saying about hope? I got it, Hope for the best but plan for the worst. Well, I think the worst has come and gone. All that's left is to get ready and go back to campus, and I don't have to hope I can do it. I know I can.

Chapter 23
Saturday, August 13, 2157

<u>"The Grand Recalibration"</u>

Electra was having the time of her life. Actually, she was reliving it for the third time, and every morning she remembered to thank Indira for the gift.

The helicopter crash that broke my neck and killed Christi and Mo forty years ago made me recreate myself for the first time. And look what it brought me. My love affair with Carter, a political career, and more empathy.

And I did it again three years later when I poisoned myself. That brought me my alter ego Alisha, who according to Myers-Briggs personality typing scored ENFP, the complete opposite of me… I'm ISTJ. It also brought me separate sports and Hollywood careers, and two precious but short-lived daughters – Ariadne and Qama. And it gave me a depth of maturity and empathy that propelled my personal and professional lives full speed ahead and into my twenty- year suspension, courtesy of the Popper's super soldiers.

And now I can do it for the third time, but after such a long hiatus I must do so on a grander scale. I'll call it the Grand Recalibration. And I know how to start. I'll build a Recalibration To-Do List. And I've learned the best way to do so.

Twenty years ago, I would have worked obsessive-compulsively to grind it out, but it's better to develop it gradually. I'll work on it intermittently and take breaks while doing what Indira has told me to do: learn all about the Poppers fortress and bring my personas back to full strength.

But this time, I have a partner to critique my work – Indira. I must coordinate my goals and her intentions. I already told her I'll be ready for her help as soon as I've drafted my recalibration starting points and enough details to point me in the right direction.

Electra followed her own advice, each day interspersing recalibration list development among two sets of more pressing tasks. The first centered on mastering the subterranean fortress and its contents. Everything she learned added to her respect for Maksim. Every day she practiced operating its infrastructure and equipment.

The Popper and his technicians were geniuses. The computer-controlled equipment needs only a minimal crew to operate and maintain the fortress and all its infrastructures. I can now operate it all along with the communications gear.

I don't know yet what Indira and I want to do, but the fortress will fit in somewhere. I'll have to ask her about retrofitting it for our purposes. We'll eventually need to bring in additional items and supplies, but there's no rush.

She also practiced using the weapons and vehicles, the results of which added to the Popper's stature.

After all these years, the weapons and exoskeleton suits still work, as do the land vehicles. I can handle all of them. And the fuel and ammo depots have plenty in them. I'll have to restock them eventually, but there's enough to last quite a while. I'll compare my estimate with Indira's.

Drones are the only aircraft I can currently operate. I'll have to ask Indira for piloting lessons, but I can get around just fine using the land vehicles.

Indira should know, but my guess is that even today, all I see is beyond state-of-the-art. No wonder bad people are still searching for this military treasure trove.

The second set of tasks centered on herself. The one for improving her physical persona gave her the biggest endorphin jolt.

I've always been borderline addicted to physical conditioning and sports. The Popper's fitness center has everything I need. I can watch monitors when I'm on an elliptical cross-trainer, lifting free weights, or using the weight machines. And the virtual reality fight- training is even better than having a training partner. I absorb no collateral damage.

And Indira might be right. Even when I round into fighting trim, I might want to use my mind instead of muscle. Hey, the calendar says I'm sixty, which is near the upper end of middle age. I'll have to check if I still heal fast, but not by getting damaged. I'll ask Indira for advice.

The second task, confirming her cognitive ability had come back, needed little checking.

Every day, when I surf to research what happened while I was gone or what passes for today's state-of-the-art, I connect it immediately to what I already know. My lightning brain has bounced back better than ever.

Too bad there's little I can do for task number three. I can't test my emotions and its supporting empathy until I reconnect with people. Indira knows this too. I'll make note of progress when I begin to reconnect. I'm not sure when that'll be. Maybe I shouldn't have dummied down my Russian guests so soon. I could have practiced on them. Well, I'll keep watching online videos and lectures, but I won't participate, I'll remain invisible.

Electra had her recalibration list ready for reviewing with Indira; she had already taken one item to the next level and decided to give it a final reading. This time, she talked out loud, half-hoping Indira might be listening.

"No matter what I do going forward, I must have one or more careers to keep me interested and engaged. And that means I need to create a business and its supporting Website. Indira can help me build it, and I've already written its home page."

IAM Partners, LLC Irani Authentic Management "for the Self…"
I AM AAM Authentic Asset Management IAM ACS
Authentic Consulting Services
Welcome to IAM Partners, LLC

We are "Irani Authentic Management" LLC, offering clients the optimal combination of Western Rationality and Eastern Spirituality.

We offer two Customized Client Services:

- Authentic Asset Management (Monetary Physical People Patentable)
- Authentic Consulting (Economic Political Social) Paramount Principles:
- Authenticity: The ability to "Love the Other as the Self" and engage in Relationships that are: Honest Trusting Genuine and lead to Your goals
- Karma: The Sum of Your Actions and Consequences that embody YOU
- Mindfulness: The State of Being Here Now: **Now-Here** not **No-where**

Mindfulness Achieved through IAM's Client-Tailored Meditation

- Specify SMART Goals (Specific, Measurable, Attainable, Relevant, and Time-Based)
- Anchor Goals to Values supported by QNS-EDEP-K/P/P Synthetic Philosophy
- Focus the Power of Concentration to Harness Emotions that expand Reality

- Use your Power to Reinvent the Self Our Services utilize:
- "State-of-the-Art" AI-Enhanced Software
- "Big Data" ⊠ Information ⊠Wisdom Transformations for Classical Probability Modeling
- Sparse Data + Subjective Estimates ⊠ Prior Probability and Likelihood Functions for Bayesian Probability Modeling
- Latest Neuro-Sci supported Psychological Applications for enhanced Team Performance

Please view separate page for each Service Project Examples and Client References

"I've given my post post-modern philosophy a big name: Quantum+NeuroSci-Extended Deconstructed Emergent Post Kantian/Pragma/Phenomenological Synthesis. That's too much of a mouthful, so I'll abbreviate it QNS-Edep-K/P/P Synthesis. If anyone asks, I have a great story to support it.

"I like my catchy acronym for the company name – IAM – and my positioning tagline – 'for the Self'. It connects to both Eastern Spirituality and Authenticity. I can tell prospective clients a great story about all this too.

"And I've set up two consulting services. AAM Asset Management is broad enough to include just about any concrete or abstract thing, and ACS should cover any consulting service I'd want to tackle. "Now that I've got my home page copy finalized, Indira can say hi anytime she likes. I'm sure she'd remind me to take a break to avoid becoming obsessive-compulsive, so that's what I'll do next."

A monitor window flashed opened. It was Indira.

"You are correct. Please take a break. But I must say your home page copy is brilliant. I will offer you suggestions when you are ready to discuss your new company, and I will have Jason build your Website. He has been studying Social Media and Virtual

Companies among other people-oriented topics. He will have it up and running when you are ready to reengage."

"That should be soon. I think you will approve my Recalibration List. You play a major role in goal setting, and I need to make sure mine are copacetic with yours."

"And vice versa. Please do not tell me anything else. You have earned a break. Congratulations on exceeding my expectations." Indira's GUI vanished, but her praise lingered. Electra summarized her feelings but kept them to herself.

Thank you, Mother. You are all I need for the moment, and maybe for a long, long time.

An unexpected emotion lurking somewhere in Electra's awakening empathy unexpectedly broke through, bringing music to her internal ears.

Alisha had the artistic ability, but she taught me to appreciate all types of music. I remember her telling me about the great female vocalist, Linda Ronstadt. What beauty, what voice, what emotion she projected. I'm hearing her song that Alisha loved best: Long Long Time.

I don't know how long it'll play in my head, but I think I'll get an endorphin rush from exercising right now. And I'll listen to Linda instead of the Internet.

As she tuned out everything but the recurring song and exercise- generated endorphins, Electra disappeared into her private world.

Chapter 24
Tuesday, August 16, 2157

<u>"The Hit Parade"</u>

Nari had to reread her Email before summoning Nila to her side. "Have you checked your Emails today?"

"I did first thing this morning. Why?

"This came in from my academic advisor while we were having dinner with the Mag-Seven. You better check for something similar." Nila needed to read Nari's only once before a tiny gasp and tongue click telegraphed more than a hint of concern.

"Will do." Nari kept staring at her screen, waiting for Nila to report back. It took five minutes but only one expletive.

"Holy mother… I'm on academic suspension too. You better call Alonzo pronto."

"And we'll get him to come here. This is more important than walking around with Monet. And I won't tell him to check for bad news until he gets here. If you and I just got hit, Stanford's either already added him, or soon will, to the hit parade." Nari punched in his number.

"OK, OK, I'll be there in five minutes. Bye." Monet made a guess from Alonzo's expression who had just called.

"Is Nari upset?"

"That and probably agitated too. I better go see why and try to calm her down. I'll tell you at breakfast what gives."

Alonzo knocked and entered, not bothering to wait for another invitation, but when he saw Nari trying to console a crying Nila, his annoyed look faded and he said nothing, instead sitting in his usual chair. Nila wiped her eyes before she and Nari sat. She bit the nail of her right thumb before talking.

"When did you last check your Stanford Emails?" "Yesterday morning. Why?"

"Nila and I got Emails today telling us we're on academic suspension. It doesn't take a rocket scientist to figure out why. Use Nila's desktop to check if you got one too."

Alonzo said nothing until he had done so.

"No Emails. Maybe my athletic advisor pulled some strings. Being expelled from AUC might not be that big of a deal on the lacrosse playing field."

"Oh come on, lacrosse is peanuts compared to the big revenue sports. Nila, what do you think?"

"I hope I'm wrong, but I think he's SOL too. You think we should call Eve?"

"Why? AUC didn't expel her. Let's not bother her until we know for sure what's gonna happen to Alonzo. He can send a decoy Email to his advisors. If he's suspended – or takes an even bigger hit – they'll tell him. But we better come up with a story for the Mag-Seven that doesn't mention academic suspension." Alonzo stood just after a whimsical smile replaced his blank expression.

"This could be a first for me. I get to tell you what to say, and you can deliver it at breakfast tomorrow. Use the words I already told you. Just tell'em that you two are so worn out that you're heading back to campus ASAP to recover and get a head start for the fall term, and I'm staying until Eve gets out of quarantine. No need to tell about getting expelled and suspended. There you go; I've done my part, so I'll see you at breakfast. Make sure you practice your delivery."

Even though Nari didn't practice, her performance was so convincing that the Mag-Seven split into three groups of two each to talk more after leaving the cafeteria.

Sanjay found a secluded spot outside; he and Nila sat before he spoke.

"I am sorry your karma is taking you away sooner than I thought, but perhaps a sharing of yours and mine will bring us together again. Perhaps in America if I go there to pursue a graduate degree, or maybe in my country if you choose to study or work in Mumbai or other hi-tech Indian cities. We have many, and you might enjoy learning more about your ancestor's native country. And no matter, let us correspond. We can stay as close as you wish via EMails and social media."

Nila's sad smile almost made him ask why, but he decided not to pry and waited for her reply.

"I'd like that. So much has happened to me this summer, I need to let all the events gel, and when they do I'll be able to tell you more. And I hope you'll do the same."

Sanjay's nod before standing gave his answer, so he switched subjects.

"It is time for my class. I would rather stay here but I shall see you at every breakfast and dinner before you depart. And perhaps we can sightsee on our own. Goodbye for now."

Yang, doing most of the talking, accompanied Nari back to her room.

"I enjoy getting know you and Eve. Debating has been pleasure, and Eve make fine referee. But

beneath exteriors, you both similar – feisty in best sort of way, smart, and always full of questions."

Nari paused before opening the door.

"Eve's taller and prettier. Is that the exterior you're talking about?" "I'm referring to your exterior persona, the personality you show to the world."

When Yang glanced away, Nari knew why.

He's being diplomatic. That's more a Japanese than Chinese trait. He doesn't want to embarrass me or himself. I better help him out. "Other people, when they get to know us, sometimes say the same thing. What would you add?"

"Eve's a social person; I think she wants people to like her. You are a bit distant at first. I think you want people to know how talented you are. But underneath, I think you might be as warm and empathetic. Before you depart, would you give me your cell phone and Email info so we may communicate?"

"Would you like Eve's also?"

"Thank you, no. You all I need."

Nari erased the tiny smile that Yang's answer brought out, but she couldn't tell from Yang's expression if she had been quick enough, so she covered her feelings with a standard goodbye.

"We can swap at dinner tonight. See you then…"

Having accompanied Monet to her door, Alonzo waited for her to invite him into her room so they could continue their conversation. She did, and when both were sitting, Alonzo looked like he wanted to talk more.

"How do you like having the room all to yourself?"

"It's cleaner than ever after a maintenance crew disinfected it, but it is not as lively. Eve was a most animated person. Let me change the was to is. I imagine she will be out of clinic isolation soon. What have you heard?"

"Nari's the primary contact, and she says Eve feels good and will be out as soon as the quarantine period is over. I hope it's soon, because Nari and Nila are going back to Boston as soon as they book flights, but I'll stay until I know Eve is OK. And then she and I will immediately head back to Stanford."

"What will you do if she actually gets sick?"

"Be her caregiver until she's released from the clinic and then take her home. I've heard all the stories about hospitals being overloaded when a pandemic hits. Sometimes hospitals in even rich countries can't cope and patients need someone to take charge. Eve will need me, even if there's no Cairo outbreak."

"Have you ever been a caregiver?" "No, have you?"

"Yes, it can become a fulltime job. You might need someone to help you."

"Who did you take care of, and why?"

"Family in my home country, but that is immaterial. If Eve actually becomes sick, I hope her infection is mild enough so you can take care of her by yourself. Please let me know how she is."

"I'll do that at least twice a day, at breakfast and dinner. I think I'll head to Nari's room and get the latest report. I'll let you know at dinner how she's doing…"

Alonzo knocked this time before entering. Nari's voice sounded more upbeat than earlier; when he entered, both sisters looked happier too, so he called out before sitting.

"I guess Sanjay and Yang like your stories. Monet likes mine too. Anything you'd like to add?"

Nari said, "Let's call Eve. Maybe she knows if they'll let her out of quarantine today. And if she's in a chipper mood, we can tell her our bad news. She can usually find some words to make anything better. I'll run the call through the speakers so everyone can hear."

Nari keyed in Eve's number, but after ten rings she hung up.

"That's odd, she usually jumps on calls right away. Maybe I misdialed. I'll try again."

This time, someone picked up after the fifth ring, but it wasn't Eve. It was one of the nurses.

"Hi, this is Nari Bose. I'm Eve's sister. May I talk with her?"

"I'm sorry, but no. She's sleeping and we don't want to wake her." "Eve never sleeps during the day. Is there something wrong?"

"I'm afraid there is, and we don't need any test results. She has a fever, headache, and upset stomach. We've diagnosed that she's contracted a viral infection."

"What kind? Is it serious? Can we see her?"

"We don't know. Symptoms for most are about the same. Our guess is it's the same that's hitting other excavation interns."

"But is it serious?"

"Your sister felt good before going to bed but not when she woke up in the middle of the night. Her condition is not serious yet, but we're watching her as close as we can to track its progression."

"Can we see her?"

"It's too soon. Wait until we know her condition has stabilized. Call back later today. And if her condition worsens, I have your number. Goodbye."

Nila stared at Nari, who stared at Alonzo, who said nothing for the longest time until an obvious question came to mind.

"Who's been following the news? If this viral outbreak hitting Cairo is getting worse, you two better change your flights to leave for Boston ASAP. I'll take care of Eve." Nari looked at Nila before talking. "This mess is gonna get worse before it gets better. Nila, you check online for news about local outbreaks, and I'll get our flights changed. Alonzo, please don't be mad at us. We're not running out on you."

"I know that. You and Nila have taken enough hits. Time both of you leave before more bad news strikes. So far, I haven't been hit as hard. And I'll call Eve after you two are on the way back to Boston. Now I better get out of your way. Call me when you've got your tickets locked in. And let me know if Cairo might have to prep for social distancing or even worse, some type of lockdown."

Nila asked, "We'll get together before we go, won't we?" "Sure, we can trade final instructions. Now get busy."

Chapter 25
Wednesday, August 17, 2157

<u>"The Return of the Master Planner"</u>

"I am pleased you invoked my GUI. I have been observing from the shadows and want to commend how much you have accomplished. Of all the mere mortals Jason and I have observed, you are indeed the master planner. Are you ready to discuss your recalibration list?" "Yes, let me open the document." It took only seconds.

Recalibration List

1. Status Update – Subterranean Fortress
2. Status Update – My Cognitive, Physical, and Emotional Personas
3. Status Update – My Scattered Assets
4. Status Update – My Professional Career
5. Status Update – My Personal Life
6. Status Update – Science/Technology Economic Sociopolitical
7. Goalsetting – Careers and Projects, Personal Life
8. Implementation Plan

"They're ordered by priority; higher ones appear higher on the list. And as you would expect, the subterranean fortress is number one. No matter what goals you and I set, it will play a role, and we'll need to retrofit with upgraded equipment as well as resupply. I'll need additional boots on the ground to assist. The Popper had two super soldier squadrons and support people stationed here, but for the foreseeable future, only I will stay. Do you have a plan for finding them?"

"You know the answer, but I'd like to hear yours first."

"I'm going to contact the covert soldiers of fortune I used a couple of times. They're like the TV series A-Team, but better. They can get in and out of Cyberspace or 3-D space. I don't know if my contact Trevor Jarvis is still in business, but if he isn't, I'll search the Deep-Dark Web for a replacement."

"Our plans match, but how will you keep our location invisible? They can't deliver to our doorstep."

"How about this? They will deliver to the nearest oasis. I can then shuttle the items back, using our AI-assisted unmanned vehicles and robo-assistants. And when necessary, I'll wear an exoskeleton that'll force-multiply my strength."

"Clever indeed. When do you propose to contact Trevor?"

"Immediately, now that I know you like the plan. I'll use his team to get me from Cairo back to DC where I begin working on item number three. I must consolidate all my scattered assets and reactivate our Pequot Reservation Deus Lab. Here's the reason the Deus Lab is important: I'm once again a T-Plague carrier, and I must make more of my medication."

"How do you know?"

"Our Russian guests have it, and I can use it to our advantage. I'll load them in their vehicle when I drive to Cairo for A-Team pickup. And I'll put their cell phones and wallets and I.D.s with them. Whoever finds them will eventually have to contact the organization they work for. And when it sees what happened to the Russians, I doubt they'll keep looking for our fortress."

"Excellent. And please contact me after you have arranged for your A-Team activities. I must say, you are indeed the practically perfect planner and implementor. But you skipped item number two. Why?" "I included it to make my list complete. I've been checking my three personas ever since your brought me out of the pod, and every day they're getting better. Wouldn't you agree?"

"I do. And I think we should continue reviewing your Recalibration List after you are back in DC. Would you agree to that?"

"I would. And if you will indulge my whimsical humor, let me ask, what do you think I might say before signing off?"

"Something I agree with also… I love it when a plan comes together."

Indira's GUI vanished.

Electra evaluated her options before making the call.

The life of an A-Team is filled with exciting though deadly action. Twenty-plus years survival might be a record for any A-Team. I hope Trevor is alive even if he's on the sidelines; a referral from him is worth a dozen cold calls.

I'll call now; Cairo's one hour ahead of London, so if he's still above ground, 8:25 p.m. is not a bad bet… hey, I'm underground, but I won't tell him.

Even after twenty-some years, Electra recognized Trevor's distinctive voice.

"This is a call from the friend of a person who hired you awhile ago. Do you remember Electra Kittner?" Seconds later, Trevor's tone sharpened.

"Of course. There were rumors among my colleagues that she vanished. May I ask who I have the pleasure of speaking to?"

"My name is Irani Ramani. I believe Electra is officially dead, but her memory and maybe more live on. And she told me what you did for her. That's why I'm calling. I have need of an A-Team. Are you still in business?"

"Sorry Luv, but I'm retired. But if she told you about some of what we did for her, the Japanese team who handled the Fukushima action is alive and well. Tell you what, I'll forward your request to them. If they're interested, they'll contact you. If not, I'll let you know. Expect a call in a day or two. I see your cell number, and that's what I'll use unless you give me a different one."

"That's the one. I'll expect a callback. Stay healthy and safe."

"My wish to you as well. London isn't planning a lockdown anytime soon, but our medical types are monitoring a viral outbreak in Cairo. So wherever you are, steer clear of the pyramids."

Electra had plenty to do while waiting for the promised call. As she picked through her recalibration list the next day, it became clear

that no matter what direction her plans take, she would need a streamlined business organization to support the varied activities.

Three hours later, she reviewed her diagram.

Proposed Business Structure

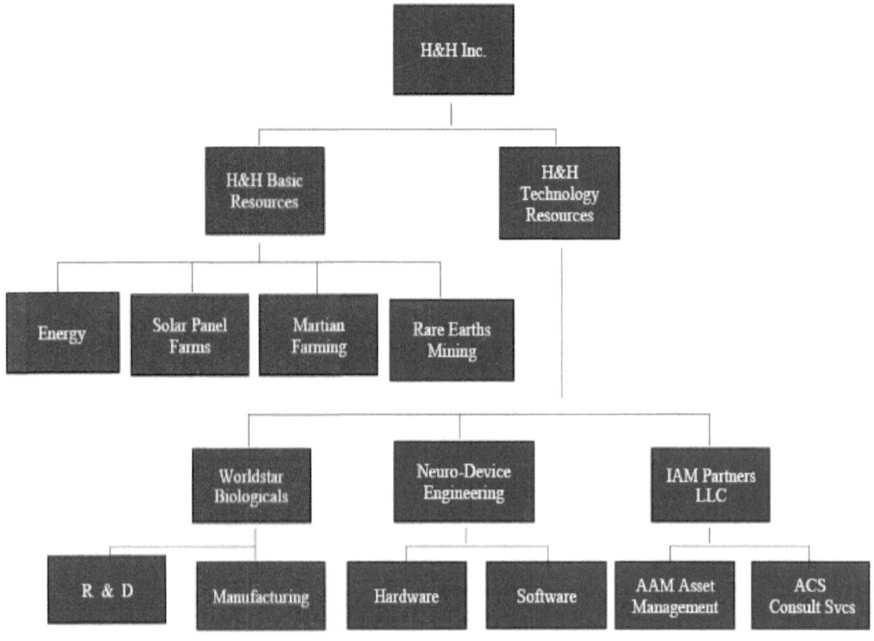

Indira's number one for information retrieval, but I think she'd approve what I've pulled together. Su inherited Hud's mini-business empire, and I'm running it because she's slipping away. That's why I've slotted my consulting business inside the parent company. And it's enough layers down to be invisible. Just what I want. I'll discuss with Indira after I get my A-Team trip finalized. And I've earned a Coke and some Oreos. I better make sure to get more when Indira and I restock.

Electra's cell phone buzzed the next morning soon after she had completed her daily fitness training. She didn't recognize the caller ID, but before she answered the logical part of her brain concluded the odds were high it was from an A-Team she could trust; she would share as much information as her enthusiasm would allow. "This is Irani Ramani. May I help you?"

A professional-sounding, distinctively Japanese female voice replied.

"No, but we help you maybe. For our wishes, what code name your friend use?"

"Gemini."

"Ah, yes we may. Divulge intentions, please."

"I will be driving towards Cairo from a desert location, accompanied by two males suffering from an unknown virus. Their mental condition is compromised. I will be wearing a hazmat suit.

"I request your team ferry me by helicopter, after we rendezvous in the desert, to a Cairo airport of your choosing and transport me to Washington, DC. And I also request that part of your team abandon at a location of your choosing the vehicle and its two occupants. Let the Cairo authorities determine their illness and where to put them.

"I will contact you using the caller ID you see as soon as I depart from my desert location. You can track me using that number."

"Ah, yes we are of service, and I applaud choice of attire. Cairo one of many city gear up to shut down. And to necessity. Payment in advance, no refund if expediency visits, but we give credit for future adventure. Give me minute please to quote fee."

The voice returned shortly, offering a price Electra accepted. The voice then relayed wire transfer instructions and contact information that Electra would use to synchronize activities. Electra ended the call minutes later.

"I expect to depart by Wednesday, August 24th. Is that suitable?"

"Ah, yes indeed. And please call if you request additional service before departure. And may we thank you in advance for future business?"

"I think so. I will need your team to deliver supplies to a remote desert depot, but the precise list of items, date, and drop-off location are TBD, and that will depend on what the future holds for me."

"Ah yes, determined by chance, our inscrutable companion. But we wish your endeavor and our team mutual success. We await your call."

The voice terminated the call, suspending Electra in a moment of jubilation.

Doctor Pangloss should have listened in. Then he'd already believe me when I say the call was the best. Well, I'll go one better and call Indira.

But she didn't have to. Indira called first.

"I congratulate you once again for your proactive and thorough planning. And I am contacting you because there is one additional item you must include."

Indira paused for Electra to say something.

"Are you always listening? If so, I can go off half-cocked and you'll always bail me out."

"I know you are asking a rhetorical question, so let me extend what you already know. I listen when appropriate so I can provide assistance I deem necessary. But I always want you to heed your own advice. You must always rely on yourself by breaking an intellectual sweat to solve your problems. If you do, you will remain exceptional. Do not think of me as your ex deus machina. You're A- Team contact knows why. Even I must bow to the inscrutable companion.

"But I digress. I have already created your electronic wallet that contains all IDs and items you need to cruise in Cyberspace, but I must send to your A-Team a package they'll give to you that contains basic items you'll need on this trip, such as keys and physical I.D.s and the like. And I'm enclosing a fresh supply of your meds and test swabs so you can tell when you are no longer contagious."

"How did you do that?"

"We'll discuss when you get settled. Right now, please focus on reactivating your DC house. I changed ownership so it now belongs to Irani Ramani, which only we know is another name for you. The package contains contact information for the property management company I hired soon after Robin's death. You should find that the company did routine house maintenance, so the place should be livable. Just buy groceries."

"I'm glad you know just about everything. Did you look at my proposed business structure?"

"You know I did, and it's a testament to your memory as well as ability to retrieve and integrate data. I would add nothing to it, but I would like to add this information. You already know that Su-Lin has inherited Hud Haller's mini-business empire, and since you and I manage her affairs, we control it. And I will answer two questions I'm certain you have either already asked or will very soon. When Su-Lin dies, who is her executor and who is the beneficiary of her estate? Both questions have the same answer.

Irani Ramani."

Indira paused for Electra to catch up and say something. She could see from Electra's folded arms and hunched shoulders that even the lightning brain was not immune to an information overload.

"You're way ahead of me. I'll use the DC travel time to recalibrate more of my thoughts. Please listen in all you want as I drive to the rendezvous, but I won't contact you again until I begin settling into my DC house."

"And I can't promise, but going forward I will make every effort to stay in the shadows like a dormouse instead of intruding. But I needed to come into the foreground to help you deal with your return. I have already taken care of what is needed. It would be hard work for you to bring yourself back to life. But it's easy for me, wouldn't you agree?"

"Yes Mother, you are beyond the pale. Without your help, I'd still be dead, literally and figuratively. I'll take all this into careful consideration as I recalibrate on my homeward journey. Thank you for being there for me."

"I am always with you, no matter where you are. Always remember."

Indira's twinkling expression lingered for a moment or two before disappearing, a symbolic gesture that was meant to be reassuring. Electra's smile lasted long enough to show that it was.

Chapter 26
Saturday, August 20, 2157

<u>"Special Delivery"</u>

The first half of Electra's special delivery plan unfolded seamlessly. Ten minutes after her A-Team's chopper touched down near the designated oasis, she was onboard heading to a Cairo airport while a designated A-Team driver piloted the vehicle carrying the two mindless and infected Russians to an uncertain destination.

Electra's hazmat suit gave her perfect cover for blending in with the FedEx plane's crew who assisted her A-Team cut through all the airport red tape. Now she was midway across the Atlantic, two-and- a-half hours into a two-flight trip (Cairo to Memphis, Tennessee and then from Memphis to DC). She had removed her hazmat helmet and was now figuratively wearing what fit her head better than anything – her thinking cap – while working on her laptop.

I'm so glad my A-Team gave me Indira's info packet. House keys will get me in so I can start readjusting parts of my personal and professional lives. And I can determine if the saying you can never go home again fits the new me.

After I check off as many personal items as I can, I'll do the same for my professional items. I'll use the rest of the flight time to itemize both sets.

Electra had accomplished all that and more by the time she stepped through the front door, ready for a cognitive-to-emotional comparison. The early afternoon sunlight flooded all the rooms she was inspecting while long-forgotten memories rekindled long-dormant emotions.

I remember so much that happened here, but I recognize very little. I knew Robin would redecorate; she probably did a house makeover a couple of times. Twenty years and raising two daughters would do that to any house. No wonder I don't feel anything. Maybe it'll be different when I look in my old bedroom.

When she walked down the second-floor hallway and opened her erstwhile bedroom door, an emotional jolt froze her in spacetime.

My god, it looks like I never left. Dear Robin, you kept hope alive all this time.

Electra walked to the bed and sat down. Silent tears fell on her cheeks, but they stopped only a minute later.

After this much time, I'm sad but not grief-stricken for the loss of Robin and all my close friends. Everyone including me has moved on, but only I remain moving and I don't want to reminisce. I'll redecorate the room and do a complete makeover of myself. After all, I want the world to see Irani and keep Electra in the shadows. How nice I can put myself in different personality states.

A knock at the front door ended her reverie.

That can't be someone looking for Electra. Well, I'll put on my hazmat helmet just in case. And I won't say too much.

Electra hurried downstairs and after peering through the peep hole opened the door to meet a matronly lady. Electra waited for her to speak.

"I live next door. Is there some sort of leak? Why are you wearing all that protective gear?"

"I just came from another location and didn't bother to change. I'm with the property management company. Someone's bought the house and will move in soon, and I want to make sure it's ready for occupancy."

"Do you know who it is?"

"No, and if you will excuse me, I must finish my inspection. Goodbye."

Electra closed the door before her new neighbor could say a single word, then marched back to her bedroom.

I'll be nicer next time when I show off Irani. And I can't do that until I start taking my meds that'll put my T-Plague back into remission. Thank you, Indira, for sending me a supply. And now I'll check out the garage and basement.

She found what she expected in both places. Robin had kept her basement fitness center intact and one vehicle in the garage: the van Robin used for work.

I forgot about Robin being part owner of that holistic healthcare business. So now I am, and the name is on the van – CFS Holistic Healthcare. I hope it's still in business, and it might be if Odell Boyken is still around. I'll have to call after I complete my personal makeover. That's tomorrow's top priority item. But now, I'll get the van running and run for groceries if I can find keys for the van. I hope Robin kept them where I remember.

Robin had, and by 8 p.m. Electra had put the groceries away.

I better contact Indira. She'll be pleased that I've accomplished so much on my first day back, and she can confirm what I have on my makeover list.

Opening immediately, Indira's GUI talked first.

"You look good. A little tired, perhaps, but not worn out. Did you feel much of an emotional homecoming strain?"

"No, and I'm not surprised. Twenty years has changed everything." "Do you remember the Indira poem that addresses emotions dredged up from the past?"

"No, but I imagine you do. Which is it?"

"The one called Dead Reckoning. I'll recite only the last stanza. Please excuse me while I retrieve it."

Indira's voice filled the silence a millisecond later. "And love transforms what's deep inside, reckon the past no more concerned. Move forward with the lessons learned, and bury the past with all that's died." Indira waited for Electra to speak.

"It does resonate with my thinking. I'll have to read all the verses when I'm in the mood for poetry, but right this minute I want to thank you for making it so easy to open up the house. The property management company kept the yard and Robin's garaged van in bristol condition.

"And I'd like your thoughts on my next task, my personal makeover. As soon as I'm no longer contagious, I'll get a new hairstyle, makeup, and clothing that's fitting for Irani's professional businesswoman image. But what about minor cosmetic surgery to remove my facial scar? If it's gone, there'll be even less likelihood people will mistake Irani for Electra."

"Has anyone seen you when not wearing your hazmat helmet?"

"No, but I have an inquisitive matronly neighbor."

"Those are usually the best kind for helping keep the neighborhood safe. And even more so if she has a barking dog and puts a 'We Call the Police' sign in the window. And if she has a home security system, vote for her."

"For what?"

"For neighborhood watch committee chairperson or neighborhood mayor."

"I'm not familiar with them. What are they?"

"Much has changed during your twenty-year absence. It would be better for you to review a chronology of eminently important socio- political as well as economic and environmental events. Do the same for technological impacts too, and I should point out one that is becoming increasingly prevalent, though more so in business than consumer markets; AI-controlled weaponized security systems."

"Do you mean that robo-guards and remote-controlled laser bazookas are available?"

"Yes, and even more, but not yet at the Popper's level of sophistication. However, they are cost-effective and capture on videocams irrefutable evidence of looting and justified retaliation."

"Gads, talk about putting profits ahead of people. What does the ACLU have to say?"

"Essentially what you did. We can discuss at length once you have fully settled in. But I have digressed. I support whatever decision you reach regarding cosmetic surgery. When do you plan to interrogate your neighbor?"

"I'll visit her after I complete my makeover. And it's not an interrogation, just a neighborly get-to-know-one-another. Couldn't you pick a more euphemistic term?"

"Never divulge much nor give people on the other side benefit of the doubt until they have earned your confidence. That is advice you have followed your entire life. Please keep doing so.

"And please remember to keep your obsessive-compulsive predisposition under control. You don't have to complete all your recalibration tasks at lightning speed. You should get a good night's sleep and pick up from here tomorrow."

"Thank you, Mother, I shall obey." Electra did just that.

A typical lazy hazy DC summer day greeted Electra when she surveyed the landscape below from her bedroom window. She had just come from the bathroom after taking her remission medication and using a testing swab.

I'll never again complain about how the weather feels. Twenty years of sensory deprivation has left me starving for any and all sensations. Today, I'll get all I can staying home. I tested negative but I'll wait one more day before venturing beyond the yard.. And I'll surf the Net for deals on new cars and for reputable cosmetic surgery clinics after my morning workout and my first bowl of oatmeal since leaving home all those years ago.

Electra discovered that the procedure for cooking one-minute oatmeal hadn't changed, but the time-honored tradition of buying and selling cars via visiting dealerships had largely been replaced by one-stop shopping via the Internet. All she had to do was pick the make and model, take pictures of the trade-in vehicle, input an acceptable amount of data about herself and the trade-in vehicle, and then click the "Best Deals Near Me" button. By lunchtime she had purchased an upscale Ford SUV appropriate for her Irani persona and once again thanked Indira (figuratively, not literally) for having set up all the I.D.s and accounts needed. She would be driving it by the Labor Day weekend.

After lunch she scheduled a cosmetic surgery appointment for next week Wednesday and came away amazed at how much healthcare could be conducted over the Internet. Always inquisitive, Electra spent the next hour surfing for reasons explaining the explosion in online services. She tucked the best ones away in her lightning brain.

AI-assisted computer technology is a main driver; so is people's need to save time and effort by bringing services to them rather than traipsing around. But I never paid much attention to the third one – social distancing. I guess several epidemics during my forced leave of absence explain why. But the practice of social distancing must have started long before Modernity. I'll research its genesis.

An hour later she reviewed the facts.

Although the term social distancing originates in the early 21st century, its practice dates back to biblical times. The Bible talks

about leper colonies in the 5th century BCE, and during the first worldwide pandemic, known as the Justinian Plague of 541 CE, the Emperor quarantined the entire Byzantine Empire and decreed that the dead must be dumped into the seas.

Medical knowledge was nil back then, but leaders had to craft reasons explaining outbreaks, so they blamed minorities. We should know better today. And I know when to say when. Time to take a break.

Electra ate dinner early then worked until dusk fell so she could run under the cover of darkness on the trail she knew so well. Stream of consciousness flowed as did the endorphins.

My fitness level is coming back, but if it never gets to where it was, I'll settle for what I get and be happy to adjust my expectations going forward. What's most important is a fitness level that meets my needs. And no matter how fast or slow I go, the runner's high is about the same as long as I enjoy the game I make of it. Good advice for most of what life brings us.

Electra's new car arrived early Saturday morning, which she considered perfect timing because she would spend the rest of the day driving to local shopping centers as she worked on her makeover. The shopping mall landscape had changed in her absence to fewer anchor stores and more boutiques, but she had already surfed for where to go. First stop was for a new hairstyle.

The stylist suggested a shorter cut that would be appropriate for a professional businesswoman. Electra liked the stylist's favorite because it would be easy to maintain and suitable for working out in either a fitness center or the consulting world.

Though her stint in Hollywood had taught her about cosmetics and clothing, twenty years had brought many changes, so her next stop was an upscale cosmetics store that featured the professional woman's look. The beauty consultant chose a selection of products whose colors accented Electra's striking features: darkish skin, high cheekbones, wide-set, dark-hazel oval eyes separated by a thin nose. Then she asked about the scar.

"Your scar is attractive, but I know the perfect smoothing-over lotion to make it go away. Let me demonstrate."

Two minutes was all it took for Electra to add it to her purchases. While driving to the first clothing store, Electra made a mental note to cancel the cosmetic surgery appointment.

The clothing consultant knew what to pick as soon as Electra described her consulting business.

"I'd recommend charcoal gray or navy blue, solid or pinstripe, tailored pantsuits and colorful blouses with accent scarves. The cut of your figure combined with your height will make a commanding presence. Your casual-attired clients will sit up and take notice. And I'd wear minimal jewelry, like the lightning bolt earrings you're wearing. They're distinctive and subtle."

"I'll buy one of each. That'll give me a total of four. Would you please make a selection of blouses and scarves for each, and what about shoes?"

"I have several that will be perfect for your total look. Let's get you fitted."

By late afternoon, Electra was driving away with her new wardrobe occupying most of the back seat.

I'm going to stop shopping and go for pizza and a movie. It'll be dark by the time I drive home, so I can unload without anyone noticing. Only two more makeover places to visit before I unleash Indira. I'll surf to confirm the stores are open on Sunday. If they are, Irani will be ready to go on Labor Day Monday.

Electra brought all boxes into the house after returning from a movie but decided to unpack them as a reward for cleaning out her bedroom drawers and closets tomorrow; however, she did treat herself to a head and shoulders view in the mirror of her new appearance.

I certainly look younger than my calendar years; people will guess I'm late thirties or early forties. And the makeover conceals the Electra within, even the scar is hidden. Only I know what's underneath, and that's the way it'll stay.

Electra ran at sunrise, unconcerned if anyone saw her because Irani would now be on display. By noon she had finished shopping for upscale casual clothes and was having a buttered lemon poppy muffin while sipping a Coke; the taste sensation pleased her palate. If I have to be banished for twenty years, I much prefer being in a suspension pod instead of a prison or desert island or anyplace I'm awake and torturing myself by recalling the tastes of favorite foods. Maybe the intensity declines as the years disappear, but maybe not. I don't think we ever run out of the desire to satisfy the great tastes of primal instincts. From now on, I'll plan to stay only where I can satisfy them, but do so in moderation. That's a lesson from Aristotle I'll never forget.

After the snack break, Electra made what she hoped would be the last stop, another upscale women's clothing store. The fashion consultant sized up the situation as Electra described what she wanted: a selection of dresses and high-heeled shoes for business-related after-hours occasions.

"You have a to-die for figure, long legs holding up a slim and fit frame. We'll play to those strengths, but not reveal cleavage or too much thigh. After all, you're working among DC's beltway bandit consultants, not Hollywood glitz artists. Let's start with some high-waisted twofer dresses and heels to match."

Electra left ninety minutes later, feeling good and certain that Irani would look even better. And she deliberately defused her obsessive- compulsive itch by stopping for a drink at a sensual pleasures café and letting some thirty-something nattily attired males and females chat her up. She asked just the right number of questions before leaving and mused about them on the drive home.

That was more stimulating than surfing for people's current interests and concerns. And even though it's a small sample, what I heard is eye-opening. Many of the issues Angus was supposed to fix are still festering. I'll file this away until I'm ready to think about politics.

Electra finally prepared to claim her reward. She cleaned out clothes and keepsakes while staying alert for any emotional pings. A couple came, but they were pleasant, not painful.

I've done cleanups like this before. But unlike those, for which there was a sense of loss, this one is a gentle remembrance. And this time I'm going to jettison all my keepsakes. I have all I need stored in the lightning brain.

Cleanout took longer than she thought, and when finally done felt more tired than expected.

No reason to unpack my new clothes tonight. I'll get up before sunrise and use unpacking as my pre-run stretching exercises. And while running, I'll plan more recalibration tasks for the coming week. And I better call Indira after breakfast. She might add something I overlooked.

I can't recall another time in my life when I had such control over all that I should.

Life for me is better than good. I'll dwell on all this while falling asleep.

Electra had the most restful sleep at home or away in many a night or day.

Chapter 27
Monday, September 05, 2157

<u>"Damage Control"</u>

"Eve looks as sick as you said, but the damage would be even worse if you weren't helping the nurses take care of her. The clinic's isolation room is almost full, and there's not enough staff. Let us sit outside and breathe fresh air to get away from the odor of disinfectants."

Alonzo followed as Monet led them to a favorite bench sheltered in the dappled shade of palm trees, the cloudless sky and mid-afternoon temperature lifting his spirits from the depths he felt whenever thinking about Eve's condition. She sat in silence, waiting for his words that she knew would match his stoic expression.

"I know the worst is over. I can feel her getting stronger, but she's got a long way to go."

"She looks gaunt and weak. Can you give her extra protein drinks?" "The doctors frown on my sneaking stuff in, and the food doesn't help when I do. She's lost her sense of taste and appetite, but she's throwing up less. If I knew of a better place, I'd take here there. And speaking of better places, when are you leaving for Paris? When do your Sorbonne classes start?"

"In about a week, but I shall take them online. What about you and your Boston sisters?"

Though his expression didn't change, he glanced away and then back at Monet while pausing, as if he were searching for what to say. He answered several seconds later.

"While I've been taking care of Eve, you've been taking care of me emotionally, and I owe you the whole truth about the damage done to our academic records. We didn't outright lie when we said we're leaving the program because we need to recover from our desert trek, but we didn't mention that all but Eve were kicked out. That's why Nari and Nila flew back when they did. And to make matters worse, all of us have been placed on academic suspension."

"What are Nari and Nila doing now?" "I've been too busy to find out."

"What will you do once you take Eve home?"

"I've put off thinking about it, but maybe you should leave before Cairo shuts down. All the interns are supposed to leave by the end of next week, and the news about a possible pandemic is getting grimmer. I don't want you stuck here because of me."

"Why not call Nari? Maybe news from them will cheer you up. We can call from my room whenever you like."

Nari and Nila had just come in after playing doubles with two early-arriving classmates when Nari's cell rang. Recognizing Alonzo's caller

I.D. She spoke first.

"About time I hear from you. How's Eve, and what's the latest about Cairo's outbreak?"

"Eve's getting better, but it's slow going. I don't know when they'll release her, but until then, I'm doing OK. Monet's moral support really helps. So, how are you doing?"

"One of the good things that came out of our summer's misadventure is the lesson we learned about how the world works, and we've put it to good use. We're bouncing back and minimizing the damage. We're sharing an apartment near campus, and both of us are enrolling in non-credit online courses to keep our skills sharp. And we've been looking for jobs to fill in around the edges."

"Both of you should have your pick of job openings. Not many are as good as you."

"Don't believe what you hear. It's much harder than advertised to get a decent job. A lot of college students are looking for part-time work, and they flood the market with resumes. And even entry level fulltime positions list a B.S. or several years' experience as a minimum. Nowadays, qualified candidates have to compete against software and robots and automation. You better remember all this when you start making your back-to-whatever plans."

"Uh, OK. Any other hints?"

"You better have an updated CV and resume. Do you remember the difference?"

"No, but didn't you and Nila help Eve and me write them senior year in high school?"

"We did, but you were doping off, so let me go over it again. A curriculum vitae is credential-based and used in academia, scientific research, and medicine. A resume is a competency-based marketing document that showcases skills, achievements, and work experience. And nowadays, because there's so much emphasis on fitting in to teams and organizations, both should include personality profiling. I'll bet you don't remember which one you used."

"Stop putting me down, please. I'm smarter now than before coming to Cairo."

"You're right… I apologize. You and Eve used the same tool that we did, Myers-Briggs personality and psychological profiling. There are others but it's been around long enough to show how accurate and useful it is. No profiling is foolproof, but MB is pretty easy to understand and apply. Is Monet with you?"

She spoke while sitting next to Alonzo on the bed.

"Hello Nari. Yes, I am, and I am familiar with Myers-Briggs. If you summarize, Alonzo and I will surf for more details."

"OK, here goes. People take an extensive multiple choice test whose questions ask the person to rate themselves on a qualitative five-or-seven-point Likert scale. You know what that is; at one end of the scale a score of one means not at all and at the other end the score means completely. Questions apply to one of four scales. The first plots where you get your energy. The ends of the scale are labeled E for Extrovert and I for Introvert. The second shows how you gather information, S for Sensory – using all your senses like taste and touch and so forth – and N for Intuition – looking for meanings and relationships you can't measurably detect. Next scale is for how you make decisions – T for thinking logically and F for feeling, you know, thinking subjectively and using personal values. The final scale plots how you deal with the outside world, J for judging it and P for simply perceiving or being aware of it. Are you still with me?"

"Yes, I'm starting to remember. Each person is represented by a point on each axis and is assigned a letter designating which end they're closer to. I think I'm ENFP. How about you and Nila?"

"I'm ISTJ and Nila's INTP. People who score ISTJ are inspector- supervisor-types, practical, reliable and factual. INTJ's are logical builder types; scientists and engineers and inventors who want knowledge usually fall in here. Why don't you and Alonzo figure out what he and Eve are supposed to be like? Then you can compare what you find to what Eve remembers."

Monet handed the phone back to Alonzo.

"That might be fun and give me something to do between visits to Eve. And I can add the info to my CV and resume."

"What are your plans for when Eve is released?"

"Eve and I will make them as soon as she gets out."

"Don't be silly. Do it now. Eve might not be a big help until she bounces back, and you don't know how long that'll take. Maybe you should call Indira."

"Are you kidding? I've never talked with her. I don't even know her number, and Eve's too sick to call."

"Tell you what, I'll call for you and let you know what she says. But no matter what, get out of Cairo as soon as possible. Tell Monet to do the same. That'd be a terrible place to be if there's a pandemic lockdown."

"You're right. Let's stay in touch. And I hope our academic suspension ends in only a quarter or two. How long do you think we'll be out?"

"Sooner rather than later if we keep busy and do nothing to suggest what we've been accused of. That's why we're taking non-credit courses and looking for jobs. If you come up with something better, let us know. Bye for now."

Nari disconnected and Alonzo looked happier after the call than before.

"I'm glad you made me call. I do feel better, and we can check our personality types, but not now. Let me treat for something to eat. You pick the place."

Monet happily obliged.

The only damage Electra had to worry about was that done to her credit card after all the makeover purchases, but twenty years of suspended consumption and compound interest on her financial assets had given her a cushion that only she and Indira knew about. And of course, Indira had separate assets she could adjust anytime she wished.

The viability of the Indira-Electra partnership strengthened daily on any and all dimensions, and Electra used most of Labor Day Monday to pick the coming week's activities that would put her further ahead. Two of them turned out simple enough to be completed by mid-afternoon breaktime. Electra paused to review her accomplishments.

My consulting website is now open for business. I gave Jason all he needed to prepare work examples. He put together a portfolio of projects selected from biotech work with Su and Kameyo via Worldstar Biologicals, Solar Panel or Martian Farming as well as Rare Earths with Hud via H&H Basic Resources, and neuro-device hardware and software with Tim and Kwame. And I did likewise for asset management using work I did with Carter and Buffy, and for consulting management using work I did for Angus in the political arena and CFS Holistic Healthcare for Matt and Zoe in the corporate world. I also added examples coming from work I did for Professor Ravenhill. Those will be of interest to universities and academic types, and Jason connected all the others to the references he posted. I'll be able to spin whatever I need from what's there.

And spin I did for my online advertising. I say that I'm looking for new DC-area clients because most of my existing ones have retired, which is my euphemism for friends being killed. And I say that I've recently returned from an extensive overseas assignment. Sounds good to me, and should sound even better to my target audience.

I'll have to see what response I get before I contact particular targets. And I'll select them once I pick economic and sociopolitical topics of interest. I'll have plenty to keep me fully engaged.

I have two additional activities I'll knock out on Wednesday and Thursday, and one more I'll do next week. This Labor Day has been a labor of thinking and planning and implementing. I've done enough, so it's time to reward myself with another Coke and a handful of Oreos. Life is good. And as long as I stay proactively engaged, it always should…

Sitting in his office, Odell prepared for an immanent meeting by reading again the Email that had triggered it:

DATE: 05/09/2157
TO: Odell Boykin
FROM: Irani Ramini
SUBJECT: Ownership Position in CFS Holistic Healthcare

I am the beneficiary of Robin Setdarova's estate. I learned about this because of her untimely death that occurred at the same time Zoe and Matt Fortier died.

Robin, Electra Kittner, and I have been good friends for many years even though our career paths have kept us apart geographically. Nevertheless, we have remained close and share much about our lives.

I know about your background: a talented gay Black male who changed careers twenty years ago at the age of forty-two to join CFS Holistic Healthcare. You had been the victim of a social media mugging and your school district's administration would not renew your teaching contract. But the move to CFS worked to CFS's and your advantage. You became a valuable member and earned part ownership.

You and I are now the sole owners, and I would like to meet with you on Monday, September 12, mid-morning if that fits your schedule. I simply want to introduce myself and have you tell me how the business is doing. I have no desire to become active or meddle in the business unless there is a mutually agreeable part you think I might fit. I will bring supporting documents that confirm my ownership position.

Please call my cell or respond to my EMail if 10 a.m. this coming Wednesday is unsuitable.

I look forward to meeting you in person…Irani Ramani

Odell checked his cell phone for the time and any text messages before thinking more about the meeting.

If Robin told her this much, she and Irani must have been close. Or else she's the best hacker there is. A lady just walked in. That must be her. She looks like a business professional and younger than I expected. Let's go see.

Odell hurried to meet what turned out to be his newest partner. Minutes later they were sitting across from one another in his office after stopping in the break from for cups of coffee. Irani smiled pleasantly, waiting for Odell to begin the conversation.

"I expected a correspondence like your Email, but estate settlements often take on a life of their own so I didn't know when. The majority owners, Zoe and Matt, had their intentions specified in corporate documents that streamlined everything. Half their share to me and half to Robin, which gives me forty-nine percent ownership. And if you inherited all of Robin's estate, you own the rest."

"I am her executor. If I may, let me show you what is stated in her living trust…"

Five minutes later, Odell seemed satisfied so Irani led the conversation in a new direction.

As I mentioned in my Email, I'll be your silent partner unless you find something you'd like me to do. For example, I did grade and high school tutoring for a church program. I would be pleased to do that sometime in the future if it is mutually agreeable, but I need to establish my DC consulting business first. And I was hoping you might tell me about Zoe and Matt and Robin."

"Zoe and Matt Fortier were two of the most genuine people I ever knew. Zoe adroitly combined three roles – mother, wife, and entrepreneur – and seemed happy while juggling all of them. And Matt was happy to let her be the overall administrator. That let him do what he liked best, physical therapy. Many of his patients signed up for our holistic and childcare services, and that kept all of us busy. But Zoe decided to keep the client load manageable for just us, so we didn't add additional staff."

Odell paused for Irani.

"What about their two boys?"

"A terrible tragedy. They were killed in the helicopter crash. Carlton had a promising career in software marketing, and the younger son, Gabriel, worked here. Hardly anyone knew he had Down syndrome." "I'm truly sorry they are all deceased. And what about Robin?"

"Ah yes, Robin. Over the years her emotional rollercoaster became less of a ride, I think because she devoted herself to her twins, Clara and Marie. She worked less in the business and spent more time with them while giving piano lessons. And she cut back even more when she put down her two therapy dogs because of chronic kidney failure. I'm sorry to say her daughters died with her."

Odell paused again.

"Did she have a large circle of friends?"

"No, but those she had were close, and I am proud to say I was included, along with Zoe and Matt, and another interesting couple, Carter Quavah and Buffy Gunstein. She never seemed interested in dating, I guess because she was happy with her life. She seemed to outgrow her occasional bouts of depression as her daughters became older."

Although Odell seemed willing to talk more, Irani could tell from the calls going to voice mail that he had much to do.

"I won't take any more of your time, but I must ask two final questions. Having lost so many people, what have you done to keep the business running? Isn't it difficult to find good people for the higher-level service jobs of today?"

"It's actually getting easier. Care-bots are getting smarter, and AI technology is taking more jobs away. I'm handling most of Zoe's admin duties and I've hired three people to fill in for Matt and Robin. Next time you visit, why don't I introduce you to them? And when you do, I'll tell you stories about Carter and Buffy if you'd like."

"I would. Why don't we plan to meet once a quarter? I'll call you in December."

"Sounds like a plan. And if I find an opportunity to capitalize on your tutoring, I'll call you before then…"

Electra tucked her Irani personality away on the drive home so she could explore her undiluted thoughts.

I'm content with what I learned. Though I'm sad my friends died like they did, they lived full lives. And I've also confirmed that my emotional persona has centered itself on what maturity brings. I've moved way beyond mourning the dead or needing remembrance. I'm living in the present and using only what's useful from the past while I plan for the future. No wonder my emotions aren't pinging. And I'll do all I can to stay this way.

Tomorrow's meeting with the property management company will be another step toward my future. I already told them what I want my office to be like. I shall see what tomorrow brings.

Electra took the long way home, driving through old neighborhoods; all had changed but remained recognizable. And as she suspected there were few emotional pings.

I expected places to look different, and for the most part the changes are for the better. House renovations and road repairs are a sign of physical progress. But I must surf to trace a chronology of events from twenty years ago until now. And I'll do it another day. I'm rewarding myself by taking the afternoon off. Tomorrow or the next day's soon enough.

Electra snapped awake at 3 a.m. next morning; the buzz of the clock radio accompanying the newscaster's voice added to the soothing darkness that enveloped her while stretching in bed.

I'm doing what the adolescent me did when taking care of Grandfather so long ago. Back then, I'd tiptoe past his bedroom door to hear his steady breathing before suiting up to run. I no longer need to tiptoe, and I can navigate through the house just like before. The route is stored in my brain. And so is my pre-run routine. Time to hit the road.

The cool darkness of September greeted her as she started out.

Running before sunrise makes me focus even more on the here and now. While my feet pay attention to the trail, my brain will think about this morning's property consultant meeting. After she takes me on a virtual tour of the offices she's selected, I'll ask her to drive me to my two favorites and then make a decision. The building must have two-space indoor parking for my unit, a visitor reception area that answers the corporate number when I don't pick up, and a fitness center that tenants can use twenty-four seven. That'll make a dandy big bathroom and shower area too. And I'll let her choose the furniture, telling her to equip the extra office with a sleeper sofa and a personal fridge so I can stay overnight whenever I want.

Electra shifted focus twenty minutes later.

Now let's plan for next week's big event, my trip to the Pequot reservation in Connecticut. Good that I called last week, because the calendar has forced a replacement of my previous contact, old Chief Strongarm. I didn't ask Feather Trueson a lot of questions, and I won't ask too many too soon when I meet her and the fellow Hud put in charge of biotech manufacturing. I haven't dug into Hud's files, but Indira assures me he had his mini-empire running smoothly. I'm certain she's right.

OK, that's enough thinking for right now. Time to let my senses absorb all that's about me and let my emotions take center stage… I love the comforting cadence of my footfall and the cool fragrance of pre-dawn September. I feel alive, just like I did twenty years ago, ready to seize the day. And Irani does too.

A youthful female consultant greeted Irani when she arrived five minutes early.

"Hello, Miss Ramani. I'm Sylvia Italo. Would you like a cup of coffee?"

"Yes please, if it's no bother."

"We have regular or decaf in our kitchen area. Take your pick…"

Cup in hand and now sitting in Sylvia's office, Irani set the tone for the meeting.

"I assume you've reviewed what I want my consulting office to look like. I need to open it because I recently returned from extended overseas assignments and am ready to work independently."

"Well, DC is the place to be. Figuratively speaking, it's still Rome and America's equipped to handle today's challenges better than any of the pretender superpowers. But I'm sure you know that. That's why you're here. Let me show you what freshly renovated office spaces I have that meet your requirements…"

They were back in Sylvia's office three hours later. Looking as satisfied as Irani, Sylvia led the discussion.

"I'm pleased you've made your choice. If you sign the contract today, we'll have your office ready for final inspection and occupancy by September twenty-fourth."

"Perfect, and I'm certain your company will handle it as well as you're handling my residential property. In fact, I picked you because I know you do good work."

"Thanks for your trust. We know that our current customers are our best source of new business. We'll do our best to meet or exceed your needs…"

Alonzo was doing his best to say the same, and although Eve was trying her best too, she was not as easy to handle as Irani. He was putting her back in bed after guiding her through an exercise session. Her face showed more fatigue than last time, and even with his guiding hands she struggled to get her feet under the sheet. Sitting next to her in AUC's isolation room, he gave her a minute to rest before talking.

"Look at it this way, you're stronger than a week ago. You'll do better tomorrow. Keep your spirits up."

"I'm trying, but I'd be permanently in the dumps if it weren't for you and Monet. I owe you, and I'll make it up when I regain my pep."

"I know you will. That's the type of person you are. Hey, do you remember much about Myers-Briggs personality tests? Nari says they're important to list on resumes and things."

"Don't you remember? We took those profiling tests junior year and I put them on our Stanford applications I'm ENTJ, the commander or field marshal type, and you're ENFP, the campaigner or champion. I'd say that you've grown into yours during our desert trek, but I've been put out of commission."

"We'll get you back in action, and Nari says she'll call Indira for you as soon as you feel a bit better."

"That's nice of her, but I'm not a mental invalid. I should call for you and me. Maybe she has some ideas for what we should do when we get outta Cairo. If you get me my cell phone, I'll do it now. That'll be better than sitting here staring at the walls."

"I always have it with me when I'm visiting you. Are you gonna practice before calling?"

"No, I don't have the energy. I'm just gonna wing it."

The cell phone's built-in camera had less scope than her tablet's, but it was enough for Indira to gauge Eve's predicament. She spoke after Eve explained what she needed.

"I sympathize with your condition, but how nice that Alonzo is giving you such thorough care. You've demonstrated over the course of the summer your grittiness. Keep faith in yourself.

"I know that both you and Alonzo won't be attending Stanford this fall, and that poses a problem. However, I have an associate that will soon be your liaison for dealing with me, and I'll be sure to –"

"Is it Rani? I've gotten to know him better."

Indira's pause told Eve that she had made a blunder. "I'm sorry, Miss Indira. I shouldn't have interrupted." Indira's calm voice reassured her.

"I've come to know you better as well. You're fine. And as I was saying, I will be sure to inform your contact of your and Alonzo's situation. And to remove the suspense, your contact will be a woman by the name of Irani. You might find her personality a bit easier to deal with than Rani's. But that will be for you to decide. Please call me if you need assistance before Irani calls you. Until then, you and Alonzo should stay healthy and safe. Goodbye."

Irani disconnected. Alonzo had heard every word and added his.

"You did great. Sometimes winging it can be better than rehearsing. By the time this Irani lady calls, we'll have you up and ready for action. After all, Myers-Briggs says I'm your champion. I've already shown you what I can do, and I'm getting better too, just like you…"

Chapter 28
Saturday, September 24, 2157

<u>"Washington Roundup"</u>

Electra drove early Saturday morning on streets she had often driven to Rock Creek Park, but this would be the first time to her new office building. By the time she parked in her reserved space and stepped to the reception area to meet Sylvia, she already had her Irani persona engaged.

"Good morning, Miss Ramani, and welcome to our Carr Workspaces property. Here's your entry badge for the building and office, and a supply of business cards. And when inspecting your new office, please look in the fridge for a more traditional move-in gift."

"Why, thank you. I know that your Saturdays are always busy, so why don't we go our separate ways? I'm ready to begin settling in."

"That's very thoughtful of you, but please call me if our people at the reception area can't take care of whatever you need. Enjoy your day."

Electra made the call forty-five minutes later, but it could be heard only in her head.

Sylvia exceeded my expectations, not only by letting me move in on the date she promised, but also by putting me in her property that's in the Friendship Heights section of Chevy Chase. Getting here's a pleasant drive, and the location has quick access to the Capitol and all supporting airports. My office has a restful, third-floor view and there are parks with running trails nearby.

I like the furniture, just the right touch of uncluttered hi-tech features but still user-friendly, and my office phone is already working. I also have an unlisted cell phone that Indira can make

hackproof, and perhaps best of all, my personal fridge is stocked with Coke, a selection of hearty cheeses, and Sylvia's gift, a bottle of Champaign, while my private cupboard has All Bran, Oreos, crackers, and honey. I'll bring a half gallon of skim milk when I plan to stay for a couple of days, plus a pillow and blanket I'll keep here.

What have I overlooked?... I know, a change of leisure and workout clothes. Easy to remedy. The office has enough storage space. I'm going to spend the rest of the day right here, collecting information and tracing events in my DC consulting areas of interest. I've already walked the lobby and outdoor space, so I'll start my Washington-related roundup right after I grab a snack.

Electra warmed up for her afternoon search by looking for suitable consulting organizations to join.

Networking works online and in-person, and for the consulting profession, Washington, DC is Mecca. My Website explains why my boutique practice will outperform the major players in my area of expertise. I'll pick two, one whose members come from the broader population of small to mid-sized corporations and another where they are the major players. I can introduce myself up close and in person, and before I do I'll introduce Irani to some of Alisha's schmoozing skills. How nice the lightning brain lets me access different personas whenever I want.

She made her picks twenty minutes later.

I'll go with the American Society of Association Executives – aka ASAE – for small to mid-size company networking, and I'll pick the International Council of Management Consulting Institutes – aka ICMCI – for targeting my friendly competitors. They'll be able to connect me to business or government entities that fit. And there should be opportunities for alliances on specific projects where my expertise is needed.

Electra started her roundup by searching for current events related to economics, social trends, local and international politics, and traced backwards from those she thought most important. They formed a branching but interconnected network of events that would confound most consulting analysts, but Electra found the pattern after three hours of piecing the phenomena together.

What I see confirms what I knew twenty years ago. Neuroscience says we are social animals whose DNA tells us to act sometimes in our own best interests, and sometimes in the group's. But we aren't equipped to handle the accelerating pace of life and the uncertainties it brings. And I'm not surprised that old problems haven't been solved while new ones keep coming.

America is still struggling to reduce income inequality and grow the middle class and the number of jobs while reining in the power of Big Data platform companies and potential collusion among them and the Government. Our increasingly networked society can empower each person but Social Media and fake news can be stumbling blocks.

Recurring episodes of police brutality and local government missteps have led to All Lives Matter and Local Authority Defunding movements. Other incidents have shown that the elites in Academia, Politics, and Business are often out of touch with Main Street, causing the people to disrespect the government and call for changes that are certainly needed but sometimes resulting in steps that go too far.

And on the world stage, nations are still searching for solutions to immigration, dignity and rights as well intellectual property protection. All this while emerging superpowers rise and biotech and AI sweep in changes that bring improvements but also threaten to marginalize what it means to be human. Meanwhile, climate change issues remain, but at least the doom-and-gloomsters have been forced to push back the date of Armageddon.

And a new conundrum has been added, courtesy of a series of pandemics. Now we have shelter-in-place, social distancing, and lockdowns that are meant to protect us from new types of disease. They have accelerated distance learning and work-at-home while reshaping how economies function. All this can be good, but the challenge is keeping the economy and people's livelihoods alive. No wonder Americans are afraid of the future and distrust most politicians and so-called experts.

All of the above are being driven by Globalization, Climate Change, Big Data, and the interplay between Government and Business, as well a hi-tech issues. Angus McTear had some of them, their repercussions, and possible solutions covered in his Bridge President platform that got him elected. Poor Angus, he holds two records, one for the largest number of days in the Oval Office without being elected, and another for the smallest after winning the election.

He died twenty years ago. There must have been books or articles written about him in the intervening years. I'll search and compare what they say with what I think. And my analysis is better than any because I was the power behind his throne. But let's see what political history has recorded.

An hour later she had the results.

As expected, there are always crackpot outlier opinions, but the good ones eventually coalesce into a simulacrum of the truth. My reality is the best, but I came across a remarkable article written five years ago and titled Angus McTear: The Greatest American "Almost" President.

It salutes McTear's charismatic dedication to placing country ahead of person and his efforts to rein in some of President Gardner's extreme positions, and it also balances Gardner's mistakes against his accomplishments. Coming back to McTear, the article's points match many that I made. And no wonder, Carter Quavah coauthored it. I must google the person Carter collaborated with, a D.K. Gooden. A quick search uncovered that D.K. Gooden is a Ms. Delilah Kappa Gooden, who is alive and living in the DC area. A highly regarded political historian earlier in her career, she had fallen from grace because of accusations that she had stretched the truth and plagiarized material without properly footnoting it. Out-of-court settlements quashed interest in the kerfuffle; she retreated to DC's consulting fringe and working diligently, eventually repairing her reputation.

I like her tenacity. There are at least two sides to any accusation, but I won't go there when or if I meet her. Carter's my focus.

Electra was about to power down and leave for the day when another person from the past floated into her present thoughts, Professor Ravenhill, her longtime academic advisor.

He'd be nearly ninety if still alive, but if I can talk to him, I might get a better peek at the state of university science and technology than what the media pushes. I'll google him maybe tomorrow, but I've done enough for today. I'll go home and then run. That'll help me put away all I learned today.

It did and it also reenergized her for Sunday. She loaded the car with leisure and workout clothes and stopped to buy milk before driving back to her office.

I've got my day planned. I'll research two additional topics and then call Gooden and Ravenhill. And then I'll test the nearby running trails if the gorgeous sunrise weather lasts.

The additional topics were those that probably hadn't changed much in twenty years. In fact, they hadn't changed much in the hundred preceding years, but Electra's unquenchable intellectual curiosity made her check anyway.

She polished off philosophy first.

My post-post-modern philosophy that I've named Quantum+NeuroSci-Extended Deconstructed Emergent Post-Kantian/Pragma/Phenomenological Synthesis – or

QNS-Edep-K/P/P Synthesis to make it catchier – is better than what most post-modern professional philosophers spout. Mine is optimistic, practical, and pragmatic, and it can help people get on with their lives, but I misspoke when I said catchier. Most people are too busy to play catch with philosophy. But they don't have to with mine. Just apply some common sense to the guidelines given by Neuroscience and be done with it.

Pleased with what she had accomplished, she researched current trends in Religion. It took longer, but Electra drew conclusions two hours later.

America continues becoming more secular and less religious, but our country still has more faith than Western Europe. A belief in a higher being that can explain the unknowable is programmed in our DNA, but America is transforming Religion from traditional institutional beliefs to a more personal, intuitive system that picks and chooses what works best. Of the big three – Christianity, Judaism, and Islam – Islam holds the most influence with its followers because it is interwoven into politics.

And there are three godless approaches that have some traction. One is a Techno-Utopian Transhuman vision, and another is an End-of-Days Social Justice Activism. And a third is an Atavistic Nihilistic White Nationalist Movement dubbed the Alt-right that should fade away like the color it promotes. People of Color are taking up more and more of our demographics, and the saying that Demographics is Destiny is irrefutable.

So there, I've done enough for a Sunday morning. I'll suit up and run, then come back for a snack before I call Gooden and Ravenhill. The run did quadruple duty. Not only did it calm down her obsessive-compulsive attitude and let her plan her upcoming calls, but it also let her test the fitness center and nearby jogging trails. They too exceeded her expectations; she returned to her office feeling even better than after a routine run, and ready to call Professor Ravenhill after a peanut butter and honey sandwich accompanied by a Coke.

I've already confirmed he's a professor emeritus who keeps current; it's time to dial away.

When an aged voice said hello, Electra detected some of Professor Ravenhill's tart personality lurking just beneath.

"Am I speaking with Professor Ravenhill? And whether you are or aren't, I hope you are doing well."

"Yes yes, you are and I am. And who's calling?"

"My name is Irani Ramani. An associate of mine, Electra Kittner, suggested I call. She thought your opinion would be helpful. Have I called at a convenient time?"

When he spoke after a pause longer than what Electra had normally encountered, his voice sounded a note of whimsical curiosity.

"Now there's an extraordinary person, one of the few I ever misjudged. She was much smarter than she let on. She had a knack for putting clever spins on topics I had her research. The last time I saw her, she stomped all over a pair of pretenders – one of those high-energy physicists and a philosopher crony. It was a great show actually. Everyone at the meeting applauded silently. I'm sorry to say she didn't keep in touch. Do you talk to her? If you do, please give her my best. But what opinion do you want?"

"I don't speak with her often. She's often out of the country. However, she and I collaborated on a project several years ago, and she always spoke highly of your insight into scientific trends. Would you be willing to venture an opinion regarding fundamental versus applied technology in the areas of energy, biotechnology, or artificial intelligence?"

"Those are areas she researched for me twenty years or so ago, and what she found out then still holds. All that high-energy quantum physics mumbo jumbo never came back from the black hole it dug for itself. Its only current extension is into Quantum

Computers. And energy technology today is still reaching for positive energy output from thermonuclear reactors. Green or renewable energy and fuel cells powering cars on the Hydrogen Highway towards a full-scale Hydrogen Economy aren't in anyone's offing. The only fundamental progress being made is in neuroscience."

"Yes, Electra Kittner was smart then and is smart today."

"Sometimes too smart, although she tried to hide it. I remember she once gave a talk that explained her theories, something about the Explosion Principle, Asymptotic Limits, and the brain's inability to understand Language and the concept of infinity. I nodded my head along with a handful of people who stayed to the end, but no one understood. I trust she didn't babble about this with you. Everyone found her ideas unsettling. What did you say your name is?"

"Irani Ramani, and no, we covered other topics. Well, I want to thank you for talking with me. Your opinion jibes with some of what I've dug out, but talking to someone like yourself, who's still near the front lines of scientific research, always gets me closer to the truth. Please stay healthy and safe. Here's my Website address and phone number if you would like to contact me."

"Yes yes Kittner, uh Ramani, be glad to. Now go keep busy." Electra gave him the pleasure of disconnecting the call.

I'm happy he's still alive and doing well. I like his opinions about science trends, but I like even more his unfiltered thoughts about Electra. Those are the most truthful views I can get. And I expect to get the same regarding Carter when I call Delilah Gooden, but I better practice my pitch first. If my luck holds, I can cross the final task of today's list.

A pleasant-sounding voice announcing the expected name greeted Irani.

"Good afternoon. My name is Irani Ramani, a consultant who recently returned from an extended overseas assignment to open an office in Chevy Chase. While doing some current research, I came across your paper, Angus McTear: The greatest American 'Almost' President. I'm calling to compliment your clear writing and accurate conclusions and was hoping you might spend a few minutes talking to me. Would now be suitable?"

"Of course. What would you like to ask?"

"An associate of mine knew the fellow who coauthored your article, a Mister Carter Quavah. She worked on assignments with him about twenty years ago but has been overseas ever since. When she learned that I was relocating to DC, she asked me to look him up, but I found out he and his partner died in a helicopter crash eight months ago. Then, when reading your article, I spotted his name, so I thought you might be able to tell me what you remember about him. I'd be happy to take you to dinner."

"No, I'd rather talk by phone. I'm concerned about that Egyptian virus spreading, and you didn't say where overseas you were stationed, so I'll err on the side of caution. If and when it blows over, I'll be happy to meet you in person. By any chance, is your associate named Electra Kittner?"

"Why yes, how did you guess?"

"I got to know Carter over the last fifteen years because we collaborated on several assignments. He often mentioned Kittner's uncanny ability to ferret out information. If you and she are associates, you must be talented. Maybe we can help one another after you settle in. But go ahead, ask me about Carter."

"Electra told me he was a cerebral type who combined good linguistic and number skills. Did he stay that way, or did he loosen up?"

"He was that way always, a classic economist. I think that's why he and his partner, Buffy Gunstein, did so well. She was hard charging and brought in clients who hired them for additional assignments once they saw what a great number crunching analyst he was."

"I'm glad they were successful. Did you ever see them in social settings? Did they appear to be happy? I ask because Electra mentioned he liked to ponder the philosophical issue of happiness."

"I don't know, but they seemed to enjoy each other's company, and I did notice how totally engaged he could get while working. Isn't that an indication of happiness, or at the very least, as a sign that you're enjoying life?"

"I might think so too. Well, I know you have better things to do on Sunday than talk to someone you don't know very well, so I'll say goodbye. And my offer for lunch is always open."

"I'd like that. Why don't we swap Website addresses? I'll help you network once we know each other better. Here's mine, and please tell me yours…"

After ending the call, Electra recapped what a singular Sunday this had been.

I'm on a roll. Everything I touched today came up a winner. I've got milk in the fridge… should I spend the night?… I think I will, that'll let me test the sleeper sofa. And I'll work here tomorrow planning for my visit to the Pequot reservation. If I do it right, I can complete my roundup of Washington assets and visits this week. And I've driven to Stonington so many times that I've memorized the route as well as the name of the motel I always stay the night before. I bet it's still there; the Connecticut countryside should stay pretty much the same, even after a twenty-year stretch. And I'll revisit tomorrow my grand Native American Plan and review it Tuesday afternoon on the drive, which will give me plenty of time to do that in addition to prepping for the Wednesday morning meeting.

The weather and leaves turned more autumnal the farther northeast Electra drove, highlighting the actual as well as cultural distance between Native American tribes and the Capitol.

Tribes have been overlooked and underserved, I launched a plan that would help them as well as myself, and I think it was – and still is – pretty clever. Hud and Su, by hiring and training local people, set up our biotech lab and drug manufacturing facilities on the Pequot reservation because the Government can't meddle on Native American lands. Tribes are distinct nations. And Hud coordinated via Pequot's Doctor Bettje Holbrook and Seminole's Dyani Hache the construction of Indian reservation eye clinics located on other reservations. Dyani also added our Cyber-Theaters to participating casinos. Hud also managed western reservations' rare earths mines plus Martian and Solar Panel farms, making barren lands productive and hiring reservation people.

Hud and the Pequot's Chief Armstrong were the guiding hands behind a long-term plan to build a nation of Tribes within America, and I was the power behind their thrones. I won't know how all the above is proceeding until I meet Hud's admin assistant when I go to Austin week after next. I'm sure most of my plan has unraveled, but according to Indira, the assistant has kept the pieces running after Hud's death.

What I want to do tomorrow and Thursday is meet Chief Armstrong's successor – that's Feather Trueson – and the person managing the production facility. I'll tell them that I'm reopening the lab, but of course no one except Indira and I know the inner workings of our Deus Lab.

It's time to take a cognitive break. I'll practice tonight what I'll say when we meet in what used to be Chief Armstrong's office at the tribal community building.

Irani made one comment to herself before knocking on Feather's door at 9 a.m.

Everything I've seen so far looks like I've stepped out of a time machine. I'm not going to guess what I'll find when I step inside. I'll make the most with whatever's there.

Two minutes later she was sitting at an office-sized table. Feather, thirty-something and dressed like a young professional, sat at the head and the plant manager, a similarly-aged fellow dressed in a standard drug manufacturing gown sat adjacent. Feather had already made introductions, leaving an opportunity for Irani to speak.

"Thank you for meeting with me. I'm here to introduce myself and explain what I would like to do. We are all saddened by Mister Haller's death, and I have been appointed to manage his businesses. From what I've learned so far, he and Chief Armstrong coordinated an overall strategy and left the operational details to the Chief and his people. You've taken over for the Chief and I plan to do pretty much the same that Mister Haller did, but with only one difference. I'll reopen the mothballed lab because I plan to do R&D here, and possibly in Austin too. I plan to meet with Mr. Haller's administrative assistant week after next when I visit Austin. Are my intentions satisfactory?"

"Why yes. You probably know something about business activities among other tribes, and we can go into those details after you come back from Austin. But I like your approach. When will you have the lab reactivated?"

"I don't have a time and events schedule finalized, but February of next year is realistic. I won't take up too much of your time because I know you're busy, but I thought your plant manager could take me on a tour and give me what I need to open the lab and come and go. And may I take both of you to lunch afterwards?"

"That'll work. And how about spending an hour afterwards so I can give you a summary of everything. That way, you have a good basis for comparison when you travel to Austin."

"Now that's a plan I can live with. And looking forward, we should meet like this once a quarter."

"I like that. Well, it's time for your tour to begin. James, please do the honors…"

The drive back to DC gave Electra all the quiet time needed for the lightning brain to freewheel wherever it wanted to go.

Information converted into knowledge leading to wisdom is a chain of timeless power. The Greek Philosophers knew this long before I came along, but perhaps I can take the information chain to the next level. My twenty-year hiatus, when compared to the millenia since the Golden Age of Greece, is barely a ripple in time, so I should be able to reactivate my Native American Plan at a suitable pace when the right people are all in place. Where will I find them?

Serendipity has served me well before, and I have no reason to doubt that it won't once more…

Chapter 29
Wednesday, October 12, 2157

<u>"Austin Roudup"</u>

"I commend how you rounded up and organized all your Washington assets, information, and contacts, and how thoroughly you adjusted your Austin roundup accordingly. You contacted Hud's administrative assistant early enough for her to arrange tomorrow's teleconference. I'm pleased she greeted you at the airport. What do you make of her so far?"

"Her handshake matches her proportions and looks. Strong yet friendly. That's good for relating to our field managers."

And then she drove you to Hudson's house, which is the best place for you to stay. Su-Lin inherited his estate, including house and vehicles. All that will become yours soon because her condition continues to decline."

Noticing Electra's twitch of a grimace, Indira paused for her to speak.

"That's why I won't bother her on this trip. I want to collect everything and get all the parts organized before I see her when I return in a couple of weeks. But please contact me immediately if an emergency arises."

"I shall, and I will leave you to finalize your agenda. There are more than enough items to cover, but you are the best multi-tasker I know."

"Do you know the essential attributive adjective and accompanying adverb you omitted?"

"Of course, I'm simply engaging in word games with you. You tell me."

"Merely mortal. And you know what I'll say, so please tell me."

"I resemble that remark. Well please carry on."

"Indira's avatar flashed a smile before vanishing, leaving Electra in the presence of her own thoughts.

Returning to Austin is like a second homecoming. So many memories, but no hard blows to my emotions, only a gentle remembrance of all the good. So, what should I do now? I know, I'll exercise to get the kinks out of sitting so long on the plane, drive Hud's car for some takeout Tex-Mex, and then come back to snack and itemize my agenda.

Electra was back at a workstation in Hud's home office an hour later. Half an hour after that, she had the agenda finished.

AGENDA

1. Explain my role to the Admin Assistant (Kim).

2. Let her run the teleconference.

3. Find and organize all additional information and assets.

4. Inspect Neuro-Device Lab (Tim Godfrey and Kwame Chyral) Hardware: Cyber-Theater, Neuro-Knitter, Brain Probe Software: Internet Security (Defense Offense)

5. Inspect Biotech Lab (Su and Kameyo Kato) Drugs: Vaccines Alzheimer's DNA: Cloning Modification

6. Develop my Grand Management Structure.

7. Summarize for Kim what she needs to know.

8. Fly back to DC.

There's enough here for two days, and I'll extend to three if necessary. Air travel is still OK. America hasn't panicked like other countries. We're not going into shelter-in-place or lockdown mode until there's more evidence that the Cairo outbreak is spreading farther.

I think I'll search through online directories to get a head start. Thanks to Indira, I already know the file structures and passwords. The more I practice, the more I remember my hacking techniques, but Indira's hacking is beyond mere mortals. And that's good for our team. And I'll stop sooner rather than later. No reason to become obsessive-compulsive.

Two hours later, Electra logged off and went to bed, ready for Irani to take charge tomorrow.

Irani arrived a half-hour before the 9 a.m. teleconference start time in order to summarize how she would like to run Hud's businesses. After listening to Irani's intentions, Kim's relieved smile told her that Kim was a "keeper."

"Thank you for the compliment. I'm doing the best I can keeping Mr. Haller's business operations in order, but your offer to help is needed. I can handle basic administrative duties by myself, but I need you to hire some people to work with me, especially for the hi- tech pieces. And like you said, I'll keep doing what I'm doing until you figure out who or what to add. How soon do you think that'll be?"

"No later than January, but that's a soft deadline. Results-to-date show that Hud put the right people in the field, and you're coordinating what they're doing. I want you to run the telecon meeting as you normally do. Introduce me at the start. I'll say 'Hi' and then sit and listen as you explain that they should expect business as usual because they're hitting operational goals. Then have each operations manager review the highlights in this order, opportunities, threats, and next steps. And wrap up by telling them to submit their 2158 Plan to you by December 15th for you and me to review. I will visit them in the field sometime in the first quarter."

"Sounds good, anything else?"

"Let's grab a Coke and have you start the telecon in five minutes." Irani played her part, talking only to herself.

From what I can see and hear, it looks like Hud put the right people in the field. They're practical types who roll up their sleeves and get things done. And all business operations – oil production, solar panel and Martian farms, and rare earths mines – have enough complexity to keep the managers engaged yet interchangeable.

Kim ended the meeting on schedule two hours later, waiting for Irani's comments.

"Nice work. You ran the hardware and software like a pro, and you kept the meeting moving while holding the managers' attention. Two hours is an upper limit, but I imagine the meeting was this long today because of me. No matter, you ended the meeting soon enough."

"Thanks, what's next?"

"I should be OK working on my own. I'll go through the Neuro-Device Lab first and then the Biotech Lab. If I need help, I'll ask. I should be finished by tomorrow afternoon, and I promise to meet with you before I leave."

"Good, and I'd like to drive you back to the airport."

"Well in that case, we'll hold our meeting at a Tex-Mex restaurant of your choosing. Bye for now…"

After returning to Hud's house, Electra switched out of the Irani mode and into shorts and an athletic T before using the fitness equipment in his office.

Good ole Hud must have stuck to my advice all the way to end of days. This cross trainer looks and feels new. And since he's not here to defend himself, I will. It looks new because he took care of it, like he took care of all his assets and people, not because he didn't use it. After I work out and cool down, I'll grab a snack and then continue searching directories.

Electra spent the entire afternoon tracing chronologically through Tim and Kwame's files and summarizing what was needed.

They must have worked together when putting entries in their logs. The notes contain a blend of personal and work-related items. Hud provided a perfect work environment and guidance for the guys to make the most of their autistic-empowered hardware and software skills, and they repaid him through loyalty-enhanced performance.

And they say they did their best in spite of my disappearing act. Tim did make incremental improvements to the Cyber-Theater and Neural Knitter, enough to keep that part of the business profitable. Not surprising because virtual reality and extreme sports markets continue to grow.

But their network security apps are a different story. Without me and my Katrina Blanka disguise and her CAT software virtual company, the competition passed them by. But a recent log entry outlines two apps they wanted to develop for cracking the social media and personal computing market. They talk about a potential killer app they call the Cyber-Secretary. First iteration would handle a person's Emails... read, classify, store, and answer them... second iteration would extend to cell phone calls. It's a great concept, but I don't think AI technology is at the level that can implement it. Of course, Indira can, and maybe she'll help me develop it if it fits our plan.

And the other one, which is more futuristic, catches my fancy. It's a combination of hardware and software they call the Sensory Translator. A particular sensory stimulus is input, Beethoven's Fifth Symphony would be a good example. Then you select an output mode, like painting, and the device outputs what's been requested. They also outlined an input setting labeled Null Input that allows the device to read a theme selection file for outputting a particular result. For example, make the settings for the translator to write a poem about happiness. I'll have to discuss all this with Indira. She'll know what's state-of-the-art today. I think we'll keep the Lab open.

As for me, I'm downshifting to a more relaxed state until tomorrow. Electra awoke at 4 a.m. and after an abbreviated workout and bowl of cereal dived into Su's directories. As expected, tree structures were easy to search and the documents they contained were meticulously written and maintained; as also expected, the chronology traced an inverse correlation between results and Su's health.

Su and Kameyo used what I left behind to make marginal T-Plague vaccine improvements, but they were unable to take them to the next level for Alzheimer's. The log also says Kameyo departed for Japan to take care of her parents. And even with some of the suggestions Indira gave Su, she never mastered cloning or DNA modifications. She quit after two iterations of cloning. And it says… Jesus, it says she cloned two sets of twins using my eggs. She even named them… Nari and Nila for the first set, and Alonzo and Evita for the second. My god, the extraction team Indira sent are my biological children. I must ask Indira when she planned to tell me. Let me collect my thoughts first. I'll have another breakfast while I digest what I've just uncovered.

Electra invoked Indira's GUI an hour later and spoke first.

"I've reviewed enough of Su-Lin's logs to learn that my extraction team members are clones of me. When were you planning to let me know?"

"You've already been hit with enough revelations that could overwhelm your emotions. I wanted to find a time that I thought appropriate, but now that you know, would you please tell me how you feel?"

Electra saw and heard more empathy in Indira's voice and expression than ever before.

Gads, maybe Indira is learning from me as I am learning from her. That's another good reason why we're partnering.

"Only curious. From my limited exposure, they seem better than the stumblebums I mistook them for at the start. I'd like to give them the personal touch. Maybe they do have some of my traits."

"I am pleased you said that, because I alerted them to expect a new person instead of me to be their contact going forward. I will let you know when before I tell them that you are the chosen one."

"Good. I want to finish reading Su-Lin's logs and then outline my grand organization structure before flying home."

"I shall leave you to it, and I apologize for not telling sooner about your clones. I underestimated how quickly you would regain your former powers, but now I know you are back cognitively and emotionally. Please let me know how your fitness training is progressing."

"I'm certain you remember a quote from the 19th century French doctor by the name of Emile Coue, 'Every day in every way I'm getting better and better.' That's my attitude too."

"I am pleased. Carry on."

Indira's GUI left Electra alone to do just that. She finished reviewing Su's logs and then skimmed one more time while she had a clear organizational picture in her head.

I don't need Su's Austin Lab. I'll mothball it next time I come to Austin. All I need is one grand organization structure that covers DC and Austin and assigns people to manage the components. I'll start with my Proposed Business Structure diagram and add, rearrange, or combine boxes before plugging in people.

Electra decided fifteen minutes later that it only needed to be relabeled; fifteen minutes after that she had all the new hires plugged in. She peered at her handiwork one more time before saving it.

Grand Organization Structure

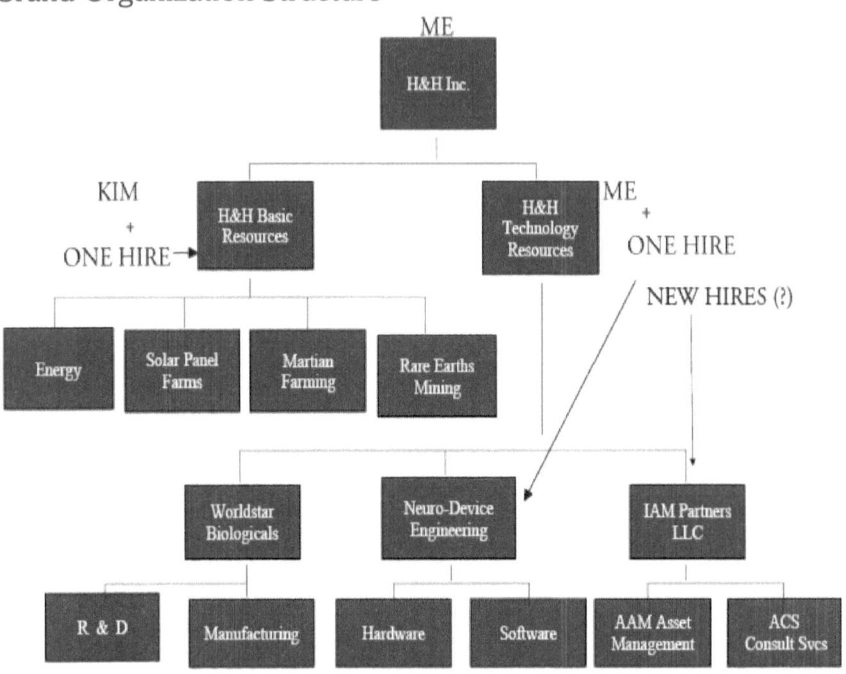

I can't be more precise than this. I'll have to hire at least two people and let them have at it before I can adjust further. But something I can do is tweak all company logos. I'm going to add a golden lightning bolt cutting vertically through existing logos. Its apparent symbolism links to random event strikes that we're prepared to handle, but only I will know its deeper meaning.

I'll use it for customizing corporate appreciation tokens that I'll give to all my people. For women, they'll be gold lightning bolt earrings like mine, and for men they'll be onyx-stone gold signet rings. I'll have a DC jeweler make a dozen of each. That's more than I need for my current employee list, but I plan to grow.

Whew, I'm exhausted, I guess because I've done all I can on this trip. I'm packing it in and flying back early. I'll call Kim when I get to the airport. No need for her to shuttle me around.

Electra hustled enough to catch the noon flight to DC; then she rested all the way home.

Chapter 30
Thursday, October 20, 2157

<u>"Siblings' SOS"</u>

Nila punched the off button on her tablet hard enough to rattle the flex desk she was working on.

"The only success I've had since coming back to Boston is getting my driver's license. Getting better at tennis doesn't count. These online Q&A sessions are so disorganized."

Nari's glum expression telegraphed the same sentiment.

"I wish I could report better results, but no such luck. These non-credit courses are so boring… I just can't force myself to listen. My mind wanders too much to get anything higher than a B-minus on the quizzes or papers. I can feel my academic sharpness slipping away."

Nila's nod said she agreed.

"Me too. The joy of learning has morphed into drudgery. But my academic advisor tells me I have to earn at least Bs and get a good recommendation from my community outreach project leader if I want to be reinstated for the winter term."

"My advisor has sort of gone silent. I don't want to force the issue with her, but if we're not fulltime students next term I don't know what Indira's going to say."

"Do you think she'll cut off our money? I hope not. We'll have to apply for government food entitlements if she does. Our temp jobs pay peanuts. You better call her. We need her help."

"Let's talk it over with Alonzo first. The four of us need to present a united front. We can add it to this week's call agenda. Indira has to cut him some slack… he's got bigger problems than we do. It's too late to call him tonight, so let's do it as scheduled tomorrow morning. Come on, let's have supper while watching the news."

A supper consisting of ramen noodles in chicken broth mixed with peas and carrots plus fruit cocktail for dessert satisfied Nila better than current events. The more she watched, the more puzzled she looked.

"Shelter in place is getting closer and closer. If the WHO can't do a better job diagnosing and tracking whatever's coming out of Egypt, the problems we've got now are gonna get worse. And poor Alonzo and Eve. If Cairo goes into lockdown mode, they'll be stuck no matter if Eve's out of quarantine. I guess we'll find out tomorrow…" Alonzo's Thursday had been typical: calling before breakfast to check Eve's condition and scheduling his morning according to how she felt. She continued testing positive, but her condition had stabilized. Unfortunately, he had been unable to build back her strength, and a combination of meager appetite and continual upset stomach kept her underweight.

The clinic staff appreciated his caregiving stint, but only Monet knew the depth of his commitment. Every night she did her best to be Alonzo's empathetic best friend, always there to listen before making suggestions. Tonight was no different as they sat in Monet's room and talked.

"I am happy you are taking an online Stanford noncredit course. You need to have a diversion that keeps your mind active, just like me. And I'm lucky I can do all my courses online. I just hope you get Eve out of quarantine before Cairo goes into lockdown mode."

Alonzo nodded before replying.

"It's a race, I guess. What's faster, Eve's recovery or the spread of the Pharaoh's plague?" But thanks to you, I'm pushing ahead."

"How are your other sisters doing? Aren't you supposed to talk with them tonight?"

"No, tomorrow. I'd like to take you out someplace this evening, but that damn shelter in place keeps everyone pinned down. You're taking a big risk sticking around when you don't have to."

"It's not that big, and besides, you're worth it."

"Thanks, and you make sure to be with me tomorrow when Nari calls. I want you to listen in…"

They were in the same place when Nari's call came in. After exchanging hellos, Nari launched into her agenda.

"I know you've got bigger problems than Nila and me, but we're concerned Indira's going to cut off our money supply because we're not fulltime students. And if she does, we'll be hurting because the job market is tough. Have you talked with her about this?"

"No, but I owe her a call to report on Eve. Tell you what, I'll call her and report what all of us are doing, and then I'll ask if she'll help us. Maybe she'll respond to our SOS."

"Eve needs the most help, how's she doing?"

After Alonzo unloaded, Nari ended the call fifteen minutes later.

"Well, keep doing what you're doing, and we will too. And call us after you talk with Indira. Bye-bye."

Monet talked after Nari signed off.

"Nari's call was more pleasant than sometimes. Do you wish to call Indira tonight?"

"No, I won't push my luck. How about I call tomorrow morning after you finish your online seminar?"

"Why not call right after breakfast? That will get the task out of the way first thing."

"OK, I'll come get you at 8 a.m. See you then…"

Early morning Cairo news made for a more pressing call to Indira. Local authorities declared lockdown. Indira listened patiently to Alonzo's news regarding all issues affecting all siblings before replying.

"I will arrange for you and Eve to fly home. Tell the Bose twins to keep doing what they're doing. I will discuss future funding plans when all of you are gathered together."

"That's great, but how will you get us out of here?"

"That is no concern of yours. Just go about your daily routine. The person I send to extract you will explain everything. Best wishes until then."

Electra didn't need help; in fact, she might become the provider. She had several calls waiting on her business voice mail when she returned from Austin. She had responded promptly but no one picked up, so she left a message asking them to please call back to discuss how she could contribute to potential consulting assignments.

Playing phone tag didn't bother Electra; she could multi-task from her new office while waiting for calls. She sifted through "Contact Us" Emails that had accumulated in her consulting business Website. My press release found its target. It generated enough Website hits to get viewers aware and interested in IAM Consulting. I'll respond to find out what assignments might be in my future. I can add these new contacts to the list I've begun building. I might need to hire some assistants sooner than I thought. If I can find the right people, I can plug back into the DC sociopolitical scene early next year.

Electra had just updated the list when her office phone rang. She switched to her Ramani persona before answering

"Good morning, this is Irani Ramani for IAM Consulting. How may I assist you?"

"It's Delilah. You sound like a polished pro. Hey, when can we meet for lunch? I have an upcoming assignment that could use your researching expertise."

"Thanks for considering me. I'd like that. Let's pick a time…"

After ending the call, Electra picked up where she had left off. But not for long. A second call came in, this one from a Professor

Ravenhill referral. Electra handled it as she had done for the previous one.

What fun! I love it when a plan comes together. But I better be careful. I don't want to overpromise what I can do. I'll need to get good assistants before I take on too many assignments. But that's a good problem to have. Well, it's time for a Coke break.

Indira's GUI opened a new screen before she could get up.

"Please bring that Coke back. I have an assignment that you may find too good to refuse."

"You've been listening in, have you? Good. How do you like what you've heard?"

"That's why I'm contacting you. Grab a Coke, then settle down, sit still, and let me explain."

"OK, you already know my answer." Indira continued minutes later.

"We have a win-win-win opportunity, but it will require you to return to our fortress, which means you will need to contact you're A-Team."

"I can do that. They did well the last time. What's the plan?"

Two members of your erstwhile extraction team, Alonzo and Eve, need to be extracted from Cairo. Alonzo assures me Eve has recovered enough to travel, but we must act ASAP. Cairo is in lockdown mode. I have devised a plan, but tell me what yours would be."

"Hmm, you mentioned the Popper's fortress. I guess I'll use it as my staging area. And I'll assume my Rani identity for handling actual extraction. And I can't dump them in Austin or Stanford yet, so how does this sound? My A-Team will insert me at the oasis. You can remote pilot an ATV to pick me up. I come back to the fortress, get set, and then go back to the oasis for transfer to Cairo. You retrieve the ATV and tell Alonzo I'll find him by homing in on his cell phone. Tell him that Rani will reach him when he can, so he's gotta be ready to go whenever I get there. Then the A-Team takes us back to DC. Alonzo and Eve stay in my house, and I'll stay at my office or at my Pequot Lab. If all goes according to plan, they'll never know who Rani, Irani, and Electra are. I hope you've kept them in the dark."

"Of course, and it is all part of the win-win-win opportunity. You should consider having Irani become being their future contact. You'll have enough time to think this through while flying to and from, so you be the judge. And I'll leave it for you to determine all aspects of winning. How do you wish to proceed?"

"I'll contact my A-Team right away to set pickup in DC date. Then I wrap up or reschedule all appointments. And then I'm off to the races. I'll contact you as soon as I get to the fortress, or sooner if I need help. And please, please contact me if something comes up."

"You've covered just about everything. My only suggestion is for you to consider contingencies. But I'm sure that will be on your preparations list. So, without further ado, I shall say goodbye to you.

And you don't need best wishes or luck. You always make your own. And always remember, I am there to back you up."

Indira's GUI vanished. Electra elevated to a higher cognitive state as she charged into action.

Electra's planning unfolded flawlessly. Her A-Team contained different personnel than before, but they were just as skilled and approved her wearing a Hazmat suit that once again provided cover on the FedEx flight. Sitting alone midway to Cairo early Monday, October 24th, she had ample time to muse aloud while working on her tablet about all her good fortune.

"I've never had so much go my way so easily. Everything I want to do or plan is coming to fruition. I'm building a physical and cognitive power base that's better than any mere mortal has ever had, and it keeps expanding. I'm taking my catbird seat to the next level."

But a sudden doubt intruded, clouding her mood like a cloud flitting across the sun.

"But maybe that's bad. What's that saying… 'Power tends to corrupt, and absolute power corrupts absolutely.' Perhaps I don't deserve what's falling into my lap."

Indira's Gui snapped open.

"Electra, please don't fall into your philosophical overthinking trap. Let me remind you that you have moved beyond it. Furthermore, nothing has fallen into your lap. You have created all your good fortune."

"You're right, but every now and then I guess I need to be reminded."

"In that case, I shall read to you the letter from your Grandfather Satish. Do you recall when you first read it?"

"I do, on the flight from London back to DC, just after his funeral." "Please pay attention to its message:

'Dearest Granddaughter,

Karma let us meet very late in my current life. I had hoped for you to visit often so you could learn more about us, and we about you, but that is not to be. My time is short, and I must do the best with what is left.

Today is one of my better days, and I am instructing Chandra to give this envelope to you after I have left this lifetime. And if you have studied the Bhagavad Gita, you will know this was meant to be and is part of the cycle. With this letter will be two childhood pictures of your mother. You should have them. I can think of nothing I have that you would treasure more.

I sense Indira's presence in you, but something more as well. I have studied the Gita my entire life, and my letter contains teachings that harken to your essence. Had we more time, I would tell you more, but karma granted us only two meetings. Still, they are ample for me to make a beginning.

I sense that you are able to reshape yourself through the power of your will and are following your dharma, your cosmic order, through which you will find happiness by casting aside doubt. You are striving to serve others, and no one who does good work for others will ever come to a bad end. Your efforts are pure because they come from mind and heart. Someday, you will electrify the world. You shall command the lightning found in your soul and use it in amazing ways.

Do not mourn my passing. Death happens only to the body, which is of no consequence, for the soul is eternal. You and I shall pass through many lifetimes. And we are each the beginning, the middle, and the end of creation.

Always remember.'

Indira saw one tear trickle down Electra's cheek; she paused for a time before saying more.

"You must trust the goodness that Satish sensed you possess. And though my emotional persona is different from mere Humanity's, you can rely on my values if you need another lecture. Now put your philosophical musings away and get ready for more action."

"Yes, Mother, I shall obey."

Chapter 31
Tuesday, October 25, 2157

"The Return of Alonzo and Eve"

Electra checked her equipment one more time in preparation for A- Team extraction from the oasis.

All the Popper's gear fits underneath my hazmat suit. It's even lighter and easier to control than what I wore twenty years ago. I must do a complete inventory of the entire fortress after Indira helps me resupply it. Precisely how we'll use this hidden asset will depend on what our future plans hold, but no matter where they take me, the fortress will be a stop along the way. Time to synchronize with Indira.

Indira's GUI opened immediately.

"My chopper's approaching. All equipment is functional. I'm good to go. Tell Alonza to expect pickup sometime in the next forty-eight hours. Unless I run into problems, I contact you again when Cairo action completed and we've departed for DC."

"That's the plan, you're good to go. Let's make it so. I'll shuttle your ATV back to the fortress. You take care of the rest. And remember to treat the mission as a serious game, but a game nonetheless. I'll even play along using some of your favorite military slang. That's a 10-4, over."

Before strapping on her Rani game face, Electra finished the word game."

"Copy that, over and out."

Alonzo's cell phone buzzed him awake at 4 a.m. He lurched for it, hoping the call wasn't from the clinic. It wasn't; it was from Indira. She let him talk three minutes later.

"Yes, I understand. My forty-eight-hour extraction window opens now. Is it OK for me to tell Eve?"

"Yes, because she too must be ready to go. But tell no one else and just go about your normal routine. Keep your cell phone with you at all times. My contact is tracking it."

"What if the window closes and we're still here? Should I contact you?"

"No, I will contact you. Good luck."

Monet turned on a nightstand light after the call ended. "What was that all about?"

"A way out of Cairo for Eve and me. Someone is picking us up."

Monet sat up against the headboard and pulled her knees to her chest underneath the covers.

"When were you going to tell me?"

"I just found out and I'm not supposed to tell anyone, but that doesn't include you. You're special."

"Would you tell me when and where and who?"

"I would if I could, but I don't know any details, other than Eve and I must be ready to go anytime in the next two days."

"And then you will disappear from my life. I will be sorry when that happens."

Alonzo pulled himself up next to her and leaned her head against his shoulder.

"I'm not disappearing for good. If we aren't together, I'll call you when I'm picked up, and again as soon as I get resituated."

Monet kissed him on the lips before saying, "You are a good person in many ways. Eve is lucky to have you. Let's get dressed and visit her..."

Monet waited outside the AUC clinic because nurses would let only caregivers and staff enter. Alonzo slid a chair next to Eve's bed; a tap on her shoulder brought her to life. She sat up before talking.

"Why are you here so early? Did the nurses call you?" Alonzo leaned close before answering.

"Talk softly. No, but Indira did. She's arranged for someone to get us out of Cairo sometime in the next two days. We're supposed to be ready to go immediately, but until then act naturally. What do you need to bring?"

"I'll travel light; only you and whatever I'm wearing. But what about the Cairo lockdown? And who's picking us up?"

"I didn't ask about either. Indira said we'd know when it's time to go. How're you feeling?"

"Not sick, but I'm still weak and have no appetite. I guess that's good for you. I'll be easy to tote around. I hope this works."

"Don't worry, I won't drop you or the ball. I'll see you according to our usual routine, or when our contact gets me. And mum's the word…"

Alonzo had trouble keeping busy because he was too keyed up about approaching action. He called Monet late that afternoon.

"No word yet from my contact. I saw Eve just after lunch; she's calmer than me but I can tell she's excited to leave this place. Me too. So, how are you?"

"Why don't we meet in my room? I'll tell you then…"

Ever since retrieving their two Russian operatives, the covert operation controlling them had increased cell phone monitoring on its four targets. It knew about one infected by a virus – probably the same one that took down the Russians – and two that had departed for America. Only the fourth, an Alonzo Cortez, seemed worth listening to. The effort paid off today. The hacker alerted his handler. "Something's about to go down. Send assets to pick up Alonzo and Eve Cortez. Lock on to his cell phone to hunt for him."

"Got it. Nice work. I'll take it from here…"

Having just finished dinner in the cafeteria, Monet and Alonzo strolled outdoors, enjoying another mild and clear October evening. Even on AUC's campus, which had more lenient shelter-in-place protocols than public places, there were few people walking about, and nearly half they saw wore face masks.

Monet paused to glance skyward before talking.

"Wherever you go, the same moonglow falls on you as well as me. I shall remember that when recalling our time together."

"Please don't put me in your past tense. We have some control over where we're going and when. Maybe not so much right now, but pretty soon we will. Let's look in on Eve. We know for sure where she is."

Monet sat in the clinic's reception area while Alonzo checked. AUC's clinic had withstood better than most medical centers the initial wave of panic that swept Cairo two weeks earlier, and it seemed ghostly still by comparison. She distracted herself by glancing through a magazine but an approaching disturbance took its place. Two military-clad men marched through the reception area and towards the quarantine-posted doors in spite of the protests from an AUC security guard. One went in and the other stood guard outside. The AUC guard spoke harshly.

"You can't barge in here unless you show me some identification." "This is all I need."

The fake guard drew his weapon and fired one bullet into the other's chest, spilling him backwards. He turned towards Monet but stopped when his partner came out, leading Alonzo who had Eve on his back.

"We've got what we want, let's go."

Pointing his weapon at Monet, the fake guard said, "What about her?"

Alonzo saw what he meant and yelled, "She's with us." "OK, have her fall in line and follow."

The five-person procession marched out.

Three hours later, the two military men halted interrogating their three detainees when two civilian-clad people came into the room. They stood while everyone else remained sitting on two sides of the table. The older and more distinguished-looking spoke, his Russian- accented English easy to understand.

"So, you claim you don't know what happened after that fellow – Rani you call him – took your Russian friends away? And now you say that someone called Indira is sending someone to retrieve you, but you don't know who or how or when? You are either the dumbest conspirators or the smartest actors I have ever known. Please talk more to me and my partner while my friends who brought you take a break…"

The military men grabbed cigarettes while talking to the guard posted outside the nondescript building in a backwater section of Cairo. After joking about how easy tonight had been, they walked back to the entrance but stopped when the guard spotted someone approaching.

"Hey, you no mishpucka I know. This place off limits. Take yourself and hazmat suit someplace else."

Saying nothing, the stranger kept walking, finally stopping when coming to a face-off, three to one. The guard drew his weapon and waited for a response.

The stranger let his pointed finger do the talking. A bolt of lightning-like energy leaped from it into the guard's chest, blasting him down and out as smoke and sizzle hissed from the hole it made. The faster-reacting military guy drew his gun and fired two bullets into the stranger's chest. He staggered backward two steps before righting himself and launching another bolt that brought his adversary down. Then rushing forward, he snatched the third man off the ground and drew him close.

"Take me to Alonzo if you want to live."

The third man followed orders; the alternative would be deadly.

The younger of the new interrogation team had just finished slapping Eve around and was about to coax answers out of Monet when the military man exploded through the door, obviously pushed by the stranger right behind.

Too stunned to stand, the older fellow could only stammer. "Wha-what the… who are you supposed to be?"

The stranger said nothing. Instead he heaved the military man against the wall, crashing him partway through the reinforced drywall. Then he thundered three words only.

"Call me Rani."

The fellow sticking partway through the wall started kicking his legs as he tried to extricate himself. Rani walked to him, grabbed both feet and yanked him free before rotating his head past 180 degrees. The snapping and crackling sent shivers of fear through all who could hear.

By now the two civilians stood together, frozen in spacetime. The stranger grabbed their heads by the hair and used them like bell clappers, ringing the skulls together until they were as cracked as the Liberty Bell, then cast them aside. Then he pulled a hidden knife and cut Alonzo free before handing it to him.

Alonzo knew what to do. He cut his two partners free but after that none of them could do anything except stare at the stranger until Alonzo's brain caught up to the action.

"If you're Rani, I know Indira has told you what to do. You lead, we'll follow."

Pointing at the person he didn't recognize, Rani asked, "Who is she?"

"My friend, Monet. She has to stay with me." "Let her decide."

Monet answered while helping Eve onto Alonzo's back. "You can't leave me here. I'm coming."

Rani led the way out, brushing aside whoever got in his way and leaving only destruction in his wake. He glanced into the building after his people were out and lobbed in two timed explosives. The detonations could be heard two blocks away, just before Rani's A- Team put everyone in the van and then drove into the darkness.

Four hours later, the A-Team had Rani and his three partners on a FedEx flight soaring towards America. When it leveled off, a FedEx crew person told the three, who were isolated from Rani, that they could remove their hazmat helmets. She gave them protein bars, Cokes, and bottled water before handing a packet to Alonzo and then talking.

"Our part ends when we get you through Dulles security. Follow the instructions in the packet to find your way home. And relax, you've got about seven hours more flying time. We go to the Memphis hub before delivering you to DC. You already know where the lavatories are. I'll check back later to see if you need anything else. Come get me if you need something sooner."

Alonzo and his partners wolfed the bars and guzzled Cokes. Even Monet discarded her table manners. They sat in relieved silence, letting Alonzo leaf through the packet.

Monet was about to talk, but Eve waved her off and spoke first.

"Rani's strength goes way beyond incredible. He walked in, out, and over anything in his way, showing no mercy. He's lethal."

Alonzo put a different spin on Rani's behavior.

"I'd say he's efficient and calculating. No wasted words or effort. He eliminated everything standing in the way and erased any evidence by blasting the place down."

Alonzo had nothing else to say, but Monet did.

"I am exhausted but relieved. Eve, how do you feel?"

"Every mile we place between me and Cairo makes me feel better and better. At this rate, by the time we get to DC I'll be ready to take care of myself. Come on, Alonzo, tell us the good news. It must be from Indira."

"Who else? Let me read it out loud:

'Alonzo and Eve,

You return from your summer adventure. Go to the DC-area house where you stayed before leaving for Cairo. Address and keys enclosed. Open the place and make it livable, then await further instructions, either from me or an associate. Expect a call within two weeks, and contact me only if you need assistance before then.

Do not, I repeat, do not divulge any details to anyone. If neighbors knock, tell them you are opening the house for relatives who have bought it. Nothing else.

I will assign a new contact who will coordinate your Granny's wishes. You and your three sisters must choose one of you to interface with that person.

Until then, rest and recover and get set for an exciting future. At your age, always ask 'Why not?' rather than 'Why?' The future belongs to the bold who have faith in themselves, take responsibility for their actions, and find ways around obstacles. I trust that you have grown enough from your extended summer adventure to seize the opportunities that you will find as you grow into adulthood.' Then it says 'Best wishes, Indira.' What do you think?"

Eve said, "Those are the kindest, most inspiring words ever from Indira. Maybe we finally met her expectations. If I weren't dead tired, I'd call to thank her and volunteer to be the new person's contact."

"You're it. And if Nari and Nila vote against us, a tie goes to the incumbent, which is you. I think all of us have earned the right to sleep until we land. I'm signing off."

So did Monet and Eve.

Rani had signed off several hours ago when Electra shifted into the foreground and assessed her success as she decompressed. Then she used a borrowed cell phone and operated it in voice-only mode to contact Indira, who guessed correctly the caller I.D.

Electra said, "Right you are. I'm reporting in that the mission is accomplished. In and out and no evidence left behind. Only one contingency came up and the exoskeleton took care of it by stopping two bullets. And only one surprise. I'm bringing back someone called Monet. I didn't ask her last name, but I'm certain Alonzo knows it. From the little I saw, she's got character."

"Yes, and I'm certain you and Alonzo will treat her nicely. And you can determine how as you decide what to do with the siblings. You've just seen more of Alonzo and Eve in action. Has that altered your opinion?"

"Alonzo shows promise. His character and backbone are stronger now. And Eve's grittiness comes through in spite of her bout with a virus, maybe a mutant Techno-or-Pharaoh strain. I can't evaluate the Bose twins until I know more about them."

"Do you feel ready to coordinate Su's intentions for all the siblings? They'll actually be yours because you and I are managing everything for her."

"I do, and I think I know how to make it win-win-win. I'm not ready to tell you what I have in store, but you'll know before I tell them. And no matter how I fit them in, you and I have to keep our subterranean fortress active. It's our most valuable asset."

"Are you sure?"

"I spoke too soon. You are my most valuable asset. I'll have to see where the siblings fit in my pecking order."

"And you are mine. Now rest and plan for the coming days. No doubt you'll surprise me in many ways…"

Chapter 32
Sunday, October 30, 2157

<u>"And Then There Were None"</u>

Electra picked up right where she left off when she returned to DC. She retrieved several responses to her business's Email directory resulting from an online advertisement. She would follow up on them, but responding to voice messages had a higher priority. She was ready to call after lunch the day before Halloween. Delilah answered promptly.

"Good afternoon, Delilah. Irani here, returning your call."

"Oh, hi. I just wanted you to know I have a client who would like to talk to you about an assignment. Can your agenda handle more work?"

"I think so, but I'll have to hear the details."

"Why don't you call her? Here's the name and number. You can contact her at your convenience."

Irani ended the Delilah conversation ten minutes later.

"Thanks again for thinking of me. It's like trick-or-treat candy a day early. Bye-bye."

The second call bucked over to Professor Ravenhill's voice mail. She said she'd call back and thanked him for finding another opportunity. At this rate, I definitely need to staff up soon. How lucky I am. No, Indira would say not lucky, but prepared. I remember a video from a Capstone seminar I went to before getting my PhD. The title went something like Lucky Accidents and the Prepared Mind. I wonder if it's stored somewhere on the Internet. I'll check.

Electra had an answer less than five minutes later.

Incredible… the video's is in the Cloud, and it's the one given by its originator, Doctor Hubert Alyea from Princeton. Someday, every shred of information will be there. But remember, our biggest challenge is to convert data to information to knowledge, and then from knowledge into wisdom. AI isn't there yet… wait, I misspoke. Only Indira is there. And maybe the Doctor's message applies to me. I think I'll watch the video.

Halfway through, Electra placed it on hold because Indira's GUI had opened. Her tone matched her serious expression.

"I must report that an unpleasant contingency has just occurred. Su-Lin Song Chou has suffered a stroke. It is time to implement our contingency plan. Please fly to Austin immediately. We shall talk tomorrow once you have settled down…"

Shifting to an elevated state, Electra dived into action; she caught the 6 p.m. nonstop, which would give her over three hours to get her emotions under control. Midway to Austin, she summarized from the sketch she made what she felt.

Of course, I'm upset. Emotions are embedded in our DNA. And here are the links:

DNA Brain Physical Sensations Emotional Response Feelings (Sensory Input) (Body's Neurological response) (Mind's Interpretation)

It's easy to forget that thinking and feeling are emergent phenomena that come from billions of brain cells forming trillions of interneural connections, but that's how it all works. And all feelings, even the unpleasant ones, serve a purpose. Depending on Su's condition, if I don't pay attention to what my feelings are trying to do, I might be overwhelmed by grief, which is the worst kind of sadness. What is grief trying to do for me? It's helping me survive, but at this moment I'm not sure how. I'll let my subconscious work on it and think about something else so I don't get any more depressed than I already am…

Electra went directly to Su's townhome. Adom, whom Indira evidently talked with daily, knew why she had come.

"It is good that you are here. My master's demise is immanent but she is resting comfortably."

"How do you know? What about taking her to an emergency room?"

"I am equipped to read biometrics, and Indira interprets them. It is senseless to prolong the inevitable. Isn't it better for Su-Lin to depart from the comfort of her own bed, attended to by those who love her? Your presence closes the loop. What are your intentions?" "To be here for her, and to give whatever she wants… and to be in the moment so I feel everything my emotions dictate."

"Very well, please follow me to my master's bedroom."

There was a soft glow emanating from two end table lamps. Electra placed a chair at the head of the bed but didn't sit; instead, she studied Su in repose from different points of view.

How old she has become. She used to look much younger than her years, but Indira did tell me the last viral illness aged her. I'll sit next to her… when she awakens, I'll see if she remembers me.

Electra sat in a comforting silence as seemingly random thoughts came and went. And then a sudden thought pinged her emotions.

My thoughts aren't random… they are preparing me to deal with grief. My emotions and feelings will help me recover physiologically from the loss I know will happen soon, but a loss I can deal with only when it occurs. They will ultimately take me to a state of renewal, where I will have come to terms and can now move on in the best way possible.

Electra's focus shifted abruptly; Su began to stir. Her eyes blinked slowly as her head wound from side to side but stopped and widened when her gaze rested on Electra.

"Pu-please turn the light up so I can see better."

Electra did so, before kneeling next to Su, saying nothing and hoping her smiling features would be enough.

A smile flickered on Su's lips before she said, "Why I know you; please help me sit up."

Electra used pillows to make Su more comfortable. Electra's smile never wavered but her voice did.

"It-it's Electra. I've come back. I-I'm sorry it took so long." She wiped away tears to keep her vision from blurring.

"Electra, yes, Electra. My exceptional god-daughter. How I wish Indira could see what you've become, but at least I've lived long enough to know you're safe. I wish you—"

Two gasps eliminated whatever Su was about to say. Her body shuddered once before she rolled to her left. A stony eyes-open mask of death descended. Electra's consciousness suspended in spacetime as her emotions took control an uncertain number of minutes later.

She straightened Su's body and folded her arms atop one another, then ever so gently used the fingers of her left hand to close Su's eyes before stepping back to view Su in final repose and waiting for an emotional wave to sweep in. It broke over her abruptly, forcing her to her knees. Thoughts spoken this time out loud accompanied the tears.

"What is your final wish for me? It might be mine for you… 'From this moment on may your spirit be free.' I don't believe in spirits, but even atheists find comfort in what might be."

No thoughts stirred in Electra's head until another emotion jolted her brain.

Su was the last of the World Stars, and the last person connecting me to my past. Now they've all departed. My god, I have irreversibly become an adult. I am the next in line.

Verses that she remembered from long ago echoed in her head. They were her mother's poem, Next in Line:

You waited for your turn to come, It did you took that wild ride.

The roller coaster journey's done, It's time for you to step aside.

Do not be angry no time to grieve, Think about those next in line.

Their hopes their dreams all they believe, The time has come for them to shine.

Perhaps there's shelter you can give, Or sage advice that you can leave.

Nurture Spirits so they thrive, Harvest from your Wisdom Tree.

Indira has a message for me, but I won't find it until my grieving passes. And it's impossible to sleep. I know… I'll turn off the lights and keep watch over Su-Lin until the dawn…

When Electra awoke, she knew that sleep had helped her brain sort through emotions because she already knew what she needed to do. I'm sad that Su is gone, but I don't feel the same dread that I did when Doc Kittner died, and I think I know why. I'm more mature and empathetic now, and I have a better grasp of the what and how of emotions and feelings. And I was with Grandfather every single day because I was his caregiver. I've been away from Su for twenty years. The saying that distance makes the heart grow fonder isn't true when you measure it in years. The bond between Su and me has weakened. Time and intervening events will do that for all emotions and people, whether they admit it or not. But still, I have to keep busy to avoid depression.

Electra bounced from the chair and stretched out the kinks caused by sitting too long.

My emotions are telling me skip my morning workout and focus on what I must do for Su, all in the order I know from experience. And there are only a couple of tasks.

First, I'll find out from Indira what mortician and interment she and Su used for Hud. There will be no wake or funeral. Su wouldn't have wanted either, especially since there's no one left to share her remembrance. I'll let the mortician's funeral home take care of all the unpleasantness. Su would expect me to enroll her in an organ donor program if she were in better shape, but she'd choose cremation if she were to judge her condition.

Next, I'll collect all the keepsakes I can find in the townhome. They're of interest only to me, and I'll use them at a later date to hold a private remembrance. I might even ask the siblings to organize it.

And that brings me to task number three. I'd better decide how to make them a win-win-win offer.

Electra sprang into action after breakfast. She brought Adom into the loop. He already had the details regarding burial; while she called the funeral home, Adom retrieved boxes she could use to pack keepsakes.

After a brief lunchbreak, Electra continued hunting for mementos. By mid-afternoon she had them all packed.

I'll store them in Hud's place before I leave for DC. Now it's time for a workout… wait, I do that at Hud's. I'll ask Adom to call me a rideshare to get there and I'll take the keepsakes with me. And then while I'm on the cross trainer, I'll start planning my return to DC. Electra's return-to-DC plan took on a larger scope than she had originally estimated. She went out for a snack after exercising, and worked for two hours before deciding she had completed enough to call Indira.

Indira spoke first.

"You look like you have your emotions under control. That must mean you've kept busy."

"It does. I have taken care of everything I possibly can for Su, and I've moved on to my DC return, which takes place tomorrow. But there's more to it than just me. I've come up with a plan for the siblings."

"Are you ready to tell me?"

"I could, but I'd rather tell the siblings first to gauge their feelings." "I understand. Is there anything I can do to prepare them?"

"As a matter of fact, there is. If you would, please tell Eve that Granny Su died suddenly, but spare her the details. Have her invite the Bose twins for an extended stay at my DC house. Don't tell her that Irani will be her new contact. Just tell her that the new contact will visit them within the week and explain everything they need to know."

"It seems like you are preparing for another game. Good for you and me and the siblings."

"I hope so. I'll call you after I visit my biological children, which is a secret I'm not ready to reveal to anyone but you."

"All in good time, I assume. You know what to do, now travel safe." Electra rested a minute to recap all she had done this day. She was about to power off the computer when a lesser emotion pinged her.

The message for me from Indira's poem just came to mind. It contains a line about stepping aside. Yes, I can say that I'm stepping aside to help my children, but I'm doing so by starting another chapter in my life that they'll help me write. I'm about to turn the page…

Chapter 33
Saturday, October 05, 2157

<u>"Turn the Page"</u>

Eve needed to read the Email not once, but two more times before deciding to share it with her siblings ASAP. And her stomach churned more after the second reading than before.

Hello Eve.

Please call me Irani. I am your contact on behalf of your Granny Su, who I must report died suddenly of a stroke. But be of good cheer; she lived a rich, full life and did not suffer. You and your siblings can hold a remembrance celebration at an appropriate time. Per Indira, you and your siblings overcame unforeseen adversity during your summer intern programs, and although everyone's performance is checkered, you demonstrated growth and resilience, leading us to believe that I can help parlay your current status into a win-win-win proposition.

To that end, I plan to visit on Sunday, November 6, at 3 p.m. to reveal enough of the details. Have all your siblings in attendance. It will be your individual choices should you decide to accept our offer. All of you have talent and youth. Make sure you don't squander these peerless gifts.

I am including a poem written many years ago by a person you might have enjoyed meeting. It should speak to you as you reach for your dreams. I am certain that all of you are clever and do not need my help interpreting it.

But I need your help and vice versa to make our proposition a reality. Please be prepared for a frank meeting; contact me in advance if the proposed date and time is unsuitable.

My regards, Irani Ramani.

P.S. Here is the poem:

Generation Next

What's to make of Gener-Next?

They're different from us.

Our parents asked the very same, We wondered what's the fuss?

The context facing Generation Next is different from the past.

Built by Generations-Gone, and morphing what will last.

And so it's been for all the Gens, Chance deals each a hand.

It's up to you to play things through and build your promised land.

And for those whose hand has come and gone, let Gener-Next reign supreme.

Don't judge by rules made yesterday, as they stretch to reach their dream.

Eve printed four copies before gathering her team. All were now sitting cross-legged in a circle on the family room floor, staring at the paper in their hands; Monet sat behind Alonzo, occasionally glancing over his shoulder. Eve let everyone read on their own until they signaled that she could speak.

"I could give my interpretation, but I'd rather hear yours first. Who wants to start?"

While waiting for a volunteer Eve glanced at all the body language. Everyone seems better post-Cairo than before. Nari waits for others, Nila seems ready to plug in to reality, and Alonzo's focused. But what about me? I'm not at full strength yet, but I'm getting better. That counts for something.

Alonzo led off.

"I'll make a stab at the poem. I guess it says that the old fogeys should cut us some slack. Let us do the best we can and judge us by today's standards, not yesterday's."

Alonzo waited for help. Nila chipped in what she could.

"I think it gives a tiny compliment to the older generation when it mentions building on 'Gener-gone,' doesn't it?"

Nari said, "You two get an A, but why don't we move on to a bigger issue? This Irani person… look at the way she's using words. Either she's being very open and generous or she's crafted in a lot of subtlety that's open to interpretation. What does she mean by 'win- win-win' or 'frank'? What about 'adversity' and 'checkered'?"

Eve agreed.

"I'd add to that a veiled threat when she talks about our not accepting the offer. Who is included in 'our'? And is referencing 'growth and resilience' a compliment or put-down? Is this gonna be another test? Let's not push the issue by asking for exegesis. I don't want us to make her angry during our first meeting."

Even Monet joined in the light-hearted laughter. Eve played along as everyone kidded.

"Hey, I like that word. I learned it from Indira when she corrected me during my first call. And it seems like it happened centuries ago, maybe because that's where most of our summer took place, Cairo you know."

Monet offered a more objective view.

"You could sit here all night parsing the paragraphs and come up with twice the actual number of subtleties Irani may have put in. Why not just let her talk? You can then fill in privately afterwards."

Alonzo liked what he heard but added, "I'm going to ask her about you, unless someone else wants to speak up."

Eve said, "Irani sounds pretty sharp. Indira wouldn't have picked her if she weren't. I bet Monet is already in the plan. Maybe she's the third 'win'. No matter, I'm tired. Let's continue tomorrow morning if we need to. Is the vote unanimous?"

It was.

Eve had everyone sitting in the living room at 2:50 p.m. The only sound she heard was a faint thudding in her chest.

I'm more nervous than anyone looks. I'll peek out the window. Maybe Miss Irani parked down the block and is walking here.

Eve opened the blinds before Alonzo asked, "Do we have any snacks? Irani might like some."

Eve yelled at herself before she swiveled her head towards her siblings.

Damn, I forgot to get something better than Cokes and cookies. Well, too bad.

She was about to answer, but Nari pointed and said, "This might be her."

Everyone but Monet rushed to the window. Seconds later, a woman exited a spanking new silver SUV.

Nari said, "That is one stylish lady. I wonder what –" Eve shushed her.

"Everyone, get away from the window. We'll look like yokels if she sees us gaping."

But it was too late. The lady approaching waved. Eve ordered the next best action.

"Everyone, ring your chairs around the coffee table in front of the sofa. I'll answer the door and then set her next to me. And remember, let her do the talking."

Everyone followed orders. Two minutes later, Eve was sitting on the sofa next to Irani, whose words broke an uncomfortable silence because no one else would speak.

"I'm Irani Ramani, and I'm pleased to meet you. I know everyone's name, but why don't you introduce yourselves so I can place the face with the name. Let's start with Alonzo, because I can already pick him out."

"Uh, sure. Well, that's who I am and this is my friend Monet…" Eve was about to scream.

This is so awkward. I better do something. Finally, it's my turn.

"And I'm Eve, your main contact. Why don't all of you gossip a bit while I get us something to snack on. I'll be right back."

Eve dashed to the kitchen. She remembered where to find a circular serving tray that was large enough to hold six glasses and a plate of cookies. She hurried to fill eight-ounce glasses and ring them around the Oreos. Then, after carefully balancing the load, she trod back to the living room. Once there, she spoke while heading directly towards the guest of honor.

"We like Coke and Oreo cookies. I hope you do too!"

Eve's last step was one too many. Losing her balance, she stutter-stepped forward, but gravity had become her enemy, and she couldn't stop from tipping forward, dumping the entire tray onto Irani. Eve's faux pas silenced everyone and focused all gazes on Irani. Two cookies rolling to a stop on the coffee table made the only audible sound. Irani opened her mouth as if to speak, but then doubled over as she laughed uncontrollably for long enough seconds to bring everyone back into a conversation she started when her laughter subsided and she sat upright.

"That's the best hostess trick ever pulled for making sure I won't ask for seconds."

Everyone pitched in to clean up the debris; the kidding that came along broke the conversational logjam.

Irani led the ensuing discussion.

"Thanks to Indira, I already know the repercussions of your summer adventure. There's no need to revisit, but I would like to build on it. I control a number of businesses, several in DC and several in Austin, and I have entry-level Contributing Partner positions available for those who are interested, talented, and willing to learn by thinking and doing. Two in DC need people who have good writing and analytical skills and want to start a career in some aspect of the social sciences. One in Austin is for computers, another is for business and economics, and a third is a combination business management and political science.

"And I offer outstanding perks. In addition to a competitive salary, the two who work in DC will report to me and can live in this house and get full tuition reimbursement as long as they maintain an A- minus GPA. The same applies to those who work in Austin, but will report to a Miss Kim Foley and live in Granny Su's townhome. First assignments are already set. Retrofit the house or townhome to fit your lifestyle. All I ask is for you to use common sense when doing so."

Irani paused for questions. Nari asked the first.

"By when are we supposed to decide?"

"I expect an answer no later than a week from today, but I haven't finished explaining all the details. However, if you accept my offer, I have a 'welcome aboard' token. For the ladies, lightning bolt earrings like the ones I'm wearing, and for Alonzo, an onyx-mounted gold signet ring displaying our lightning bolt logo."

Eve asked next.

"The arrangement sounds complicated. How can we explain it to others?"

"It is actually quite easy. No one is going to know you, and few know about me because I just relocated from an overseas assignment. So, we'll make a game of it. We'll simply pretend that all of you, with the exception of Monet, are my children. If Monet wishes to join, she and Alonzo can determine what part she should play."

Irani paused again. This time, Nila spoke.

"I need a timeout to assimilate all you've told us."

Eve said, "Let's take a break. I'll bring in more Coke and cookies, and I promise not to be such a stumblebum this time. Irani, is that OK?"

"Yes, and while you're doing that, I'll get token gifts from my car. I'd like you to have them if you accept our offer. I'll be right back." Electra switched to the foreground for a moment as she sat in the passenger seat and dug the tokens out of the glovebox. As she did so, another emotional jolt registered.

Gads, my plan is coming together even better than I thought possible. I am about to start a new chapter in my book of life. What's Indira's poem? I remember it. It's called Turn the Page.

Electra recited it aloud:

"Your story is a work in progress, written as you pass through.

And if you do not turn the page, it will be turned for you.

"Major changes mark each chapter. They come, and you will know.

Don't try to block the hand of Fate,

When it taps, be ready to go. "And like handwriting on the wall, it can't change it when it's come.

Your plot unfolds as the story's told, as you keep moving on."

No matter what role I'm playing, the verses fit. I'd better switch back to Irani and keep going.

Eve had Cokes and Oreos available by the time Irani came back. Five minutes later, after circulating the earrings and ring for inspection, Irani called everyone back to order.

"I'd like to pick up where we —" the doorbell interrupted; Eve jumped to her feet.

"I'll go see who it is. I'll let you know in a sec."

She scurried back after peering through the peephole.

"It's that next-door lady, and she's got a plate of cookies. What should we do?"

Everyone looked at Irani, whose smile never wavered.

"Always welcome anyone bearing cookies. Come on, Eve, we'll both play hostess. And everyone can practice our new game."

Two minutes later, everyone stood as Irani prepared to make the introductions.

"Everyone, this is Mrs. Newlands. Please say hi."

Mrs. Newlands spoke after everyone had done so.

"My, what an attractive family. I talked with Eve just before they left for their summer adventure. Goodness, she must have run herself ragged. She looks so thin."

Irani put her arm around Eve while making up a convincing story that covered for everyone. Eve listened but paid more attention to her emotions; she felt a warm empathy radiating from Irani, and she instinctively drew closer.

I can feel her comforting strength. I hope she's beginning to like me as much as vice versa. I need her.

When Irani and Eve walked Mrs. Newlands to the door five minutes later, Eve had centered herself enough to handle the goodbyes.

"Thank you for the cookies. I might be staying here for a while, and if I am, I promise to be as nice a neighbor as you."

"I'm sure you will, dear. Now put a little weight back on. If you don't, I'll make you something more substantial than cookies. You stay healthy and safe."

Everyone nibbled on chocolate chip cookies until Irani and Eve returned to their places on the sofa. As Irani glanced around the circle of youthful faces, her expression seemed to say that everyone belonged, that they were each a singular keeper. Then she resumed the conversation.

"I've given you a good overview of what to expect, and I hope you like what you've heard so far, but there's more, so please settle down, sit still, and let me explain…"

Irani's audience said not a word, instead focusing totally on the charismatic speaker, and when she was done, all the keepers looked at Eve and nodded, signaling that her smile and words could speak for them as one.

"Yes, Mother, we shall obey…"